OTHER BOOKS BY JAE

Conflict of Interest

Under a Falling Star

Good Enough to Eat

The Hollywood Series:
Departure from the Script

The Moonstone Series:
Something in the Wine
Seduction for Beginners

The Oregon Series:
Backwards to Oregon
Beyond the Trail
Hidden Truths
Lessons in Love and Life

The Shape-Shifter Series:
Second Nature
Natural Family Disasters
Manhattan Moon
True Nature
Nature of the Pack
Pigeon Post

Damage
CONTROL

JAE

ACKNOWLEDGMENTS

Being a full-time writer would be a lonely profession if not for my wonderful creative team. A big thank-you to my critique partners and fellow Ylva authors RJ Nolan and Alison Grey for encouraging me and keeping me on track and to my beta readers Erin Saluta and Michele Reynolds for taking the time out of their busy lives to help me with this book.

I'm also grateful to Andrea Lowescher, Nancy Jean Tubbs, and Edie Stull for reading the manuscript in a very short time and providing me with helpful feedback.

Thanks also go to the wonderful team at Ylva Publishing—Nikki Busch for editing, Gillian McKnight for proofreading, Glendon Haddix for creating a beautiful cover, and the rest of the "pack" for their hard work and support.

Last but certainly not least, a big thanks to my readers for continuing to read my books and for taking the time to let me know how much you like them. You certainly keep me motivated!

CHAPTER 1

WHEN A RAPID-FIRE STACCATO OF steps echoed through the foyer and Grace's mother swept into the living room without knocking, Grace regretted giving her the security code to her Hollywood Hills home. Her mother's habit of waltzing into Grace's house unannounced really had to stop.

With the dramatic flair of a former actress, her mother flung a magazine onto the coffee table and stabbed the offending print with a manicured finger. "What is this?"

Sighing, Grace put down the script she'd been reading and sat up on the couch. The magazine on the table was *Tinseltown Talk*, one of the trashiest celebrity gossip rags around. "Let me guess. Either it's another photo of me picking up my dry cleaning without makeup, or I'm secretly pregnant with twins, suffering a mental breakdown after gaining two pounds, or having a torrid affair with Neil Patrick Harris."

"Neil Patrick Harris is gay." Her mother lowered her voice and added, "And so are you, apparently."

"Uh, what?"

Her mother sank into an armchair and shoved the gossip rag across the table.

Grace picked it up and turned it around so she could read it.

The most prominent headline on the cover read in scarlet, two-inch-tall letters: *Exposed! Grace Durand caught cheating on Nick! Secret GAY tryst!* Below it, they had added in smaller letters: *See a shocking photo of Grace and her LESBIAN lover only in this issue of* Tinseltown Talk.

Grace snorted. Whatever photo they had was probably as fake as the breasts of some of her co-stars.

"I told you something like this would happen," her mother said.

"Mom, this is bullshit. I'm not having a secret gay tryst."

"I know. But if they're already writing ridiculous things like this, can you imagine the headlines once they find out what's really going on with you and Nick?"

Grace could, and that was why she hadn't told anyone but her mother and her lawyer yet. She said nothing.

The silence in the living room was deafening.

Her mother leaned forward. Her gaze darted back and forth between Grace and the open French doors leading to the stone patio. "You aren't…you know?" she asked, her voice lowered to a whisper.

"Gay?" Grace asked.

"Hush! You don't want the neighbors to hear you." Her mother's gaze went to the French doors again, even though Grace's home was perched on a hillside bluff high above the city, with no neighbors living nearby. "No, I mean, are you drinking again?"

Grace gritted her teeth. She hadn't touched a drink since she'd been seventeen years old. She'd worked hard to live up to her mother's expectations and to make up for the sins of her youth, but apparently, it wasn't enough to make her mother trust her. "Why would you think that?"

Her mother waved at the magazine.

Frowning, Grace flipped through the gossip rag until she found the page with the headline about her "secret gay tryst." She skimmed the article, noticing with amusement the exclamation points after almost every sentence, probably meant to let readers know they were reading something scandalous and exciting.

According to the article, Grace had been out partying after she'd wrapped up shooting her latest movie and had gotten drunk with her cast mates.

Grace huffed. *Never going to happen.* After spending fourteen hours a day, six days a week with her co-stars, she didn't want to hang out with her colleagues, no matter how much Roberta, her publicist, urged her to.

Well, this probably wasn't the kind of headline Roberta had been looking for. Being caught in a compromising situation with a fellow actress was not the way to promote a family-friendly movie about a heterosexual love story.

Grace searched the article to see which actress *Tinseltown Talk* was putting her in bed with.

Oh, shit. Jill.

Her gaze jumped to one of the pictures on the page. It was a little grainy and had apparently been taken with a telephoto lens. In the picture, she and Jill had their arms wrapped around each other while they swayed up the steps to Jill's trailer. The caption beneath the photo said, *Grace Durand and Jill Corrigan stumbling into bed for a drunken tryst.*

"Would you excuse me for a minute?" Grace threw the magazine back on the table and reached for her cell phone. She walked past her mother as she scrolled through her contact list and dialed Jill's number. Her mother's disapproving stare drilled into her back, but she ignored it for once. This was more important than placating her mother. When Jill picked up, Grace stepped out onto the patio and closed the doors behind her.

"Hi, stranger," Jill said. "Long time no hear. Are you busy writing your Oscar speech?"

Grace laughed. "Hardly." They both knew the romantic comedies she usually starred in wouldn't get her one of the coveted Academy Awards, but they had made her a household name, celebrated as a younger, hotter Meg Ryan. "How about you? How are you doing?"

"No Oscar speeches in my near future either, but otherwise, I'm fine," Jill said.

"Good." With her back to the house and her mother, Grace sank onto one of the lounge chairs next to the pool. "Listen, I'm not just calling to say hi. Have you, by any chance, seen the newest issue of *Tinseltown Talk*?"

"Can't say that I have. I try to stay away from trash like that. So, who's pregnant—you or me?"

"Neither," Grace said. "At least I don't think so. It would be pretty hard to become pregnant from a lesbian affair."

Jill let out a wolf whistle that nearly pierced Grace's eardrum and made her pull the phone away from her ear for a moment. "They seriously think the two of us are doing the horizontal mambo?"

"Yeah." Morosely, Grace stared down at the skyline of LA beneath her.

"Well," Jill said after a moment of silence, laughter in her voice. "I'm honored to be sleeping with the woman who has been voted one of the sexiest women alive, but please tell Nick not to kill me." When Grace didn't laugh, Jill sobered too. "What's going on?"

"They photographed us going to your trailer, with our arms wrapped around each other. You have to be more careful."

Jill sucked in an audible breath. "Damn. You didn't tell them anything, did you?"

"No, of course not." It hurt that Jill even had to ask.

"Sorry. I didn't mean to imply that you would…"

Grace sighed. "It's all right."

The irritating sound of fingernails tapping on glass interrupted her. When Grace turned, her mother stood on the other side of the doors, staring at her through the glass.

"I have to go," Grace said into the phone. "Please take good care of yourself."

"Will do. You too, okay?"

"I will." Grace said good-bye and ended the call.

Her mother stepped onto the patio. "Who was that?" She gestured toward the phone.

"Jill."

"Was that really necessary?" Her mother frowned as much as that was possible after her recent Botox injections.

Grace pocketed the phone and squeezed past her mother, back into the house. "You don't think she deserves to know what the tabloids write about her?"

"Well, yes, but you have to think of yourself and your career first and foremost. You worked too hard to let rumors like that," her mother waved in the direction of the magazine on the coffee table, "destroy everything."

Before Grace could think of an answer, the phone in her pocket started to ring. Not sure if she should be relieved or annoyed at the interruption, she pulled it out and glanced at the display. "It's George."

"I know," her mother said. "I called him as soon as I saw that article in *Tinseltown Talk*. We can't have them write something like that about you."

Grace suppressed a sigh. She was grateful for everything her mother did for her, but sometimes Katherine took her duties as Grace's manager a bit too far, acting on her own instead of asking Grace what she wanted first. She swiped her finger across the screen to accept the call and lifted the cell phone to her ear. "Hi, George."

Not bothering with a greeting, her agent asked, "Did you see the newest issue of *Tinseltown Talk*?"

Grace groaned. "Yes, I did. Mom just brought it to my attention. You know it's not true, right?"

"Where are you?" he asked instead of answering her question.

That had to be the most-asked question since the invention of cell phones. "At home," Grace said. "Trying to read scripts."

"Can you meet me in Westwood in half an hour?" George asked.

"Westwood?" Grace wanted to go back to reading the script, not drive all over Los Angeles. "Why? What's in Westwood?"

"Your new publicist."

Lauren cursed herself for agreeing to the nine o'clock slot the reporter had suggested for the interview. It meant that she had to spend an hour crawling through rush-hour traffic on Sunset Boulevard instead of working through the two hundred e-mail messages in her in-box.

The light mist of LA's infamous June Gloom coated her windshield, and she eyed the low-hanging clouds as she crept east. At least she had booked the photo op for Ben's new album for this afternoon, when the fog would have burned off.

Just as she lifted the paper cup of black coffee to her mouth, a car crossed into her lane without signaling, forcing her to stomp on the brake to avoid a collision. Coffee dribbled down her chin and soaked her blouse.

Great. This day was getting better by the minute. Lauren hurled a curse at the reckless driver in front of her while putting the coffee into the cup holder and dabbing at her blouse.

Her cell phone rang through the car's speakers.

She didn't even have to look at the number on her dashboard display. She had gotten two calls in the last five minutes, both of them from Ben Harrison. She pressed a button on the steering wheel and accepted the call. "Hi, Ben," she said in a pleasant, upbeat tone, forcing herself to be a professional and forget her shitty day. "Don't worry. I'm almost there. We're now going almost thirty miles an hour, which is practically a high-speed race here in LA."

Ben didn't laugh as he usually did when she made a quip like that. Only silence filtered through the line.

"Ben?"

"No, it's Marlene."

Of course. She should have expected it on a day like this. A call from Marlene Chandler, founder and president of Chandler & Troy Publicity Inc., usually meant one of their clients had gotten into trouble and Lauren was expected to handle the resulting PR nightmare.

"Sorry, boss," Lauren said. "I thought it was Ben Harrison. He needs a lot of hand-holding."

"I'll let Judy know," Marlene said.

"Judy?" Lauren frowned. Why did one of her colleagues need to know about Ben's jitters?

"There's been a change of plans. Judy will take over as Ben's publicist."

What the hell...? Was this supposed to be another punishment for the Tabby Jones disaster? "But Ben has an interview in half an hour, and he'll be a nervous wreck if I'm not there to field questions."

"Judy is already on her way."

"And he's got a photo op scheduled this afternoon."

"Judy will handle that too," Marlene said. "I need you in the office right away."

It irked Lauren to hand over a client just like that, but she knew protests were futile. She made a quick right turn into Vine Street and headed toward Santa Monica Boulevard, which would take her to the CTP offices in Westwood.

"What happened?" Mentally, she went through her client roster, searching for the most likely up-to-their-necks-in-trouble candidates. Her money was on either Brittany posting R-rated photos of herself on Twitter again or Leroy being caught cheating on his wife with the au pair.

"We've got a new VIP client," Marlene said.

Lauren braked at a red light and eyed the cement truck in front of her. With the kind of luck she was having today, being behind that thing made her a little nervous. "I thought Ben was VIP."

7

"Well, if Ben is VIP, this new client is VVIP."

Despite her curiosity, Lauren knew better than to ask who it was. They never discussed the names of their VIP clients on insecure cell phones. She'd have to wait until she got to the office to find out more.

"We need absolute discretion," Marlene said, emphasizing every word.

In the PR business, the need for discretion went without saying. Having her boss remind her of it was unusual. When the light turned green, Lauren sped across the intersection and switched lanes, leaving the cement truck behind. She couldn't wait to get to the office and find out what was going on.

Lauren pulled into her spot in the office's underground parking garage and got out of her car. She waved at the security guard in his booth and marched past him to the employee elevator. A quick swipe of her ID card and the elevator doors slid apart.

When they opened again on the twelfth floor, the controlled chaos of a typical Monday morning in the PR business engulfed her. The phones were ringing; people were tapping away at their keyboards, and someone was humming a song that sounded like "Rehab" by Amy Winehouse. She weaved around the desks of hard-at-work publicists, careful not to collide with the interns running around, asking questions, and putting together press kits.

As she passed one of the desks, someone grabbed her arm.

Lauren turned.

Tina, one of the account executives on Lauren's team, looked up at her with a desperate expression. She was on the phone and now pressed one hand against the receiver, covering it. "It's Mark. He called me twice already because he wants to go on *Ellen*. Should we try to get him a spot?"

"God, no." Lauren firmly shook her head. "*Ellen* is perfect for a witty client with a good sense of humor, but Mark is about as funny as going through a bout of norovirus with no toilet in sight."

Still covering the phone, Tina chuckled before her expression switched back to panic. "You're right, but I can't tell him that. How do I talk him out of it? He thinks it's a genius idea."

Knowing Marlene was waiting for her, Lauren didn't have time for long explanations. She waved at Tina. "Give me the phone."

Tina handed it over with a sigh of relief.

"Hi, Mark. This is Lauren Pearce. How are you doing?"

The actor paused for a moment. "Oh, hi, Lauren. I'm fine. Did Tina tell you about my idea? I think it'll really boost the DVD sales of my last movie."

His last movie had been a laugh-out-loud comedy, and if his audience realized Mark was funny only if he had a script, they'd be disappointed. Few things were worse than disappointed fans. "*Ellen* is a great idea."

Tina stared at her as if she'd grown a pair of green antennae.

"See?" Mark said. "I told Tina you'd think so too."

"Yes, but the thing is, you don't have enough movies out yet to secure the lead guest spot."

"Yeah, you're probably right." Mark was silent for a moment. "Doesn't matter. The second guest spot is still great, right?"

"Depends on where you want your career to go," Lauren said.

"What do you mean?"

Lauren grinned. She had him now. Like all of her clients, he, of course, wanted his career to go all the way to the top. "Well, if you always accept the second guest spot, people will begin to think of you as second-best. I really think it's better to pass and hold out for the lead guest spot."

"Oh." Mark sounded like a little kid who'd just learned that Santa Claus didn't exist. "I guess we should wait until I have a few more movies under my belt."

"Definitely." With any luck, Ellen would have done the Oprah thing and retired her talk show by then. "I'll hand you back to Tina. I'm sure she can find you another great interview opportunity." Preferably one with a reporter who would send them the questions beforehand so they could go over the best answers with Mark.

Tina took back the phone and mouthed, "Thank you, thank you, thank you."

Lauren nodded and walked past her in the direction of her office. She needed to change into a new blouse, one without coffee stains, before meeting with Marlene.

But luck wasn't with her today. Marlene's office door opened just as Lauren walked by. Marlene crooked one finger at her.

Sighing, Lauren changed course, feeling like a child being called to the principal's office. She had always liked working for Marlene, but since she'd been taken off the Tabby Jones account, she wasn't sure where she stood with her boss anymore. Reluctantly, she entered the corner office.

"Close the door, please," Marlene said.

Lauren did.

Marlene rounded her large desk and sat in her executive chair. The black leather almost seemed to swallow her diminutive five-foot frame, but Lauren knew that appearances were deceiving when it came to Marlene Chandler. She might look like a fragile toy poodle, but she had the attitude of a pit bull. "Have a seat."

Lauren walked past Marlene's freshwater aquarium, peeking at the Siamese fighting fish, a male and his harem. Some of her colleagues said that the fish became aggressive whenever Marlene was in a bad mood. If that was true, Lauren wasn't looking forward to the conversation with her boss, because the male flared his fins and gills.

Lauren slid onto the visitor's chair in front of the desk and waited for what Marlene had to say, knowing better than to ask and hurry her along.

For long moments, Marlene sat there without saying anything, just studying Lauren. She raised a brow at the coffee stains on Lauren's blouse.

Well, nothing she could do about them now. Lauren managed not to fidget under Marlene's disapproving gaze.

Finally, Marlene returned her attention to Lauren's face and leaned forward. "I'm sure you've heard of Grace Durand."

"Who hasn't?" She wasn't too fond of the type of movies Durand starred in, but Lauren had to admit the woman was hot.

Marlene nodded. "Right. Well, her mother—who is also her manager—just fired her publicist and wants us to take over."

"Shouldn't be too hard," Lauren said. Unlike many other former child stars, who had become tabloid fodder, ending up in rehab, prison, or reality TV, Grace Durand had avoided any scandals so far. Other than attending the occasional red-carpet event with her husband, Nick Sinclair, the golden boy of action movies, she'd stayed out of the limelight and hadn't created any PR nightmares for her publicist to clean up.

"That's what you think," Marlene said. "Her agent didn't want to discuss it over the phone, but apparently, there's been a recent development that needs to be nipped in the bud. You'll find out the details when they get here."

Lauren's eyes widened. "You want me to take over as her publicist?"

Marlene nodded calmly. "Yes."

If the other PR consultants found out that their firm was now representing Grace Durand, they would fight over the account like sharks over a piece of meat. Why was Marlene handing it to her? She couldn't shed the feeling that she was being tested, and she didn't like that feeling. In her eight years with Chandler & Troy, she had proven herself time and again. There had been talk of promoting her to account supervisor when she got back from touring with Crashing Guitars, the new, hip girl group. Instead, she was now back at square one.

"Do you feel up for it?" Marlene asked.

Lauren's spine stiffened. "Of course."

"Good. I scheduled a meeting with Ms. Durand, her agent, and her manager for ten."

Lauren glanced at her watch. That would give her just enough time to change into a clean blouse and get herself another coffee. She had a feeling she'd need it.

CHAPTER 2

"Is THIS REALLY NECESSARY?" GRACE asked when she met her agent at the address he'd given her. "Why do I have to meet with a new publicist? I already have one."

"No, you don't," her mother said as she climbed out of the SUV. She frowned back at Grace's Ford Escape as she did every time she had to get into *that vehicle* and shouldered her purse the way a soldier shouldered his rifle. "I fired Roberta."

Grace whirled around. "You did what?"

Katherine raised her chin. "I fired her. She didn't do a good enough job as your publicist. Otherwise, your last movie wouldn't have flopped at the box office."

Thanks for the reminder. Grace bit her tongue. A sarcastic comment like that would serve no purpose and only hurt her mother. "It wasn't Roberta's fault."

"Your mother is right," George said. "Roberta wasn't bad, but she doesn't run with the big dogs, and these guys do." He pointed at the high-rise building next to them, built of white travertine marble. "In fact, they eat other big dogs for breakfast. They're one of the top damage-control firms in town."

"Damage control?" Grace repeated with a frown. "You think I need damage control, just because of what *Tinseltown Talk* wrote about me and Jill? No one takes a tabloid rag like that seriously, right?" She looked back and forth between her mother and George.

"Probably not, but what if other, more widely read magazines or blogs pick up the story?" George ran a hand through his salt-and-pepper hair. "You can't afford headlines like that. Not this close to the premiere of *Ava's Heart.*"

Grace sighed. Maybe they were right. Better safe than sorry, right? It couldn't hurt to at least check out the new firm before making a final decision.

The three of them walked past a glassed-in outdoor workspace, where employees sat, drinking coffee and typing away at laptops.

Grace whistled appreciatively. *Nice workplace.*

They crossed a plaza between two buildings that looked almost identical, except for the fact that one of the towers was a little higher than the other. Palm trees swayed back and forth in a light breeze like kelp in the tide, and the water in a long pond rippled as several orange and white koi drifted close to the surface. A few employees sat outside on benches, enjoying their coffee break in the sun.

Grace wished she could join them and just sit under one of the palms with a good book for an hour. It had been a while since she was able to truly relax.

But even if she'd had the time, it wasn't meant to be. Heads started to turn as she walked past. If your face regularly graced the big screen, you couldn't fade into the woodwork. Grace straightened and put on an automatic smile when she felt gazes on her.

Right before they could escape into the building, a young woman in business attire stopped her. "Oh my God! You're Grace Durand, aren't you?"

Her mother tugged on Grace's arm. "Let's go in. We don't have time for this."

But Grace had promised herself that she would always make time for her fans and not become one of the arrogant divas who thought talking to ordinary people was beneath them. Gently, she pulled her arm out of her mother's grasp.

"Yes, I am," she said to the young woman, giving her a friendly smile. "Nice to meet you."

Red-cheeked, the young woman shook Grace's hand with a little too much enthusiasm. "I'm a big fan. I've seen all of your movies." She jumped up and down and waved to three of her colleagues, who sat on the raised marble edge of the pond. "Come here, guys! It's her!"

The woman's colleagues and other passersby joined them. Soon, Grace was surrounded by people. It always amazed her how fast a crowd could gather. She wondered if all of them even knew who she was. Several people took out their phones and snapped photos while others handed Grace scraps of paper to get her autograph.

Grace gamely signed her name, laughing when one young man bared his biceps and had her sign it.

Finally, the crowd dispersed, transforming from excited fans back into serious-looking business people.

Her mother pulled her into the building before new people could walk up to them.

Grace paused in the lobby for a moment to get her bearings. The interior of the building was as impressive as the outside. The lobby, with its shiny floor, was clearly designed to wow visitors. To the left, the clinking of porcelain came from a café, and to the right was a fitness center for employees. Grace scanned the directory listing the companies housed in the building—mostly real estate agents, investment bankers, and lawyers.

The PR firm really had to be a big dog to afford renting space in this building.

George herded them to the elevators and pressed the button for the twelfth floor.

A short time later, the elevator opened into the PR firm's reception area. *Wow.* Chandler & Troy Publicity seemed to occupy the entire floor. Soft recessed lights reflected off a marble-topped desk and several leather lounge chairs. Tasteful works of modern art hung on two walls while a flat-screen TV filled the wall opposite a designer couch.

A frosted glass door opened and closed to their left as someone entered, revealing a large room with cubicles to the left and right.

Grace followed George and her mother across the cushy, burgundy carpet.

The young brunette behind the reception desk smiled at them, obviously used to people pausing to take in their impressive reception area. "How may I help you?"

"This is Grace Durand," Katherine said before Grace could introduce herself. "I'm her manager, and this is her agent." She pointed at George. "We have an appointment with Ms. Chandler."

The receptionist's smile didn't waver. She never even stared at Grace. In her line of work, she was probably used to dealing with celebrities. "I believe your appointment is with Ms. Pearce, one of our senior account executives," she said without consulting an appointment book or her computer. "She's expecting you. Let me take you to her office."

While they followed the receptionist, Grace glanced at her wristwatch and winced when she realized they were late. Her encounter with the fans in front of the building had held her up longer than she'd realized. Maybe her mother was right and she did have to learn to say no to her fans sometimes. Being almost fifteen minutes late wasn't the way to make a good first impression.

The receptionist knocked on a closed door. When no answer came, she knocked again, hesitated, and then opened the door to peek in. "Oh. Ms. Pearce must have stepped out for a moment. Why don't you wait in her office, and I'll let her know you're here." She opened the door wider and let them enter. "Please have a seat. Can I bring you anything?"

"No, thanks," Grace said before her mother could bother the receptionist with an extravagant coffee order.

"All right. Ms. Pearce will be with you in a moment." The receptionist closed the door, leaving them alone in the office.

Grace looked around. The office wasn't overly large, but the panorama window behind the desk made it look bigger. It offered a great view of Century City, West Hollywood beyond, and the Santa Monica Mountains in the distance. The large desk took up one entire side of the room. It was covered in stacks of papers and files, yet didn't look messy at all. Quite the opposite, actually. The papers were neatly stacked and the folders sorted by color into piles of red, yellow, and green.

Did the colors mean anything? Maybe they symbolized the importance of the clients or how difficult they were to handle. Grace wondered what color she rated.

The office revealed no hints of the occupant's private life—no photographs of family members, no personal knickknacks, not even framed diplomas. Instead, autographed photos of celebrities lined the walls, probably famous people Ms. Pearce had worked with.

Grace turned and stepped back to take a closer look at some of the photos next to the door.

Five minutes earlier, Lauren had been sitting behind her desk, drumming her fingers on a stack of files. Every few seconds, she glanced at her watch.

Grace Durand was late. Fashionably late, some of her colleagues might have called it, pointing out that no one was on time in Hollywood.

Lauren didn't care about that. She hated when her clients were late for appointments. It didn't bode well for her working relationship with Ms. Durand. *You don't have to like her,* she reminded herself. *You just have to make sure everyone else does.*

A few more minutes ticked by and still no sign of the famous actress.

Huffing, Lauren grabbed her empty mug and stood to get herself another cup of coffee. Of course, as soon as she had entered the kitchen and was about to press the button for a cup of strong, black coffee, Carmen, the firm's receptionist, stopped her cold.

"Oh, there you are," Carmen said from the doorway. "Ms. Durand is here. She's waiting in your office, along with her manager and her agent."

Figures. Her caffeine fix had to wait. "Thanks, Carmen." Lauren put down the mug and headed back to her office. Before opening the door, she glanced down at her unstained blouse and the dark gray slacks, making sure she was presenting a professional image. When she was convinced that she looked fine, she swung the door open—only to be met with resistance.

The door hit something or rather someone, she realized. And not just any someone. She had never met her newest client in person, but she had seen her a million times before, on TV and celebrity blogs, in magazines and newspapers. The golden locks cascading halfway down her back, the contrasting dark eyebrows, and eyes as blue as a sunlit ocean were unmistakable. Lauren had just hit Golden Globe-winning actress Grace Durand.

The actress's full lips formed a startled "oh" as she stumbled back, rubbing her arm.

Still gripping the door handle, Lauren stood frozen in the doorway. "I'm sorry. I didn't mean to... I thought you'd be..." Uncharacteristically rattled, she gestured to the visitor's chair in front of her desk, where she'd assumed the actress would be sitting.

Grace Durand directed her world-famous smile at her. "It's all right," she said. "Despite reports to the contrary, I'm not made of glass." Her voice was husky and melodic, with faint undertones of a Southern drawl, which, as Lauren knew, were holdovers from portraying a character from Georgia in her last movie.

Lauren had never found a Southern accent all that sexy, but now she instantly changed her mind. She couldn't stop staring at the actress's classically beautiful face and her eyes. She had always assumed that those blue eyes she'd seen in movie posters were photoshopped, but up close, the color looked real. The rest of Ms. Durand didn't look as if it needed airbrushing either. She wasn't exactly a size zero like most other actresses in the business, but Lauren had never liked stick figure women anyway. She much preferred Ms. Durand's luscious curves.

Yeah, okay, she's gorgeous. So what? Each and every one of the women Lauren worked with was beautiful, but she had never let herself be impressed by their beauty. Much too often, the gorgeous shell hid a bitchy attitude, egoism, or shallowness. Reality never matched their kind, sometimes heroic on-screen personas, and this time wouldn't be any different. Besides, growing up around celebrities had made Lauren immune to being starstruck.

Oh yeah? You sure aren't acting like it. She gave herself a mental kick and moved forward, holding out her hand.

Grace Durand readily stepped forward. Her handshake was unexpectedly firm, and she looked Lauren straight in the eyes, although she didn't quite match Lauren's five foot ten.

Even up close, Lauren could detect no trace of makeup—not that Ms. Durand needed it. Admittedly, she was even more appealing off-screen, if that was even possible. "Good morning, Ms. Durand. I'm Lauren Pearce, senior account executive here at CT Publicity."

"Thank you for meeting with us on such short notice. And please, call me Grace."

Lauren nodded, even though she would have liked to keep a little more professional distance from this client. But the customer was king, so she said, "Call me Lauren, then." She realized she was still holding the actress's hand and quickly let go to greet the other two people in the room, George Benitez, an agent she'd dealt with before, and a peroxide blonde she guessed to be in her fifties. Lauren had done her homework, conducting some research while she waited for the actress and her entourage to arrive, so she knew that the older woman was Katherine Duvenbeck, Grace's mother. A quick search on Wikipedia had revealed that Katherine had been the one who had encouraged her daughter to go into acting, taking her to her first audition for a diaper commercial when Grace had been just six months old.

At least my folks never did that.

"This is my mother, who's also my manager, and George Benitez, my agent," Grace said.

They shook hands, and Lauren gave them polite nods. "Mrs. Duvenbeck, nice to meet you. George, it's great to work with you again."

Katherine Duvenbeck's eyes, not quite the same startling color as her daughter's, widened when Lauren addressed her with the correct name.

Lauren smiled faintly. "Can I get you anything before we start?"

Grace started to shake her head, but her mother said, "That'd be nice. If you have it, I'd like to have a freshly pulled espresso with steamed low-fat milk that forms a foam cap, no higher than half an inch."

Lauren nodded, but Mrs. Duvenbeck wasn't through yet.

"It should be flavored with just a hint of sugar-free vanilla syrup and garnished with a sprinkle of cinnamon—organic, of course."

Years of practice enabled Lauren to keep a straight face, even though she was inwardly cringing at the culinary crime Mrs. Duvenbeck was committing on a perfectly good cup of coffee. "Of course," she said calmly.

Grace sent her an apologetic gaze, surprising Lauren.

Since Grace had been a child star, Lauren had expected her to be just as spoiled as her mother. Lauren pressed a button on the office intercom. "Carmen, can you do me a favor and get Mrs. Duvenbeck a coffee?" There was a moment of silence when she repeated the woman's coffee order, but then Carmen gamely promised to deliver the coffee in a minute.

Lauren rolled her desk chair toward a small, round table and nodded at the three chrome-and-leather chairs surrounding it. "Why don't we get started by talking about where you want to take your career and what, exactly, you feel your brand is? Or is there something in particular you wanted to discuss?"

Mrs. Duvenbeck gingerly settled herself into the chair next to Lauren instead of reserving that seat for her daughter. "Oh yes, there is." She rummaged through a giant purse that probably held half the product line of Lancome and finally flung a magazine onto the table. "We need you to make this go away!"

Lauren read the sensational headlines and skimmed the article, managing not to raise an eyebrow at the mention of a gay tryst. She peered over at Grace, who met her gaze with an anxious expression. The actress didn't set off Lauren's gaydar, but then again, Tabby Jones hadn't either, and the photo of Grace with Jill Corrigan looked awfully cozy. "Mrs. Duvenbeck," Lauren said, deciding to be straightforward. "I'm a publicist, not a magician. I can't just make this go away, especially not if there's any truth to it." She looked back at Grace. "If this is just news you weren't yet ready to put out, you should realize that the reporters are going to find the truth sooner or later. You might want to bite the bullet and—"

Grace, George, and Mrs. Duvenbeck all spoke at the same time, with Mrs. Duvenbeck's enraged voice drowning out the others. "My daughter isn't gay!"

There was no way they could have a productive discussion like this. If there was any truth to the gay rumors, Grace certainly wouldn't confirm them while her mother was in the room. Ignoring Mrs. Duvenbeck, Lauren turned toward Grace. "Maybe the two of us could go over to the conference room to talk while your mother enjoys her…coffee in peace."

Mrs. Duvenbeck's makeup-covered face flushed. "I'm perfectly capable of talking while I enjoy my coffee."

"I don't doubt that for a second," Lauren said, managing to hide any hint of sarcasm. "But the thing is, if I want to represent Grace to the best of my abilities and handle this situation as efficiently as possible, I need to get a good feeling for who she really is as a person, and I can do that better if we're alone."

Grace got up and put one hand on her mother's shoulder. "She's right. We'll be right back, I promise." As soon as the door closed behind them, she lightly touched Lauren's forearm. "I'm sorry. My mother means well, but sometimes, she can be a little…"

Lauren said nothing. She'd learned the hard way that it was best not to comment on things like this. The loyalty of celebrities could be fickle and change faster than wind direction. Pulling her arm away from Grace's touch, she pointed down the hall. "This way, please."

Grace kept her shoulders squared as she followed her new publicist to the conference room. At least they'd left behind that damn magazine in Lauren's office, but Grace knew she wouldn't be able to leave the rumors behind as easily.

They settled facing each other at one end of the long table in the conference room.

Lauren put her phone on the table and turned it off, giving Grace her full attention. For several moments, she didn't say anything; she just sat and looked at her.

Grace took the opportunity to study her too. In a city where even waitresses were drop-dead gorgeous, Lauren Pearce wouldn't rate a second glance. Her chin was a bit too assertive, her jaw too energetic, and her body a little too sturdy for her to ever make it in front of the camera, but she certainly looked like someone who could do wonders behind the camera, single-handedly rescuing reputations and changing public opinion. Grace guessed her to be a few years older than her own twenty-nine—certainly not the elderly PR veteran she'd expected, but old enough to have a lot of experience in her job. She radiated confidence as she tucked a strand of her chin-length chocolate-brown hair behind one ear with a steady hand. The hazel eyes behind the horn-rimmed glasses were so light that they almost looked golden.

"So," Lauren finally said, "let's talk openly."

Grace nodded. "I'd appreciate it." Most people in Hollywood were masters at beating around the bush, never coming right out and saying what they meant, so Lauren's straightforward style of communication was a nice change of pace.

"Look, I know many managers, agents, and even publicists try to keep their clients in the closet, fearing it'll ruin their careers."

"But I—"

"Yeah, I'm not a big fan of that strategy either," Lauren said. "I'm not saying it'll be easy. Coming out will cost you a few roles, but nowadays, it won't ruin your career. It's different for gay leading men, but for women—"

"I'm not gay," Grace burst out. She felt her cheeks heat, and she cursed her fair complexion.

"Okay," Lauren said calmly. Nothing seemed to rattle her. "Then what was going on in that picture? You have to admit the two of you looked pretty friendly."

Grace took a deep breath and tried to sound less defensive as she repeated, "I'm not gay. If Jill and I looked friendly, it's because we are. Just friends. Nothing more. I'd like for you to set the record straight."

The corner of Lauren's mouth twitched at her choice of words, and even Grace felt her tense features relax into a smile.

"No pun intended," she added. "What do you think we should do? Give a press conference, stating that I'm straight?"

Lauren firmly shook her head. "That would only drag attention to that gossip rag that most people don't even know exists. Besides, the more you swear you're not gay, the more it'll look like you're either in denial or outright lying."

"But I'm not!"

"That doesn't matter," Lauren said. "We both know that perception is everything in this business."

Grace slumped against the back of the leather chair. "So you want me to just do nothing? I can't afford any negative publicity right now. My new movie is premiering in two months, and I need it to do well at the box office, especially after my last movie didn't gross as much as the studio had hoped."

"What's the new movie about?" Lauren asked, appearing genuinely interested. "Some love story set in Georgia, right?"

"Yes. I'm playing a widow from small-town Georgia. Her husband died in a farming accident, and she stopped believing that life has anything good in store for her." Grace realized that the Southern accent that she'd worked on for months was back full force, and she tried to shake it off. "By the end of the movie, she finds her faith again and a good man to love."

Lauren tapped her chin. "Hmm. I have to admit that doesn't sound like the kind of movie that would benefit from having the media out its lead actress."

"No," Grace said, gritting her teeth. "It sure doesn't. So, what can we do to stop this madness?"

"In my experience, one of two things will happen. One," Lauren raised her index finger, "some starlet is caught driving under the influence or something else happens in Tinseltown that draws the paparazzi's attention. They'll simply forget about you. Or, two..." Lauren lifted her middle finger as well.

"I don't think I'm going to like option number two," Grace murmured.

"Two," Lauren said, "if it's a slow news week or something else happens that gives those gay rumors any ammunition..."

Grace shook her head. "Nothing like that will happen; I can assure you."

"Okay, then let's hope for option number one." Lauren looked as if she'd prepare for option two nonetheless. She sent Grace a warning glance. "From now on, refer all media inquiries to me. If you do address the press, keep it short and simple. Remember that you can't be caught lying or dodging questions, or your credibility will be shot."

Grace nodded tersely.

"Lay low for a while and stay out of the headlines," Lauren continued in the same stern tone. "No parties, no drinking, no warm embraces with other actresses that could be construed as something more."

It irked Grace that Lauren thought she was one of the fun-loving party girls. *Come on. What do you care what she thinks?* But she couldn't change her nature. She cared what people thought of her, always had and probably always would. Her livelihood depended on people liking her. "I'm not into any of that anyway."

"Embraces with other actresses?" Lauren asked, a tiny smile lurking at the corner of her mouth.

Against her will, Grace had to smile as well. She felt herself relax a little. "Drinking and partying. I don't mind the embraces—in a strictly platonic way, of course."

"Of course," Lauren said, now completely serious again.

"So that's it?"

Lauren nodded. "Yes. That's our plan of action. Letting the fire die down by not pouring more fuel into it. It also wouldn't hurt for you to be seen out and about with that handsome husband of yours, as long as it doesn't seem like you're putting on a show for the press."

That would be much harder to do. Her interactions with Nick had stopped long ago to feel loving and passionate. They were affectionate, but more like old friends and less like two people still madly in love with each other. Not wanting to discuss it with her new publicist, though, she just nodded.

They got up, and Lauren walked her to the door, where they paused to shake hands.

Lauren's fingers around hers felt strong and capable, and Grace allowed herself to relax and believe that Lauren would guide her through this situation. "Thank you." She gave Lauren's hand one last squeeze and walked out to gather her mother and George and make it out of the building with as little attention from fans or the media as possible.

CHAPTER 3

"DINNER AND DANCING?" LAUREN REPEATED, glad that Peyton couldn't see her lack of enthusiasm through the phone.

"Yes. You know, that thing normal people do on weekends," Peyton said, her tone teasing.

After five business lunches, two cocktail parties, and one premiere this week, the last thing Lauren wanted to do in her free time was to get dressed up and head out again, yet she found herself saying yes anyway. Too bad most women didn't consider hanging out on the couch in sweatpants a proper dating activity.

An hour later, Lauren met Peyton in front of El Niu, the trendy restaurant Peyton had suggested.

"Hi, you." Peyton kissed her on the lips. "Long time no see," she said as the hostess led them to their table. Her voice held an undertone of accusation.

Lauren suppressed a sigh. "Yeah, it's been a busy week."

"More like a busy month," Peyton said.

"That too." Sometimes, Lauren wondered why she even bothered with dating. Her relationships never worked out anyway.

It wasn't as if she was too picky or had unrealistically high expectations. The only requirement she had was that her date couldn't have anything to do with the entertainment industry. She wanted a girlfriend whose only connection to show business was going to a movie theater to enjoy a film, popcorn, and tacos on a Saturday night.

As a dentist, Peyton definitely met that requirement. She was also pretty and intelligent, but Lauren still found her attention drifting as they studied the menu and talked about what food they'd order. Behind the cover of the menu, she discreetly peered at her phone, which lay next to her on the table, wondering whether Judy had remembered to keep track of Ben's social media.

Her cell phone vibrated, indicating that she had new messages, but she valiantly ignored it and kept listening to Peyton's adventures on her three-day cruise to Ensenada.

Just when the waiter approached the table to take their orders, Lauren's phone rang. She had kept it turned on, explaining to Peyton that it was just in case of emergency. Of course, an emergency for one of her clients could be anything from a broken nail without a manicurist on set to a dead body in bed next to them. A quick glance at the display showed her that Marlene was calling. "I'm sorry. I have to take this. It's my boss."

Peyton nodded with a stony expression.

Lauren pressed the button to accept the call. "Marlene?"

"K-Cee just got evicted from a hotel in Vegas," Marlene said, not bothering with a *hi* or a *how are you?*

"What did he do this time?"

"He took a swing at the concierge. Lauren, I need you to talk to the hotel manager and convince him not to press charges."

Lauren tightened her grip on the phone. "I'm not sure if we should continue to represent him. This is the third mess he's created since we took him on last month. No matter how often I talk to him, he just doesn't want to understand that the old adage 'the only bad publicity is no publicity' stopped being true two arrests ago."

"Let's discuss this another time," Marlene said. "Take care of this matter first."

"All right." It was Marlene's company, so she got to make the decisions. Lauren just hoped she was billing K-Cee enough for having to pull his ass out of the fire time and again—on a Saturday night to boot. "I'll be there in thirty minutes." Lauren slowly lowered the phone, pocketed it, and met Peyton's resigned gaze. "I'm sorry. I have to go. One of my clients got himself into trouble. Why don't we try for dinner sometime next week? Things should have settled down by then."

Peyton refolded her napkin and put it on the table. "I don't think so. By then, you'll probably have another fire to put out."

Lauren couldn't even deny it. She'd canceled their second date at the last minute, too, because something had come up at work. If she was perfectly honest with herself, her job had always come first.

"As nice as it's been, I'm not into ménages à trois."

Halfway out of her chair, Lauren froze. Ménages à trois? What the heck did Peyton mean?

Peyton gestured to the spot on the table where Lauren's phone had been. "You, me, and your phone."

Ouch. Lauren winced but again didn't try to defend herself. She rounded the table and took Peyton's hand. "I'm sorry," she said again, meaning it. "Let me at least pay for your dinner so you can stay and enjoy the rest of the evening."

"No, that's okay," Peyton said, now sounding a little more friendly. She stood, leaned up on her tiptoes, and kissed Lauren, lingering for a moment.

They both knew it was a kiss good-bye not just for tonight.

As Lauren headed for her car at a fast clip, she felt like a loser. She did damage control for celebrities every day, yet couldn't control the damage her job did to her private life.

The waiter walked up to their table. "Good evening, ladies. My name is Marc. I'll be your waiter for—" His gaze came to rest on Grace. He did a double take and paused in the middle of introducing himself. "Uh, you are…"

Long since used to it, Grace just smiled and said, "Good evening."

"Can I get you something to drink while you look over the menu?" Marc asked when he recovered. "Our wine list is excellent."

"I'll have a glass of pinot grigio, please," Katherine said.

"Right away, ma'am." The waiter turned a questioning gaze on Grace.

Grace suppressed a sigh. On days like this, it was really tempting to order a glass of champagne, her drink of choice in the past. But, as she had every day for the last thirteen years, she shook her head. "Just a Pellegrino for me."

"Very well." After bowing slightly, he walked away and returned with their drink orders within less than five minutes. He started to recite the specials of the day, but Grace's mother stopped him with a shake of her head.

"My son-in-law will be joining us," Katherine said, apparently enjoying calling Nick that as long as she still could. "We'll wait to order until he arrives."

"Very well. Let me know if you need anything else." After one last lingering glance at Grace, the waiter walked away.

By the time they had both emptied their glasses, there was still no sign of Nick. Grace was beginning to doubt he would arrive anytime soon, if at all.

"What's keeping Nick so long?" her mother asked.

"I have no idea, Mom. Maybe he's stuck in traffic or something." She bit her lip when she realized she was falling into the old habit of finding excuses for him.

Her phone vibrated, rattling around in her clutch, and when she checked, a message from Nick had arrived.

Sorry. Can't make it. Rooney had us do fifty takes on this damn scene, and now I'm just fried.

"Nick can't make it," she told her mother. "He got held up on set."

While her mother went on and on about neither of them putting any effort into saving their marriage, Grace shook her head at herself. *Serves you right.* Normally, she wasn't the calculating type, but after her new publicist had suggested she be seen out and about with her husband, she had let her mother talk her into meeting Nick for dinner in this restaurant, where the waiters were known to tip off the paparazzi as soon as a celebrity arrived. Now they could photograph her having dinner with her mother.

Her mother stopped mid-rant and stared at something at the other end of the room. "Isn't that your new publicist?"

Grace turned her head. From their discreet corner table, she let her gaze sweep through the room.

Most of the guests were couples holding hands across the table, the candles throwing flickering shadows over their engrossed features. Grace didn't recognize any of them. "Where?"

"There." Under the pretense of fluffing her hair, her mother reached up and pointed.

Grace looked in that direction. "Yes," she said. "I think that's her."

At one of the smaller tables, Lauren and another woman were sharing a bottle of wine. Well, the woman was gulping down wine while Lauren was on the phone. Probably an occupational hazard. Just when Grace was about to look away, Lauren stood and rounded the table. She took her companion's hand and kissed her on the lips, lingering a little too long for it to be a gesture between friends.

What the...? She's gay? Grace swiveled around to face her mother. "Did you know about that when you hired her?"

Katherine clutched the table with both hands and looked as if she were about to faint, so apparently she'd been as clueless as Grace. "Oh my God," she whispered. "What on God's green earth was George thinking? Hiring a lesbian to handle your PR?"

"I have no idea," Grace murmured, still watching Lauren, who now turned and walked toward the exit.

"Call him!"

"Now? It's almost nine already."

"Call him," her mother repeated. "This can't wait until tomorrow."

Grace pulled her phone back out of her clutch. She hesitated for a second before pressing the icon with George's picture on it. "Hi, George," she said when he answered. "Sorry to bother you this late, but...did you know that Lauren Pearce is gay?"

George didn't answer for several seconds. "Uh, yes, I knew. Why's that important?"

Grace wasn't sure it was, but somehow, it felt that way. "I don't know, but I would have liked to know before I decided to hire her."

"So you wouldn't have hired her had you known?" George asked, sounding stunned.

Honestly, Grace had no idea how to answer that question. "I probably would have hired her anyway, but…"

Her mother waved at her to hand over the phone, but Grace pretended she hadn't seen. If she let her talk to George, her mother would only shout at him, and George didn't deserve that.

"Ms. Pearce comes highly recommended," George said. "Everyone I talked to has good things to say about her. In the last few years, she has made a name for herself as the go-to publicist for celebrities wanting to come out as gay. She's the best in the business for that kind of thing."

"Yeah, but this isn't *that kind of thing*! I'm not gay." Grace realized she'd spoken more loudly than intended and quickly lowered her voice. She looked left and right, glad when she found that no one seemed to pay them any attention in their secluded booth. "My publicist is a reflection on me, and I'm trying to convince people that I'm straight, so do you really think it's a good idea for me to work so closely with a gay person?"

George was silent for a moment. "You already do," he said quietly and took an audible breath. "I'm gay, Grace."

In the sudden silence, the background buzz of the restaurant sounded incredibly loud. "I know," Grace finally said just as quietly.

"You…you knew?" George stuttered. "You never said anything."

"I wasn't sure." George wasn't exactly obvious, but since she'd worked in showbiz all her life, Grace could usually tell when she met a gay man. That skill apparently didn't extend to lesbian women. She hadn't even considered for a second that Lauren might be gay. "And it just didn't matter to me." Grace peered over at her mother, who watched her impatiently. "Listen, George, this isn't about Ms. Pearce's sexual orientation. I couldn't care less about whom she does or doesn't sleep with. I just don't want people to think I'm preparing to come out."

George sighed. "Do you want me to hire someone else?"

Grace hesitated.

"What is he saying?" her mother asked.

"He's asking if I want him to hire someone else."

"Yes," her mother said immediately. "Tell him to fire her and hire someone else. There have to be plenty of competent straight PR consultants in this town."

Grace nibbled her lower lip until her mother's disapproving stare made her stop.

"Grace?" George asked. "Are you still there?"

"Yes."

"Do you want me to—?"

Grace made a split-second decision, for once listening to her gut instead of her mother. "No," she said. "Sorry for bothering you with this. I'll talk to you later." She hung up.

Her mother stared at her. "Why didn't you tell him to fire her?"

Slowly, Grace put her phone away and looked into her mother's eyes. "Because it's not right to hire or fire people based on their sexual orientation."

For a moment, she thought her mother would start ranting and raving again, but Katherine just sighed. "You get that from your father. He was too soft to make it in this business too. Good thing you have me, or people would take advantage." She got up and gestured for Grace to put a couple of bills on the table. "Let's get out of here."

CHAPTER 4

LAUREN HAD BEEN GOING NONSTOP since she'd arrived at work, coffee in hand, shortly before eight o'clock. She'd checked HootSuite and skimmed various blogs, websites, magazines, and newspapers. Then, satisfied that none of her clients had gotten into trouble overnight, she'd settled down to answer e-mails and return phone calls.

Now she was clicking back and forth between a press release that one of the interns had written and that needed to be checked, the Twitter strategy for one of the sports stars she represented, and an e-mail marketing campaign for Grace Durand's new movie.

"Lauren?"

She looked up from her computer screen.

Marlene stood in the doorway, her expression unreadable. "I need to have a word with you."

"Sure." Lauren saved what she'd been working on.

When Marlene entered and firmly closed the door behind her, Lauren began to suspect that nothing good would be coming. Marlene settled her petite frame into the visitor's chair and regarded Lauren as a mother would her wayward child. "I really don't understand it. You're a good publicist. Scratch that. You're a great publicist."

Lauren knew better than to thank her for the compliment, sensing that there was something else coming.

"How on earth did you manage to have your client fire you so fast?" Marlene asked with a shake of her head.

Lauren's first thought was that K-Cee had dropped her as his publicist after her candid words to him. *Well, good riddance.* She wasn't exactly sad to see him go. "He just didn't like it that I called him on the carpet for his self-destructive behavior; that's all."

Marlene put both hands on the desk and leaned forward. "I'm not talking about K-Cee. I'm talking about Grace Durand."

Stunned, Lauren sank against the back of her chair. She hadn't seen this coming. After talking to Grace alone in the conference room, she'd thought they were on the same page about how to handle the situation and that Grace was willing to trust her and follow her lead. Apparently not. "Grace fired me?"

"Yes. Well, her mother did." Marlene leaned back. "Maybe she was afraid that it would turn out like the Tabby Jones debacle."

If she never, ever heard that name again, it would be too soon. Lauren gritted her teeth. "This doesn't have anything to do with...that."

"Her mother implied that—"

"Whatever she said is bullshit!"

Marlene's gray eyes narrowed to slivers of rock. "I beg your pardon."

Lauren rubbed her face. Normally, she had much better control than this, but the news that Grace—or rather Mrs. Duvenbeck—had fired her really rattled her. "Sorry. But you can't take whatever she said seriously. I bet she's just pouting because I practically kicked her out of the meeting."

"You did what?"

"It was like trying to have a conversation with a three-year-old while her controlling mother is hovering," Lauren said. "I needed to talk to Grace without her mother interrupting every two seconds. Grace is my client, not her mother."

Marlene slapped one palm down on the desk, making Lauren's mug rattle. "Your client is whoever I say it is. Losing this account is not an option. Go and apologize. Do whatever it takes to get them to change their mind."

Lauren had to unclamp her teeth before she could speak. "Okay," she finally got out.

Marlene shoved the chair back and stood. When she reached the door, she turned back around. "I didn't want to put any more pressure on you, but... This account is your chance to prove yourself. Use it."

When the door closed behind Marlene, Lauren picked up a pen and hurled it across the room. On days like this, she remembered why she had never wanted to be a celebrity publicist. After attending Boston University—a university as far away as possible from her producer mother, her director father, and Hollywood in general—she had worked in the marketing department of a nonprofit organization. Right now, she wished she'd stayed there instead of switching to a more exciting job. Her life might have been a lot less interesting, but at least then she wouldn't have to apologize to a spoiled actress and her arrogant mother for a perceived wrongdoing she didn't even understand.

Lauren steered her Honda Civic along the narrow roads zigzagging through the Hollywood Hills. One glance into the red file with Grace's name on it had shown her that, of course, Grace owned the mandatory multi-million-dollar mansion in Laurel Canyon. Lauren's navigation system led her to the end of a quiet cul-de-sac. It had been a relatively short drive, just minutes from Sunset Boulevard, yet up here everything felt peaceful and secluded. Grace's house, a Spanish-style residence, was set back from the street, surrounded by massive stone walls.

Lauren stopped the car in front of a wrought-iron gate, letting the engine idle, and peered through the iron bars to the circular driveway beyond. The security camera mounted on the left side of the gate was outfitted with a motion sensor; it rotated toward her. She lowered her window and pressed the call button on the speaker to her left.

For a minute or two, nothing happened; then the speaker crackled.

She'd expected to be greeted by an employee, but it was Grace's unmistakable, slightly husky voice that came through the speaker. "Yes, what can I do for you?"

Lauren looked into the camera right above the call button and held her CT Publicity ID card up to the camera's lens. "Lauren Pearce."

The electronic gate swung open.

She closed the window and drove through. The gate clanged shut behind her, making her feel as if she were trapped in this uncomfortable situation with no way out. Gravel crunched under her tires as she steered the car along the driveway, flanked by palms and tall cypress trees. Lauren parked in front of the mansion and climbed the stone steps toward the massive front door. More security cameras peered down on her, making her stand ramrod straight as she waited to be let in.

After a moment, the door was opened, and Lauren stepped into a large foyer with high ceilings.

Once again, it wasn't an employee who greeted her but Grace Durand herself. She had obviously been exercising before Lauren arrived. Her long hair was pulled back into a ponytail, highlighting her sculpted cheekbones. A few blonde tendrils had escaped and were now clinging to her flushed face. A damp, white tank top clung to her chest, and a pair of red running shorts showed off her long, shapely legs. When she reached up to pull out her ponytail, the tank top slid up, revealing a tantalizing glimpse of her flat belly. She shook her head, and her hair streamed down to her shoulders like a golden waterfall.

Jesus Christ. Lauren instantly understood why *Playboy* had offered Grace a six-figure sum for an in-the-nude photo spread. As her publicist, she was, of course, glad that Grace had refused. Nude photos didn't fit Grace's squeaky-clean girl-next-door image.

"Come on in," Grace said while she put her ponytail up again.

Dry-mouthed, Lauren followed her, keeping her gaze fixed on Grace's no-name running shoes.

No housekeeper or other staff showed up as Grace led her through the hall that opened into a spacious living room looking like a showpiece out of *Architectural Digest* more than a comfortable place to relax. The coffee table next to the white leather couch was a glass-and-chrome contraption that seemed to be held up by some gravity-defying magic. Abstract paintings hung in perfect alignment on the walls, but Lauren realized that there was no sign of a TV anywhere. *Interesting choice for an actress.* Well, maybe there was a media room somewhere in the mansion.

Lauren took in the cobalt-blue armchair, white rugs, and silver lamps, and she couldn't imagine living here. Not even the brick fireplace could lend this sleek, modern room a hint of warmth.

A spiral staircase led upstairs, but everything was quiet there too. Grace's husband was nowhere to be seen, and not even a personal assistant was hanging around. As far as she knew, she was completely alone with Grace Durand.

Lauren swallowed. "I'm sorry to barge in on you without making an appointment, Ms. Durand."

"It's okay." She tilted her head. "And didn't you agree to call me Grace?"

Lauren was caught off guard again. Why was Grace so nice to her? She wasn't behaving like someone who had just fired her. Was it possible that Grace had no idea what her mother had done? "Uh, right...Grace."

"There aren't any new gay rumors about me, are there?" A tiny wrinkle formed between Grace's brows, indicating that she, unlike many other actresses approaching thirty, hadn't helped her naturally good looks along by engaging a plastic surgeon.

"Oh, no, don't worry. Nothing new on that front. I just thought we should talk."

Grace let a long breath escape. "Okay. Let's go outside to the patio. Can I offer you something to drink?"

Lauren shook her head. Even though her mouth was still a bit dry, she didn't want to draw this out any more than necessary.

"Do you mind if I get myself a bottle of water?"

"Uh, no, go ahead," Lauren said, surprised that Grace would even ask. Was this polite consideration for other people just a well-practiced act, or was it real? Lauren wasn't sure. Grace was unlike any celebrity she had met so far.

"Go on ahead, if you want," Grace said. "It's just through the French doors. I'll be right with you."

Glad for a moment alone, Lauren crossed the shiny hardwood floor and stepped through the open doors onto the stone patio. Grace's Olympic-sized pool and the landscaped backyard with its Japanese rock garden screamed money. What drew Lauren's attention, though, was the great view of downtown LA. She could only imagine how this might look at night.

Just as Lauren had settled on one of the patio chairs at a round glass-top table, Grace stepped outside with a bottle of water, now wearing drawstring pants and a clean T-shirt. She sat on the chair next to Lauren's, unscrewed the bottle, and took a healthy swig before she said, "I'm all yours now. What is it that you wanted to talk about?"

"I just wanted to understand why."

Grace frowned. "Why what?"

Lauren wanted to tell her to drop the innocent act, but she bit her lip and forced herself to stay calm and professional. "Why fire me?"

"What?"

"Why fire me?" Lauren repeated. "I mean, if you think I didn't do a good job handling your publicity, it's your right to look for another PR consultant, but it's only been a week. You didn't even give me a chance to prove myself."

Grace screwed the cap back on the bottle with jerky movements and put the bottle down on the table. "I didn't fire you."

"I know. Your mother did." *Same difference.*

"I didn't tell her to do that. I didn't even know, and I certainly don't approve. Consider yourself hired back."

Lauren blinked. This situation was giving her emotional whiplash. "Just like that? Then why fire me in the first place?"

"I didn't fire you," Grace repeated with a hint of exasperation. "My mother just…" She sighed. "She probably thought she was acting in my best interest."

Anger churned inside of Lauren like the bubbling La Brea Tar Pits. She struggled to keep her voice down. "How is firing me in your best interest?"

"It's probably not. She just thought…" Grace averted her gaze and stared down at the city below them.

"Thought what?"

Grace continued to study LA's skyline.

"Thought what?" Lauren repeated with a little more force behind it.

Slowly, Grace turned her head until her disturbingly blue eyes met Lauren's. "She…we…thought… We were wondering if it's such a good idea to let myself be represented by a gay publicist."

Lauren stiffened. Of course, she had faced discrimination once or twice in her life, but, usually, her sexual orientation was no big deal for her clients. She hadn't thought that the friendly, approachable Grace would care one way or another. *You should know better by now. Nothing is real in this town. It's all just an illusion.*

"Whatever you think of my competency as a publicist," Lauren said, carefully modulating her volume, "I want to make one thing crystal clear: I'm not in the habit of making passes at straight women, especially not straight women who are clients of mine." Just the opposite. She'd just been put on probation for rejecting the advances of a supposedly straight female client who'd made a drunken pass at her.

Grace shook her head, making her blonde hair fly. "I'm not implying that you would. Really." She reached across the table and touched Lauren's arm.

When Lauren stared down at the warm hand on her forearm, Grace quickly pulled her fingers away.

"Personally, I couldn't care less whether you're gay, straight, bi, or sleeping with your dog."

Lauren made a face. "Nice comparison."

"I didn't mean it like that." Grace rubbed her face and then peeked up through her fingers. "I'm really making a mess of this, aren't I?"

The sheepish expression on her face almost made Lauren smile. *Oh, no, don't let that pretty face fool you. You're angry with her, remember?* "Yeah, I'm afraid you are."

Grace sighed. "That article in *Tinseltown Talk* has really made me a bit paranoid. When I saw you…"

"Saw me?" Lauren frowned. "Saw me doing what?"

Grace nibbled on her lip.

"If you want me to continue as your publicist, we need to learn to be completely honest with each other."

Staring at the bottle on the table, Grace said, "You suggested that it might be a good idea for me to be seen with Nick, so I went to El Niu on Saturday to have dinner with him."

Lauren connected the dots in one point five seconds. Grace had seen her with Peyton, had probably seen them kiss good-bye. "Oh." *Damn.* Sometimes, even a city the size of Los Angeles was too small. Lauren wasn't ashamed that Grace had seen her kiss another woman, but she liked to keep work and her private life separate.

For a moment, they were both silent. The pumps in the pool came on, circulating the water.

"All I could think of was that I might look guilty by association," Grace finally said. "I didn't want anyone to think that I'm gay just because I hired a gay publicist."

Lauren wanted to hold on to her anger but found that she couldn't. As silly as such an assumption was, she couldn't promise Grace that none of the gossips in Hollywood would think that. "Do you want another publicist? I think I could talk Ms. Chandler into taking you on herself."

"No," Grace said with a vehement shake of her head. "No, I don't want another publicist. I told my mother that. You were right with what you said earlier. It hasn't even been a week, and I want to give you a chance to prove yourself."

Great. One more person she had to prove herself to. *No pressure or anything.*

Grace studied her face. "But I'd, of course, understand if you don't want me as a client anymore."

Lauren had thought she'd kept her feelings hidden behind a shield of professionalism, but apparently, Grace was good at reading people's expressions and sensing their moods. "No, that's all right. I'd like to keep working as your publicist."

Grace flashed her legendary smile. "Good. Thank you."

"So you'll let my boss know that I'm back on your account?"

"I'll have my people call your people," Grace said with another smile.

Even Lauren had to grin. She cursed the actress's charm, which made it impossible to stay angry with her. "I'd better get back to the office, then." She got up and followed Grace back through the living room and the foyer to the front door.

They both paused in front of the open door.

"I'm really sorry," Grace said. "It was never my intention to—"

"Let's just forget it and move on."

Grace nodded. "Okay."

Lauren slid her hand into her pocket, searching for her car keys. "If you want, call me later to talk about the campaign for your movie. I contacted the studio, and they sent me the posters they want to use. I worked on an e-mail campaign all morning, and I have some ideas I want to run by you."

"Sure. I'll call you later." Grace's smile faltered, and her full lips formed a tight line. "But first, there's another call I have to make."

Grace hated fighting with her mother. It didn't happen often, because Grace gave in most of the time, but when they did fight, her mother usually used any argument she could, no holds barred, bringing up every transgression she could remember from Grace's childhood. For a moment, Grace considered hanging up before her mother could answer the phone, but then she sternly told herself to woman up and clutched the phone more tightly.

"Hello, darling," her mother said. "We should really try to get you on *The Tonight Show* a week or two before the premiere. I just watched an episode with that new guy, Jimmy, and—"

"Mom, you're my manager, not my publicist. Don't you think you should leave it for Lauren to decide what talk shows would be best for me to do?"

Her mother was silent for a moment, which would have alerted Grace to the fact that something was going on, even if she hadn't already known.

"About that," her mother said and cleared her throat. "I called Ms. Chandler this morning and told her we'd prefer to go with another publicist."

Grace took a deep breath. "No, Mom. We are not going with another publicist." There. She'd said it.

"Darling, I'm afraid you don't understand."

"No. You are the one who doesn't understand. You can't keep making decisions like this without even consulting me first. This has to stop—now!"

Her mother sucked in an audible breath, not used to Grace talking to her in such a firm tone. "I'm only trying to do what's best for you."

Grace sighed. "I know," she said, more softly now. "And I appreciate it. I really do; you know that. But firing one publicist in a week is more than enough. I say we stick with Lauren for now."

"But she's gay," her mother said.

"Yes, she is. That doesn't make her a bad publicist."

"Maybe not, but what if people think—?"

"What if they think I fired her just because of her sexual orientation? I can't afford to alienate any demographic group," Grace said, using the only argument she knew would work with her mother. "Being caught discriminating against employees is a serious thing."

Her mother gulped. Finally, she said, "At the very least, she should be more discreet if she wants to continue working as your publicist."

No way was she telling Lauren that. Grace said nothing.

"So," her mother said, "what do you think about doing *The Tonight Show?*"

Lauren knocked on Marlene's door at nine the next morning.

Marlene was on the phone but waved her in.

While Lauren sat in the visitor's chair and listened to Marlene artfully buttering up an Academy member, she mentally went over her to-do list for the day.

After a minute or two, Marlene ended the call and gave Lauren her full attention. "What can I do for you?"

"Have you checked Twitter this morning?"

"Not yet. What's going on?"

"K-Cee got into a fight with a fan who tweeted that he didn't like K-Cee's new album."

Marlene groaned. "How bad was it?"

"Let's just say I learned a few new cuss words," Lauren said. For a man who wrote such boring lyrics, he'd come up with some pretty imaginative insults; she had to give him that. "This is the fourth PR nightmare he's created in as many weeks. Or is it the fifth? I've lost track."

"What do you recommend?" Marlene regarded her as if she was testing her again, trying to see if she'd stick to her principles.

Lauren calmly met her gaze. "We should give him the ax. Life's too short to work with clients who never listen. If he continues like this, he won't just harm his own reputation but ours too."

Marlene tapped her chin twice and then nodded. "Okay. Do you want me to let him know, or do you want to do the honors?"

"I'll do it." It wasn't that Lauren enjoyed dropping clients from her roster, no matter how difficult they were, but this was her last duty as K-Cee's publicist, so she didn't want to shirk it.

"Good." Marlene turned her attention to her computer screen, wordlessly dismissing her.

Lauren got up and walked to the door.

When she opened it, Marlene's voice reached her. "Ms. Durand called me yesterday."

Lauren turned back around.

"She said it was all just a misunderstanding."

A misunderstanding. Sure. Suppressing a huff, Lauren nodded. "I went over to her house yesterday, and we cleared the air between us. I'm confident there won't be any other problems."

"Let's hope not," Marlene said.

Lauren heard what she wasn't saying: *or your career at CTP will be toast.*

CHAPTER 5

Lauren's phone rang for the fifth time since she'd sat down to put together the PowerPoint presentation. Still clicking away on the slide she was working on, she reached for the phone and tucked it between her shoulder and ear so she could continue to work. "Chandler & Troy Publicity, Lauren Pearce speaking."

"Hi, Lauren," a man's voice came through the receiver. Before Lauren could place the familiar voice, he added, "This is Stan. Stan Zaleski. I wanted to give you a heads-up about one of your clients."

Stan regularly blogged for *Hollywood Affairs*, a website that posted news about the love lives and sexcapades of celebrities. Lauren had managed to build a relationship with him in the past year, knowing good connections to the media paid off, even if she personally didn't like their style of reporting. She bolded the improved social media statistics in the presentation. "Thanks, Stan. You know I always appreciate that. So," she said with a laugh, "who got caught cheating this week?"

"Grace Durand."

The phone slipped and nearly crashed to the floor. Lauren caught it just in time and hurriedly brought it back to her ear. "I didn't think you were reading drivel like *Tinseltown Talk*, Stan. You know that nine times out of ten, they just pull the stories they run out of their asses."

Stan chuckled. "True. But not this time. I did some digging, and I've got a source who swears that Grace spent the night with another actress at the Ocmulgee Riverside Inn while they were shooting in Macon."

Lauren closed the presentation, her attention now fully on the phone call. "People think they see celebrities all the time. They imagine all kinds of things; you know that," she said, trying to sound casual even though the tiny hairs on the back of her neck stood on end. Things didn't look good for Grace. News like that fit right into Stan's monthly column, *The Celluloid Closet*, in which he often outed celebrities.

"So you think my witness also imagined them booking the room using a credit card that was registered to someone named Betty G. Duvenbeck?"

Shit. Lauren instantly recognized Grace's less-than-glamorous birth name. "Even if it were her—and I'm not saying it was—can't two colleagues share a hotel room without people misconstruing it as something else?"

Stan barked out a sarcastic laugh. "When was the last time you shared a hotel room with a woman in a purely friendly fashion?"

Lauren gritted her teeth. "That's different. I'm gay."

"And so is she," Stan said.

"Stan, you know me. You know I always advise my clients to come out. Don't you think I would have told her the same if she were gay?"

That made him pause for a second. "If she's not, she can tell me so herself. I'd really like to include a direct statement from her before I put the article online."

"What's your deadline?" Lauren asked. She hated playing his game, but she knew he would post his article with or without her help. At least this way, she could have some control over what he wrote.

"I want to post it before the people on the East Coast are asleep."

"Today? I don't even know if I can get a hold of her that fast. Come on, give me some time," Lauren said. "If what you say is true, it'll still be a big story tomorrow. But if you're wrong, it'll make the entire *Celluloid Closet* series look dubious."

He hesitated.

Lauren sensed that she had him hooked. Now she needed to reel him in slowly, using another bait. "Give me until tomorrow, and I'll throw in an interview with one of my high-profile clients."

"Deal," he said. "But I need her statement by noon tomorrow, or I'll post what I have. I'm sick of celebrities hitting it rich with straight flicks while leading a double life, as if being gay were a dirty little secret they needed to hide." Stan, gay himself, was passionate in his belief that the stars and starlets had a social responsibility to come out and make it easier for gay and lesbian teenagers to do the same.

Lauren knew he wouldn't hesitate to pull the trigger on his column, with or without a statement from Grace. "I'll get you a statement on time." She ended the call and jumped up. Leaning over her desk, she powered down her computer. On her way out the door, she stopped at Tina's desk. "I need you to clear my schedule for the rest of the day."

Tina opened Lauren's calendar on her computer screen. "Even the event with your parents tonight?"

Especially the event with my parents. "Tell them I'll try to make it."

When she stepped out of the elevator, she reached for her phone and called Grace, not wanting to show up unannounced a second time.

The call went straight to voice mail.

Cursing, Lauren got into her car.

Nick aimlessly walked around the living room, touching the armchair, the coffee table, and the lamp in the corner as if refamiliarizing himself with everything after being gone from the house for months.

From her place on the couch, Grace watched him without saying anything. He looked good—the quintessential action star with a healthy tan, windblown dark hair, and impossibly broad shoulders.

Finally, he turned to face her. "Are you sure you wouldn't rather have your lawyer here to talk about this?"

Grace had considered it for a while, but now she shook her head. "I told you I don't need a lawyer to talk to you. I think we can handle this on our own for now."

His dark brows knitted together as he regarded her across the coffee table, the suspicion obvious on his handsome face.

Was this what Hollywood had made out of them? Two people who no longer trusted each other's intentions? That was one of the reasons Grace had decided not to get her lawyer involved just yet. She didn't want to believe that Nick would try to go after her money.

After studying her for a few moments, Nick plopped into the armchair and gave her one of the boyish grins that had won her heart three years ago.

Grace barely felt like the same woman anymore.

"Some days, I think I'm crazy for letting you go so easily," he said with a slight shake of his head.

Nothing about this was easy for Grace. Even though she knew it was the right thing to do, she'd struggled with this decision for months. But Grace had been an actress all her life, so she drew on her acting skills to hide her feelings and return his smile. "Well, you clearly are."

His grin broadened. "Oh, yeah? What about you? You're just as crazy for giving me up." Sobering, he put one of his ankles on his opposite knee as if he needed a bit of a barrier between them. "Why are you?"

He'd asked before, when she'd told him it might be a good idea to take a break, some time apart to think. She hadn't had a satisfying answer then, and she didn't have one now. How could she explain to him what she barely understood herself? "I don't know, Nick. I just think there's something missing. Obviously, you felt the same way or you wouldn't have found someone new so fast."

He tilted his head and studied her. "You're not jealous, are you?"

"Not even a little bit." It was the truth. Being replaced within weeks by a twenty-one-year-old dancer with abs to die for hurt her ego, but not her heart. "And that tells me that getting a divorce is the right thing to do." As far as she was concerned, their marriage was over for good. Now it was just a matter of making it official—and that was what worried her most. "Let's just hope that the media and our fans will think so too."

Nick's frown deepened the little scar on his forehead. He liked to tell people that it was from one of the stunts in his movies, when he'd actually tripped in the bathroom and hit his head on the toilet. "You don't think it'll hurt your career, do you? I mean, you're rock solid, right?"

"Let's hope so. The divorce won't be final until the end of the year, long after the release of *Ava's Heart*, so I should be fine."

"Shailene and I will keep a low profile until then," Nick said.

"Thanks." Grace shifted on the couch. She didn't want to think about the headlines the press would print once they found out about the divorce and Nick's new girlfriend, so she instead reached for the paperwork Nick had brought over. "What's this?"

"My lawyer has drawn up a generous alimony package for you."

"Alimony?" Grace was careful not to smile since she didn't want to hurt his male ego. She made more money than he did and had from the very beginning. When they'd first met, Nick had been a stuntman while Grace had already been nominated for her third Golden Globe. "Nick, I appreciate the gesture, but it's not like I'll starve to death after the divorce."

"Okay, then let's forget about the alimony and talk about the house." He swept his muscular arm to indicate the Laurel Canyon property.

They had bought it together when they'd married fourteen months ago. Grace looked around, taking in the living room where they had hosted dozens of parties. None of it held any meaning to her. Nick and his interior decorator had picked out the furniture and the ultramodern decor while she'd been on location. She'd thought she would come to like it or at least get used to it over time, but it hadn't happened. The house, impressive as it was, had never truly felt like a home. She bit her lip to stop herself from saying it out loud. "You can have the house."

"Did you just say…?"

She nodded. "That you can have the house. It's too big for me alone anyway. I just want the cottage in Topanga Canyon."

He stared at her with eyes as round as an owl's. "You prefer the cottage to the house?"

Before she could answer, the gate buzzer sounded.

Nick glanced toward the foyer. "Are you expecting someone? Your new boyfriend?" he asked casually.

A little too casually, Grace thought. Clearly, he couldn't help being a bit jealous of any new man in her life. "I don't have a new boyfriend."

"No? I thought maybe you and Russ… You looked pretty cozy on set."

Grace burst out laughing. "It's called acting, Nick." Kissing her co-star on film had probably been the most unromantic moment of her life. "Be right back."

Lauren parked in the same spot as the last time she'd been here and climbed the stairs to the Durand/Sinclair mansion.

Again, Grace was the one who opened the door, with no sign of any employees around. "It seems we're making a habit out of these impromptu meetings," Grace said when she stepped back to let her in. She was smiling, though, and didn't sound annoyed at the interruption. In a pair of faded Levi's and a *Central Precinct* T-shirt, she was more attractive than any woman had a right to be.

For some reason, that annoyed Lauren even more. She didn't return the smile. "We need to talk."

Grace looked back over her shoulder, toward the living room. "Now isn't a good time."

"Now is a very good time," Lauren said. "If we don't talk about this now, you can read all about it online tomorrow."

Grace's eyes widened. "What—?"

A man stepped into the foyer, interrupting them. "Sorry," he said. "I didn't want you to think I was intentionally eavesdropping on your conversation."

The surprise and worry disappeared from Grace's face as if she'd pressed an emotion-controlling button. With a practiced Hollywood smile, she said, "Nick, this is Lauren Pearce, my new publicist. Lauren, this is Nick Sinclair, my husband."

Lauren would have recognized him even without the introduction. She'd met him only once, but he'd been photographed with Grace often enough. Admittedly, they made a striking couple, his black hair and broad shoulders contrasting nicely with Grace's blonde hair and feminine curves.

"I think we met at an after-party a few years ago," Nick said.

"Right." Almost against her will, Lauren was impressed that he remembered her. With all the classically beautiful actresses who'd paraded around the party in plunging dresses, she hadn't thought that he'd paid her much attention.

They shook hands before Lauren looked back at Grace. "We really need to talk."

"I'll go," Nick said.

"I didn't mean to—"

"That's okay. I'm expected back on set in an hour anyway." He turned toward Grace and pulled her into his arms.

Lauren averted her gaze, giving them some privacy, but out of the corner of her eye, she saw that he just pressed his lips to her cheek instead of claiming her in a passionate kiss. "Thank you," he said.

Grace hugged him tightly. "You're welcome. Just be careful on set, okay?"

"Will do. See you tonight." He jogged down the stairs, got into his gleaming black Corvette, and drove off.

They stood in the foyer for a few seconds, looking at each other, before Grace closed the front door and said, "Let's go to the patio."

They settled on the same two patio chairs they had used a few days ago.

Lauren decided to get right to the point. "I just had an interesting call from a blogger for *Hollywood Affairs*. He found a source who swears you spent the night with a fellow actress in a hotel in Macon."

Grace gripped the armrests of her chair with both hands, but her carefully schooled features gave nothing away.

"He says you paid with a credit card registered to your birth name," Lauren added and watched Grace's face for any kind of reaction.

Grace stared out over the city without saying anything. After a few moments, she got up and walked toward the edge of the pool. She dipped the toes of one sandaled foot into the water as if to buy herself time to think. "What do we do now?"

Lauren followed her and stood next to her so that she could see her face. "The first thing you need to do is to stop lying to me. You can't be caught lying. Not to the media and certainly not to me."

"I'm not lying," Grace said, still staring down into the rippling water.

The impulse to shove Grace into the pool gripped Lauren. Maybe that would wake her up. But, of course, she couldn't do that. "You sure as hell didn't tell me the truth either. What happened with Jill Corrigan? It was Jill with you in that hotel, wasn't it?"

Stan hadn't mentioned the other actress's name, but he'd implied that the *Tinseltown Talk* article was true.

"That's none of your business," Grace said, her voice carefully controlled, no anger leaking through.

"None of my business?" Lauren shook her head. "Your public image is my responsibility. If you don't give me the information I need to do my job, I can't keep working with you."

Slowly, Grace turned toward her. "You want to drop me as a client?"

"No. I don't want to." God knows, Marlene would kill her if she did. "But I will if you constantly keep me in the dark. We've been broadsided by this because you didn't trust me."

"How can I trust you? I hardly know you." Grace's Hollywood mask wavered a little. Her eyes, bluer than the water of the pool, reflected so much vulnerability that Lauren was speechless for a few moments.

Lauren understood. There were no friends and no secrets in the showbiz jungle. If you trusted someone with your secrets, it was entirely possible that you could read about it in the tabloids the very next day. "I know you don't. But you know my reputation. I want to make partner or even run my own PR firm one day. What do you think would happen if I broke the confidentiality clause in my contract?"

"No one would ever hire you again," Grace said.

"Exactly. I might not be an actress, but image is everything in my profession too. If I did anything that harmed my reputation, it'd be game over for me. So it's in my own best interest to protect your secrets."

Grace sighed. "I believe you, but…it's not my secret to tell."

Lauren studied her. *She's protecting someone.* One person came to mind immediately. *Jill Corrigan.* "Is Jill gay?"

"I can't tell you."

Her stubborn refusal to tell her the truth made Lauren grit her teeth, but at the same time, she couldn't help admiring her loyalty. In Hollywood, that was rarer than a fifty-carat diamond. "Grace, I need the facts so I can put together a strategy for how to deal with the media."

"No, I mean, I can't tell you because I don't know. I don't think she is, but we never talked about it. All you and everyone else need to know is that we're not having an affair." Grace turned abruptly and walked back to the patio table.

Again, Lauren followed her, sensing there was something Grace wasn't telling her. They sat facing each other.

"That won't be enough for the media," Lauren said. "We have to give them something, or they'll keep digging. If you don't talk, they will find someone who will. They'll bribe your housekeeper, your assistant, your gardener…"

"I don't have an assistant, and my cleaning service and the company that keeps my yard up come in when I'm not here," Grace said.

So she'd been right. Grace kept no employees around, probably because she didn't want strangers leaking intimate details of her life to the press. Once again, Lauren wondered if there was a reason why Grace was so private. Was she hiding something? "Doesn't matter," she said. "They'll snoop through your private life until they find something."

Grace gulped audibly. She raked her fingers through her long, blonde hair.

"There is something to find, isn't there?" There always was. Lauren had found that out early on in her life. Nothing was ever as it seemed in Hollywood. Still, she'd hoped that it would be different with Grace. She liked her, no matter how often she told herself not to be fooled by her warm, friendly facade. It was probably just that—a facade.

"Yes," Grace whispered.

Lauren said nothing, not pressuring her. She sensed that Grace needed to say this in her own time.

"Nick and I…" Grace rubbed both hands over her mouth as if part of her wanted to hold back the words. But then she dropped her hands and looked into Lauren's eyes. "We're getting a divorce."

Lauren sank against the back of her chair. She wasn't sure what she had expected Grace to say, but certainly not that. She cursed under her breath. "And you're only telling me this now? Christ, Grace, I need time to prepare a strategy. You can't just spring this on me out of the blue and expect me to adjust!"

Grace lowered her gaze to the stone patio. "Sorry," she mumbled. "I'm not trying to make things difficult for you, but like I said…"

"You don't trust me." Lauren sighed. Thoughts and media strategies ricocheted through her mind. "Their golden couple separating… Your fans won't be happy. I bet they didn't see this coming." She sure hadn't. Grace and Nick's relationship had seemed to be one of the few stable ones in Hollywood. "There were never any jealousy dramas, ugly fights, or separation rumors."

"No," Grace said. "And there won't be any in the future either. It'll be an amicable divorce. No breaking dishes, no screaming, no tears."

No passion? Lauren wondered. "So if everything is so harmonic between you, why get divorced?"

"It's not because either of us is having an affair, if that's what you're asking." A hint of defensiveness crept into Grace's tone.

"It's not," Lauren said. "I'm not trying to be nosy. But that's the first thing the press will want to know."

Grace curled one leg under herself on the patio chair and tugged on the hole in one knee of her jeans, making it larger. She pulled a few of the threads free and watched them being blown away by the breeze. "With both of us constantly gone, shooting three movies a year, we didn't get to spend a lot of time together," she said after a while. "Let's face it, actors make lousy spouses."

Oh yeah. If there was one thing Lauren had learned growing up, it was this. "So there are no other people involved?"

Grace hesitated but then said, "Nick has a new girlfriend. They got together three weeks after we separated, but he swears he never cheated on me. I believe him."

Lauren wasn't sure she did. Sometimes, cheating seemed to be a popular hobby for celebrities. Lauren herself wasn't exactly a by-the-book girlfriend, but she had never, ever cheated, and she would never tolerate it from a partner. She'd had to endure the sham her parents called a marriage for too long to want that kind of relationship. "The press will still call it an affair. If they find out that Nick and his flame got together while he was still married to you—"

"I don't want the press to tear him to shreds as a cheating bastard." Grace's eyes glittered with determination.

"Let's focus on you and your career and let Nick's publicist worry about his, okay?"

Grace clearly didn't like it, but she nodded.

"So, what about you? Is there someone new in your life too?" Lauren asked. Maybe Grace had found someone else too, and that was why she was so forgiving.

Grace shook her head. "There's no one else."

Either she was telling the truth, or she was an even better actress than Lauren gave her credit for. "Okay, but if there's ever someone new in your life, I need to know before you even tell your mother or your best friend. I don't want to be blindsided again. No more surprises. If there's ever anything, call me immediately."

"You'll be the first to know," Grace said.

Lauren couldn't tell if she was being sincere or if there was a hint of sarcasm in her voice. She wondered if Grace ever stopped acting and was just herself. She glanced at her watch and realized it was noon already. Just twenty-four more hours until she had to give Stan something. "This couldn't come at a worse time."

"I know. Which is why I'm trying to keep it a secret until after the release of *Ava's Heart*."

Lauren nodded. It wouldn't help promote a film with strong Christian undertones if the public found out the lead actress was getting divorced from her movie-star husband. "That's the best strategy for now. But we still have to give *Hollywood Affairs* something."

"Do they know who the other actress in Macon was?" Grace asked.

"Stan—the blogger—didn't name names, but I'm sure he knows. If he thinks he can out someone, he's like a bloodhound."

A flush of annoyance crept into Grace's cheeks, and Lauren realized that she again wasn't wearing makeup. She was by far the most low-maintenance actress Lauren had ever met.

"What gives him the right to make that decision for someone?" Grace asked, a bit of heat in her voice now.

"The constitution," Lauren said.

"Freedom of the press." Grace's lips compressed into a thin line. "What about my freedom? Or Jill's?"

Lauren answered with a helpless shrug. "I know it's not fair. I don't like it either, but that's the way it is, and we…you have to deal with it."

Grace sighed. "Sorry. I didn't mean to take it out on you." After one last tug on the by-now frayed hole in her jeans, she uncurled her long legs, shoved her chair back from the table, and got up. "I'll talk to Jill and then get back to you with something we can tell this Stan."

We. For the first time, Lauren felt as if they were really working together as a team. She nodded and got up too. "I need something before noon tomorrow."

Grace accompanied her to the door. "I'll try my best."

They could only hope that it would be enough. Lauren reached for the doorknob. "I'll see you tonight, then."

"Uh, tonight?"

"You're still going to Russ Vinson's handprint ceremony, aren't you?"

Grace raised one perfect eyebrow. "You know my schedule?"

"I'm your publicist," Lauren answered.

"So you plan to attend all of my public appearances with me from now on?"

"Wouldn't be a bad idea. But I'd be there tonight anyway. Until then." Lauren walked away with a short wave. Her private and her professional lives were about to collide, and—as always when that happened—she didn't like it one bit.

CHAPTER 6

THE LIMOUSINE THE STUDIO HAD sent turned onto Hollywood Boulevard, making its way past souvenir shops and tourists strolling over the star-cemented Walk of Fame.

Frowning, Grace leaned forward and pressed the button to lower the privacy screen that separated the rear of the limo from its front. "Excuse me," she said to the driver. "Aren't we picking up Ms. Corrigan?" She'd tried to reach Jill all day—to no avail so far, but since she knew she would see her at Russ's handprint ceremony, she hadn't been too worried.

The driver looked at her in the rearview mirror. "She was on my list, but then they told me at the last minute not to drive by her house. Apparently, she won't be able to make it."

How weird. Jill was as focused on her career as the rest of them. She wouldn't just skip this event, knowing the studio expected her to be there and show her support for her cast mate.

"Looks like you'll have to make do with us," Russ said, grinning at her and at Nick, who lounged next to Grace on the leather backseat.

The driver pulled the limo to a halt alongside the curb in front of the TCL Chinese Theatre. Paparazzi and fans instantly crowded the limo, trying to see through the dark-tinted windows to find out who had arrived. The security team struggled to keep them back but barely stood a chance against the excited crowd.

"Ready to face the hordes?" Russ asked.

Grace snapped open her compact and checked her hair and makeup.

"Don't worry," Nick whispered in her ear. "You look beautiful."

No longer sure if it was a sincere compliment or just what he thought she wanted to hear, Grace simply said, "Thanks," and nodded at Russ.

The driver got out and opened the door for them.

Nick climbed out first and reached back to offer Grace his hand.

Grace took one last deep breath and put on her screen-goddess persona everyone expected to see before she took his hand and stepped out of the limo.

Cameras clicked and flashes erupted around them, blinding Grace for a moment as the paparazzi snapped picture after picture. Dozens of voices called out her name.

"Grace! Grace, turn this way!"

"Give us a smile, Grace!"

"Look this way!"

"Over here, Grace!"

Grace turned this way and that, posing for the cameras the way they wanted, and kept smiling through it all, even though her face was starting to hurt and her strappy stilettos were already making her feet ache.

"How does it feel to have to watch Russ being immortalized this way instead of leaving your own set of handprints on Hollywood Boulevard?" one of the reporters shouted.

"It feels wonderful, thanks for asking," she answered with the biggest smile she could manage. "I'm very proud of Russ."

"We all are," Nick added.

She held on to Nick's arm with one hand and wrapped her other arm around Russ. Together, the three of them made their way toward the roped-off area in the theater's forecourt, where hundreds of famous actors and actresses had already left their handprints and footprints in cement.

"Remind me again why we put up with this," Nick whispered out of the corner of his mouth.

"Because we're crazy," Grace whispered back.

"Yeah, we established that this morning."

They grinned at each other, and for a moment, Grace wondered why they were going through with the divorce. He was her best friend and, with the exception of Jill and her mother, the only person she trusted in this crazy town. *Because that's not enough. He deserves more—and so do you.*

Russ went ahead to where the block of wet cement was waiting for him.

"Wait up, Russ!" Nick called and followed him. "I'd better join you in case you get stuck and need me to pull you out."

Grace stayed back, glad that she wasn't the center of attention for once. She waved at the fans behind the barricades, who were holding up their camera phones, busily snapping away. For a moment, she didn't pay attention to where she was stepping. Her high heel caught on something, making her stumble.

A strong hand closed around her forearm, catching her and holding on until she'd regained her balance.

Grace thought it was one of the security guards, but when she looked up, she gazed into Lauren's eyes, which glittered like gold in the sunlight.

"Careful," Lauren said. "I don't want to deal with headlines like 'Grace Durand breaks her foot on red carpet' tomorrow morning."

A grin formed on Grace's lips. She marveled at how different it felt from the trained Hollywood smiles she'd given the paparazzi. "Thanks for the heartfelt concern."

Lauren doffed a nonexistent hat.

Compared to all the actresses and celebrities around, she should have looked average at best, but to Grace, she stood out in a pleasant way. Lauren was wearing tailored trousers, sensible leather shoes, and a short-sleeved blouse that revealed toned arms. Her sunglasses were shoved up on top of her head, keeping her wind-tousled hair from being blown into her face.

Grace envied her a bit for being able to dress comfortably instead of wearing what was expected of her.

The crowd started cheering, making Grace look away from Lauren and toward Russ.

He knelt on a red velvet cushion and pressed his hands into the wet cement. Flashes went off when he stood and stepped onto the cement, leaving his footprints as well. Finally, he signed his name and the date in the corner of the concrete block.

Someone—Grace wasn't sure whether it was one of the organizers of the event or a studio lackey—ushered her over to Russ and Nick so more photos could be taken of them posing in front of the cement block.

Russ leaned close, pretending to grab her ass with his cement-smeared hands.

Grace smiled even though she wanted to slap his hands away. She just hoped that they had more chemistry on-screen than off-screen and tried not to think about how their romantic movie, *Ava's Heart*, would do at the box office come August. Her gaze swept the crowd in search of Lauren, and when she found her, she sent her a secret get-me-out-of-here gaze.

Lauren just shrugged and grinned.

After what felt like hours, the cement was covered to cure, and the stars and their guests relocated to the theater's lobby for a party. By now, Grace's feet were killing her, but she circulated through the room with an ever-present smile, exchanging chitchat with the movers and shakers of the entertainment industry. It was part of her job—not a part that she liked, but a necessary one. Being nice to the top producers and directors might pay off when it was time for them to pick the actors for their next blockbuster.

From time to time, she saw Lauren doing the rounds too. Her publicist clearly knew how to work a crowd. She shook hands and talked to all the important power players in the room.

Eventually, they both ended up in the same corner of the room. When Grace walked past Lauren to greet the director of *Ava's Heart* at the other end of the room, she overheard a bit of Lauren's conversation.

"What did you have to pay them to let Russ leave his prints?" Lauren asked a woman who was old enough to be her mother.

Grace blinked and stopped midstep. She didn't disagree—there were many actors who would have deserved to have their prints on Hollywood Boulevard before Russ—but she couldn't believe that Lauren would talk so openly to someone who clearly stood above her in the Hollywood food chain.

Then the woman shifted a little, allowing Grace to see her face more clearly.

Isn't that Olivia Pearce? She'd met the successful producer once at a charity fundraiser, back when Mrs. Pearce had been the president of production at Universal Pictures, one of few women to head a film studio in Hollywood. *Wait a moment! Pearce?* The woman wasn't just old enough to be Lauren's mother; she probably *was* her mother.

They didn't look anything alike—Lauren had a more solid frame compared to her almost fragile-looking mother—but they both had that intense gaze.

Grace realized that Mrs. Pearce had caught her looking and turned toward her. "Good evening. It's nice to see you again, Mrs. Pearce."

"Olivia, please." The producer pointed to the man next to her. "Have you met my husband, Leonard?"

Grace hadn't yet met Leonard, but she'd heard of him, of course. He'd given up acting for the most part and had drifted into directing, but he was still very handsome. His tan looked as if he spent more time on California's beaches than in the director's chair.

They shook hands.

"Nice to meet you," Leonard said. His gaze swept down, away from her eyes.

Had he just checked out her cleavage with his wife right there, watching him? Grace pulled back her hand as fast as she could without being impolite.

His wife either hadn't noticed or didn't care. "And this is my...our daughter, Lauren."

"We know each other, Mom," Lauren said. "Grace is one of my clients."

"Lucky you," Olivia said to Grace. "Lauren is the best publicist in the business."

Lauren groaned. "Mom..."

Grace watched with amusement as the normally confident woman blushed.

"What? It's true, isn't it, Leonard? She really should go into producing."

As much fun as it was to see Lauren squirm, Grace decided to step in before they could embarrass Lauren even more. "I hear we'll work together next month," she said to the director.

"We will?" Leonard blinked.

Grace nodded. "I'm guest-starring in one of the *Central Precinct* episodes you're directing."

"Oh, wonderful, wonderful." He launched into a discussion of camera angles he thought worked best for a fast-paced TV show like *Central Precinct.*

Lauren and Grace peered at each other.

"You'll have to excuse us now," Lauren said after a minute. "Grace and I have a lot to discuss." She gripped Grace's elbow and led her away before either of her parents could protest.

One of the waiters circulating the room walked up to them with a tray of champagne glasses.

"Thanks." Lauren took two of the glasses and handed one to Grace before taking a long swig. When she lowered the champagne flute, it was half empty.

Grace took the offered glass because she knew it was expected of her but just held it in her hand without drinking.

"Sorry," Lauren said, gesturing in the direction of her parents.

Grace smiled. "No need to apologize. They're proud of you. That's nothing to be ashamed of."

"I guess." Lauren took another sip of champagne, not gulping it down this time. She craned her neck and scanned the crowded room. "I thought Jill Corrigan was supposed to be here."

"I thought so too, but the studio's driver said she couldn't make it."

"Missing this shindig isn't going to earn her any points with the studio. She has to know that. What's going on with her?"

Grace rolled the stem of the champagne flute between her fingers. "I have no idea. I couldn't reach her all day."

"Want me to take that for you?" Lauren asked.

Grace looked up, startled. "Uh…what?"

Lauren gestured at the glass. "Everyone else around is on their third glass, and you haven't even taken a sip. You obviously don't like champagne."

I liked it a little too much. At the last moment, Grace held herself back from saying it. *Christ, what's wrong with you?* Just because she'd told Lauren about the divorce didn't mean she had to spill all her secrets. "I'm just not thirsty." She put her untouched glass on the tray of another waiter and breathed a sigh of relief as he carried it off.

Lauren looked from the bubbles in her own glass to Grace's face. "How long has it been?"

Grace stared. She couldn't be asking what she thought she was asking, could she?

"Since you last had a drink," Lauren said, her voice so low that no one else around could hear.

Only years of practice kept Grace's smile from faltering. *Damn.* Was it that obvious, or was her new publicist just too observant for her own good?

"You don't have to tell me if you don't want to." Lauren looked around. "Want to get out of here and see if we can reach Jill?"

Grace nodded.

It took them fifteen minutes to make it to the door because people kept stopping one or both of them to talk.

Grace detoured toward Nick, who was demonstrating what was either a dance move or a stunt choreography to a captive audience.

When he saw her coming, he stopped and wrapped his arms around her, drawing her near so no one could overhear them. "You okay?"

"Yes. I'm leaving."

Nick's brows bunched together. "Already? It's barely ten."

"I know. I want to look in on Jill."

"You think something's wrong with her?" Nick asked.

Grace hesitated but then said, "No, I'm sure she's fine." She leaned up on her tiptoes and kissed him good-bye, wondering when the butterflies had stopped swarming and her body had stopped reacting to his closeness. All she felt was warm affection.

She waved at Russ and then returned to Lauren's side.

"You're a good actress," Lauren whispered as they reached the door. "That was very convincing."

For a moment, Grace looked at her, not sure what Lauren was talking about. Then she understood. "That wasn't an act. I really love Nick."

"You're just not in love with him," Lauren said quietly.

Grace didn't answer. Followed by Lauren, she left the building.

It had gotten dark outside, and the temperature had dropped, so it was a little chilly now.

Genius. Grace realized she'd brought neither a jacket nor a car.

Camera flashes lit up the night sky around her.

Grace was tempted to try to escape or at least turn away, but she knew it wouldn't do her any good. They would just keep following her. If she posed and smiled for them, letting them get the shots they wanted, they'd leave her in peace afterward. At least she hoped they would.

"Why are you leaving alone?" one of the reporters shouted. "Where's Nick?"

Of course the paparazzi had noticed. As casually as possible, Grace pointed over her shoulder. "Still inside. Boy talk with Russ. But for me, business is calling. I have some things to go over with my publicist." She pointed at Lauren. It couldn't hurt to let them know who Lauren was. Otherwise, they might run a photo of them with the caption: Grace Durand leaving the party with an unidentified woman.

Fans hurried over, handing her autograph books, postcards, scraps of paper, and even napkins to sign.

Two studio bodyguards rushed forward, trying to stop the fans from approaching Grace, but she waved them away. Even though she was impatient to finally get away and check on Jill, she tried to smile while she signed her name over and over until her hand started to cramp.

Luckily, some other celebrity stepped out of the theater's lobby, and the fans and paparazzi diverted their attention away from Grace. She used the moment to step out of the limelight and led Lauren to a quieter corner, where she fished her cell phone out of her clutch and called Jill for the dozenth time that day. Once again, the call went straight to voice mail. "Voice mail," she said to Lauren.

"Why didn't you leave a message?"

"I left three already." Grace put the phone away and rubbed her arms. "What now?"

Lauren shrugged. "Not much we can do. Maybe the blogger called her publicist too, and now she's laying low."

Grace hoped that was all it was. She couldn't help worrying. "You wouldn't happen to have a car here, would you? It seems my carriage turned into a pumpkin." She gestured to the spot on the curb where her limousine had been. Another car now idled there.

"But it's not midnight yet," Lauren said.

"Apparently, modern-day fairy tales stick to different curfews." The driver had probably been forced to circle the block and park somewhere else to make room for other arrivals. One call would be enough for her to be picked up, but she didn't want to use the studio's limo for what she had in mind.

Lauren chuckled. "Seems like it. I left my car in a garage two blocks from here. What did you have in mind, Cinderella?"

"If you don't mind, I'd like to look in on Jill, see if she's home."

Looking at the photographers and fans crowding around the entrance of the theater, Lauren asked, "Want me to get the car?"

Grace hesitated. Maybe it would have been the sensible thing to do, but she didn't want to stay behind alone. "No. For once, I'd like to walk, like a normal person."

"All right. Then let's go." Lauren marched off, her long strides quickly creating distance between them, forcing Grace to hurry after her.

The two studio bodyguards followed them.

"Not so fast," Grace called after her. "I'm wearing stilettos!"

"I noticed," Lauren said and slowed down to a more leisurely stroll. *Oh, yeah, I definitely noticed.* The four-inch heels made Grace's legs look even longer. Lauren had also admired the white spaghetti strap dress that Grace wore. Simple but classy, it showed off Grace's toned shoulders and just the right amount of cleavage. Not that Lauren had allowed herself to look for too long. Grace was a client after all—an especially gorgeous one, but still a client.

Tourists with cameras around their necks started turning their heads as they passed.

At first, Lauren thought they were admiring Grace's dress too, but then a loud voice cut through the night. "It's her! It's little Amber!"

Grace let out a low groan, but when she turned around, she was all smiles.

An elderly lady who looked as if her hair dye job had gone horribly wrong dragged her overweight husband over to Grace.

The two studio bodyguards jumped in to stop them, but Grace waved them away. "It's okay."

When the security guards stepped back, the woman grasped both of Grace's hands as if she were a long-lost relative, completely ignoring Lauren in the process. "Oh, I always wanted to meet you and tell you how wonderful you were on *Everything That Counts.*"

Grace smiled as sweetly as the little girl she'd played on the long-running TV sitcom.

"You were just so cute."

For a moment, Lauren thought the woman would reach up and pinch Grace's cheek, but she didn't.

"I never understood why they sent you to that boarding school in Europe," the woman continued and clucked her tongue in disapproval.

"Well," Grace said. "Education is important."

The bodyguards, who were hovering nearby, burst out laughing, but Grace looked completely serious.

Lauren didn't know how she could keep a straight face. Apparently, she was used to fans who confused the real Grace with the roles she played on TV.

"Oh, of course, dear." The lavender-haired woman patted Grace's hands, turned toward Lauren, and squinted at her. "Weren't you the one who always tormented poor little Amber?" She looked ready to whack Lauren with her giant purse.

Lauren held up both hands. "Uh, no, no. It wasn't me, I swear."

Grace giggled.

"She's the one, isn't she?" The woman turned to Grace for confirmation.

Grace's ocean-blue eyes glittered with mischief.

For a moment, Lauren thought she would nod. She gave the security officers a beseeching look, but they just smirked and apparently had no intention of protecting her from the wrath of this little old lady.

Finally, Grace shook her head. "No. She's one of the good girls. Really."

"Oh, that's all right, then." The woman thrust her camera at Lauren. "Can you take a picture of us with Amber?"

Lauren took the camera and zoomed in a little. On the digital camera's small screen, it was easy to see that Grace was shivering in the cool night air, but she gamely wrapped one arm around the elderly lady's shoulders and the other around the woman's husband, smiling as if she'd just won an Oscar. *Amazing.* Lauren snapped a few pictures and then handed back the camera.

The woman did a little happy dance. "Thank you, thank you. Oh, just wait until I get home and tell my friends!"

Grace said good-bye, and they continued toward the parking garage, the bodyguards following them at a respectful distance.

Lauren looked back over her shoulder. "What the hell was that? She was about to strangle me with her purse straps for something that somebody did to your character twenty years ago!"

"Now do you understand why these gay rumors are so bad for my career?" Grace asked with a serious expression, talking so quietly that neither the security guys nor the tourists passing by could hear her. "A lot of people still remember me as Amber Haynes. America's little darling can't be one of *those people.*"

Are you? Lauren still couldn't tell. With an actress like Grace, it was hard to say what was real and what was an act. "Trust me, I get it." If Grace had starred in action movies or had been a character actress in dramas, maybe her sexual orientation wouldn't have mattered so much. But she had always played Ms. Perfect, the pretty girl-next-door, the one you wanted the movie's hero to fall for. "I just didn't think it would be that bad." Lauren pointed over her shoulder to where the elderly lady had stopped them.

"I thought she was pretty sweet, actually."

"Yeah," Lauren grumbled, "because you weren't the one she threatened with her monster purse."

Grace laughed, a gesture that didn't seem at all rehearsed.

"Thanks for not throwing me under the bus, by the way," Lauren said.

"You're welcome."

Grace had expected Lauren to drive a BMW or a Lexus, but when Lauren pressed her key fob, the lights of a gray Honda Civic flashed. Most of the PR types she'd met were concerned with status symbols, but apparently, Lauren wasn't.

Lauren looked at her over the roof of the car. "Something wrong?"

"No, nothing," Grace said and quickly got in.

Lauren settled in the driver's seat and looked over with a slight smile. "The carriage not to your liking?"

"It's fine. I just..."

"You thought I'd drive something a little more...flashy?"

Grace nodded, embarrassed to admit it. She rubbed her goose-bump-covered arms. "Would you mind turning up the heat a little?"

"I can do better than that."

Their shoulders brushed when Lauren turned and reached through the gap between their seats. "Here." She handed Grace a red Boston University sweatshirt.

"Thanks." A hint of Lauren's perfume—a fresh, citrusy scent with spicy undertones—clung to the fabric, making Grace inhale deeply as she slipped the garment over her head. *Hmm. Nice.*

"So?"

Grace looked over at Lauren. "Excuse me?"

"I'm going to need Jill's address."

"Oh. Of course." Grace told her and tried to reach her friend again while Lauren punched the address into her GPS and started the car.

Still no answer from Jill. Grace was really starting to worry.

For once, there wasn't much traffic, so they covered the eight miles to Jill's home in Glendale in less than half an hour. The house sat on a corner lot, surrounded by an ivy-covered brick wall. Jill valued her privacy just as much as Grace did.

They got out of the car and pressed the call button next to the gate.

Nothing.

"Seems she went out," Lauren said.

Grace peered through the iron bars toward the house. "I don't think so. Her car is in the driveway, and the light is on in one room."

"Then why isn't she answering the intercom?"

A reason instantly popped into Grace's head. She closed her eyes against the image, but it kept intruding. "What if she slipped and fell?"

"Why would she slip?" Lauren asked. "Is she drinking?"

"No." Grace didn't offer more of an explanation. Maybe bringing Lauren here hadn't been such a good idea.

Lauren stepped closer and pressed the call button again—with the same lack of response. "If you're really worried, maybe we should call the police."

"No!" Jill wouldn't like that kind of attention.

"But don't you want to check on her?"

"We will."

Lauren eyed the brick wall surrounding the house. "You're not suggesting we climb the wall, are you?"

"Dressed like this?" Grace gestured to her stilettos and the sweatshirt-covered dress. "No, thanks. I have the security code, but I never used it without her knowing that I'm coming."

If Lauren wondered why Jill had given her access to her home, she didn't show it. She waited patiently while Grace typed the code into the panel.

The gate sprang open.

"Come on." Grace waved at Lauren to follow her, and they entered the property.

Loud barking from the front of the house stopped them in their tracks just a few feet from the gate.

Lauren froze. "Oh, shit. You didn't tell me she has a dog."

"She didn't the last time I was here." Grace tried to make out the dog in the darkness, but she could see only a shadow on the porch. "Nice doggie."

The barking started again. It sounded like a big dog. One with sharp teeth. And the barking was coming closer.

"Let's get out of here!" Grace shouted.

Lauren didn't have to be told twice. She sprinted toward the gate.

Nearly twisting her ankle in her stilettos, Grace followed. When she slid to a stop next to the code box, Lauren gripped her arm to steady her.

Her heart hammering wildly, Grace entered the code, but the gate wouldn't open. "Shit!" Hastily, she peered toward the house and thought she saw a big shape charging toward them. "Climb!"

Next to each other, they grabbed handfuls of ivy and clambered up the wall.

Part of the ivy pulled from the wall, almost sending Grace plummeting to the ground.

Lauren gripped the sweatshirt and held on until Grace had grabbed hold of another handful of ivy.

One of Grace's feet found a brick that stuck out of the wall, giving her a more secure hold. Her heart still slammed against her ribs as she peered down, trying to see where the barking dog was.

"Jesus Christ," Lauren said next to her. "I don't think this is covered in my contract."

For some reason, this struck Grace as funny. She laughed hysterically, almost falling off the wall in the process. Her stilettos scraped over the wall until she found her foothold again.

When the dog continued to bark, lights went on in the house. The door opened. A figure, backlit by the light in the house, appeared in the doorway and then stepped onto the porch. "Who's there?"

Was that Jill? She sounded strange somehow, but maybe it was just the blood rushing through Grace's ears. "Jill? It's me," she called, "Grace."

"What are you doing up there?"

"Uh, hanging on for dear life?" Grace glanced into the shadows where the dog lurked. "Can you call the dog back, please?"

"Tramp! Come here!"

Grace and Lauren looked at each other. "Tramp?" they mouthed at the same time.

56

Lauren breathed a sigh of relief when the dog gave one last bark and then raced toward the house.

After waiting a few seconds to make sure the dog wasn't coming back, Lauren jumped down, congratulating herself for wearing sensible shoes. Once Grace had climbed down a little, Lauren reached up to put her hands on Grace's hips. "I've got you."

Still gripping the ivy, Grace slowly slid down and into Lauren's arms.

A whiff of perfume teased Lauren's nose, and for a moment, she wanted to pull Grace close, bury her nose in her fragrant hair, and hug her for all she was worth. *Are you crazy?* Grace was still a client, even though they'd just shared an adventure that seemed right out of an action movie. Quickly, she let go and stepped back.

Grace took one step toward the house and immediately stumbled as one of the stiletto heels finally gave out and snapped.

Lauren quickly caught her before she could fall. With their arms around each other, they tottered across the lawn toward Jill. Lauren could only imagine what a pathetic sight they must be, both of them scraped and covered with ivy and Grace with just one good shoe and wearing an old sweatshirt over her dress.

Jill still leaned in the doorway, holding on to the dog with one hand while gripping the doorjamb with the other.

Now that there was some light on the porch, Lauren realized that Tramp wasn't the large, mean guard dog she'd imagined when she'd heard him bark in the dark. He was medium-sized, with a golden, curly coat that made him look like a cuddly teddy bear. Wagging his fluffy tail, he strained toward them, apparently eager to greet them and be petted.

Lauren groaned and traded glances with Grace. "That's the monster dog we ran from?"

Grace shrugged with an impish grin. "It sounded like a much bigger dog." She called over to Jill, "When did you get a dog?"

"I went to an adoption fair when we got back from Georgia. It was love at first sight, so we adopted each other." Jill's voice sounded slurred. The light from the house shone on her gleaming red hair, styled in a cute pixie cut that looked a little messy. Had she already been in bed, and that was why she hadn't answered the doorbell?

Lauren stretched out her arm so the dog could sniff her hand. "What kind of dog is it?"

"He's a labradoodle," Jill said with a proud grin. At their questioning expressions, she added, "A cross between a Labrador retriever and a poodle. But let's go and talk inside." When she stepped back to let them in, her legs refused to carry her and she started to fall.

One arm still around Grace, Lauren managed to catch Jill with the other. All three of them tumbled against the doorjamb, both actresses clinging to Lauren.

God, if Marlene could see me now... I think I dreamed of something like this when I was younger, but this wasn't exactly what I had in mind.

"Jill?" Grace peered around Lauren. "Are you okay?"

"Fine," Jill said but sounded as if she had trouble talking.

Was she drunk? Somehow, Lauren didn't think so. This close to the actress, she would have smelled alcohol on her breath if that were the case.

The dog jumped around them, barking excitedly and nearly making them topple over, until Jill told him to go lie down.

Lauren caught a glimpse of a couch through an open door. "As pleasant as this is, ladies, I think we should go sit down."

"One second." Grace let go of Lauren and knelt to take off her ruined shoes. Carrying the stilettos in one hand, she squeezed past Lauren and wrapped her arm around Jill from the other side.

They led Jill to the couch, where she plopped down heavily. Grace and Lauren sat on either side of her.

After several moments, Lauren remembered her manners and reached out to offer Jill her hand. "Now that we already got up close and personal, maybe I should introduce myself. Lauren Pearce, Grace's publicist."

Jill gave her a friendly smile and took the offered hand. "Jill Corrigan." She gazed at Grace. "What happened to Roberta?"

"My mother," Grace said.

"Could someone please tell me what's going on?" Lauren asked.

"I was just about to ask the same," Jill said. "What were you doing climbing my wall in the middle of the night?"

Grace rubbed one knee that was covered in scratches. "It's barely ten thirty."

"That's not the point."

"I wanted to check on you," Grace said. "I tried to reach you all day, and you didn't show up at Russ's ceremony."

Her gaze on Lauren, Jill said, "I'm fine."

Clearly, she wasn't. She leaned heavily against the back of the couch and looked as if she was about to fall asleep sitting up. Her speech was slightly slurred and slow, as if she had to focus to form words. She didn't seem the type to take drugs, but in Hollywood, you never knew. Whatever was going on, Jill was clearly reluctant to admit it in front of Lauren.

"I think we can trust Lauren," Grace said.

"You *think*?" Lauren repeated. "I nearly got beaten up by an old lady and then eaten alive by Tramp the vicious labradoodle, all because I was trying to help you out. You'd think that would rate a more enthusiastic expression of trust."

Grace smiled. "Right. Jill," she said, her voice firm, "I *know* we can trust Lauren. You should tell her."

Tell me what? Lauren wanted to ask but sensed that it was better to keep quiet.

The two actresses looked at each other for several moments as if having a silent conversation. There was definitely a connection between them, but Lauren didn't get the impression that it was anything more than the loyalty of friends who'd been through a lot together.

Finally, Jill inhaled and exhaled loudly and looked at Lauren. "I..." Faltering, she bit her lip and sent Grace an imploring gaze.

Grace took Jill's hand. "Jill has MS."

Lauren couldn't help staring. *But she's too young,* she wanted to say but then remembered a former client of hers who'd been an athlete in her mid-twenties— Jill's age—when she'd been diagnosed with MS.

When Lauren said nothing, Grace added, "Multiple sclerosis."

"I know. I mean...I know what MS means." All the pieces of the puzzle suddenly fit together. That was why Jill had problems talking and walking and why the paparazzi had caught them stumbling up the stairs of Jill's trailer and going to a hotel together. Grace had probably helped her keep it quiet and covered for her whenever Jill wasn't doing so great.

Lauren looked from Grace to Jill. The actress's green eyes were so vivid and full of life that it was hard to imagine that she had an incurable neurological condition. She finally decided to say exactly what was on her mind. "I don't know what to say."

"Say that you'll keep it to yourself," Jill said. "Please."

"I will, but why? Why not just be open about it?"

Jill shook her head. "I don't want to be known as the actress with MS. I want to be known for my acting skills, not for this condition."

"Do you really think you can manage to keep it quiet for much longer? I mean..." Lauren gestured at the actress who sat slumped against the backrest.

"Today's a bad day, but it's not always like this. I'm not sure yet if it's a relapse or just my normal symptoms acting up. When I got up this morning, my legs felt like limp noodles." She looked at Grace. "That's why I wasn't at Russ's ceremony. I was so tired that I camped out on the couch all day. I heard the phone ring a few times, but it's upstairs, so..."

"It's okay," Grace said. "I'm just glad you're all right."

"What was so urgent that you had to come over here and break in?" Jill asked.

Grace hesitated as if debating whether to burden her friend with this.

"She needs to know," Lauren said gently. "It could impact her career too."

Jill looked back and forth between them. "Could someone please tell me what's going on? Preferably before I pass out from exhaustion."

"Do you want us to take you up to your bedroom first?" Grace asked.

"So the two of you can have your way with helpless little me?" Jill shook her head and then grinned. "Not that I'd put up much of a struggle."

Grace slapped her leg.

Lauren watched them interact. Was Jill just trying to lighten the mood, or was she gay after all? But surely then Grace, who was deathly afraid of being thought of as lesbian, wouldn't keep hanging out with her. Or maybe she would. After tonight, Lauren was beginning to think there wasn't much Grace wouldn't do for her friends.

"Tell me, please," Jill said.

Grace blew out a breath. "The paparazzi are at it again. They somehow found out that we shared a hotel room in Macon. So now they're putting one and one together and coming up with three."

Painfully slow, Jill reached up and massaged her temples. "Shit."

"They're expecting a statement about our affair from me before noon tomorrow," Grace added, making air quotes with her fingers.

Jill made a face as if she'd just bitten into a lemon. "Can't we just tell them 'no comment'?"

"Only if you want them to think you've got something to hide," Lauren said. "Saying 'no comment' to a reporter is like waving a red flag in front of a bull. It'll only make them dig deeper. Didn't your publicist tell you that?" It was usually the first thing she told clients that were new to the entertainment business.

"I don't have a publicist," Jill said. "Like I said, I always wanted my acting to speak for itself, so I stayed away from any other publicity as much as I could. But it seems I really need a publicist now." She grinned at Lauren, crinkling her lightly freckled nose. "You wouldn't happen to know a good one, would you?"

Lauren knew she should say no. It wasn't only that this was shaping up to be a PR nightmare that would have her working overtime in the very near future. Somehow, this felt personal for her, and she usually preferred to be all business when it came to her job. But when she felt the pleading gazes of the two actresses on her, saying no was not an option. "All right. I'll need to talk this over with my boss, but as far as I'm concerned, you've got yourself a publicist."

When she reached over to take Jill's hand in both of hers, she hoped like hell that she wouldn't end up regretting it.

CHAPTER 7

THEY WERE BOTH SILENT ON the half-hour drive to Grace's home. Lauren kept glancing over, but Grace seemed deep in thought, looking out the window, and Lauren was content to let her be and just drive in silence. It had been a long, eventful day for both of them.

When Lauren turned left, taking the Laurel Canyon Boulevard exit, Grace cleared her throat. "Thirteen years."

Lauren looked over at her with a small smile. "I hope it won't take us that long to get you and Jill out of this mess."

"No, I mean, that's how long it's been since I had a drink."

Lauren sensed the importance of this moment. Grace, who was notoriously closemouthed about her private life, had just trusted her with a secret that could harm her career. None of her fans had the slightest inkling that the golden girl of romantic comedies had once succumbed to addiction, and it was best to keep it that way. "Thirteen years," Lauren repeated, not sure how to react to that big proof of trust. "Which means you stopped drinking when you were...?"

The tension visible on Grace's face relaxed into a smile. "Is this your subtle way of asking me how old I am?"

"I know how old you are," Lauren said. "Twenty-nine, like so many other actresses have been for years."

"I'm really twenty-nine."

Lauren grinned at the indignant tone. "I know. Which means you stopped drinking when you were sixteen."

"Almost seventeen," Grace said.

"Wasn't that when you left that TV series?"

"No, that happened earlier, when I was fourteen. The drinking began when they kicked me off the show."

"They kicked you off?" Lauren asked. "Why would they do that?"

"Ratings, why else?" Grace sighed.

"But you had a lot of loyal fans, didn't you? I mean, purse lady clearly still remembered you fondly after all these years."

Grace stared through the windshield. "Yeah, but I bet she remembers the cute little girl, not the pimply-faced teenager. As I grew older, I wasn't so cute anymore."

Somehow, Lauren doubted that. The actress was cute, even barefoot, scratched, and in a stained dress. Lauren could hardly imagine her as an awkward teenager.

Grace must have seen her skeptical expression, because she said, "No, really. It was bad. I had acne like you wouldn't believe, and keeping the weight off was a constant battle. After the powers that be sent little Amber off to boarding school in Europe, I had trouble finding work for a year or two. My mother dragged me to every dermatologist and to every cattle call in town. God, that was humiliating."

Lauren had accompanied a few of her clients to casting calls, so she knew how demoralizing they could be. She could only imagine how Grace must have felt as a teenager—when her self-esteem was low to begin with—having to face casting directors who eyed her every pimple and each extra ounce of fat on her body and told her she wasn't good enough for a role.

"That's when the drinking got bad," Grace said.

"How did you manage to keep it quiet?" Lauren asked. "I've worked in PR for eight years now, and I never even heard rumors about it."

Grace shrugged. "Acting was the only thing that meant something to me. I always stopped drinking early enough to be sober when call time came. My mother was also very creative when it came to covering for me."

Her mother had covered for her instead of putting her into rehab? Lauren couldn't believe it. She didn't know what to say to that, so they drove along in silence, only the hum of the engine filling the space between them.

A loud growling noise interrupted the silence.

Grace pressed a hand to her stomach. "Sorry."

"No need to apologize for being human," Lauren said. Truth be told, she was pretty hungry too. She'd skipped lunch and dinner, and by now, her stomach felt as if it were ready to digest itself. She looked over at Grace. "Do you want to stop somewhere for something to eat?"

"At this hour?"

"Hey, this is LA, the city that never sleeps."

"That's New York," Grace said.

Lauren playfully rolled her eyes. "Smart-ass." She paused when she realized what she was doing. When had their interaction become less professional and more like the banter between friends?

But Grace didn't seem to mind. The teasing probably introduced a normalcy she didn't often get in her interactions. "Yeah, but I'm a barefoot smart-ass with scratched-up knees. Even if we find a place that is still open, we can't walk into a restaurant looking like this."

She was right, of course. People usually just saw the freedom that money could buy celebrities—a shopping trip to Paris, vacationing on the Bahamas, a new sports car every year—but there were actually a lot of things Grace couldn't do. Lauren wondered if she'd ever had a beer at a corner bar or taken a stroll through the park in a pair of old jeans and no makeup. "Right," Lauren said. "Can you imagine the headlines I'll have to deal with tomorrow if you show up in a restaurant like that?"

"Are you implying that I look less than my usual gorgeous, sophisticated self?" Grace asked in a faux haughty tone.

Lauren looked away from the street for a moment. The headlights of oncoming cars bathed Grace in streaks of light, so Lauren could take in Grace's scraped knees, the ivy stains on her white dress, and the baggy sweatshirt that kept slipping over her hands. "You look beautiful." She cursed herself as soon as she'd said it.

Just when she was about to add something such as, *For an actress who'll soon turn thirty,* Grace said quietly, "Thanks."

In the awkward silence, the gurgling of another stomach—this time Lauren's—sounded overly loud.

"Guess I'm not the only one who's hungry," Grace said with a mild smile.

Lauren nodded. "I could eat a horse."

"Well, I don't think I have any ungulates in my fridge, but there should be enough other stuff to throw together a salad and sandwiches. You're welcome to join me."

Lauren wanted to accept the invitation, sensing that Grace rarely if ever had guests over, but she knew it wasn't a good idea. "It's not that I don't want to, but..."

"You want to keep things professional," Grace said. "I understand." She turned her head and stared out the side window to the darkness beyond.

The playful mood was gone, and Lauren almost wished she would have accepted the invitation. "I wouldn't put it beyond Stan to keep an eye on your house to see who's coming and going. Can you imagine what he'd write in that *Celluloid Closet* column of his if a known lesbian was seen sneaking out of the home of Grace Durand in the middle of the night?"

Grace groaned. "Jesus Christ. Sometimes, a sandwich is just a sandwich."

"Not when you're in show business, Dr. Freud."

"I guess." Grace looked out the window again.

"Well," Lauren said when the silence in the car continued, "I'm fairly sure Stan isn't keeping an eye on my place."

Slowly, Grace turned her head and looked at her.

"We need to talk about what to tell Stan tomorrow anyway, and we might as well eat while we do that," Lauren added.

When Grace nodded her acceptance and said, "I'd like that," Lauren started to wonder whether she'd picked her socks up off the floor in the living room before leaving for work this morning.

Grace suppressed a giggle as they glanced left and right and then, when they were sure no one was watching, snuck into Lauren's apartment building in Brentwood. She hadn't done something like this since she had been a teenager, sneaking out to party with some of her older co-stars.

Luckily, everything was quiet as they made their way down the corridor, with no neighbors peeking out of their apartments. Lauren stopped in front of the last door to the right and unlocked it. She reached in to turn on the light before letting Grace enter ahead of her.

Still barefoot, carrying her stilettos in one hand, Grace squeezed past Lauren and looked around.

By the standards of her Hollywood acquaintances, the apartment was small, but Grace instantly liked it. The front door opened directly into a long living/dining room, with no space wasted on a hall. Four chairs were placed around a square dining table on which a stack of bills and magazines waited for Lauren's attention. To the right, an open archway led into a small, but fully functional kitchen.

The apartment was quiet except for the hum of the stainless steel refrigerator. Grace realized belatedly that she hadn't asked Lauren if she lived alone. She was curious but didn't want to appear nosy by asking about Lauren's private life. Lauren was her publicist, after all, even if she was starting to feel almost like a friend. *I guess scrambling up a brick wall together can do that to you, but you'd better be careful.* She'd been burned by new friends more than once. People she'd thought she could trust had revealed all kinds of personal information to the media. Nothing scandalous, but still, it rankled her to read in magazines about her battle to keep off weight or about how much she'd paid for her couch. As a result, she'd become slower to trust over the years. Despite her internal admonition, she had a feeling that Lauren wouldn't betray her, even without a confidentiality clause.

Lauren walked past her and opened the sliding glass door leading to a small balcony. Fresh air streamed into the apartment. She gestured at the camel-colored microfiber couch in the living room. "Please, have a seat while I rustle up something to eat."

When Lauren moved to the kitchen, Grace stood by the open balcony door for a moment, breathing in the fresh air. Through the palm trees and greenery surrounding the building, the lights of the city glittered in the distance. "Nice," she said when she finally turned and settled into the plush couch cushions.

"Thanks," Lauren said from the kitchen, her voice sounding muffled as if she had her head stuck in the refrigerator. "Nothing special, but I like it here. It's not like I'm home that much anyway, so it's enough for me."

"How long have you lived here?" Grace asked as she eyed the stack of scripts on the coffee table. Was Lauren reading them for one of her clients?

The refrigerator door thudded closed, and then pots banged. "About eight years."

"And before that, you lived in Boston?"

Lauren stepped around the breakfast bar separating the kitchen from the living room and sent Grace a startled gaze. "Did you google me or something?"

Grace laughed. "No." Grinning, she pointed at the sweatshirt she was still wearing.

"Oh." Lauren went back to the part of the kitchen Grace couldn't see. "Yeah, I went to BU, but I was born in LA."

"Oh, wow. You're probably the first LA native I've met."

The sound of a jar popping open and Lauren's chuckle drifted over. "What can I say? We're a rare breed. Onions?"

"Uh, excuse me?"

"Do you want onions?"

What the heck was Lauren making? "No, thanks."

"How about you?" Lauren asked and leaned over the breakfast bar to look at Grace. "Where were you born, Betty G. Duvenbeck?"

Grace winced at the use of her birth name. "What? That big red file you have on me told you my birth name but not where I was born?"

"How do you know it's a red file? There are other colors too, you know?"

"After my mother fired you your first week, I have a feeling I rate the red file," Grace answered. She realized that she liked Lauren's gentle teasing. It was so unlike the reverent tone most other people used when talking to her. Lauren seemed unimpressed by her celebrity status and made Grace feel as if she could for once be herself—whoever that was. Sometimes, after spending months getting into the head of a character, it was hard to remember.

A drawer opened and closed in the kitchen. "I'm pleading the fifth. So, where were you born?"

"Londen," Grace said.

"London? You don't sound British."

"Not London. Londen." Grace spelled it for her. "A tiny little town in Illinois, with nothing but cornfields and one stop light."

"Did you like it there?" Lauren asked from the kitchen.

Grace curled her bare toes into the soft carpet. "I guess it was okay. I didn't really spend enough time there to be sure. I spent a lot of my childhood in LA and Toronto, shooting commercials, TV shows, and later movies."

"We have that in common," Lauren said. "Well, not the shooting, of course. But I practically grew up on various movie sets too. My whole family is involved in the entertainment business."

"You mean other than your parents?"

"Yeah. Let's see... We have several actors, two screenwriters, and a costume designer. Oh, and my godfather and godmother are studio executives. Our family dinners looked more like production meetings. I knew long before I entered school that I never wanted to end up in show business. It's a crazy line of work, and you have to be a bit nuts to survive in it. Um, no offense intended," Lauren added as if only now remembering who she was talking to.

Grace smiled. "No offense taken. So what happened to make you end up as a publicist for the people in this crazy business?"

"I guess I missed the California sunshine," Lauren said.

"That's your answer? You missed the California sunshine, and that's why you went into PR?"

"Well, not directly," Lauren said. "After four winters in Boston, I moved back here. I worked in the marketing and communications department of a nonprofit organization for three years."

Grace could see her in that line of work, maybe helping underprivileged children, homeless people, or animals in need. Somehow, she got the impression that Lauren was a person who'd throw herself into her job and be good at it, no matter what it was. "What happened then?"

"I did someone a favor," Lauren said. "An old friend of my family, who is a talent agent, needed something written for one of his clients, so I helped out for a while."

"And you were hooked."

"Yeah."

Grace wished she could see into the kitchen area and watch Lauren's face. She couldn't quite figure out whether Lauren regretted going into PR or thought it was the best thing that could have happened to her career. Before she could open her mouth for another question, Lauren asked, "Ready for my award-worthy midnight snack?"

As if in answer, Grace's stomach rumbled again. "Beyond ready."

Lauren rounded the breakfast bar with a tray. "Mind if we eat here, or do you want to move to the dining table?"

"Here is fine." Grace craned her neck to see what Lauren had prepared.

After pushing the stack of scripts out of the way, Lauren set the tray on the coffee table.

Steam rose off four hot dogs. Other bowls held condiments such as onions, relish, and shredded cheese. Bottles of ketchup and mustard balanced at the edge of the tray.

Grace's mouth watered as she caught a whiff. "Oh, God. Do you know how long it's been since I had one of those?"

"Oh. I didn't think... Is it okay?" Lauren asked.

"I really shouldn't..." Her mother would have a heart attack if she saw her eat junk food, especially this late in the day.

Lauren pointed at the fridge. "If you'd rather have a salad, I can—"

"No. This is fine." Grace decided that she'd just spend an extra half hour on the elliptical trainer tomorrow and reached for one of the soft, white buns.

Lauren settled on the recliner across from Grace and watched her pile condiments on her hot dog. During her career, she'd had lunch with many actresses, and most of them just picked at their salads instead of eating heartily.

Not so Grace. She pushed up the sleeves of Lauren's sweatshirt, picked up the hot dog, eyed it for a moment, and then took a big bite. "Oh God. So good."

The moans and little sounds she made while she ate made Lauren squirm. She'd watched love scenes in movies that sounded less erotic.

Grace looked up and licked a bit of mustard off her fingers. Somehow, she managed to make even that look sexy.

Lauren averted her gaze and reached for her bottle of water, feeling the need to cool off. Bringing Grace here, into her private life, hadn't been one of her brightest ideas. Apparently, her libido wanted to share more than just hot dogs.

"Thank you," Grace said when her first hot dog was gone.

"It's just hot dogs."

"Not just for the hot dogs. For everything you did today. Like you said, running from a dog and climbing a brick wall isn't covered in your contract, so thanks."

Lauren reached for her own hot dog so she didn't have to look at Grace and see the gratefulness in her eyes. It was easier to think that she'd just fulfilled her duties as a publicist, nothing more. She tilted her head in silent acknowledgment and said, "That second hot dog is yours."

"I shouldn't," Grace said, even as she reached for it.

Chuckling, Lauren heaped relish on her own hot dog.

After polishing off the last crumb of her second hot dog, Grace insisted on doing the dishes.

"That's not necessary," Lauren said. "I have a dishwasher."

"Does it rinse the plates and put the food back into the fridge too?"

"Uh, no."

Grace sent her a telling gaze. "Well, then I guess one of us needs to do that. And since you cooked…"

Lauren gave up and followed her to the kitchen with a clipboard. She leaned against the breakfast bar and watched Grace put the mustard and ketchup back into the refrigerator and rinse the plates and bowls. How surreal this was. Grace Durand, three-time Golden Globe winner, was in her kitchen, doing the dishes. Lauren shook herself out of her haze and lifted the clipboard. "Let's talk about what to tell Stan tomorrow morning."

"Not much we can tell him," Grace said. "Not as long as Jill isn't ready to tell the public that she has MS." When she bent to put the plates into the dishwasher, her dress slid up a little, revealing a smooth expanse of thigh.

With some effort, Lauren forced her gaze back onto the blank page. "She should really think about doing it soon."

"I understand why she's hesitating. She mostly plays spunky sidekicks, characters that are upbeat and full of life. What if casting directors think someone with MS can't convincingly portray those characters once the public finds out?"

Lauren didn't have a good answer for that. Life as an actress sometimes simply wasn't fair. "Okay. Then what do you want to tell Stan?"

Grace closed the dishwasher, turned, and leaned against it. "Can't we simply tell him that Jill and I are just two friends who wanted to spend a quiet night away from the set?"

"That sounds too much like a romantic getaway," Lauren said. "But I like the premise. How about we rephrase it a little?" She scribbled something down, describing the stressful life on set—five o'clock call times, fourteen-hour days, endless repetitions because the director wanted one more take—and then stating that the two actresses had retreated to the hotel for its whirlpool and room service. That was how most people viewed actresses anyway. She held out the clipboard so Grace could read it.

When Grace finished reading and looked up, admiration sparked in her eyes. "Brilliant. You really have a way with words."

"The inn did have a whirlpool, didn't it?" Lauren asked. Stan was an old-school journalist. He'd check out each and every little detail of their story.

A tiny wrinkle formed on Grace's forehead. "I have no idea. Once I finally had Jill in bed, I didn't leave the room."

Lauren pointed at her with the pen. "Don't say that to the press."

Grace rolled her eyes. "You've got a dirty mind."

Chuckling, Lauren led her back to the living room.

Grace sat in Lauren's recliner, both feet up, Lauren's MacBook on her lap while Lauren rummaged around in the next room.

"Did you find anything?" Lauren asked when she returned with a first-aid kit.

Grace nodded and pointed at the website on the laptop's screen. "They do have an outdoor whirlpool."

"Great. I'll send Stan the statement tomorrow morning, then." Lauren put the first-aid kit on the coffee table and opened it. "Now let me see your knees."

"They're just a few scrapes, nothing serious."

"Even scrapes can get infected," Lauren said. "It's better not to take any risks. I don't want to have to handle headlines like 'Grace Durand hospitalized with an infection she contracted when she climbed the wall surrounding Jill Corrigan's property in a sapphic midnight remake of *Romeo and Juliet.*'"

Grace had to laugh at the headlines that Lauren kept making up. "You're right. We can't risk that. I prefer movies with happy endings."

Lauren soaked a cotton ball with antiseptic and knelt next to the recliner.

They both looked down at Grace's legs. Several scratches covered her knees, a few trailing down to her shins. Most of them hadn't broken the skin, but some had been bleeding. Half-dried blood and bits of dirt now clung to her legs.

"This might sting a bit." Lauren lowered the cotton ball, hovering just an inch from Grace's skin. "Ready?"

Grace nodded and braced herself. A burning pain flared through her when the antiseptic touched her skin. She clamped her hands around the armrests of the recliner and looked at Lauren, the dark head bent as she worked on getting the dirt out of the wounds.

Lauren's hands, broad, with long fingers, moved gently over her skin.

Grace couldn't remember the last time someone had taken such tender care of her.

When Lauren was done with the antiseptic, she squeezed out a bit of antibiotic ointment and used cotton swabs to dab it onto the scrapes without touching them directly.

Grace thought it was overkill for a couple of harmless scrapes, but she didn't have the heart to tell her.

Finally, Lauren placed Band-Aids over the deepest cuts, re-capped the tube of ointment, and clicked the first-aid kit shut. "There." She smiled up at her. "All better now."

Grace cleared her throat. "Thank you, Dr. Pearce." She put Lauren's laptop on the coffee table and stood.

"Do you want me to drive you home now?" Lauren asked.

"That's not necessary. I'll call a service that I sometimes use to drive me to the airport. They're very discreet."

Lauren frowned. "I can drive you."

"Thanks for the offer, but remember the headline you quoted earlier? How would you like to handle a headline about Grace Durand getting out of the car of a known lesbian in the middle of the night, wearing said lesbian's clothes?" Grace tugged on the sweatshirt she was still wearing.

"Hmm. You might have a point there."

Grace called the service. By the time the driver arrived, it was nearly two in the morning. Yawning, Grace walked to the door and turned back to Lauren.

They smiled at each other.

"Thanks again for everything," Grace said, meaning it.

"You're welcome. Good night."

"Good night." One foot already outside the apartment, Grace remembered something and turned back around. "Your sweatshirt." She moved to take it off, but Lauren shook her head.

"Keep it. Remember—"

"Yeah, yeah. I know. You don't want to handle headlines about Grace Durand catching pneumonia."

"Exactly."

They shared another grin, and then Grace left.

What a crazy day, Grace thought as the door closed behind her. Somehow, though, Lauren's presence had made it all okay. She hoped tomorrow would go just as well.

CHAPTER 8

LAUREN JERKED AWAKE. AFTER UNTANGLING herself from the sheets, she rubbed her eyes and sat up. Remnants of a dream still clung to her hazy mind like cobwebs, images of running across a lawn with Grace, scrambling up a wall, and then patching up Grace's knees. Pretty much a realistic repeat of last night—only that when Lauren had glanced up with the cotton ball in hand, Grace had lowered her head and kissed her.

She pressed her hand to her tingling lips and tried to tell herself that it was perfectly harmless. Millions of people worldwide had dreams like that about Grace Durand, right?

Yeah, but those people don't have to work with her. Maybe she should put some professional distance between them and cut out the friendly banter that had somehow made it into their interactions.

Finally more awake, she realized that bright sunlight was filtering in through the shades. Her head swiveled around.

The glowing numbers on her alarm clock told her that it was already after eight. Why hadn't the damn thing gone off? Had she forgotten to set the alarm before finally drifting off to sleep around three?

No time to figure it out now.

She jumped out of bed without checking her e-mail, as she usually did right after waking up. She was showered, dressed, and on the way to the office in record time. When she walked into the lobby of CTP, there was only one thing on her mind: coffee.

"Lauren!" Tina's urgent voice reached her before she could start her search for a cup of the coveted beverage. "Thank God you're here. I've been trying to reach you for the last hour. The press has been calling all morning for a comment from you or Ms. Durand."

Frowning, Lauren reached into her pocket and pulled out the phone she'd grabbed on her way out. She'd turned it off before the handprint ceremony yesterday and had then uncharacteristically forgotten to turn it back on.

Now, as she powered it back on, it chimed frantically. She had eleven missed calls, three of them from Stan Zaleski, three from the office, and five from various reporters.

Oh shit. Whatever was going on, it wasn't good. "What happened?"

"Uh, maybe you should just listen to your messages or read your e-mail," Tina said, clearly not wanting to be the one who gave Lauren the bad news.

Nearly plowing down an intern, Lauren rushed to her office and powered up the computer while she listened to her messages.

The first one was from Stan. "Lauren? This is Stan Zaleski. There's been a change of plans. Can you call me back, please?"

The next one was from him too. "Stan again. I'm in a bit of a predicament. One of our writers didn't send in his article on time, so my boss wants the article about Grace Durand to go live sooner. Can you send me her statement tonight?"

Lauren started cursing.

Then Stan's voice came again. "The article just went live. I'm sorry."

Listening to the messages of bloggers and reporters who wanted more information about Grace's newfound sexual orientation, Lauren clenched her jaw and opened her browser. Seconds later, Stan's blog post appeared on her computer screen.

Lauren skimmed it quickly.

Unlike the sensational garbage *Tinseltown Talk* had published, this article was intelligently written, and Lauren agreed with a lot of what was said. Instead of focusing just on Grace, Stan Zaleski had written about the don't-ask-don't-tell policy of Hollywood studio heads and casting directors who pressured actors and actresses to stay in the closet, fearing they'd lose money due to the part of their audience that might not like gays and lesbians in leading roles. The sad thing was that many of the studio execs, agents, and other power players were gay themselves—and Stan vowed to expose their double lives, starting with Grace Durand.

He'd included the picture of Grace and Jill climbing the stairs to Jill's trailer, holding on to each other, and romantic snapshots of the Ocmulgee Riverside Inn at sunset.

At the end of the article, he'd stated that "neither actress could be reached for comment," which made them look even more as if they had something to hide.

The blog post had gone live not even twelve hours ago, but it already had hundreds of comments, some of them from fans claiming they'd always known that Grace was a lesbian and Nick just a "beard," while others were links to blogs and websites that had already picked up the story.

Lauren shoved back the keyboard tray. She didn't want to even glance at Twitter, knowing that a storm of speculation had most likely descended upon them. What had started out as a mention in a gossip rag that no one took seriously had now turned into a media hurricane.

She itched to pick up the phone to call Stan and rip into him, but she knew it wouldn't do her any good. What was done was done. Now she needed to focus on damage control—and fast.

A hand on her shoulder startled Grace awake, nearly making her jump out of bed—and out of her skin. She bumped her head on the headboard as she jerked upright and clutched the sheet to her chest.

Her mother loomed over her in a pink skirt suit.

For a moment, Grace thought she was still dreaming, having one of the nightmares in which her mother dragged her out of bed and to a casting call, where Grace stood in front of the casting director naked and utterly unprepared. But when she pinched herself, the image in front of her remained.

"What are you still doing in bed?" her mother asked, her hands on her hips. "Haven't you seen what's going on?"

Well, apparently not, since I was sleeping. Grace bit her lip so she wouldn't say it. "I had a late night after Russ's party," she said instead. No need to tell her mother where she'd been. It would only lead to discussions since her mother wasn't a big fan of Jill—or Lauren.

Her mother took a step back and stared at something on the floor. The color drained from her heavily made-up face. "That ugly thing isn't yours, is it?" Her gaze went to the bathroom door. "Oh my God! Is there someone in there?"

Still not fully awake, Grace glanced from the bathroom to her mother and finally to the floor. Lauren's Boston University sweatshirt lay beside the bed next to her dress, where she'd stripped it off before falling into bed last night. "Oh, you thought...? No, that's just Lauren's."

But that didn't seem to calm her mother's concerns—quite the opposite. "Lauren?" she screeched. "That...that publicist? You mean you and she...?"

Grace sighed. Why did she have to deal with all this drama so soon after waking up, after a night like the last one? She reached for the bathrobe draped over a nearby chair, slipped out of bed, and put it on. "No, Mom. Nothing's going on between Lauren and me. She just lent me her sweatshirt; that's all. I'm not gay, remember?"

"Then what's this?" Her mother reached into her large purse and threw a printout of a celebrity website onto the bed.

Grace caught a glimpse of her own face in a photo before her mother threw another website printout on top.

"And this?"

This one had a photo of Grace and Jill on the set of *Ava's Heart*, their shoulders touching as they looked at a page of last-minute script changes that Jill held.

A glossy magazine landed on top of the printouts. "And this?"

With trembling fingers, Grace picked up the magazine and leafed through it until she found the article about her and Jill. It was peppered with photos of the inn where they had stayed while shooting in Macon. The tabloid called it their *romantic little love nest*.

Shit. Grace plopped down onto the bed and reached for the cell phone on her nightstand. Just when she was about to call Lauren, the phone started to ring and Lauren's name flashed across the display. Grace quickly accepted the call. "Did you see it?" she asked instead of a greeting.

"Yes," Lauren said, sounding as if she was gritting her teeth. "Stan ran the article last night, and a couple of other bloggers picked up the story within an hour."

"It's not just the bloggers. There's at least one gossip rag that worked really fast and printed the same nonsense." Loud honking made Grace jerk the phone away from her ear. Cautiously, she moved it back. "Where are you?"

"On my way to Glendale," Lauren said.

That could mean only one thing. "You want to talk Jill into telling the press the truth."

"Yes. It's the only way out of this mess. By now, not telling them is hurting both of your careers much more than revealing the truth ever could."

Grace blew out a breath. "I think you're right. Drive carefully."

"I will. Please be careful too. Don't leave the house if you don't have to," Lauren said. "I bet the paparazzi are somewhere out there, just waiting to jump on you."

"I'll try to stay in," Grace said. Not much else she could say or do, so she ended the call.

"Telling the press the truth?" her mother repeated, sounding alarmed. "What truth is that?"

"I can't tell you that," Grace said.

Her mother's lipstick-red mouth formed a startled O. "But...but you always told me everything."

"And I would, Mom, but this isn't my truth to tell. Have some patience, okay? I promise you'll find out soon." Grace wanted to crawl back into bed and pull the covers up over her head, shutting out her mother, the media jackals, and the entire world, but she knew she couldn't. With her mother's disapproving gaze following her, she headed to the bathroom to get ready for whatever this day would have in store for her.

74

Rush hour still hadn't ended, so it seemed to take forever until Lauren reached Glendale. When she finally turned the last corner and Jill's house came into view, she started cursing and smashed her fist against the steering wheel. *Dammit.* She should have known the paparazzi would get there faster than she did.

Half a dozen vehicles lay in wait in front of Jill's house, most of them SUVs with dark-tinted windows, which were typical for celebrity-hunting photographers.

If she went in through the front door, she'd end up in the tabloids. The press vultures might even try to follow her in, not caring that they were breaking the law.

Lauren stopped her car two houses down, ignoring the fact that she was blocking someone's driveway. For a moment, she contemplated climbing the wall at the back of Jill's property, where the paparazzi couldn't see her, but she immediately dismissed that crazy idea. She didn't want to even imagine what the media would write if she got caught doing that.

Just when she was about to pull out her cell phone and call Jill, a black town car rounded the corner. It slowed in front of Jill's house, but the SUVs were blocking the front gate. The town car stopped, and one of the doors in the back opened.

Lauren craned her neck to see who was getting out. "Jill, if that's you, stay in the car," she murmured.

Of course, it was Jill. Her red hair gleamed in the sun as she climbed out of the car.

The paparazzi crowded around her before she could take even one step toward the gate. Cameras flashed, making Jill flinch back. One of the men pulled out a reporter's notebook.

"Oh, no, no, no. Don't say anything, Jill." Cursing, Lauren jumped out of the car and locked it hastily. As she sprinted over, the paparazzi peppered Jill with shouted questions.

"How long has it been going on?"

"Does Nick know about the affair?"

"Does he know his wife is gay?"

"Nonsense," Jill said. "Grace isn't gay."

Like a shark scenting blood, one of the reporters pressed closer. "But you are?"

"No!" Lauren shouted and ran faster to reach them before it was too late. "Don't say anything, Jill!"

But apparently, Jill didn't hear her over the snap of cameras and the shouts of the paparazzi. She had shrunk back, clutching the open door of the car for support. Now she slowly straightened. "Yes," she said and lifted her chin. "Yes, I am."

More flashes went off.

Lauren pushed past the paparazzi, nearly getting an elbow in the eye, and took up position in front of Jill. "That's enough, gentlemen." *And I use that term very loosely.* "We'll prepare a statement with more details. If you leave me your cards, I'll e-mail it to you."

The paparazzi grumbled, but when Lauren stood her ground, they finally handed over their business cards and backed off. They climbed into their SUVs and cleared the driveway, but they didn't drive off, hanging around just in case something else exciting happened.

Jill let go of the car door, closed it, and stumbled away from the town car, which slowly drove off. She looked at Lauren with wide eyes. "Oh, shit. Did I really say that?"

Lauren sighed. "Yes, you did."

"Jesus, Grace is going to kill me."

Only if I don't do it first, Lauren thought and helped the shell-shocked actress into the house.

Jill sank onto the couch and raked her fingers through her hair, thoroughly messing it up. Tramp ran over and leaned his muzzle on his mistress's leg, whining as if he could sense that something was going on.

Lauren got a glass of water and pressed it into Jill's hands. "Here."

Jill gulped down the water. "I wish I could have something stronger right now, but the doctors don't think it's a good idea."

"What were you thinking?" Lauren asked.

"The only thing going through my mind was 'whatever you do, don't say *no comment.*'"

Lauren groaned. She should have instructed Jill more carefully about how to handle the press, but there had been no time last night, and she hadn't thought things would move so quickly. Perching on the other end of the couch, she studied Jill's face. The actress was pale but seemed to be doing better than she had last night. "So you're gay?"

Jill threaded her fingers through Tramp's curly coat and looked up. A hint of humor returned to her green eyes. "Aren't you supposed to be able to tell? You're gay too, right?"

"Yes, I am. But it seems being chased up a wall by a dog puts my gaydar out of order," Lauren said with a shrug.

Jill snorted. "He hardly chased you up a wall. Tramp might bark, but he's more likely to invite intruders in for a petting session."

"Does Grace know?" Lauren asked.

The light in Jill's eyes dimmed. Pressing her lips together, she shook her head. "I don't think so. She might suspect, but I never came right out—no pun intended—and said so."

"Then we'd better figure out what to tell her *and* the media." Now that Jill had outed herself, even the more serious press might print articles about her possible involvement with Grace.

Moaning, Jill buried her face in the dog's fur and then peeked up at Lauren. "Can't you do it for me?"

"Me?"

"You are my publicist, aren't you?"

"I'll handle the press. You handle Grace."

Jill let go of Tramp and fell back against the couch. She sent Lauren a pleading gaze. "Can't we do it the other way around?"

Lauren raised her brows. "You aren't afraid of her reaction, are you?" While Grace hadn't reacted too well to finding out she'd hired a lesbian publicist, Lauren hadn't gotten the impression that she was homophobic. Grace had seemed totally relaxed when having hot dogs in Lauren's apartment with her.

"I don't want her to think…" Jill looked down to where she painted invisible patterns onto the armrest of the couch.

"What?"

"Do you know how many people pretend to be her friend in the hopes of getting something from her—her money, her body, a role in her next movie, a bit of the limelight…?" Jill shook her head. "I don't want her to think I'm one of them."

"Why would she think that?" Lauren asked. "Just because you're gay doesn't mean you're a gold digger or out to seduce her."

Jill said nothing.

Lauren hesitated, wanting to grant Jill some privacy, but she needed to know. There'd been too many surprises blindsiding her already. "You're not in love with her, are you?"

"No," Jill said quickly. A little too quickly, perhaps.

Lauren kept looking at her.

Red-cheeked, Jill threw a pillow in her direction, making Tramp strain to jump up on the couch because he wanted to join in on the game. Jill pushed him back down. "Oh, come on. She's gorgeous. What dyke wouldn't be just a tiny little bit infatuated with her?" She looked into Lauren's eyes. "Aren't you?"

Images of her dream flashed through Lauren's mind, and she again felt Grace's soft lips on hers. She stiffly shook her head. "This isn't about me."

"Oooh." Jill's wolf whistle made the dog bark. She soothed him before sliding closer to Lauren on the couch. "Do tell!"

Lauren gritted her teeth. "Nothing to tell. And don't try to change the subject."

"Said the pot to the kettle," Jill murmured.

"Jill," Lauren said with a warning undertone. "Seriously."

Jill held up both hands. "Okay, okay. So, to answer your question, I might have a little bit of a crush, but I'm not in love with her. I'm her friend. How do we get the media and the fans to believe that?"

Sighing, Lauren pinched the bridge of her nose. "That's the million-dollar question."

CHAPTER 9

WHEN GRACE REALIZED SHE HAD read the same page of the script three times without remembering one word, she threw the stapled stack of paper on the coffee table and got up from the couch. She restlessly prowled the house and finally settled down in the breakfast nook, where she'd left her laptop.

Her mother looked up from the smoothie maker that she was trying to figure out. "What is it, darling?"

"Nothing." Grace forced a smile. "Just checking my e-mail."

"You really should hire a housekeeper who's here twenty-four/seven, you know?"

Grace got up, walked over to her mother, and put the pieces of the smoothie maker together before sitting back down. When she opened the lid of her laptop, a notification alerted her of new messages. She accessed her in-box and glanced at the unread e-mail, most of them messages from George and some that Lauren's office had forwarded her. None of them looked urgent.

No new messages from Lauren, though. Was she still talking to Jill?

She frowned when she saw an unread e-mail from someone whose name she didn't recognize. Probably just spam. She clicked on it to make sure. After reading the first sentence, she realized it was from a fan. How the heck had he found out her personal e-mail address? *Great. Like things aren't bad enough.* Now she'd have to change her e-mail address—again.

She skimmed the rest of the message. It was from someone who'd signed the e-mail "a former fan" and promised her that she'd burn in hell. A wave of anger swept over her with such force that she nearly shoved the laptop off the table. Why was someone who had been a fan suddenly sending her hate mail just because of these stupid rumors? Sometimes, she just didn't understand people.

Calm down. Lauren will make it go away. She took several deep breaths before deleting the e-mail and emptying the trash.

There. The message was gone forever. She hoped she wouldn't get another one like this but knew better. Instead of opening the other unread messages, she logged out of her e-mail program.

Her e-mail provider displayed a colorful page of celebrity news.

Grace rolled her eyes and was just about to close the browser when one of the pictures caught her attention.

It showed a redheaded woman getting out of a town car, her eyes wide as if the photographer had surprised her.

Grace's finger froze on the trackpad. She leaned closer to the screen to study the small image. *That's Jill!* The caption beneath the picture said, *Yes, I am.*

Huffing, Grace clicked on the picture just to see in what clever way the tabloids had distorted the truth this time.

The headline of the short article was set in all caps, practically screaming, YES, I AM—JILL CORRIGAN COMES OUT AS GAY!

"Yeah, sure," Grace mumbled and started to read.

> *Jill Corrigan, best known for her role in the popular TV show* Coffee to Go, *has recently been photographed getting up close and personal with Grace Durand, even spending the night at a romantic little inn with her.*
>
> *We caught up with the actress in front of her Glendale home this morning to hear what's up with the two hotties.*
>
> *When asked if she's gay, Jill said, "Yes, I am," confirming the rumors in true Ellen DeGeneres-style.*
>
> *Grace still hasn't commented one way or the other, so stay tuned!*

Grace blinked and reread the article. The "yes, I am gay" echoed through her head. Part of her wanted to dismiss it as fake news made up by a couple of reporters out to make money, but the photo had clearly been taken in front of Jill's house. After her adventure last night, Grace was intimately familiar with the ivy-covered brick wall in the background of the picture. If the photo was real, maybe the rest of the article was too.

Had Jill indeed said that? Or had the media made that up or somehow taken it out of context?

The website didn't provide any answers, no matter how long she stared at it. She slammed the laptop closed and jumped up. No more rumors and lies. She needed answers—now.

She got her cell phone from the coffee table and called Jill.

The call went directly to voice mail.

Jesus! Can't she pick up for once?

Grace pressed the end button without leaving a message. She wanted answers now, not whenever Jill got around to checking her voice mail. She thought about calling Lauren but then shook her head. Lauren had probably gone back to the office by now, and she didn't want to add more stress to the publicist's already stressful job.

Her mother abandoned the smoothie maker as Grace reached for her car keys. "Where are you going?"

"I need to talk to Jill," Grace said on her way to the door.

"Now?" Her mother rushed after her. "But you can't—"

Grace stopped and turned. "I can't just sit around here and be the last one who finds out what's going on. This is my career. My life!" She tapped her chest.

"Then I'm coming with you," her mother said in a tone that brooked no further discussion.

For a moment, Grace considered staying home. The conversation she needed to have with Jill wasn't one she wanted to have with her mother in the room. Well, she could just tell her to wait outside and keep Tramp company. The thought made her grin despite her tension.

"Let's go."

Several cars and SUVs were parked in front of her driveway, blocking the now-open gate.

Her mother tugged on Grace's arm. "Let's go back inside and—"

"No." Grace clutched the steering wheel. She didn't want to be a prisoner in her own home, having to find out from the tabloids what was going on. Instead of putting her Ford Escape into reverse, she leaned on the horn.

Four men and a woman came running around their cars and stopped at the open gate, cameras at the ready.

Grace bit her lip. Somehow, a female paparazzo—a paparazza, she supposed—felt like a betrayal. She honked again, but they didn't back away or move their vehicles. Slowly counting to three, she lowered the driver's window and tried to sound civil as she said, "If you don't mind, could you—?"

Flashes went off in her face, blinding her. For a few moments, stars danced in front of her eyes. She threw her arm up to shield her face. "Please," she said politely, but firmly. "Back off and let me leave."

The intruders kept snapping away, still blocking the gate.

She had always tried for an amicable relationship with the press, but this was too much. "Enough!"

More flashes went off.

"If you don't move your cars right this instant, I'm going to call the police!"

"One question, then we'll leave," one of the men said.

Grimly, Grace nodded at him to ask his question.

"Are you gay?"

Her mother leaned across Grace's lap to shout at him. "That's outrageous! I'll have you sued for slander!"

The paparazzo just grinned and snapped a photo of her. "Is that a yes?"

"That's a no comment!" her mouther shouted. "And now get out of the way, you insolent little punk!"

Great. Now that her mother had waved the *no comment* red flag, they'd never leave her alone. Grace groaned and hastily stabbed the button to close the window before her mother could do even more damage.

The paparazzi trotted to their vehicles, got in, and backed up enough so Grace could leave the property. As soon as she had driven a few yards, they followed her.

Determined to lose them once they hit Laurel Canyon Boulevard, Grace kept driving, keeping an eye on them in the rearview mirror.

Her mother pulled her phone from her oversized purse. "I'm calling that publicist of yours! She has to do something about this rabble!"

"Mom, Lauren told you she's not a magician."

Of course, her mother didn't listen. She lifted the phone to her ear, tapping her index finger against the cell phone's plastic shell as she waited for Lauren to pick up.

Lauren leaned back in the armchair and watched Jill return from the kitchen with a bottle of water. "I think it's time to come out to the media and the public."

"I thought that's what I just did." Navigating carefully so she wouldn't lose her balance, Jill rounded the coffee table.

Lauren was tempted to jump up and help her to the couch, but she sensed that Jill didn't want that kind of attention—which would make her next words not very popular with the actress. "I'm not talking about coming out as gay. I'm talking about coming out as someone who has MS."

Jill flopped down on the couch. "Are you sure I wouldn't just be shooting myself in the foot?"

Lauren tilted her head. "What do you mean?"

"As an actress, it's my job to convince people that I'm someone else." Jill let her hand dangle down, resting it on top of Tramp's back. "If I tell them too much about myself, especially things that contradict the roles I'm playing…"

"I understand. You'd like to be a blank canvas."

Jill nodded. "Something like that."

"I don't think that's possible. People are too nosy to just ignore your private life. If you don't fill that canvas, the tabloids will do it for you."

"And sling some mud on Grace's canvas too while they're at it," Jill said, sounding resigned.

"I'm afraid so. This is quickly turning into one big public-relations mess, and it's starting to hurt both of your careers much more than just telling the truth ever could."

Jill scratched the dog behind his ears, making him let out a contented groan. She trailed her fingers through his golden coat before finally looking up and at Lauren. "All right," she said. "I don't like it, but I'll do it."

For Grace. There was no doubt about it in Lauren's mind. She respected Jill for taking a personal risk for a friend. "I'm sorry that it has to be like this."

"It's not your fault," Jill said.

"I can still be sorry, can't I?" Lauren was sorry for more than just the situation with the media. A person like Jill didn't deserve to have multiple sclerosis. *No one does.*

The ringing of a phone stopped Jill from answering.

"It's mine," Lauren said and pulled her phone out of her pocket. It was a minor miracle that they hadn't been interrupted by calls before.

The display indicated that Katherine Duvenbeck was calling.

"It's Grace's mother." Lauren couldn't help groaning and then realized that she was practically bad-mouthing one client to another. *Damn.* Somehow, she had gotten too familiar with these two actresses. "I mean…"

Jill laughed. "Don't bother. I met Katherine."

Lauren lifted the phone to her ear. "Mrs. Du—"

A high-pitched scream nearly shattered her eardrums.

She jerked the phone away from her ear. *What the…?* Slowly, she moved the phone back. "Mrs. Duvenbeck? Are you all right?"

"Did that sound like I'm all right?" Grace's mother yelled after a few seconds of silence. "These men are trying to kill us!"

"What?" Lauren jumped up from the armchair. "Calm down and tell me what's going on."

"They're hunting us like rabbits!"

Lauren's adrenaline spiked. "Who's hunting you? Where's Grace?"

Jill sat up and slid onto the edge of the couch, mouthing, "What's going on?"

Lauren held up one finger in a give-me-a-minute gesture.

"Right next to me," Mrs. Duvenbeck said.

"Can you give her the phone?" Obviously, Grace's mother was hysterical, so she wouldn't get a clear answer from her.

"No, I can't!" Mrs. Duvenbeck nearly shouted. "She's trying to get us away from the paparazzi."

The paparazzi were chasing them? Images of high-speed chases and accidents flashed through Lauren's mind. She paced up and down the living room, nearly wearing a hole in Jill's carpet.

Tramp, sensing her agitation, let out a low whine, but Jill kept him next to her.

"They keep following us," Mrs. Duvenbeck said in that tone of voice that reminded Lauren of chalk screeching across a blackboard.

"Goddammit!" Lauren wanted to hurl the phone across the room but kept it pressed to her ear instead. "What are you doing out there? I told Grace to stay in the house!"

"Don't talk to me in that tone," Mrs. Duvenbeck answered.

Lauren took a deep breath, then another. *Okay, okay, don't upset her while they're driving.* "All right," she said as calmly as she could. "Where are you right now?"

"How am I supposed to know?"

A rustling sound reverberated through the phone; then Grace's voice came through the line. "We're a mile or two from Glendale. Are you back at the office or still with Jill?"

"Dammit, Grace! What are you doing—trying to get yourself killed?" Sometimes, Lauren wanted to put some of her clients over her knee. She hadn't thought that Grace would be one of those clients.

"Don't worry," Grace said, sounding much calmer than her mother. "It's not as bad as my mother made it sound. The paparazzi are backing off a little now. Maybe they realized they're scaring us."

Lauren snorted. "You think they care? No, they probably realized where you're going so they know they can catch up if they lose you."

Grace sucked in an audible breath, as if only now realizing that she was leading the paparazzi right to Jill's doorstep. "Maybe I'd better turn around and head back."

The thought of Grace driving all the way back with the paparazzi tailing her made Lauren frown. "No," she said more sharply than intended. "Keep driving. You're almost here now. We'll have to deal with the press sooner or later anyway."

Grace sighed into the phone. "I had hoped it could be later."

Well, you should have thought of that before you left your goddamn house, Lauren wanted to say but held her tongue. She could tell Grace exactly that as soon as she made it here in one piece. "If they catch up with you, just tell them that you and Jill are preparing a statement, okay? Remember not to say 'no comment.'"

Silence filtered through the line; then Grace murmured, "Too late."

"What do you mean?"

"Mom already waved the red flag."

Lauren rubbed her face with her free hand. Why oh why did she have to deal with amateurs who thought they were God's gift to public relations? "Just get here in one piece, okay?"

"Will do," Grace said and ended the call.

Within thirty seconds of entering Jill's house, Grace wished she would have stayed outside with the paparazzi. Tramp rushed over, greeting her like a long-lost friend, nuzzling her hand, and letting her pet his soft fur.

Lauren's greeting was less friendly. Her gaze swept Grace from head to toe, and as soon as she had made sure Grace was fine, she started shouting. "Dammit, Grace, what were you thinking?"

Grace opened her mouth to explain or defend herself, but Lauren wasn't finished yet.

"Life isn't one of Nick's action movies! If a car chase goes bad, you can't just yell 'cut' and do another take." She was shaking with anger, and her eyes sparked with intensity.

"Don't you think I know that?" Grace asked, struggling to rein in her own anger. She hated being treated like a misbehaving child. Her mother was doing enough of that, and she didn't need it from Lauren too.

A strand of Lauren's chin-length hair fell forward, into her eyes, and she shoved it back with an impatient hand. "You sure don't act like it! You took a big risk coming here—and not just a risk to your career."

Before Grace could reply, her mother pushed past her. "Don't you dare talk to my daughter like that!"

"I wouldn't have to if she'd done the sensible thing and stayed in." Lauren turned away and added more softly, "Not every injury can be patched up with a Band-Aid."

"Band-Aid?" Grace's mother asked, catching up with Lauren, who stomped into the living room. "What do you mean? What happened?"

"Nothing," Lauren and Grace said in unison.

"Grace? What is she talking about? I demand to—"

"With all due respect, Mrs. Duvenbeck," Lauren said. "I think you should stay out of this. You've already done enough damage."

Grace's mother paled, and then a flush swept up her neck, matching her pink skirt suit. "Why, you—"

Jill walked over, swaying almost imperceptibly, and gently gripped her sleeve. "Why don't you help me make some coffee, Katherine? I have a feeling you'll all be here for a while."

When her mother dug in her heels, Grace walked over to her. "Please, Mom. I promise that I'll explain everything later."

"All right." After one last glance back, Grace's mother let herself be pulled to the kitchen. Tramp trotted after them.

Lauren's gaze followed the trio. "You know," she said, more calmly now. "You're not doing yourself any favors letting her handle the media."

Grace opened her mouth to defend her mother but then closed it again without saying anything. Even though she didn't like to hear it, she knew Lauren was right, and she admired her for telling her straight out what no one else had the courage to say. She sighed. "I know. But she's my mother."

"Then maybe she should be just your mother, not your manager too."

If only things were that simple. Her mother had managed her for nearly thirty years and had gotten Grace to where she was today. How could she now, after all these years, come right out and tell her mother that she didn't want her as a manager anymore?

Knowing she wouldn't be able to resolve that particular problem anytime soon, Grace decided to focus on the situation at hand. "I read an article online that said Jill confirmed she's gay. Did they pull that out of their asses too, or…?"

"I think you should ask Jill that question," Lauren said.

Grace knew a confirmation when she heard one. She squinted at Lauren. "Was that a *no comment?*"

"What? No! I…" Lauren plucked her horn-rimmed glasses off her nose and started to clean them as if she needed an excuse not to look at Grace. "Just talk to Jill, okay?"

"Okay," Grace said. "I'll go talk to Jill, and you'll keep my mother entertained and out of the kitchen."

Lauren froze with her glasses halfway to her nose. "Uh…"

Grace smiled and then sobered. She took a step toward Lauren. "I really didn't mean to cause any trouble by coming here. In hindsight, I should have stayed home, like you told me to, but Jill didn't pick up her phone and I was sick of sitting around, not knowing what's going on."

"And I didn't mean to shout at you," Lauren said, the anger and gruffness now gone from her voice. "That wasn't exactly professional behavior."

They looked at each other for several moments.

Grace glanced into Lauren's hazel eyes and realized that Lauren hadn't just been angry with her because her presence at Jill's house might have messed up whatever PR tactic she'd planned. Lauren hadn't just been worried about Grace's public image; she'd been worried about Grace as a person. A hint of a smile played around her lips as she walked over to the kitchen. What a nice surprise. For once, she had a publicist who didn't see her as only a paycheck.

When Grace entered the kitchen, her mother and Jill were leaning across the sink, peering through the blinds.

"Are they still there?" Grace asked.

At the sound of her voice, Jill whirled around and then swayed.

"Careful!" Grace hurried over and gripped Jill's arms to help steady her.

"Thanks," Jill said. "I'm fine now. Just turned a little too fast. And yes, the paparazzi are still around. Well, at least they are no longer blocking the gate."

Grace slowly let go of her. She glanced at her mother, who watched them with an expression that Grace had learned to interpret as a post-Botox-injection frown. "Mom, would you mind taking the coffee to the living room?" She gestured at the tray that held coffee mugs, milk, sugar, and cookies. "We'll be there in a second."

"I'm not—"

"Please."

With a dramatic sigh, her mother reached for the tray and carried it out of the kitchen, mumbling something under her breath. Tramp bustled after her, his tail wagging, as if he hoped she'd drop one of the cookies.

Grace watched them go and then turned toward Jill.

Jill sent her a puzzled grin. "Are you sure it's a bright idea to leave her alone with Lauren?"

"I'm sure they'll be fine for a minute. There's something I need to know. Is it true?"

"Is what true?"

For some reason, Grace suddenly found it hard to say the words. Maybe because the media had made it sound so much like a scandalous thing. She sucked in a breath, held it for several seconds, and then said in a rush, "Are you gay?"

Jill gripped the kitchen island. For a moment, Grace thought she'd try to divert, but then Jill raised her chin, looked her in the eyes, and simply said, "Yes."

"Wow. I think I need something stronger than coffee now," Grace mumbled. They had known each other for years and worked together on two movies. How was it possible that she hadn't known something so essential about her friend?

"Did you really never suspect?"

Grace mutely shook her head.

"You didn't wonder why I'm never photographed with a man, not even at red-carpet events?" Jill asked.

"I thought you were just dating in private, away from the cameras." And very likely, that was what Jill had been doing; she just hadn't dated men. "Why didn't you ever tell me? You could have trusted me, you know?"

"I know. It's not that I didn't trust you. It just didn't matter between us."

Grace thought about it. Would Jill's sexual orientation matter if not for the media circus? Nothing had changed between them now that she knew. Jill was still the same person. Straight or gay, she was still the loyal friend who'd run lines with her until three in the morning when a scene had given Grace trouble.

"I know I sometimes joke around, but..."

Grace gave a dramatic little gasp. "Joke around? You mean you're not actually head over heels in love with me?"

Jill stepped closer and gave her a little shove. "Sorry to flatten your ego, Ms. Big-Shot Actress. Although God knows how I manage, because you are just too damn charming for your own good."

Grace hip-checked her and then quickly held on to her when Jill stumbled. "Sorry."

"It's okay. Damn MS is messing with my balance. One more reason why my sexual orientation doesn't matter," Jill said. "It's not like I'm good dating material anymore."

Oh, no. Grace couldn't let her friend believe that. She took Jill's face between her hands and forced her to look into her eyes. "Any woman would be lucky to have you."

Jill's chest heaved under a big breath, and then she smiled. "Any woman? Is that a come-on, Ms. Durand?"

"You wish, Ms. Corrigan. I meant any lesbian woman."

"What are you doing?" Grace's mother demanded to know from the doorway, looking back and forth between them.

Grace let go of Jill's face but forced herself not to step away from her. She had nothing to hide and wouldn't feel guilty for being Jill's friend. "Just talking to my friend, Mom."

"The coffee is getting cold," her mother said.

"We'll be there in a second."

Her mother lingered in the doorway for several moments before sending Jill one last glare and then marching off.

When Jill moved to follow her, Grace held her back. She'd tried for weeks to get up the courage to tell Jill but had postponed it time and again, telling herself that it wasn't the right moment. Maybe that right moment was now. "While we're making personal confessions, there's something that I have to tell you too."

Jill leaned against the kitchen counter and regarded her with a curious gaze. "What is it? You're not gay too, are you?" She grinned weakly.

Grace rolled her eyes. "No. But Nick and I..."

"Oh my God!" Jill eyed Grace's belly. "You're pregnant!"

"Only if immaculate conceptions are back in style," Grace muttered.

A wrinkle formed between Jill's brows. "What's that supposed to mean? You and Nick...you don't...?"

Grace wasn't in the mood to go into details about her troubled marriage or her lack of sex life, especially not with her mother and Lauren in the next room. "We're getting a divorce."

Jill sank against the kitchen counter. "What?"

"We're getting—"

"I heard you the first time. Why didn't you ever say anything? I know you. You wouldn't just give up on a relationship. This must have been going on for quite some time."

Grace had thought about it often, but she still had no idea when she and Nick had stopped being happy together. If she was perfectly honest with herself, maybe getting married had been a mistake, but after being together for two years and living together for nearly as long, saying yes had seemed like the right thing to do when Nick had proposed. "I don't know. I think I didn't want to face it."

"But you're sure it's over for good?" Jill asked.

Grace nodded. There was no way back for her and Nick.

"Come here." Jill spread her arms wide, and Grace willingly stepped into an embrace. "Are you okay?"

"I'll be fine. I'm more worried about what the divorce might do to my career. Does that make me sound like a cold-hearted, selfish bitch?"

Jill let go to look into Grace's eyes. "Only to people who don't know you. Jesus, I couldn't have picked a worse moment to out myself. I'm sorry, Grace."

"You couldn't know," Grace said. "At least now one of us doesn't have to pretend anymore."

"So you and Nick will pretend to still be crazily in love with each other?"

"Just until after *Ava's Heart* is released."

Jill frowned. "That's two months away."

"I know." Probably the two longest months of her life. "Come on." She wrapped one arm around Jill to help her keep her balance. "Let's go to the living room before Lauren quits because my mother drove her crazy."

This time, it was Jill who held her back. "Are we okay?"

"We're okay," Grace said without hesitation. She just wished she could say the same about their careers and the situation with the press.

Just as Lauren wanted to go after Mrs. Duvenbeck and haul her out of the kitchen, the woman marched back into the living room. She moved the blinds aside with two pink-painted fingernails and peeked out the window before whirling around to face Lauren. "My daughter isn't like that. You have to make them," she stabbed a finger toward the window, "realize that."

"Like what?" Lauren asked even though she knew exactly what Mrs. Duvenbeck meant. She couldn't help baiting Grace's mother a bit.

Mrs. Duvenbeck gestured. "Like…like…well, like you."

Lauren put down her mug of coffee and enjoyed the much-needed caffeine surge for a moment. "Oh, you mean she isn't as tall as I am? I think the press noticed that already."

With her hands on her hips, Mrs. Duvenbeck glared at her. "You know exactly what I mean."

"I do. Just let me do my job without interfering."

"Interfering?" Mrs. Duvenbeck repeated in a much higher pitch. "I have been guiding my daughter's career long before you even knew how to spell PR. If you're implying—"

"You two didn't eat all of the cookies, did you?" Jill asked as she entered the living room with Grace.

Lauren regarded the two actresses.

Grace had her arm wrapped around Jill's waist, helping her keep her balance. If Jill had really told her, Grace was earning points with Lauren for not shying away from Jill now that she knew she was gay.

"I'm not in the mood for cookies," Mrs. Duvenbeck said. "We need to find a way to deal with the media. What do we tell them?"

"The truth," Jill said.

Grace studied her. "Are you sure that's what you want to do?"

"Yes. Just give me twenty-four hours. I need to tell my parents first."

Grace's eyes widened. "You haven't told them?"

"Told them what?" Mrs. Duvenbeck asked.

No one answered.

Jill shook her head. Tramp ran over and nosed his mistress's hand as if feeling her anxiety. "They know I'm a lesbian, but I haven't told them about—"

Mrs. Duvenbeck gasped. "You're a…a lesbian?"

Jill looked her right in the eyes, not ducking her head. "Yes, Katherine, I am. I hope you won't hold it against me, just like I'm not judging you for being straight."

Go, girl! Lauren wanted to clap her on the shoulder but abstained from doing so.

"B-but the photos…the things those reporters wrote…" Mrs. Duvenbeck looked back and forth between her daughter and Jill. "They aren't…?"

"No, Mom," Grace said. "I'm not gay. You know that. The reporters misinterpreted the situation. I was merely helping Jill to her trailer; that's all."

"Then you need to tell them that," her mother said. "Now. Why wait around, eating cookies, while the world thinks that you're..." She lowered her voice. "... gay?"

Normally, Lauren would agree and deny Jill the twenty-four hours she'd asked for. When it came to doing damage control, a rapid response was essential. With the Internet, news traveled fast, so they needed to act quickly before rumors snowballed out of control.

But when Jill and Grace looked at her, she nodded reluctantly. "Twenty-four hours," Lauren said. "Not one second more."

CHAPTER 10

TEN MINUTES LATER, LAUREN REALIZED that Jill was fading fast. The actress was slumped against the back of the couch, looking as if she'd just run a marathon. Lauren and Grace exchanged glances; then Lauren gestured at the door, and Grace nodded.

"I think it's time for us to leave," Grace said.

"Leave?" her mother echoed, her eyebrows hiked up her forehead as far as they would go. "But the paparazzi are still outside. I don't want them to take more photos of you, writing all kinds of ridiculous things about you and Jill."

"You're parked right in front of the house, inside of the gate, right?" Lauren asked.

Grace nodded.

"Good. Mrs. Duvenbeck, are you up for playing the decoy?"

Mrs. Duvenbeck eyed her warily. "What do you mean?"

"I want you to put on a baseball cap or something, take Grace's car, and drive out of here as fast as possible," Lauren said. "Hopefully, the paparazzi will follow you."

"I won't be able to fool them for long," Mrs. Duvenbeck said.

"Doesn't matter. By the time they realize it's just you in the car, Grace and I will have made it out of here too, with no photos taken."

Mrs. Duvenbeck didn't seem happy, but she allowed Grace to outfit her with a coat to hide her pink skirt suit and one of Jill's hats, all the while complaining about it ruining her hair.

Tons of hair spray had turned her platinum-blonde hair into what looked like a helmet, and Lauren idly wondered how a hat could possibly mess up the bulletproof creation.

Finally, Mrs. Duvenbeck was ready. Acting as if she were an actress stepping onto the red carpet to accept an Oscar, she left the house and got into Grace's SUV.

"Ready to head out too?" Lauren asked.

Grace nodded. She hugged Jill, whispering something in her ear that made Jill clutch her a little more tightly.

Lauren averted her gaze to give them some privacy, but she couldn't help wondering what Grace had said.

After a moment, Grace joined her next to the front door.

"We have to be quick, just in case any of the paparazzi are still around," Lauren said.

"No problem. I'm not wearing stilettos this time." Grace held out one sneaker-covered foot.

A chuckle escaped Lauren. Somehow, she'd ended up in the most adventurous situations since becoming Grace's publicist. She turned her head and nodded at Jill. "I'll send you the statement for tomorrow as soon as I have it. We should hold the press conference in the CT Publicity offices, with both of you there."

"Okay," Jill said. "Be careful out there. The paparazzi are crazy."

She opened the door for them, and they hurried toward the gate with Lauren in the lead. A quick peek revealed that their plan had worked—the paparazzi's SUVs were gone. Still, Lauren took Los Feliz Road instead of choosing the direct route, heading west on the freeway, as Mrs. Duvenbeck had probably done. She didn't want to encounter any of the paparazzi who had surely turned around when they realized their mistake.

"You didn't seem surprised to hear that Jill is gay," Grace said after a few minutes of silence.

Lauren gave a vague shrug, not wanting to break any confidences. After all, she was Jill's publicist as well as Grace's. "Well, you know, we lesbians are supposed to have gaydar."

Grace turned toward her in the passenger seat, her knee pressing against the middle console. "Gaydar?"

"Like radar, just...gay."

"You mean lesbians can tell if another woman is gay, just by looking at her?" Grace sounded baffled.

Lauren glanced into the rearview mirror to make sure they weren't being followed. Luckily, the coast was still clear. "Some can."

"How about you?" Grace asked. "Can you do that?"

"Sometimes." Very aware that she was talking to a client, she would have preferred to talk about something else—anything else.

The sound of the tires on the road sounded overly loud in the silence between them.

Lauren risked a quick glance to her right, wondering what was going on in Grace's head.

Before she could ask, Grace cleared her throat. "What about me?" she asked quietly.

"You? Are you asking if you have gaydar?"

"No, I don't need to ask that. I already know that I don't," Grace said. "I had no clue that Jill is gay, and it never occurred to me that you could be too. But that's not what I'm asking. I mean…what does your…that gaydar thing say about me?"

"Why are you asking?" Wouldn't any straight woman just assume that Lauren's gaydar would identify her as heterosexual?

"Well, if gaydar works on me, at least my gay fans—if I have any—should realize that I'm straight, no matter what nonsense the press writes, right? So, what does your gaydar say about me?"

Lauren clutched the steering wheel and pretended to need her full attention for driving. "Um…Nothing."

"Nothing?"

"My gaydar didn't say anything about you." *Probably because it got drowned out by my libido.*

"Hmm." Grace seemed to think about it for a minute or two.

"Besides," Lauren added, "gaydar isn't exactly a scientific measuring method. Sometimes, it's affected by wishful thinking."

Grace tugged on the seat belt so she could turn even more toward Lauren. "What do you mean?"

Lauren tapped the indicator before making a right onto Franklin Avenue. "Your straight audience likes to imagine that you're just like them, someone they could hang out and be friends with. The men might even fantasize about—"

Grace pretended to stick her fingers into her ears. "Lalalalala," she sang loudly. "Nope. No way. Never happens."

Lauren laughed. "If that's what you'd like to think, I'll try not to ruin your illusions."

"Thanks. So you think my lesbian fans might do the same and wish the rumors about me and Jill were true?"

Mentally repeating the comments her lesbian friends made about actresses like Grace, Lauren nodded.

Grace sighed. "No matter what I do, who I am, I can never satisfy everyone, can I?"

"No one can do that," Lauren said and wondered why she would even want to try.

"Sometimes," Grace said very quietly, as if talking more to herself than to Lauren, "I think the Native Americans were right."

The non sequitur made Lauren turn her head to look at her before returning her attention to the road. "Right how?"

"They believed that if you have your picture taken, you'll lose your soul. Sometimes, I think that happens to actors and actresses too." Grace stared through the windshield.

Lauren braked at a red light and looked over at her. "I know what you mean. But...if that's what you think, why did you go into acting?" Then she remembered that Grace had been in front of cameras since she'd been in diapers and added, "I mean, why did you continue in acting as you grew older?"

Grace glanced over.

Once again, the disturbingly blue eyes startled Lauren. She sat staring for several moments until the driver behind her started honking. Quickly, she cleared the intersection.

"My father died when I was eight," Grace said quietly.

Lauren wanted to reach over and squeeze her arm or her knee, but she was very aware how inappropriate that would have been, so she kept both hands on the steering wheel. "I'm sorry," she said, hoping Grace could hear the sincerity in her voice.

Grace nodded her acknowledgment. "Thanks. I'm not saying it to make you feel sorry for me, though. Back then, I was devastated, of course. I have always been a daddy's girl, right from the start. My father really got me. I could talk to him about anything, while my mother..." She bit her lip. "I think she coped by throwing herself into managing my career. So I learned to do the same. When I was in front of a camera, I forgot about everything else. I could strip off all the pain and the expectations and just...be someone else for a while."

Lauren thought about Grace's words while she drove beneath an overpass and continued west.

"Do you think that's weird?" Grace asked when Lauren didn't comment immediately. For such a famous person, she sounded remarkably insecure.

"Not at all." Lauren understood her better than she liked to admit. Her last girlfriend had accused her of doing the exact same thing—avoiding her relationship issues by escaping into her job, where she could deal with other people's problems instead of her own. "It's not that different from what a lot of people are doing—using their jobs to avoid dealing with other, more painful areas of their lives."

"Christ, you make me sound like someone who could use a lot of therapy," Grace murmured.

Lauren smiled. "You mean you don't have a therapist? Don't you know that it's a status symbol?"

"You saw my car," Grace said. "I'm not into status symbols."

True. Grace's mother had driven off in the compact SUV that clearly was a few years old, and now Lauren peeked over at Grace's Levi's and sneakers. She decided she liked Grace in jeans.

Apparently, neither wanted to delve more deeply into the topic of therapy or their private lives, so they spent the rest of the drive in companionable silence.

Lauren navigated the narrow, curvy road, every now and then glancing left to enjoy the incredible view of the city below them. When she rounded the last bend, past the bougainvillea-hung villa at the corner, and caught sight of Grace's home, she slammed her foot down on the brake.

Reporters and paparazzi were camped outside of Grace's mansion. Either they had waited here the entire day, or they were the same ones who'd been in front of Jill's house and they had driven straight to the house when they'd realized it wasn't Grace in the red SUV. Their vehicles were blocking the gate.

Lauren put the car in reverse and backed up before the paparazzi could spot them. "What now?" she asked as she used a neighbor's empty driveway to turn the car around. "Is there somewhere you could stay? Some place the paparazzi won't know about?"

Grace nibbled on her lip as if considering whether she should tell Lauren about whatever hideaway she might have. Finally, she nodded. "Go back to Laurel Canyon Boulevard and then take the Ventura Freeway west."

"And then?" Lauren asked. Where was Grace leading her? Did she own another luxury villa, maybe in Malibu or some other place where the rich and famous lived?

But Grace gave nothing away. "You'll see."

"Turn left here," Grace said as Lauren navigated the constant twists and turns of Old Topanga Canyon Road.

Lauren eyed the dirt road to the left. "Are you sure this is the right way?"

Grace smiled. "Trust me. It is."

"All right." Lauren slowed to a near crawl. Her poor car bumped along a steep, winding dirt road that constantly narrowed. With damp palms, Lauren clutched the steering wheel, hoping that no rocks would damage the bottom of her car. She was beginning to understand why Grace drove an SUV. Just when she thought the road would end in the middle of nowhere, the car made it up an incline and a cottage lay in front of them.

"This is it," Grace said, a pride in her voice that hadn't been there when she'd invited Lauren into her multi-million-dollar mansion.

Lauren parked where Grace indicated, and they got out. Bending, Lauren checked to make sure the oil pan and the car's undercarriage had survived the drive up. Everything seemed to be fine, so she straightened and looked around. The cottage was nestled among a grove of trees that screened it from view. The scent of sagebrush hung in the air. Lauren lifted her nose into the light ocean breeze and inhaled deeply. It was hard to believe they were just forty minutes from LA.

Grace led the way to the cottage's front door and unlocked it.

This small, modest home was as different from her Hollywood Hills luxury villa as possible. Grace's little hideaway up in the Santa Monica Mountains was all wood from floor to ceiling, including the simple furniture. A rocking chair, a pockmarked oak coffee table, and a couch with a brown-and-white afghan faced a wood-burning fireplace. A tiny kitchen was tucked into one corner of the room, and a ladder led up to a loft, probably a bedroom right under the eaves.

The tense set of Grace's shoulders seemed to relax as soon as she entered.

This was her home. Lauren sensed it without an explanation. "This is nice," she said and realized she had lowered her voice as if she were in a sacred place. Maybe she was. She would bet her next paycheck that Grace didn't bring visitors here very often.

"Wait till you see the view from the patio." Grace opened the sliding glass door and waved at Lauren to follow her.

Several small lizards that had warmed themselves on the patio darted away when they stepped outside.

The cottage was nestled high up in the mountains, and the patio offered a breathtaking view of the canyon, which was blanketed in thick, blue-green stands of chaparral and sage. Lauren thought she could even detect a very distant glimpse of the ocean.

At a piercing cry above them, she looked up and saw a red-tailed hawk soaring in large circles against the blue sky.

Lauren made a living with words, but now she didn't know what to say. "Wow. This sure isn't the luxury beach house in Malibu I expected." She bit her lip when she realized what she'd just blurted out.

But Grace didn't appear insulted. She just grinned. "Disappointed?"

"God, no. I could see myself hiding out here. Well, if not for the fact that you probably don't have Internet or phone reception."

"Yeah, phone reception is pretty spotty here, but the Internet works most of the time. If you want to stay and write that statement for tomorrow…"

Lauren thought about it. She wanted to stay and enjoy some peace and quiet for a change, but was it really the proper thing to do? If the media found out they had stayed together overnight in this little cottage with just one bed, it would start the rumors flying. But then again, if the paparazzi found their way up here, she didn't want Grace to have to face them alone. If she returned to LA, she'd leave Grace stranded without a car or a means to call for help should anything happen. The thought made her shiver despite the warm sunshine. "I'd love to," she said firmly.

Grace nodded. "Let me get you my laptop." She returned with a sleek, silver device, settled down at a small wood table, and opened the laptop's lid. "I just need to send my mother a quick e-mail to let her know I'll be staying here, then the laptop is all yours. Feel free to use the Internet or try the phone reception out here on the patio if you need to let anyone know where you are."

"No, it's okay." It was a bit sobering to realize that no one would miss her if she didn't make it home. By now, it was Friday evening, so unless there was a PR fire to put out, no one at the office would wonder where she was either.

After a minute of hunt-and-peck-typing, Grace closed her e-mail program and got up. She swept her arm toward the laptop. "All yours. Can I get you anything while you work?"

"Coffee would be great, if you have it," Lauren answered as she settled at the table.

"Sure. How do you take yours?"

Remembering Mrs. Duvenbeck's coffee order, Lauren gave her a horrified glance. "No milk, no sugar, no extra flavor."

"Oh, you're one of those people." Grace nodded knowingly.

"Those people?"

"The ones who like their coffee so strong that the spoon stands up in it."

Lauren chuckled. "Guilty as charged."

"One coffee, John Wayne style. Coming right up."

Lauren watched her walk away, even managing not to ogle her firm backside in the formfitting jeans. *Grace Durand is serving me coffee.* Sometimes, her life was just crazy. With a shake of her head, she slid the laptop closer and got to work.

Grace stretched out in the hammock under the ancient oak tree, gently swaying back and forth, while Lauren sat at the table, working. The sun soaked into her skin, and the warm, dry breeze ruffled her hair. She closed her eyes and felt the stress of the last two weeks melt away. This was the most relaxed she'd been since the media circus had started.

Up here, the typical noise of the city was absent. The only sounds drifting over were the chirping of crickets, the soft warbling of birds, and Lauren's typing. Strangely, the rapid-fire clickety-clack of the keyboard didn't disturb her, and neither did Lauren's presence. Other than Nick and Jill, no one had ever stayed in the cottage with her. This was her refuge from the world, so she had been a little hesitant to bring Lauren here. To her surprise, though, Lauren's presence didn't feel like an intrusion.

Lazily, Grace opened one eye and watched Lauren type. Her long, strong fingers darted over the keyboard without Lauren having to look down. Grace watched her for a while and then closed her eyes again, content to let Lauren deal with the problem. Hiring Lauren back after her mother had fired her had definitely been a good idea. Grace realized that she trusted her in a way that she'd never trusted Roberta, her previous publicist.

The sound of a car door slamming shut interrupted the peacefulness. Seconds later, the doorbell rang.

Alarmed, Grace opened her eyes and sat up, nearly tumbling out of the hammock in the process.

But Lauren was already closing the laptop and getting up. "Stay put," she said, her tone brooking no discussion. "I'll deal with whoever that is." She strode inside and then turned to close the sliding door. Their gazes met through the glass, and Lauren gave her a soothing nod before crossing the living room.

Grace's heart drummed a rapid beat against her ribs. Had the paparazzi found them up here? *Calm down. They wouldn't ring the doorbell.* It was probably just her mother, who had jumped into her car as soon as she read Grace's e-mail, horrified about her daughter spending the night in the cottage with a lesbian. Grace sighed. When had her life started to revolve around her sexual orientation?

"What are you doing here?" Nick's voice, loud and gruff, drifted over. "Where's Grace?"

"On the patio, but I'm not sure—Hey! You can't just barge in here and—"

"The hell I can't!" Nick shoved the glass door open.

Lauren hurried after him and grabbed his shoulder to stop him.

Nick whirled around, towering over her, but Lauren didn't back off.

For a moment, Grace thought he would hit her. "Nick! No!"

Nick turned toward her and rolled his eyes. "What? Do you honestly think I was about to hit her? Don't worry; I won't touch your little girlfriend."

"What's that supposed to mean?" Grace asked, her hands on her hips.

"You tell me." He folded his muscular arms across his chest. "You and Jill are all over the tabloids, and now I find you here with her." He pointed his thumb over his shoulder, indicating Lauren. "You never bring anyone here. What the fuck is going on? Is this why you wanted a divorce?"

Grace really didn't need this kind of drama on top of everything else, but she knew she had to deal with it. And he had every right to be angry. She had reminded herself to call him when she'd seen the paparazzi at the mansion but had then forgotten about it, so now he'd gotten ambushed by the media circus. *Damn. We used to be better at communicating.* "It's okay," she said to Lauren, who was still hovering nearby as if she were Grace's bodyguard instead of her publicist. "We'll just talk—civilly," she added in Nick's direction.

"I'll be right inside," Lauren said. It sounded like a message to Nick, warning him to be on his best behavior.

Nick stepped onto the patio and closed the glass door. Calmer now, he sat on the chair that Lauren had vacated a minute ago.

Grace took a seat on the other side of the table. She reached out, saved the document Lauren had been working on, and then closed the laptop.

"What's going on?" Nick asked. "When I got up this morning, you and Jill were all over Twitter. Hundreds of websites swear that Jill just came out as gay and that she confessed to having an affair with you."

"Do you remember when the tabloids wrote about you and that stuntwoman the year before we got married?"

"Why are you bringing up that bullshit now? I told you there was nothing going on between her and me."

"Yeah, and I believed you over the tabloids," Grace said. "Now you can give me the same courtesy. Jill and I are friends, nothing more. We'll give a press conference, clearing that up, tomorrow."

Nick slumped against the back of the chair. "I knew it couldn't be true. Just because we haven't exactly steamed up the bedroom the last year or two doesn't mean you're gay."

Grace's cheeks heated. She just hoped their voices didn't carry through the glass door.

"And neither is Jill," Nick continued. "I think she has a pretty big crush on Russ."

Grace nearly barked out a laugh. Jill couldn't stand Russ and had come up with some creative excuses for why she couldn't sit next to him on the plane to Georgia and back. "Actually," she said and took a deep breath. "Jill is gay."

Nick's Adam's apple bobbed up and down. "So it's true?"

Grace nodded.

"And...and you?"

"I'm not," Grace answered, not feeling the need to add anything else. Having to discuss her sexual orientation was getting old.

"What about her?" Nick pointed to the cottage.

Grace turned her head and looked through the closed glass door.

Lauren sat on the edge of the couch, ready to jump up and come to her defense at any moment should it become necessary. When their gazes met, Lauren tilted her head in a silent question.

Grace lifted her hand, silently telling her to stay put. "She's my publicist."

"But she's a lesbian, isn't she?"

Her patience ran thin. She had no intention of discussing Lauren's sexual orientation in addition to her own. "She's my publicist," she repeated. "And a damn good one. Anything else is none of my business—and none of yours either."

Nick rubbed the scar on his forehead. He looked as if his head was spinning. "You're right," he finally got out. "It's just... I'm trying to understand. I don't want to sound conceited, but I really don't get why you suddenly want a divorce. When I told you about Shailene, I was prepared for a temper tantrum, a breakdown… anything. But you just sat there and said nothing, never once appearing to be even a little jealous, for old times' sake."

A temper tantrum? Grace shook her head. He didn't know her as well as she'd thought. "I had my last temper tantrum when I was three years old and my mother forbade me from wearing my worn denim overalls to a casting call."

"All right, maybe I wasn't really expecting a temper tantrum, but *some* kind of reaction. At first I thought you were acting, because that's what you do when you're hurting. But I couldn't shake the feeling that there was something else going on. When I read that shit about you and Jill, I thought maybe that's why…"

Grace sighed. "It had nothing to do with Jill or any other person, man or woman."

"Then what else is going on?"

She hesitated.

"Come on, Grace. Help me understand."

"I guess I just…" She studied the wood pattern of the table, not wanting to look at him and see the hurt in his eyes. "I fell out of love with you somewhere along the way."

For several seconds, the chirping of the crickets was the only sound on the patio.

"When?" Nick asked, his voice hoarse.

"I don't know."

"When?" he repeated more forcefully. "When did you realize you don't love me anymore?"

Grace kept her gaze on the table. "I do love you," she said softly. "I'm just not in love with you anymore."

"Semantics," he grumbled. "When did you realize?"

She knew he wouldn't back down until he got an answer. Biting her lip, she peered up at him. "I'm not sure. Maybe when I was shooting in New Zealand." They'd spent nearly five months apart, and it had dawned on her that she didn't miss him as fiercely as she should. While some of her cast mates spent almost every available moment on the phone, calling their loved ones at home, she had taken trips and tried to see as much as possible of the beautiful country.

His chair scraped over the stone patio as he shoved it away from the table—and from her. "But…but that was two years ago!"

Grace said nothing.

"That was before we got married!" He jumped up and paced around the table.

The glass door slid open, and Lauren stuck her head out. "Everything okay out here?"

"Yes," Grace said. "Nick was just about to sit back down."

He glared at her and at Lauren but then sat. "I'm sitting, see?" He lifted both of his hands as if showing Lauren that he was unarmed.

Without another word, Lauren closed the sliding door and returned to the couch.

Nick stared at her retreating back. "Jeez! For someone who's just your publicist, she's damn protective of you."

Grace groaned. *Not that again.* "Nick…"

"Okay, okay." He swiveled on his chair and studied her across the table. "Why did you marry me if you weren't in love with me?" His voice was calm now, almost defeated.

"I didn't know," Grace whispered, her head lowered. She glanced over at him. "I thought that's how people felt after being together for a while. I never meant to hurt you."

He didn't answer, instead turning away from her to gaze out over the canyon. "Guess it doesn't matter anymore."

Grace saw right through his stoic action star routine. "Now who's acting?"

He turned and glared at her, but one corner of his mouth soon curved up into a hint of a smile. "Dammit. You know me too well." He eyed the sliding door. "Think I can get up and leave without your guard dog trying to bite my ankle?"

"She's my—"

"Yeah, yeah, your publicist, I know." He rose and walked to the door, this time without a hug, their customary good-bye. "Be careful, okay? There was a horde of paparazzi hanging around the villa when I was there, looking for you."

"I know. That's why I'm staying at the cottage. Are you sure no one followed you here?"

"One hundred percent sure. I'm Special Agent Ray Harper, remember?"

"You play him on TV," Grace said.

He shrugged. "Still. I learned enough from him to trick the paparazzi." He tipped an imaginary hat, slid the door open, and stepped inside.

"Nick?" Grace called.

He turned back around.

Grace nibbled her lip and hesitated, knowing that she would sound like a cold-hearted, career-driven bitch, but this needed to be said. "Even after Jill and I make a public statement tomorrow, the media will probably still keep an eye on us. It's more important than ever for us to appear happily married. Do you think you can pull that off after…everything?"

He huffed. "Please. I'm an actor." He threw a fleeting glance over his shoulder at Lauren. "Have your publicist call me, and we'll set up a date where I'll make doe eyes at you in a very public place."

"Thank you," Grace said quietly.

The sliding door clicked shut behind him. He crossed the living room with long steps and stopped in front of the couch, where Lauren sat.

Grace tensed, but before she could get up and hurry inside, he said something and then left. Exhaling sharply, she folded her arms on the table and buried her face in the bend of her elbow. God, and she had thought the day couldn't get much worse.

When the door closed behind Nick, Lauren got up and walked to the window, watching him get into his car and slowly make his way down the dirt road until he disappeared around a bend. Everything was quiet outside, so apparently he had managed not to lead the paparazzi here.

Lauren crossed the room and reached out to open the sliding glass door but then paused.

Grace was sitting at the edge of the patio, her knees pulled up to her chest, her arms wrapped around her legs, and her forehead pressed to her knees.

Maybe it was better to give her a few minutes to collect herself.

Lauren went back to the couch. Had she ever been in such an awkward situation with a client? She didn't think so. She had been on tour with bands, had witnessed them fight like sworn enemies and then hug each other like the best of friends for the cameras, but she'd never been in the middle of such a personal crisis. Perhaps it would have been better if she left and went back to LA, but one glance at the figure outside made her want to go out there and comfort Grace instead. Besides, the sun would set soon and she didn't think she could safely navigate the dirt road in the dark.

When Grace lifted her head off her knees, Lauren slid back the glass door and joined her, sitting next to her. "Hey," she said quietly. "Are you okay?"

Grace nodded without looking at her. Her expression was calm and collected, but Lauren still didn't believe her. Grace hadn't won three Golden Globes for nothing. "I'm sorry you had to witness that," Grace said. "He's usually not such a…"

"Asshole?" Lauren provided.

For a moment, Grace looked as if she wanted to defend her soon-to-be ex-husband, but then she nodded. "Something like that, yes."

They sat side by side in silence, watching the sun set over the canyon. As the sun dipped lower and then sank below the horizon, ribbons of orange, crimson, and purple stretched across the sky. The moon was already rising, reflecting the orange light of the setting sun. Wisps of clouds drifted on the breeze, casting shadows over the canyon.

Lauren turned her head in Grace's direction to say something but promptly forgot what she'd been about to say when she caught sight of Grace. The sunset bathed her in a dusky golden glow, weaving specks of light through her hair. She looked as if she were in a scene from one of her romantic movies.

"What?" Grace asked as if sensing her gaze.

Lauren looked away. "Nothing. It's just…beautiful out here."

Grace gazed toward the horizon, where only a single band of orange remained. "It is," she said quietly.

As darkness fell, the full moon rose over the hills and the stars came out. There were no neighbors and no street noise, just crickets chirping and a coyote howling in the distance. An owl hooted in a nearby tree.

Finally, Grace unwrapped her arms from around her knees, leaned back on her hands, and looked at Lauren. "What did Nick say to you before he left?"

"He gave me his card so I can call him to set up a public date for the two of you and then he told me to take good care of you." A little too patronizing for Lauren's taste, but he honestly seemed to care about Grace.

Grace sighed. "I need a good soak." She walked over to the above-ground redwood hot tub and flipped a switch.

"Now?" Lauren asked. The temperature had dropped after the sun had set.

"It's either that or a drink. Feel free to join me. The hot tub is large enough for two."

A picture of her and Grace, their wet bodies pressed together in the hot tub, rose in front of Lauren's mind's eye. Her breath caught. *Very, very bad idea*, she firmly told herself even though her body said something else. "Uh, no, thanks. I didn't bring a swimsuit."

"I have one I could lend you," Grace said.

Lauren's thoughts raced, trying to come up with an inconspicuous reply. "Thanks, but I think I should try to get that statement written for tomorrow." She marveled at how calm and professional she sounded. Maybe Grace's acting skills were rubbing off on her.

"Right." Grace got up and went inside.

Lauren fled to the small table on the patio and opened the laptop, planning on being totally immersed in her work by the time Grace came back out in her swimsuit or—God help her—a bikini.

She didn't look up when she heard the sliding door open a few minutes later. Out of the corner of her eye, she caught a flash of a shapely leg and skin that looked soft in the moonlight. *Work! You're here to work, not to ogle a client.*

But that was easier said than done as the sounds of a towel being dropped and then water splashing drifted over. Lauren cursed her overactive imagination, which showed her the water rising up a bare belly as Grace lowered herself into the hot tub. Droplets slid down her neck and into her bikini top and—

Lauren roughly shook her head. Christ, what was wrong with her? She'd never fantasized about any celebrity, and now was not the time to start. Turning the laptop a little so that the screen blocked her line of sight to the hot tub, she focused on finding the right words to tell the public that Jill had multiple sclerosis.

Grace sank onto the built-in seat, letting the warm water envelop her until she was submerged to her neck. The tension in her shoulders was killing her, so she slid a little to the side until her back was against one of the jets. She hoped a good soak would loosen her muscles and help clear her head.

Moonlight glittered on the surface of the swirling water. Steam wafted up into the darkness as she reached up to tug a strand of damp hair behind her ear.

Taking a deep breath, she slid down until the churning water closed over her head. The sounds of the crickets and Lauren's typing faded away, and she felt as if she were in a world of its own—a silent realm where none of her problems mattered.

She emerged only to take a deep breath and then went down again, staying under water for as long as possible. When her lungs started to burn, she pressed her feet against the bottom of the hot tub and shot upward. Her head broke the surface, and she looked directly into Lauren's eyes.

Lauren stood next to the hot tub, regarding her with a worried expression. "Jesus, Grace! You scared me half to death. I was about to reach in and pull you out."

Grace brushed her wet hair away from her face with both hands. "Nah. Don't worry. I'm a good swimmer."

"Lots of pool parties in your youth?" Lauren asked, now sounding calmer.

Grace placed her arms along the edge of the hot tub, enjoying the difference in temperature and the steam wafting up from her skin. "I wish. No. My mother thought swimming was a good form of exercise for a girl, so she made me get up an hour early every day so I could swim before school."

Lauren didn't comment. "I'd better get back to work. Try not to drown on my watch, okay? I'd hate to have to deal with the headlines."

Grace grinned and leaned back against the jets.

When the tips of her fingers started to prune, she finally climbed out, dripping water onto the stone patio as she headed over to the chairs, where she'd left her towel.

Lauren was still tapping away at the laptop. Every now and then, she stopped typing, pushed up her glasses, and rubbed her eyes.

Grace regarded her with a shake of her head. "You're a worse workaholic than I am, and that's saying something."

Lauren's head jerked up as if she hadn't heard Grace get out of the hot tub and walk over. "Uh, what?"

"I said you're a worse workaholic than I am," Grace repeated. She took the towel off the back of the chair and rubbed it over her arms before bending to dab it over her legs.

"It's not always like this," Lauren said. "Just..." She trailed off, sounding distracted, and stared at something.

"Just?" Grace straightened and tried to see what Lauren was looking at, but the silver moonlight reflected off her glasses and made it impossible to see her eyes.

"Uh, just... Okay, it's like this a lot of the time." Lauren raised her hand to cover her mouth as she coughed.

A cool breeze brushed along Grace's back, making her shiver. Goose bumps raced over every inch of her skin. She wrapped the towel around herself. "I'd better get inside and change into something dry. You should come inside too before you catch a cold. That cough doesn't sound good." A wave of protectiveness swept over her, surprising her. But perhaps it was only logical. She needed Lauren healthy so she could do her job as her publicist.

"I'm fine," Lauren said and coughed again.

Grace raised one brow at her.

"Really," Lauren said. "I'm not sick. I always start coughing when I'm tired."

"You cough when you're tired?" Grace squinted at her. She'd never heard of such a thing.

"I swear it's true. My doctor couldn't explain why. It's just a weird little thing."

Grace kept studying her. "But he's sure that it's nothing bad?"

"Yes. It's just a cough or two, not like I'm hacking up a lung or anything," Lauren said. "I don't get it very often, just when I'm really exhausted."

"Well, it's been a long day."

Lauren nodded. "You can say that again. And tomorrow probably won't be any better."

"So come on in and let's go to bed," Grace said.

The chair creaked as Lauren shifted her weight. "I'll just finish this up and be inside in a minute."

"Okay." Another gust of wind made Grace hurry inside. Shivering, she went into the cottage's tiny bathroom, dropped the towel, and stripped off her swimsuit. The wet material peeled off her goose-pebbled skin and hit the floor. Routinely, she swept her gaze over her naked form, taking in every ounce of fat on her hips with a critical eye and then traveling up. Her nipples had hardened into tight peaks in the cold. She reached into the shower to turn on the hot water, then froze and looked back down at her chest. Blood rushed to her cheeks, heating them. Was that what Lauren had been staring at?

She considered it for a moment and then rolled her eyes at herself. *Don't flatter yourself.* If she thought that everyone desired her, she'd definitely been in Hollywood for too long. With a shake of her head, she stepped into the shower.

As soon as Grace had disappeared inside, Lauren closed the laptop and fanned herself with both hands. Despite the dropping temperature, she was overheated. Being kissed by Tabby Jones, the attractive singer who'd been on the cover of both *Rolling Stone* and *Playboy*, had left her cold, but the sight of Grace in just a swimsuit, the wet material clinging to her chest, water dripping down her curvaceous body...

Jesus! Stop it! The woman is your client—your straight, married client. She'd probably fire her, this time for good, if she knew where Lauren's thoughts were headed. Lauren had worked with models, beauty queens, and actresses, all of them gorgeous, some of them lesbian or bi, and a few even interested in a quick adventure with their publicist. Still, it had never been this difficult to keep her libido in check and stay professional. What the heck was it about Grace Durand that made it so hard to think of her as just a client?

Minutes went by, but Lauren didn't find an answer. Maybe she was just building this up in her mind, making more out of it than it really was. Only a person in a coma would be able to resist taking a peek at Grace Durand in a swimsuit. Being attracted to one of the sexiest women alive was perfectly normal for a lesbian, right? It was just a physical thing, easy to ignore.

With that kind of encouragement in mind, she picked up the laptop and went inside.

Everything was quiet in the cottage. Just when Lauren started to wonder where Grace had gone, the door in the corner of the living room opened.

Grace stepped out, wearing nothing but a towel. The damp material did nothing to conceal the shape of her full breasts or her curvy hips. Her cheeks were flushed from her shower. She had wound her golden-blonde hair into a knot on top of her head and secured it with a clip, giving Lauren a view of her elegant neck and her bare shoulders.

Lauren struggled not to stare. *This is so not fair.*

"Sorry," Grace said when she saw Lauren standing frozen in the middle of the living room. "I forgot to take a change of clothes into the bathroom with me. Feel free to take a shower too."

"Thanks. I'll definitely take you up on that offer," Lauren said, managing to sound fairly normal. She needed a shower—a cold one.

"I'll put out something for you to wear." Barefoot, Grace padded past Lauren and climbed up the ladder to the loft.

See? Just a physical thing, Lauren repeated her new mantra. *No problem, right? Easy to—*

Grace's towel rode up, revealing a glimpse of bare thigh and the rounded bottom of her ass.

Lauren quickly looked away and clamped her teeth around her bottom lip to suppress a groan. Marlene couldn't have picked a better test for her. Determined to prove her professionalism, she marched to the bathroom for a cold shower.

Twenty minutes later, Lauren entered the living room in the clothes that Grace had put just inside the bathroom door for her. Grace had to smile as she caught sight of her. The sweatpants were too short for her by a few inches since Lauren was a bit taller and heavier, but she didn't seem to mind. She wore them with the same confidence as she would a pair of tailored slacks. Her hair had apparently been towel-dried and finger-combed; it hung loosely around her face.

Grace decided that she liked seeing her that way. It was a refreshing change of pace from the high-maintenance divas she often worked with.

"Was there enough hot water left?" Grace asked from the tiny kitchen unit.

"I didn't...uh, yeah, thanks. And thanks for the clothes."

"You're welcome." Grace carried the tray she'd prepared over to her and gestured at Lauren to take a seat on the couch. "I thought we should eat something before we go to bed." With an apologetic shrug, she put the tray of cheese, salami, and crackers on the coffee table. "Normally, I hit the store in town before driving up to the cottage. I don't keep much food here, so it's not exactly haute cuisine."

"Unlike the extravagant meal I prepared for you yesterday," Lauren said, grinning.

Grace had to think for a moment before she grasped her meaning. Somehow, it seemed much longer than just a day since they'd eaten hot dogs at Lauren's place. "Yeah, we seem to make a habit out of this. Let's not tell my mother, or she'll put me on a diet."

Lauren snorted. "Please. You don't need a diet."

Grace popped a piece of cheese into her mouth and studied Lauren while she chewed. "Why, Lauren Pearce," she said with a teasing smile. "Was that a compliment?"

"It's in my contract, isn't it?" Lauren assembled layers of crackers, cheese, and salami into a mini-sandwich. "The publicist shall provide the aforementioned client with daily compliments. Any delay or failure to perform this obligation will result in an immediate termination of the contract," she said, sounding as if she were reading from a legal document.

With a cracker halfway to her mouth, Grace paused. Now no longer teasing, she said, "While we're exchanging compliments... I think I should tell you that I'm really glad I didn't allow my mother to fire you. You're doing a good job as my publicist."

Lauren stopped chewing. A hint of red tinged her cheeks.

Grace smiled, charmed by her modesty.

"Uh, thanks, but I don't think I deserve that praise," Lauren said. "I didn't get your statement to the blogger on time, and things went downhill from there."

The self-critical response was a surprise. Most people Grace had worked with so far were quick to blame everyone else when things didn't go well. "He posted his story long before the deadline he gave you. That's hardly your fault."

Lauren reached for a slice of salami and held it in her hand without eating. "Still..."

"Stop beating yourself up for something that wasn't within your control."

"I'm not."

"Good." Grace gave her a smile. "Or you'd have to handle a headline tomorrow about Grace Durand beating some sense into her publicist."

Grinning, Lauren popped the piece of salami into her mouth.

Finally, when the last crumb of their impromptu dinner was gone, Grace cleared the table and then settled back on the couch. She gestured at the laptop that Lauren had brought inside. "Can I see the statement you prepared for tomorrow?"

"Sure. We should talk about how to handle the press conference anyway."

Grace pulled the laptop over and opened the lid. The document that Lauren had left open appeared on the screen, and Grace read through it. "Hmm," she said when she looked back up. "I don't think Jill will like this. It makes her look like a helpless damsel."

"It makes her look like someone who has a neurological condition and therefore needs help on occasion," Lauren said. "It's the only way to make people stop questioning your presence in Jill's trailer and her hotel room."

True, but still... For the first time, Grace wondered whether it had been the best idea for Lauren to become Jill's publicist too. "So you phrased it like that for me? What about Jill? Shouldn't we use a statement that protects her?"

Lauren looked her in the eyes. "I honestly think this is best for Jill too. I don't know her very well, but from what I've seen so far, I think her MS will become obvious to the people she works with sooner rather than later. What if she has a flare-up in the middle of shooting a scene or during a press event?"

Grace had asked herself the same thing before, but she didn't have an answer.

"If she stops pretending everything is all right and openly discusses the limitations that come with MS, I think people will only respect her more."

After thinking about it for a moment, Grace nodded slowly. "Maybe you're right."

"Yes. But there's something else you probably won't like."

Not sure she wanted to hear it, Grace gestured at Lauren to tell her anyway.

"I want to allow a few questions from the media at the end of the press conference," Lauren said.

Grace sucked in a breath as she imagined the kind of questions the reporters would ask. "But won't that open us up for questions that we really shouldn't answer? What if they bring up my marriage to Nick?"

"We're taking a bit of a chance, but if we just read the statement without answering the reporters' questions, it will only feed the media frenzy and make them even more hungry for additional information."

Unfortunately, she was right. Grace played with the laptop's trackpad, making the mouse arrow stagger across the screen. "So what do I tell them if they ask about Nick and me?"

"Don't lie, but don't tell them the truth either. You could tell them that Nick is just as outraged as you about the accusations of infidelity. In fact…" A cough interrupted her. "Sorry. It would be a good idea to have Nick there for the press conference, showing his support. I should have thought of it when he was here earlier, but…"

"It's okay. I don't blame you for being thrown off stride by that little bit of celebrity drama." God knows she had been caught off guard by it too. "I'll call him first thing tomorrow morning and ask him to come."

"Why don't you let me do it?" Lauren said. "I need to coach him on what to say anyway."

Grace studied her. Was Lauren trying to spare her the indignity of having to ask her future ex-husband a favor? Well, after today's conversation with Nick, she wasn't too proud to accept that offer. "All right. Thank you."

Lauren coughed again.

"Come on. Let's go to bed before you do cough up a lung." Grace got up and made up the couch with a spare set of sheets while Lauren made a quick trip to the bathroom.

Finally, with their teeth brushed, they stood facing each other in the middle of the living room.

"Good night," Grace said. "And thanks for today. Driving me up here and everything. Giving compliments might be in your contract, but I know most of the other things you did today aren't." She hesitated but then gave in to the impulse.

Quickly, she leaned forward and hugged Lauren for just a second before backing away.

She was halfway to the ladder before Lauren's "you're welcome" reached her.

Smiling, Grace climbed up into the loft and crawled into bed.

From below, the sounds of Lauren getting settled on the couch drifted up.

It should have been slightly awkward to sleep practically in the same room, especially here in her private sanctuary, but for some reason, Grace found it comforting to know that Lauren was down there. She turned off the light, closed her eyes, and listened to Lauren's soft coughing until she drifted off to sleep.

CHAPTER 11

BY THE TIME LAUREN WOKE, the gray light of dawn had crept into the cottage. She reached for her wristwatch that she'd set on the coffee table serving as her nightstand. It was barely after five. She listened for a few moments, but upstairs, in the loft, nothing moved.

As quietly as possible, she gathered her clothes and tiptoed to the bathroom.

Finally, armed with her cell phone and Grace's laptop, she went outside to the patio so she wouldn't wake Grace.

The signal strength icon on her phone showed a single bar. Despite a momentary flash of guilt because of the early hour, she called Tina and told her which reporters to invite to the press conference. Just when she contemplated whether it was a good idea to call Nick so early, the glass door behind her slid open and Grace joined her on the patio.

"Good morning." She set a mug of steaming coffee on the table next to Lauren and kept a second one for herself.

"Morning. Thank you." Lauren peeked into the mug and grinned. Grace had remembered her preference; the coffee was black and hopefully strong.

They sat next to each other at the small table, their hands wrapped around their mugs for warmth, slowly sipping their beverages while they watched the fog roll in and sweep through the canyon below. The first hue of dawn lit up the mountains and hills surrounding them. With a view like this, Lauren understood why Grace didn't keep a TV in the cottage.

Neither of them seemed to feel the need to fill the silence with small talk, and Lauren was grateful that Grace wasn't one of the chatty stars she represented.

Finally, when her coffee was gone and the sun was climbing higher, she turned toward Grace and took in the faint shadows under her eyes. Grace probably hadn't slept too well, maybe going over possible questions and answers in that state between sleep and wakefulness.

"Don't worry," Grace said as if guessing Lauren's thoughts. "Nothing a little concealer won't cure."

"All right. I'll call Jill and Nick to let them know when to be at CTP, and then let's get going. We need to stop by my apartment so I can get changed, and I want to coach Jill on what to say before we head to the office for the press conference."

Grace tugged on the sweatpants and the long-sleeved T-shirt she was wearing. "Any advice on what to wear?"

Lauren considered it for a moment, her mind showing her flashes of the clothes that Grace might have in her closet. She quickly discarded the more elegant dresses, no matter how beautiful Grace might look in them. "Pick something that says 'helpful friend' rather than 'sexy vixen.'"

"You've got something against sexy?" Grace asked, a light smile playing around her lips.

Oh, not at all, believe me. Lauren bit her lip and stopped herself from saying it. "No. I just think we should play on your friendly girl-next-door image. We want them to see you as Jill's friend, not as a woman she might lust after."

"Got it. Helpful friend it is." Grace got up and headed inside.

Lauren squared her shoulders and walked over to the corner of the patio where she had the best cell phone reception. When the display finally showed one bar, she pulled Nick's business card out of her pocket and typed in the number.

The phone rang and rang and rang.

Just when Lauren thought voice mail would pick up, Nick's groggy voice came from the other end of the line. "Yeah?"

"Nick, it's Lauren Pearce." When only silence answered, she added, "Grace's publicist."

Sheets rustled. "Is she okay?" he asked, sounding wide-awake now.

"She's fine," Lauren said quickly. "I'm sorry to bother you this early on a Saturday, but I need a favor."

"A favor?" he drawled.

"We're going to hold a press conference at ten, trying to stop the rumors once and for all by telling the press that Jill has MS."

That stunned him into silence for several seconds. "MS? What the fuck? Is this some PR trick?"

"No. I wish it were, but sadly, it isn't. I would never say something like that if it weren't true."

"Damn. I had no idea." Nick sighed and then asked, "Does Grace know?"

Lauren hesitated, not sure how much Grace would want him to know.

"Don't bother. Of course she knows. Why didn't she tell me?"

"I don't know. Jill probably didn't want her to," Lauren said, feeling the need to defend Grace.

Nick huffed out a breath. "And now she suddenly wants to tell the whole world?"

"She's doing it for Grace."

"You know, Grace said the rumors aren't true, but sometimes, I really wonder what's going on between those two," Nick muttered.

"It's called friendship, Nick." Not that she, herself, had a friend like that in her life.

Soft noises indicated that Nick was getting out of bed. "So now you want me to be her friend too and show up for the press conference, right?"

"Right."

He sighed. "When and where do you need me?"

The paparazzi had picked up their trail somewhere on the way from Lauren's apartment to Glendale and followed them to Jill's house.

Grace gritted her teeth in the passenger seat when she saw the SUVs and the cars behind them. "Damn."

"Don't worry," Lauren said. "We'll clear up what's really going on in an hour anyway, so even if they post the photos they'll take of us entering Jill's home, it won't matter anymore."

True. Grace just hoped things would settle down after the press conference. She couldn't take this constant hide-and-seek with the paparazzi for much longer.

Jill's housekeeper opened the door when they rang the bell. "Oh, thank God you're here, Ms. Durand," she said, clutching Grace's shoulders and nearly dragging her inside.

Tramp ran up to them, wagging his tail so hard that his rear end shook from side to side.

Grace gently freed herself of the housekeeper's grip and petted the dog while she looked at the stairs leading to the master bedroom. Concern gnawed at her, but she stopped herself from rushing upstairs. "Is Jill all right? Are the symptoms worse today?"

"Oh, no, it's not that. She's just a nervous wreck because of the press conference. She's been upstairs in her room since you called earlier."

"Would you mind waiting down here?" Grace said to Lauren, who had entered after her. "I'll go up and see if she needs any help getting ready."

"Sure," Lauren said. "I'll keep Tramp company. Come on, boy." When she patted her thigh and walked off in the direction of the living room, Tramp bounded after her.

Grace climbed the stairs, taking them two at a time.

The door to the master bedroom was closed, so she knocked.

A grunt answered.

Hesitatingly, Grace opened the door a few inches and peeked inside the room.

Jill stood in front of the mirrored closet doors, wearing just a pair of panties. She held a bra in her hands but seemed to struggle with the tiny hooks.

"Jill? Can I come in?"

"Sure, if you don't mind seeing me in my birthday suit."

Grace had seen Jill half-dressed before and had even helped her undress in the hotel in Macon, when Jill hadn't been able to manage on her own. Now that she knew Jill was gay, it felt different, though. *Oh, come on. That's stupid. She's the same old Jill.* She gave herself a mental push and entered.

Her lips pressed together, Jill continued to fumble with the bra closure. "This goddamn clasp just won't...argh!" She threw the bra across the room.

It ricocheted off the doorjamb next to Grace and hit her in the chest. She caught it reflexively and raised one brow. "Do you think this is a new phase in my career? I never had women throw their bras at me before."

Jill stared at her and then began to laugh. The frustration fled from her expression. "You're one of a kind, you know that?"

Grace shrugged and closed the door behind her. "So, what's wrong with the bra?"

Jill scowled at the offending garment. "Nothing. The MS is just messing with my fine motor skills, so I can't get the clasp to close."

"Want some help?"

"Yes, please," Jill said after a moment's hesitation. "I don't think Lauren would want me to show up at the press conference without a bra."

"I doubt it." Grace carried the bra over to her friend and then looked back and forth between Jill's face and the article of clothing. "Uh, how do we do this?"

"I don't know. You just put it on."

"Easier said than done." Grace's attempt to give Jill some privacy by not looking at her naked chest wasn't making it any easier. "I never helped another woman put on her bra before."

"Me neither. My experience is limited to taking them off." Jill grinned and winked.

Grace socked her in the arm, and some of the awkwardness disappeared. She helped Jill slip first one arm, then the other through the bra straps before walking around to fasten the hooks.

Jill adjusted her breasts in the cups. Grinning, she watched Grace in the mirror. "You're not blushing, are you?"

"No, of course not!" Grace pulled on one bra strap, letting it snap against Jill's skin.

"Ouch! Hey, you're here to help me, not to relive junior high."

Reaching over Jill's shoulders, Grace adjusted the bra straps for a more comfortable fit. "Well, I never really went to high school, so..."

Jill turned to face her. "You didn't?"

"I was schooled at home and on sets by my mother and tutors," Grace said. At the mention of her mother, she sobered, remembering that Jill had wanted to tell her family about her MS. "Did you call your family yesterday?"

Jill just nodded. She walked over to her closet and pulled out a dress, holding it out for Grace to see. Except for its color, it resembled Grace's light blue summer dress, so it probably fulfilled Lauren's helpful-friend-not-sexy-vixen criteria. Grace nodded her approval.

"How did they take it?" she asked while she helped Jill pull the dress over her head.

Jill put up a brave front most of the time, hiding behind witty comments, but this time, her expression was serious as her face reappeared through the dress's opening. "It was bad, like I expected. My mother cried as if I would fall over dead any moment, and my brother declared it my punishment for being gay."

Grace nearly ripped the fabric of the dress she'd just straightened. "Excuse me? What kind of brother would say that?"

"My homophobic asshole brother."

"He doesn't deserve a sister like you."

"I know," Jill said, now with her trademark impish grin.

Grace pointed at the jewelry on Jill's dresser. "Jewelry?"

Jill batted her lashes at her. "Isn't it a little soon in our relationship for that?"

"You!" She backhanded her across the shoulder but couldn't help returning Jill's grin. She knew that humor was Jill's way of dealing with things. "I meant do you want to wear any jewelry?"

"No, thanks," Jill said. "I think I'll go *au naturel* today."

Grace fastened a pair of flat sandals for Jill and peeked up at her. "Will any of your family be there for the press conference?"

"No. I don't want them to come. How about your mother? She'll be there, right?"

Only now did Grace realize she'd forgotten to call her mother to let her know about the press conference. She pressed her hand to her mouth. "Oh, shit."

"What?"

"I forgot to let her know." Grace looked at her watch. It was too late now. Her mother would never get ready in time.

Jill laughed. "I think I'd rather call my mother again to tell her I have MS than call your mother and tell her you forgot to inform her about the press conference."

Grace stepped up to the microphone and adjusted it, ignoring the camera flashes. She gazed down at the sea of reporters that had crowded into Chandler & Troy Publicity's conference room. There were even two news teams with cameras and microphones.

Even though she was shaking inside, she flashed her Hollywood smile and gave them a friendly nod. "Good morning, ladies and gentlemen. Thank you all for coming."

Next to her, Jill gripped the side of the podium with both hands.

Grace wasn't sure if her friend had problems with her balance again or was just nervous. She reached out and wrapped one arm around Jill.

More flashes went off.

Grace glanced to the left, where Lauren stood slightly behind them, with Nick by her side. In a gray suit and a purple blouse, she looked calm and composed. She gave Grace an encouraging nod.

Squeezing Jill's shoulder, Grace took a deep breath. "You probably all followed the headlines about me and Jill that have flooded the media in the last two weeks. We called this press conference to set the record straight—pun intended."

A few of the reporters chuckled, and Grace smiled. Lauren had written a great beginning for their press conference, making sure to keep the tone friendly and not turn the entire event into a confrontation with the media.

"Yes, it's true that I accompanied Jill to her trailer on more than one occasion while we were on location, and we also booked a hotel room in Macon together," Grace said and paused to let the hastily scribbling reporters catch up. "But I'm afraid the reason is not nearly as exciting as you think."

She turned toward Jill, who was so pale that her freckles stood out in stark contrast.

Jill leaned closer to the microphone, shifting some of her weight onto Grace. "I found out last year that I suffer from MS—multiple sclerosis."

A collective murmur went through the conference room. One or two of the reporters even had the decency to look ashamed for the bullshit they'd been writing.

Jill lifted one hand, asking for silence. "Most of the time, I manage just fine," she continued, skipping over the list of symptoms in Lauren's original statement, "but the long days on set take their toll, so Grace helped me when I was too exhausted to make it back to the trailer alone." She turned her head to look at Grace.

To Grace's surprise, tears shimmered in Jill's green eyes.

"She has been a good friend to me throughout a very difficult time in my life, and I ask you not to repay her kindness by spreading lies about her. Thank you."

Lauren stepped up behind them. "We will now take a handful of questions, but we ask you not to tax Ms. Corrigan's energy too much, so please stick to relevant topics."

Every reporter in the room raised his or her hand. A few waved like overeager students.

A lump formed in Grace's throat as she waited for the first question. She was grateful for Lauren's soothing presence behind her.

Lauren pointed past Grace to one of the reporters in the first row. "Mr. Abner, right?"

"Yes."

"Go ahead and ask your question," Lauren said.

The man stood. "How long have you known about Ms. Corrigan's...condition?"

Grace relaxed a little. She glanced at Jill, who gave her a nod. "She told me right before we started shooting *Ava's Heart*."

"Will you give up acting?" another reporter asked, addressing Jill.

"Hell, no," Jill said.

Several journalists laughed at the energetic response.

"Seriously, I will continue to act for as long as possible. The kind of MS I have is called relapsing-remitting, which means that I get episodes of symptoms and then fairly long periods of remission."

"But won't your symptoms get worse over time?" another journalist asked.

Jill shrugged. "They do for about fifty percent of patients with relapsing-remitting MS, but I don't know yet if that's true for me too. I'm hoping for the best, but I'm prepared to muddle through even if the symptoms get worse."

Grace squeezed her softly, once again impressed with her friend's braveness. She didn't want to even imagine how she would handle having a disease like MS.

"Ms. Corrigan, can you confirm what you said about your sexual orientation yesterday?" another reporter asked.

Jill lifted her head and looked directly at the man who'd asked the question. "Yes. I'm a lesbian."

After Jill had answered two other questions, Lauren said, "All right, ladies and gentlemen. One more question, then let's wrap this up."

Before any other reporter could step in, a man in a tweed suit rose in the last row.

Grace knew him. He had followed her career for various magazines and newspapers over the last twenty plus years and had practically watched her grow up. While they weren't exactly friends, the articles he wrote about her had always been favorable, so she breathed a sigh of relief and nodded at him to ask his question.

"Ms. Durand, while I commend you for your loyalty toward Ms. Corrigan, isn't it true that your relationship with your husband is less loving?"

It stung that this probing question came from him. Forcing down her anger, she looked him straight in the eyes. "If you're asking whether I'm having an affair, the answer is no."

"What about Mr. Sinclair?" Abner asked. "Is he having an affair?"

Grace's mind reeled. How could she answer that without lying? "Nick would never cheat on me behind my back." Technically, it was the truth. While Nick was with someone else now, it had happened after their separation and he'd been up-front about it.

"So everything's fine between you and Mr. Sinclair?" Abner asked. "He didn't move out of your villa and into an apartment in Silver City?"

Damn. How had he found out about that? The apartment in Silver City wasn't even in Nick's name. She glanced at Lauren, hoping she'd step in and end the press conference, but Lauren almost imperceptibly shook her head. Grace understood. If Lauren cut off the reporter's question, it would have the same effect as saying "no comment." It would make the media even more suspicious, so they would dig deeper to find out what was going on.

Before Grace could think of something to say, Nick walked past Lauren and pointedly wrapped one arm around Grace and the other around Jill. "Since I'm here, why don't you ask me directly, Mr. ...?"

"Dinsmore," the reporter said. His gaze drilled into Nick. "So, why did you move out?"

"Who says I did?" Nick countered. "I'm just staying in the apartment in Silver City for a few weeks. It's more convenient right now, since it's so close to the studio where I'm shooting *Hard as Steel III*. I will continue to live in the villa in the future."

Which was true, since Grace would move out once they no longer needed to hold up appearances.

Nick pressed a kiss to Grace's cheek. "We love each other," he said, radiating sincerity. "My wife never cheated on me, not with Jill and not with anyone else." He paused and then grinned and winked at the reporters. "Even though these two would be damn hot to watch, don't you think?"

The reporters laughed and started to gather their notes.

Grace didn't know whether to kiss him or to kick him in the shin for that last remark. "I seriously underestimated your acting skills," she whispered as the last of the journalists filed out of the room. "Thank you."

He let go of her and Jill and stepped back. "You're welcome. I need to get back on set. We're working on a new stunt."

"Be careful, please," Grace said.

"Will do." He walked off, passing Lauren on the way to the door.

"That went well," Lauren said as she joined them. "Although I could have sworn there was a sentence or two about the symptoms of MS and how they affect you somewhere in that statement." She gave Jill a pointed look.

"Oops." Jill grinned. "Guess I forgot to mention that. You do know that MS can affect people's memory, right?"

"Right." Lauren looked at her for a moment longer before turning to Grace. "The media circus should settle down now, but try to lay low anyway."

"You mean no climbing walls in stilettos at midnight?"

"None of that," Lauren said sternly but then cracked a smile.

Grace smiled in return. "Okay." She wouldn't miss the tabloid craziness and being hunted by the paparazzi. Still, she had enjoyed working so closely with Lauren the last three days. A strange feeling of regret washed over her, but she quickly shook it off.

"Do you want me to drive you home now?" Lauren looked back and forth between Grace and Jill, who'd both driven to the CTP offices with her.

"That'd be nice," Grace said. "Can you drop me off at my mother's? I still need to pick up my SUV from her."

"And tell her about the press conference," Jill added.

A groan escaped Grace before she could hold it back. *Oh, God.* She'd forgotten about that or maybe shoved it back into the recesses of her mind. But, of course, she had to face her mother sooner or later.

"Is that going to be a problem?" Lauren asked.

"No. I just forgot to tell her with all the chaos going on yesterday and this morning."

Lauren kept studying her with her much-too-perceptive gaze. "Do you want me to tell her?"

"Thanks, but no." This was something she had to do, or her mother would be even angrier with her.

"Are you sure?" Lauren asked. "Remember we're trying to avoid making headlines, including one about Grace Durand being clobbered to death with her mother's makeup case."

Amazing how she could make Grace laugh even in the tensest of situations. Grace chuckled and put her hand on Lauren's arm for a moment. "I'm sure. Thanks, though. I appreciate the offer."

Lauren looked down at the place on her arm where Grace's hand had been a second ago, then cleared her throat and jingled her keys. "All right. Then let's get going."

"I gave you the security code. Why do you keep ringing the doorbell?" her mother asked when she opened the door.

Grace stepped into the Beverly Hills home. She'd lived here for a few years as a teenager, but it felt even less like a home than her mansion in the Hollywood Hills.

"I didn't want to give you a heart attack by walking into your home unannounced." *The way you keep doing,* she mentally added.

"Ah, pish-posh." Her mother peered over Grace's shoulder before closing the door. "How did you manage to lose the paparazzi?"

"Um, why don't we take a seat in the living room?"

Her mother dug in her high heels and stopped in the middle of the tiled foyer. "What's going on?"

There was no way to delay the inevitable. She took a deep breath and said, "The paparazzi backed off because we just held a press conference and gave them the information they wanted."

Her mother's mouth gaped open. She looked at Grace as if she'd just told her that aliens had landed in her backyard. "You...you held a press conference? Without me?"

Grace bit her lip.

"I have been there for every press conference, for every single event in your entire career, from the moment your backside became the official derriere of Dry 'n' Tender Diapers! I changed all of those diapers too! I gave up my own life to get you where you are today, and now you suddenly no longer find it necessary to at least let me know or ask my opinion?"

For a moment, Grace contemplated telling her that she hadn't asked her to give up her life or to be dragged to cattle calls when she'd been a toddler and to spend her childhood in front of a camera, but, once again, she held back, not wanting to open that particular Pandora's box. "I'm sorry, but we couldn't wait—"

"We?" Her mother's voice went quiet. Dangerously quiet, like the silence settling over a town before a tornado blew through.

Grace swallowed. "Jill, Nick, Lauren, and I."

"I see." Her mother stalked past her and strode into the living room, where she stood by the window and stared out.

Grace squeezed her eyes shut, stood in the foyer with slumping shoulders for a moment, and then followed her. "Mom..."

Her mother held up one hand but didn't turn around. "No, that's all right. I understand. You're listening to other people's advice now and don't need me anymore."

God, how Grace hated that exact tone of voice. Still, it never failed to have its desired effect—making her feel guilty. "That's not true." She pulled her mother around by one shoulder. "I still value your advice and always will."

"Then why didn't you talk this through with me? That's not like you, Grace. You've never made any decision without consulting me first. At least not regarding something that could affect your career."

"I just forgot to tell you. Things were so crazy yesterday, and then we ended up staying at the cottage, where I don't have cell phone reception most of the time, and this morning—"

"We?" her mother repeated.

"Um…" *Shit.* She'd jumped out of the frying pan, right into the fire. "Lauren drove me to the cottage and then stayed because you still had my SUV and she didn't want to leave me without a car."

"How considerate of her," her mother said, sounding anything but appreciative.

Grace studied her mother's face. What was it about Lauren that made her dislike her so much? Grace didn't get it. Was it just the fact that she was a lesbian? Or was it that Lauren, unlike everyone else Grace's mother surrounded herself with, told her straight out what she thought? Grace found it refreshing, but her mother apparently didn't appreciate it. "Mom," she said, treading carefully, "you were the one who fired Roberta and told George to find a new publicist."

"Yes, but I never meant for her to repl—" Her mother bit her lip and turned back toward the window.

Was that what this was all about? Her mother was jealous because she felt that Lauren was replacing her in Grace's favor? *Oh, for heaven's sake.* Not for the first time, Grace understood why Lauren initially hadn't wanted to get involved in show business. The egos of many people in the entertainment industry were so unbelievably fragile. "Mom, she's not replacing you."

Her mother didn't answer.

Again, Grace pulled her around.

The tears in her mother's eyes made her reach out and pull her close. "Oh, Mom."

Katherine clutched her with both hands, clinging to her the way she had after Grace's father had died.

Grace shoved that memory aside. She stroked her mother's hair with one hand, even though the hair spray made it stiff and unyielding. "Lauren is my publicist, and I value her advice. That doesn't mean I don't value yours anymore. Where's that sudden insecurity coming from?"

"I just don't want you to shut me out of your life," her mother said in a near whisper. "You're all I have."

"I won't. I promise to involve you more in the future. Okay?"

Her mother sniffed and nodded against her shoulder. "Okay." After a few more moments, she pulled away and wrinkled her nose. "You smell like dog."

"Oh, that's Tramp."

"You mean Jill's dog?"

"Yes. Let me tell you about my first meeting with Tramp." Grace pulled her mother over to the uncomfortable white designer couch. She'd probably get an earful from her mother, but she'd promised to involve her more and not make her feel left out. A promise was a promise, after all.

CHAPTER 12

LAUREN DRAGGED HER TIRED SELF out of bed at eight. She stared at her red eyes in the bathroom mirror. "What am I doing?" It was Sunday, and she'd worked late last night, getting some of the gossip rags to print retractions and admit that they'd jumped to conclusions about Grace and Jill. Why was she getting up instead of staying in her cozy bed for some much-needed sleep? Clearly, she'd worked in Hollywood for too long and all the craziness had rubbed off on her.

Speaking of Hollywood craziness... She made herself a cup of coffee and settled on the couch with her laptop. A notification popped up on the screen when she opened the lid, informing her that she had new e-mail. *What else is new?* She always had new e-mail. Ignoring the notification, she opened her screenwriting program instead.

It had been a while since she'd last found the time to work on her script, so she started by rereading the last few scenes. She liked the parts in which her characters struggled to survive the earthquake and then the fires destroying the city, but the scenes that came afterward somehow fell flat. Her third act wasn't working, and she had no idea why. What was she missing?

She reached for her mug and took a sip of coffee, making a face when she realized it had gotten cold. She got up to reheat it. While the mug rotated in the microwave, she poured chocolate cereal into a bowl and opened the fridge. *Damn.* She'd forgotten to buy milk during the media crisis of the last few days. Now she would have to do without.

She carried her now-hot coffee and the bowl to the couch and made herself comfortable again. Inspiration still refused to strike. She typed a line of dialogue and then deleted it again when it didn't ring true to her characters. In moments like this, she was tempted to delete the entire script and never write again. Why was she even bothering? Even if she finished this script at some point, it didn't stand a snowball's chance in hell of ever being made into a movie. She wasn't sure if that was what she wanted anyway. Becoming a screenwriter would make her a part of the Hollywood factory, something she'd sworn she'd never be. But every time her finger hovered over the delete button, she just couldn't bring herself to press it.

Writing called to her in a way that even working in PR didn't, so she finally decided that she'd dabble in it just as a hobby, with no intention of ever letting anyone see one of her scripts. No harm in that, right?

But even with that resolution, the words wouldn't come today. She stared down into the dry cereal. *I might as well pretend it's popcorn and see what's on the tube.* Maybe watching a few lines of a good movie would inspire her. *Yeah, right.* Even knowing she was procrastinating, she reached for the remote control. Her laptop still open next to her and the bowl on her lap, she flicked through the channels and crunched a handful of her improvised popcorn.

She nearly choked on the cereal when Grace's face appeared on her TV screen. It seemed there was no getting away from her clients, even on a Sunday. Still, she didn't change the channel. Glued to the scene on the screen, she popped a handful of the chocolate-flavored cereal into her mouth without looking at the food.

It had to be one of Grace's many romantic comedies, probably an early one, because she appeared to be several years younger. In this scene, Grace—or rather the character she played in this movie—walked down the aisle in a dream of a wedding dress that enhanced her generous curves and revealed just a hint of cleavage.

Lauren stopped chewing. *Beautiful.* She rolled her eyes at herself. Of course Grace was beautiful, but so was every other person in the movie. They made a living looking good for the camera, after all. Still, Grace stood out. She was also the most talented actress in the movie by far. The tears in her eyes looked real as she repeated the marriage vows. Lauren wondered what she'd been thinking of to make herself cry. Grace's fingers even trembled as she pushed the wedding ring on her fictional groom's finger. Her acting skills were totally wasted on the type of movies she made, Lauren decided.

The happy couple on her TV screen met in a kiss, Grace's full lips moving against those of the lucky guy who played her new husband. Lauren swallowed against her suddenly dry mouth. With a grunt, she dragged her gaze away and flicked off the TV. She didn't need that kind of inspiration; she wasn't writing a love story after all, and she certainly didn't need any more erotic thoughts about Grace.

She reached for the laptop and tried to immerse herself into her own fictional world, imagining her characters wandering the streets of their burned-down city. They would stop at the top of a hill, look down at the smoldering ruins of San Francisco, and then...

Yeah, what then? The only image flickering through her mind was of the two women kissing. One of them suddenly looked suspiciously like Grace, even though Lauren had described her as having red hair in the opening scene, and the other one—

The phone rang, making her jump.

With a sense of relief, Lauren reached for it and accepted the call without even glancing at the display. "Lauren Pearce."

"This is Grace. Grace Durand. I'm so, so sorry to disturb you this early, especially on a Sunday, but Jill just called me and now I have a question and I think I already know the answer, but…"

Lauren laughed. So even world-famous actresses sometimes rambled. *Cute.* "Don't worry about it. You saved me from…"

"From what?"

My bad writing. "Getting bored," Lauren said. She hadn't told anyone about her writing and intended to keep it that way. "I was just hanging out on the couch, watching sappy movies. So, what can I do for you?"

Grace was silent for a moment and then said, "I'm thinking about walking in the gay pride parade today."

Lauren shook her head. She hadn't expected that. Grace was certainly keeping her on her toes. "So this is the call you promised me?"

"Uh, I promised you a call?"

"Yeah, informing me when you got involved with someone, especially a woman."

"What? No, no, I'm not…"

"Relax," Lauren said. "I'm just joking."

"That's so not funny," Grace grumbled. "You'd better keep your day job."

Yeah, she's got that right. Lauren looked down at her script and then reached out with one hand to close the program. "Okay, seriously, what's this all about?"

"Jill called me an hour ago," Grace said. "Now that she's out, they asked her to march in the parade, and she's thinking about going, but she doesn't want to do it alone, so I was thinking about going with her. It's set to start at eleven, so I need to make a decision fast. What do you think?"

Resolutely, Lauren closed the laptop with a slap of her hand. "I'm thinking there's no way in hell I'd agree to that."

Grace sighed. "I told Jill you'd say that."

"Grace, as a lesbian, I really appreciate your willingness to support Jill and the rest of the LGBT community, but do you honestly think being photographed marching between a guy in a studded leather thong and a woman in assless chaps is a good idea?"

"Thanks for that lovely mental image," Grace said dryly. The phone speaker crackled as she blew out a long breath. "I know you're right. I just hate to tell Jill she'll have to go alone."

Lauren understood more and more how little freedom Grace really had, despite all her money and fame. "I'm sorry. Maybe in a few years, things will be different for you, but right now, it would only make all the rumors start up again."

"I know. Thanks for setting me straight…so to speak."

Lauren gave a faint smile. "You're welcome. Is everything else okay at your house? The paparazzi are gone, right?"

"I think one or two are still hanging out, but most of them are gone," Grace said. "There are rumors that Amanda Clark is pregnant, so they're probably camped out in front of her house, hoping for a snapshot of the baby bump."

Well, if that was true, then Amanda's partner was more talented than Lauren had given her credit for, because she was fairly sure *Central Precinct*'s leading lady was gay. She wasn't in the habit of outing one actress to another, though, so all she said was, "Good."

"Again, sorry for disturbing you. Have a nice Sunday."

"You too."

When they ended the call, Lauren stared at her closed laptop. She knew she wouldn't get any more writing done today. *Might as well get some fresh air.* She reached for her cell phone again and scrolled through her contact list on the way to the bedroom to get dressed.

A shiver of dread skittered down Grace's spine when her mother waltzed into her living room—again without an invitation or a warning—and threw a glossy magazine onto the coffee table.

The last two days had been wonderfully quiet on the media front, with no new headlines about her, and Grace had just gotten used to the new feeling of peace. *I should have known it wouldn't last long.* Nothing good in her life really seemed to. What had the damn hacks written now? She reached for the magazine.

Her mother plopped down on the couch next to her. "Your friend," she said, giving the word a derisive emphasis, "really shouldn't make such a spectacle out of herself."

So this wasn't about her and Nick. But Grace couldn't relax just yet. Had Jill somehow gotten herself in trouble? She flicked through the magazine until she got to a headline saying, *Out and proud—Jill Corrigan living it up at the LA Gay Pride parade.*

Grace glanced at the first picture and rolled her eyes. In jeans and a T-shirt with a rainbow-colored peace sign on the front, Jill looked downright tame compared to the guy in drag next to her and a half-naked man behind her. "She's hardly living it up, Mom. I think she's just celebrating that she doesn't have to hide anymore."

"Volunteering for an MS fundraiser would have been a better way to do that," her mother said.

"You know what? That's actually a good idea." The pride parade was a little too wild for Grace's taste too, but if it was Jill's idea of fun, she had still wanted to support her. "Maybe Jill and I should look into that. We could—"

The ringing of her cell phone interrupted.

Grace smiled when she saw who was calling her. *Speak of the devil...* She swiped her finger across the display to accept the call. "Hi, Jill."

Her mother let out a huff and stalked to the kitchen.

"I hear you were living it up at the parade," Grace said into the phone.

Jill snorted. "Who said that?"

Grace looked up to make sure her mother was out of hearing range. "A little bird brought over the newest gossip rag."

"Oh, I think I know that mockingbird."

"Jill..."

"I don't know why you keep defending her," Jill said.

Grace lay back on the couch and stared at the ceiling. "She's my mother."

"And that gives her the right to control everything you do, including who you make friends with?"

"No, of course not. It's just..." Grace didn't want to get into this topic now. "Tell me about the parade. How was it?"

"Crazy," Jill said with a laugh. "But it was really cool to see all the people out on the street, supporting gay rights. Must have been a few hundred thousand. It was such an empowering feeling. I wish you could have been there."

Grace rubbed the back of her hand across her forehead. "I'm really sorry you had to go alone."

"Who says I was alone?" Jill said, a hint of teasing in her voice.

"Oh." Grace had never known her friend to date, but maybe Jill just hadn't told her because she'd dated women and hadn't wanted Grace to know. Or had she attended the parade with an acquaintance? "You weren't?"

"No. Guess who called me and offered to go with me?"

"I have no idea. Angelina Jolie?"

Jill laughed. "I wish. No. Lauren."

"Lauren who?" Grace's eyes widened. "You mean our Lauren? Our publicist?"

"Yes."

A warm feeling flowed through Grace, and she smiled into the empty living room. Lauren had gone with Jill because Grace had mentioned that she hated for her friend to go alone—and she hadn't said one word about it. Their publicist was one classy lady. *Amazing.* Few people in Grace's world would do something so selfless, giving up her own weekend plans and maybe even risking her boss's disapproval for ending up in a gossip rag instead of creating PR.

"Guess your little bird didn't tell you that, did she?" Jill said.

"No, she didn't. Let's see..." Grace reached for the magazine on the coffee table and took a closer look at the pictures of the parade.

There she was. In one of the photos, Lauren was marching next to Jill, laughing about something that Jill must have said. Instead of the tailored business suits that Grace was used to seeing her in, she was wearing jeans and a simple white T-shirt. A pair of sunglasses dangled from the T-shirt's V-neck.

"She looks good in her lesbian uniform, doesn't she?" Jill said as if she knew what Grace was looking at.

Yes, she does. Grace glanced at the picture again before closing the magazine and throwing it back onto the coffee table. "I guess."

"Oh, come on. You're straight, not blind. Even you can acknowledge when another woman looks good, can't you?"

"All right, she does look good. Happy now?"

"Yes," Jill said, sounding as if she was grinning broadly.

"By the way, I thought the lesbian uniform was a plaid flannel shirt?"

"Not in LA," Jill said.

"Right." Grace sat up. "So, no regrets?"

"About the way Lauren dressed for the parade?" Jill laughed. "Heck, no."

"About coming out."

Jill hesitated for a moment. "None so far, but it's too soon to tell if or how it'll affect my career."

"Do you have anything lined up for the rest of the year?"

"Just some voice-acting for an animated movie, lending my voice to a little piglet." Jill let out a series of loud oinks.

Not exactly a dream role. And on bad days, the MS made it hard for Jill to speak clearly, so voice-acting wasn't the ideal job for her. "Do you want me to ask around and see if—?"

"No," Jill said and then added more softly, "Thank you. I know you mean well, but this is something I have to do on my own."

Grace could respect that, even if she worried about her friend.

Banging and clanging sounds came from the kitchen.

"I'd better go before my mother destroys my smoothie maker," Grace said. "They have an ongoing feud."

"Who's winning?"

A loud cracking noise drifted over. Grace grimaced. "My mother."

"All right. Talk to you soon."

"Take care." Grace ended the call and hurried to the kitchen.

Elbow-deep in Grace Durand posters, Lauren realized she'd again skipped lunch when her stomach made itself heard.

"I like that one." Zachary, their newest intern, pointed at one of the posters spread across the large table in the conference room.

I just bet you do. Not that Lauren could blame him.

In the movie poster he'd pointed at, Grace was standing in the middle of a cornfield with rain pouring down on her, her off-white sundress clinging to her curves.

"It's good," Lauren said. "But don't think about what you like or don't like. Think about what our target audience—"

"Lauren?" Carmen, their receptionist, called from the doorway.

Lauren turned.

"This was just delivered for you." Carmen held out a big, white box with a red bow and a little envelope.

Frowning, Lauren rounded the conference table. She wasn't expecting anything. It didn't look like a PR-related delivery. Who else could possibly be sending her something here? Even when she'd been dating, her girlfriends had always known better than to send gifts to the office. "Who is it from?"

"I have no idea. The security guard brought it up. All I know is that it smells heavenly."

It smelled heavenly? Had someone sent her flowers?

One of the interns giggled. "How sweet. You have a secret admirer."

Lauren ignored the girl's comment and took the box from Carmen. "Thanks."

Instead of returning to her desk, Carmen lingered in the doorway, clearly waiting for Lauren to open the box or at least the envelope.

Oh, no. Lauren had no intention of letting her co-workers see whatever was in the box. "Why don't you take your lunch break now, and we'll meet back here in an hour?" she said to the interns. With the box in her hands, she squeezed past Carmen and went to her office.

Once she had settled in her desk chair, she removed the envelope that was taped to the box. Lauren's name was scripted across the front in black ink. When she opened the envelope, a small card slid out.

Thank you.
G.

That was all the card said. Lauren mentally leafed through the women in her address book. If she left out business contacts, it was a rather thin book, and no woman whose name started with G came to mind.

Maybe the contents of the box would give her a clue. She removed the red ribbon. Carmen was right. Whatever was in the box smelled heavenly, but not like flowers. More like some kind of baked goods. She opened the lid of the box.

Muffins?

There had to be at least half a dozen different kinds: blueberry, chocolate, banana, lemon/poppy seed, corn, and one that Lauren couldn't identify by sight alone.

Her stomach loudly growled its approval.

She glanced at the card again. A vague idea began to form in her mind. Had Grace sent the box? It couldn't be, could it?

As if on cue, the phone rang and the display revealed that it was Grace calling.

Laughing, Lauren lifted the phone to her ear. "Muffins? You're sending me muffins?"

"I thought everyone liked muffins. Don't you?"

"Of course I do." As if to prove it, she picked up one of the muffins she hadn't yet identified and bit into it. The taste of cinnamon, apple, and a subtle coffee flavor exploded on her tongue. "Oh my God." She moaned into the phone.

Grace cleared her throat.

"Sorry," Lauren said and quickly swallowed. "I just discovered the cinnamon/coffee ones."

Grace chuckled. "I thought you'd like those."

Lauren popped another little piece into her mouth. "I do. But I thought you wanted us to stop eating junk food?"

"I said that *I* shouldn't eat it, but you're not on the Hollywood diet. Besides, I thought sending flowers to another woman might not be the best way to follow your order and lay low, so..."

"So you sent me muffins," Lauren said, still a little puzzled.

"I wanted to say thank you." Grace's voice had gone serious now.

Lauren dusted a little cinnamon off her blouse and shook her head, even though Grace couldn't see it. "You don't need to thank me. I get paid to do my job."

"I'm not thanking you for getting me out of the hot water with the media, although I'm grateful for that too. This is for what you did on Sunday."

"Oh." Lauren rubbed her cheek with her free hand. So Grace had heard that she had accompanied Jill to the LA Gay Pride. A little uncomfortable with Grace's gratefulness, she said, "Well, I got paid for that too. I'm Jill's publicist, remember?"

"I'd bet my salary from *Ava's Heart* that the time you spent marching in the parade won't show up on the bill your company will send Jill," Grace said.

Damn. She's beautiful and perceptive. A dangerous combination. "I have a confidentiality clause in my contract, so I can't discuss what I might or might not bill another client for," Lauren said, trying for a dignified, businesslike tone.

Grace laughed. "That's a 'no comment,' right?"

Lauren just chuckled and said nothing.

"Seriously, though, thank you," Grace said. "It meant a lot to Jill—and to me."

"You're welcome." Lauren eyed the muffins and picked a banana one.

Before she could take a bite, a knock sounded at the door and Carmen poked her head around the doorjamb. "Sorry for the interruption. Sheryl Blackstone-Wade is here."

Lauren frowned and covered the receiver with one hand. "She doesn't have an appointment, does she?"

"No, but she's wondering if you have a minute."

So much for her lunch break. Lauren suppressed a sigh. "All right. Give me a minute, then send her in."

"Will do." Carmen turned away.

"Carmen?"

The receptionist showed up in the doorframe again.

"Catch." Lauren threw her the banana muffin.

"Ooh, thank you." Beaming, Carmen caught it and hurried back to her desk.

Lauren took her hand off the phone's receiver. "Grace? I'm sorry, but I have to go. Duty is calling. I'll contact you later this week to go over movie posters, okay?"

"Okay," Grace said. "Enjoy the muffins."

"I will." Lauren ended the call, closed the box of muffins after one last, regretful glance, and put them in her bottom desk drawer, hoping there would be time to indulge her sweet tooth later.

CHAPTER 13

LAUREN WAS IN THE CONFERENCE room, showing two of the interns how to put together EPKs—electronic press kits—when Carmen burst into the room. With a sense of déjà vu, Lauren hoped there wasn't another box of muffins waiting for her or her team would start to think that she had a new girlfriend.

"Mrs. Duvenbeck just called," Carmen said. "She wants you to call her back right away."

Lauren frowned. In the three weeks that she'd been Grace's publicist, Mrs. Duvenbeck had never called her before. "Did she say what she wanted?"

"Just that she has an assignment for you."

An assignment? Lauren didn't like the sound of that. She enjoyed working with Grace, but her mother was another story. "I'll call her back when we're finished here."

Once they had chosen the music clips, bios, and interviews for the press kits and she'd sent the interns off to work on other things, Lauren went back to her office and reached for the phone. "Mrs. Duvenbeck. This is Lauren Pearce. Our receptionist said you were trying to reach me?"

"Finally! I've been trying to reach you all day."

Lauren was used to exaggerations from the Hollywood divas she worked with, so instead of reacting to the implied complaint, she asked, "What can I do for you?"

"My daughter's birthday is July 3. It's her thirtieth," Mrs. Duvenbeck added in a whisper, as if giving away a national secret, "so I'd like to do something special and surprise her with a party."

Lauren relaxed a little. "That's a great idea. I'm sure she'll love that."

"Yes, but the thing is, I can't plan the party without her finding out about it ahead of time."

It couldn't be that hard, could it? They didn't even live in the same house. The tiny hairs on the back of Lauren's neck stood on end as she started to suspect where this was going. "So you're calling me because…?"

"Because you're her publicist, of course. You could put together a wonderful party, invite all the guests, and—"

"I'm a publicist, not a party planner."

"For three hundred dollars an hour, I'd think you'd do whatever I wanted."

Lauren bit back a sharp reply at the last second and abstained from telling her that it was Grace's money, not hers. "Mrs. Duvenbeck," she said, trying for a patient, calm tone. "Grace is my client, and I doubt she'd want me to waste my billable time on—"

"Ms. Chandler already okayed it," Mrs. Duvenbeck said, stopping her midsentence.

Dammit! That manipulative witch had gone straight to Marlene, who had okayed it, of course. If Lauren took over the party planning, it meant more billable hours for the firm. "With all due respect, but maybe my boss wasn't the right person to ask. If Grace is going to have to pay for it, she should be the one to okay it."

"You want Grace to okay the surprise party we're planning for her? That would defeat the purpose."

For once, Mrs. Duvenbeck was right. It still irked Lauren that she was spending her daughter's money as if it were going out of fashion, but if Grace didn't rein her in, it certainly wasn't Lauren's place to do so.

"So," Mrs. Duvenbeck said, "are you going to take over the party planning?"

There was no way she could refuse. Not while she was still on thin ice with Marlene. But she didn't want to give in without at least trying to appeal to Mrs. Duvenbeck's sense of reason—if she had any. "Do you really think this is the best use of my time, just eight weeks before the release of your daughter's new movie? I should be focused on promotion right now."

"Who says you can't do both? You haven't given me a chance to explain what kind of party I want."

That you want? Shouldn't it be about what Grace wants? "I'm listening," Lauren said, even though she wanted to hang up.

"I'll send you a list of producers, filmmakers, directors, and actors I want you to invite," Mrs. Duvenbeck said. "That includes my son-in-law, of course. And I want you to invite selected members of the press—the ones that'll give us the best exposure."

It finally dawned on Lauren why Mrs. Duvenbeck wanted her to plan the party instead of doing it herself—Lauren had better connections to all the right media people. *I can't believe that she seriously wants to turn her daughter's birthday party into a promo event.*

"I'll leave the choice of venue and food up to you, but please make sure that no alcohol will be served," Mrs. Duvenbeck continued.

Well, at least she had that much consideration for her daughter. "I'll make sure of it."

132

When Lauren didn't question the reason behind the order, Mrs. Duvenbeck noticeably paused, probably astonished that her daughter had trusted Lauren with that secret. "One more thing," she finally said. "It might be better not to invite Jill Corrigan."

"What?" Lauren thought she hadn't heard correctly. "Why? As far as I know, she's Grace's best friend, so why wouldn't we invite her?"

"You should know better than anyone that it's not in my daughter's best interest to be seen with Jill all the time," Mrs. Duvenbeck said, her voice as cold and cutting as steel.

"Mrs. Duvenbeck—"

"I expect you to honor my wishes."

Before Lauren could think of a reply that wouldn't put her job at risk, Mrs. Duvenbeck said good-bye and ended the call.

Lauren smashed her fist onto the desk, making her pens rattle in their holder. "Goddamn bitch!"

A gentle knock on the door interrupted her cursing.

"What!"

The door was opened, and Grace peeked into the room. "Um, is this a bad time? I thought I'd drop by to see the posters you were talking about, but it sounds like this might not be the best time."

Lauren's anger subsided. "No, it's fine. Come on in. Sorry you had to hear that."

"Don't worry. I heard it all before. When they have to do thirty takes in the pouring rain, even the most well-bred actors start to curse like sailors." Grace smiled as she walked toward Lauren, casually dressed in a pair of formfitting black jeans and a sleeveless cream top. "But maybe I should have brought muffins. That sounded like you're not having the best of days."

It just got a lot better. At the mention of doing thirty takes in the pouring rain, Lauren's mind flashed to the poster of Grace in the nearly see-through wet dress. She gave herself a mental slap and got up from behind her desk. "No, I think I should lay off the muffins. They go right to my hips." She patted the body parts in question.

Grace's gaze swept down her body and then back up to her face. "Nonsense. You look fine."

Lauren blinked. Heat crept up her chest. *Did she just check me out?* She imperceptibly shook her head at herself. Even straight women could look at other women. It didn't mean a thing. "Come on. I'll show you the posters."

At least she wouldn't have to deal with the guest list for the party while Grace was here.

133

Sometimes, Grace thought that her mother must have cameras installed in her living room. Every time she sat down to read one of the scripts George had sent her, her mother showed up or called. Sighing, she put the script aside and answered the phone.

"Are you doing anything important?" her mother asked.

"Reading a script."

"Oh, good. Then I'll pick you up in half an hour. We're going shopping."

Grace groaned. "Shopping? Now?"

"Yes. I saw this exquisite dress in one of the boutiques on Rodeo Drive. It will look marvelous on you."

Rodeo Drive meant the paparazzi would be there within seconds, following them from store to store. "Mom, I've got two closets full of dresses. I don't need a new one."

"Trust me, you do," her mother said firmly.

Something about her tone made Grace suspicious. Why would she need a new dress even though the premiere of *Ava's Heart* was still nearly eight weeks away? "You're not planning on throwing me a birthday party, are you?"

"What would make you think that?"

Grace switched the phone to her other ear. "I don't know. Maybe the fact that you want me to buy a new dress? Or that you're answering a question with another question?"

"Can't I want to spend a nice afternoon shopping with my daughter? I miss spending time with you."

Shopping on Rodeo Drive with a horde of paparazzi following them around wasn't Grace's idea of a nice afternoon, but she had to admit that she hadn't spent much time with her mother lately. "All right. We'll go shopping. But you've got to promise me, no party." While she appreciated the effort her mother put into planning parties for her, Grace knew she'd have to attend countless parties and red-carpet events to promote her movie very soon. She didn't want to spend her birthday holding on to a glass of champagne that she couldn't drink, making small talk with the movers and shakers of the entertainment industry. "Please, Mom."

"All right. I promise that I won't plan a party. Happy now?"

"Yes. Thanks, Mom. See you in half an hour." Grace got up and went to get her credit card.

Lauren sat at her desk, clicking through possible venues for Grace's birthday party. They were all equally luxurious, impressive, and high-priced. Any of these

Michelin-starred restaurants and glamorous ballrooms would probably make Mrs. Duvenbeck happy, but Lauren kept hesitating. Was this really how Grace would want to spend her birthday, a milestone birthday no less?

When the phone rang, she bookmarked the websites and accepted the call. "Chandler & Troy Publicity, Lauren Pearce speaking."

"Do you ever sleep or go home?" Jill's cheerful voice came through the phone.

Lauren glanced at the clock in the task bar of her computer and realized that it was after nine. "Every once in a while, when you Hollywood stars don't keep me too busy." She swished her chair from side to side. "How are you doing? You sound good."

"Thanks. I am. No complaints at the moment. Well, maybe one," Jill said. "I hear there's going to be a surprise party for Grace, and I have no idea what to get her for her birthday."

Lauren froze mid-swivel. "Where did you hear that?"

"Russ told me," Jill said.

Thanks a lot. Now she had a problem. Of course Jill assumed she was invited, and Lauren had to find a way to politely uninvite her. She felt like such a traitor. Jill didn't deserve this. "Sorry," she said lamely, "but I have no idea what to get her for her birthday either."

"Actually, I do have an idea. Instead of a present, how about we throw her a party she'll never forget?"

"That's what I'm trying to do."

Jill made a tsking noise with her tongue. "Not one of those awful parties her mother usually throws for her."

"Grace doesn't like them?"

"She hates them!"

Lauren stared at the open tabs on her computer screen. "She does?"

"Oh yeah. For once, I would like her to have a party that is really for her, not for publicity's sake. That's why I'm calling you."

"Me? I hate to point it out, but I'm the publicity gal."

"Yes, but you're also the person who's putting together this year's party, right?"

"Uh, yes. But—"

"I have a fun idea for where to have the party." Jill's enthusiasm was unstoppable. "It's a bit crazy, but...well, it's been a crazy year, so maybe it fits. I think Grace will love it."

Lauren's gaze lingered on the gourmet restaurant on her screen, which had been her top choice so far. Now was the moment when she had to tell Jill that she had already put together a plan for the party—and that she wasn't on the guest list. But then a mental image of Grace's face as she bit into the hot dog flashed through her mind. She still vividly remembered how much Grace had enjoyed such an ordinary thing, probably because she didn't get to experience it very often.

Her middle finger hovered over the right mouse button. Two clicks and she would delete the bookmarks for the restaurant and hotel websites. *No, don't do it. That's career hara-kiri.*

"Lauren? Are you still there?"

To hell with it. This was Grace's birthday, not Katherine's. She deleted the bookmarks and closed her browser. "I'm listening."

CHAPTER 14

LAUREN WIPED ONE CLAMMY PALM on her slacks as she walked up the stairs to Grace's home, her other hand clutching the gift basket she carried. She hadn't been this nervous since her first date. *Oh, come on. Don't be ridiculous. This is not a date.*

It was Grace's birthday—and the day Lauren figured she had a good chance of getting fired. Maybe she did have reason to be nervous. She squared her shoulders and rang the doorbell. Seconds ticked by slowly while she waited, basket in hand.

Finally, the door was opened.

Instead of Grace, Katherine Duvenbeck stood before her. "Is everything ready?" she whispered.

Lauren nodded. "Everything's ready." *Just not the way you wanted.* Mrs. Duvenbeck would find that out soon enough, but Lauren wasn't in a hurry to reveal it.

Grace appeared behind her mother. "Lauren? I thought we wanted to meet at your office for the interview?"

"Yeah, well, I wanted to say happy birthday without the media around. And I wanted to give you this." Feeling a little awkward under Mrs. Duvenbeck's watchful eyes, Lauren thrust the basket at her.

"Oh. That's so nice of you. Thank you." Grace took the basket, studied the assortment of fruit, chocolate, jams, and jellies, and laughed at the bright streamers and the helium birthday balloon tied to the basket's handle. "This is great. Thank you. Come on in."

Lauren followed her into the living room, where a floral scent greeted her.

A sea of bouquets covered almost every available surface of the room—roses, orchids, and other flowers, all of them looking expensive.

Lauren began to think bringing Grace a gift basket had been a bad idea. The balloon in particular might make it look a little juvenile next to the classy bouquets. Well, too late. She ran her empty hands down the outer seams of her slacks.

But then Grace touched her arm and sent her a smile. "I love the balloon. My father got me some of those every year for my birthday."

Was Grace just saying that to make her feel better? Lauren couldn't tell. "I'm glad you like it."

"I do."

Lauren returned her smile and relaxed, finally deciding that Grace genuinely liked her gift basket. "Happy birthday."

"Thank you," Grace said quietly.

Their gazes met and held.

Mrs. Duvenbeck pushed between them and eyed the gift basket. "Do you have any idea how many calories these things are?"

"Mom, please. Not today."

"Whatever." Mrs. Duvenbeck waved one manicured hand. "Let me put the chocolates in the fridge while you go change into something more elegant."

Lauren turned away, pretending to inspect the flowers Grace had gotten. If this was how Mrs. Duvenbeck treated her now, she didn't want to even imagine what would happen once she found out what kind of party Lauren had put together. It would truly be a surprise party—and not just for Grace.

Grace started to smell a rat when her mother told her for the third time she had to change into something more elegant. "I think slacks and a blouse are just fine. It's an interview with a local newspaper, not an official reception with the president. Right, Lauren?" She looked over at her publicist, who was wearing similar attire.

"Uh…"

What was going on with Lauren? She looked more nervous than Grace had ever seen her, even at the tense press conference.

"Trust me, darling," her mother said, drawing Grace's gaze back toward her. "You really want to change."

Lauren cleared her throat. "Actually, what you're wearing is just fine."

"How can you say that? It's not—"

"Trust me, Mrs. Duvenbeck," Lauren said and glanced at her silver wristwatch. "We should be going."

Grace followed her outside and raised her brows as she saw the limousine in her driveway. It seemed Lauren had decided she should travel to the interview in style, since it was her birthday. She didn't protest when her mother climbed in after her, insisting on coming with her to the interview.

As the limousine navigated the curving roads and then the busy city streets, she quietly reflected on what a strange way to spend her birthday this was. Well, at least the interview would be over in an hour and she didn't have to spend the entire rest of the day at a party. Sometimes, playing the role of Grace Durand could be tiring.

She spent the half-hour ride mentally going over each question the reporter could possibly ask. It took her a few minutes to realize they had already passed Lauren's office in Westwood, where they were supposed to meet the reporter, and were heading toward Santa Monica. "Uh, Lauren…"

Lauren grinned over at her. "Don't worry. Just a little change of plans."

Grace's head sank against the backrest. "Let me guess. There is no reporter waiting for us."

"Oh, yes, there is," Lauren said, still grinning. "Several of them, actually."

Damn. So her mother had put together a party and invited the press after all. Somehow, she'd even roped Lauren into helping.

"Don't worry," Lauren said quietly. "You'll like it." She glanced at Grace's mother. "I think."

As the driver turned left onto Colorado Avenue and headed toward the Santa Monica Pier, Lauren nervously shifted on the leather seat.

The limousine approached one of the expensive seafood restaurants. Mrs. Duvenbeck stopped complaining about her daughter dressing so casually and gave Lauren a grudging nod, apparently thinking that was where the party would be held.

But the limo continued on, passing the restaurant and also another one on the pier, famous for its lobster bisque.

"Where on God's green earth are we going?"

"Just a little farther," Lauren said.

"Farther?" Mrs. Duvenbeck screeched. "But there's nothing but the ocean!"

The limousine crossed the bridge and rumbled over the boardwalk.

"Actually, there is."

The driver pulled the limousine to a stop in front of a metal barricade.

"We'll have to walk the rest of the way," Lauren said. "It's just a few steps." She led Grace and a grumbling Mrs. Duvenbeck toward a building directly on the pier. Security guards blocked the entrance, but they quickly stepped back when they realized who was approaching. Lauren pulled Grace inside before she could stop to ask questions.

Three dozen people jumped out from behind video game machines, air hockey tables, pinball machines, and a shooting gallery, loudly shouting, "Surprise!"

Grace jumped and pressed both hands to her chest. "Oh my God! You're throwing me a birthday party at an arcade?" she shouted over the chaos toward her mother.

Stiffly gripping her purse, Mrs. Duvenbeck glared at Lauren. "I certainly did not!"

Grace looked at her too. "You did this?"

A lump in her throat prevented Lauren from speaking, so she just nodded. She nearly tipped over when she suddenly found herself with an armful of Grace.

Laughing, Grace hugged her for all she was worth. "This is fantastic. Thank you!"

The subtle scent of Grace's perfume made Lauren dizzy. Or maybe it was the feel of her curvaceous body pressed against hers. She didn't want to examine that too closely. Very aware of all the people watching them, including Mrs. Duvenbeck and several members of the press, she awkwardly put one hand on Grace's back. "You're welcome. I'm glad you like it. There are some reporters here, but I made sure they're the friendly, reputable kind. There are no video cameras, and they are only allowed to take photos for the first hour. After that, you can relax."

"Thank you," Grace said again and looked as if she wanted to say more, but then she was whisked away by her guests.

Grace's laughter trailed after her, and Lauren couldn't help grinning at the childlike glee.

"What on earth were you thinking?"

Mrs. Duvenbeck's voice was like a bucket of ice-cold water, instantly dousing her joy. Slowly, Lauren turned around. She knew she was about to face one of the biggest battles of her career. "Well, you wanted me to pick the venue...so I did. It has all the requirements you wanted—there's no alcohol being served, and I invited several reporters."

"Don't play innocent. You knew this isn't what I wanted!" Mrs. Duvenbeck stomped one high-heeled foot.

"What about what Grace wants?" Lauren asked softly.

A flush rose up Mrs. Duvenbeck's neck until Lauren thought steam was about to come out of her ears. "How dare you presume to know what my daughter wants? I'm her mother. I single-handedly raised her while you've barely known her for a month! I'm going to call your boss right now and tell her about this...this..." She swept her hand around, indicating the arcade. "This travesty!"

Lauren watched with gritted teeth as she pulled her cell phone out of her purse and pressed a few buttons. *Figures that she'd have Marlene on speed dial.* Her boss wouldn't like this one bit.

The phone rang, and Mrs. Duvenbeck waited for Marlene to pick up, her triumphant gaze directed at Lauren.

"Oh, Mrs. Duvenbeck! There you are!" A blonde woman of about Grace's age rushed over and took Mrs. Duvenbeck's shoulders in an enthusiastic grip, showering her with air kisses left and right.

Mrs. Duvenbeck blinked rapidly. Her hand with the phone dropped to her side as she stared at the newcomer.

"This is such a wonderful idea," the blonde said, twirling once to indicate the entire arcade. "I just told Mr. Garner from the *LA Times* what a great event it is and that you are the one responsible for it. He was very impressed."

"Uh, he was?"

"Yes, of course! I mean, how could he not be impressed? It's a genius idea to have the wealthy guests pay for tokens and then have the proceeds go to a nonprofit organization raising money for MS research."

Mrs. Duvenbeck looked back and forth between the blonde and Lauren.

A muffled voice came from the phone hanging limply in Mrs. Duvenbeck's grasp. She lifted it to her ear. "Yes?"

Lauren recognized Marlene's voice but couldn't tell what she said. Probably the polite PR equivalent of "Why are you calling me on a Friday evening?"

"I just wanted..." Mrs. Duvenbeck's gaze veered up to the blonde, who gave her a sweet smile. "I just wanted to thank you for all the great work CT Publicity has been doing for my daughter," she said with an expression as if she'd been forced to drink a gallon of sour milk.

Weak-kneed, Lauren bit back a relieved grin.

Just as Mrs. Duvenbeck ended the call, the sound of Grace's laughter drifted over from a nearby video game.

Both Lauren and Mrs. Duvenbeck turned their heads.

Gripping a plastic gun with both hands, Grace was fighting virtual zombies shoulder to shoulder with Jill.

Mrs. Duvenbeck whirled back around and stabbed an accusing finger in Jill's direction. "What is she doing here? I told you not to—"

"Actually, Mrs. Duvenbeck, she's my plus one since my partner is away on a photo shoot and couldn't make it," the blonde said, once again saving Lauren's ass.

"Oh. Well, then... I'll go greet the reporters." Mrs. Duvenbeck's gaze drilled into Lauren. "I will talk to you later. Don't think for a minute that you're going to get away with this." After one last glare, she marched off.

Lauren blew out a breath. She wanted to hug the blonde, but instead stuck out her hand. "Thank you. You saved my life—or at least my career."

"It was my pleasure." The stranger took Lauren's hand in a grip that was unexpectedly firm for such a slender woman. "I met Grace's mother when we were shooting in Vegas, so I know how she can be."

Shooting in Vegas? Lauren took a closer look at the blonde. "Oh, wow. You're Amanda Clark." Jill had probably put her on the guest list. Lauren had seen her on TV, but once again, the old adage about the camera adding ten pounds was true. The actress looked different than she did on *Central Precinct*, the TV show she starred in.

Amanda grinned and tipped an imaginary hat. "In the flesh."

"Lauren Pearce. I'm Grace's publicist."

"I gathered that when I saw Mrs. Duvenbeck spitting fire at you because of the party," Amanda said.

"Thanks again for slaying that dragon." They shared a grin. "But you know, I didn't invite anyone from the *LA Times*."

Amanda shrugged. "Yeah, but Mrs. Duvenbeck doesn't know that, does she?"

Laughter bubbled up from Lauren's chest. "Guess not."

"I think I'll go say hello to the birthday girl before she saves the world from the second attack of the zombies," Amanda said, pointing over to where Grace was just finishing a game.

Lauren nodded and watched her go. What was suddenly going on with Hollywood? This was the third actress she'd met within the last few weeks who actually seemed to be a decent human being.

Grace hugged her colleague, for once omitting the air kisses and the fake, minimal-body-contact embrace so common in Hollywood. "Oh my God, don't tell me this is a member of the *Central Precinct* cast out and about before midnight?" She let go of Amanda and pressed her hand to her chest in pretend shock. Then, becoming serious, she asked, "Has your shooting schedule become any lighter?"

When she had guest-starred in an episode of the popular TV show last year, they'd rarely finished shooting before eight or nine o'clock in the evening, sometimes working for fourteen or more hours a day.

"I wish. But I didn't want to miss this, so we did some creative rearranging of scenes, and here I am." Amanda greeted Jill with a hug too and then looked around. "This is great."

"Yes, it is." Grace took in the large arcade, which had more games than she had ever seen in one place in her entire life. Since she'd spent most of her childhood in front of a camera, that didn't say much, but this place made her feel like a giddy preschooler.

In one corner of the room, Nick and Russ were wielding plastic shotguns; across from them, the director of *Ava's Heart* was gobbling ghosts at a Pac-Man game, and a reporter Grace had seen at the press conference was making rock star poses with a guitar controller.

Grace reached out and squeezed Jill's arm. "Thank you again."

"I wish I could take all the credit, but I just came up with the idea," Jill said. "Lauren did most of the work, booking the arcade for the day and sending out most of the invitations."

Grace looked around. She hadn't seen Lauren since they'd entered the arcade. "Where is she?"

"Probably hiding from your mother who wasn't too happy about this *travesty*," Amanda said, making air quotes with two fingers of each hand. She held on to Grace when she wanted to march off and rescue Lauren from her mother's wrath. "Don't worry. I calmed her down by telling her how much the journalists like it."

Grace again let her gaze sweep the room. There was still no sign of Lauren, but the reporters did indeed seem to enjoy themselves. They probably were as sick of boring cocktail parties as Grace was.

Jill hooked her arms through Grace's and Amanda's. "Come on," Jill said and pulled them with her. "Let's see what kind of mischief we can get into. Ooh, they have Skee-Ball! Let's play."

Grace looked at the different-sized rings at the end of an inclined ramp. "I have no idea how to play."

Jill was already feeding tokens into the machine, making nine wooden balls clatter down into a chute. "Don't worry. It's not rocket science."

While she listened to Jill's explanation of the rules, Grace let her gaze wander through the arcade again. She was beginning to think that maybe Lauren had gone home now that the party was in full swing when she finally found her bent over the air hockey table.

Grace couldn't make out whom she was playing since the other player's back was to her. Lauren's face, bathed in the glow of the bluish light in the arcade, was intent like that of a warrior readying for battle. Grace wondered if she approached every part of her life with this intensity. For a moment, an image of Lauren in a heated embrace with another woman flashed through her head before she forced the thought from her mind.

Lauren shoved an unruly strand of hair out of her face and glanced up.

Their gazes met.

The puck shot past Lauren's paddle and clattered into the goal slot while Lauren's opponent let out a triumphant cry.

"Sorry," Grace mouthed.

Lauren grinned and shrugged.

Jill tugged on her sleeve. "Hey! You're not paying attention."

Grace turned back toward her. "Go ahead and show me. I'm watching your every move with complete and utter attention."

Jill swung her arm as if she were bowling and rolled the first ball up the inclined ramp.

Lauren wandered the arcade, every now and then stopping to play a game with someone who hadn't yet found a partner. Even though Mrs. Duvenbeck had already left in protest, she was sure she hadn't heard the last of it from her, so if she was in for more ass-chewing, the least she could do was make sure everyone else thoroughly enjoyed the party.

Grace certainly did.

Grinning, Lauren looked over to the Skee-Ball ramps, where Grace was playing with Jill and Amanda. It was hard to believe that she was watching three well-known, seasoned actresses. They looked more like carefree children as they competed against each other and did little victory dances when they hit one of the high-score slots.

When it was her turn, Grace took one of the wooden balls, pretended to spit on it, and rolled it down the lane. It launched off a short ramp, gave a little hop, and landed squarely in the fifty-point ring at the top.

Grace threw her arms up and cheered.

Lauren's grin grew. This made the confrontation with Mrs. Duvenbeck worth it. She would bet her next paycheck that Grace had never gotten to play in an arcade as a child or teenager and was glad that she had helped give her a chance to experience it now.

She leaned against an out-of-order Galaga machine and watched as the three women wandered over to the shooting range to try something else.

Russ and Nick were already there, and they happily showed the women how the game was played. Nick wrapped his arms around Grace from behind, pressing against her back, his hands covering hers as he showed her how to aim the plastic rifle.

Lauren's grin withered, and she mentally gagged. *Oh, come on.* As Grace's publicist, she knew she should be happy that Nick was willing to play along and pretend that he and Grace were still the deeply in love, touchy-feely couple. Still, she didn't like it. It wasn't that she was jealous, she told herself. She just didn't like them putting on a show, acting even though the cameras weren't rolling. She'd had enough of that at home growing up.

She pushed off the out-of-order machine and headed toward one of the shooting games. Blasting up some zombies was exactly what she needed now.

After a few more games, Grace realized they'd lost Amanda somewhere in the crowd and that Jill was getting tired. Her movements were slower than before, and she blinked repeatedly as if she had trouble seeing in the dim, bluish light of the arcade. "How about we take a break?"

Jill dug in her heels when Grace tried to drag her away from the games. "No. I demand a rematch."

Christ. Women. Why did they have to be so stubborn? Grace glanced around for something that would help distract her friend. "But there's a fortune-telling machine over there." She pointed in the direction of the oak-and-glass cabinet. "Let's go and see what the future holds for us."

"I'm not so sure I want to know," Jill muttered.

Grace rubbed Jill's arm. "Hey, come on. It's my birthday. No morose thoughts allowed."

"Sorry. I don't usually—"

"I know," Grace said. Now completely serious, she looked into Jill's eyes. "You never complain, and you always seem happy and upbeat. I know it's probably not like that deep inside. If you ever have a bad day and want to bitch or cry or whatever, you can call me any time. You know that, don't you?"

Biting her lip, Jill nodded. She hugged Grace for a moment and then pushed her away. "Come on. Your bright future is waiting." She dragged Grace over to the fortune-teller puppet in the oak cabinet and pressed a token into her hand.

When Grace put it into the slot, the life-sized puppet started to move, sagely nodding her head, which made her red-and-gold headscarf sway. The crystal ball in front of her lit up as she circled her bracelet-adorned hand over it. "Come closer and listen to what Zamira the Gypsy has to tell you."

Jill nudged Grace forward.

"Here's my wisdom for you," the gypsy said, her mouth opening and closing. "Your hard work will pay off in the future."

"Oooh," Jill whispered. "There might be an Oscar in your future after all!"

"But laziness pays off right now, so use this day to relax and enjoy yourself. You deserve it." The puppet's mouth snapped shut, and the crystal ball went dark.

"That's it?" Grace said. "That was all?"

Jill grinned and elbowed her. "What were you hoping for?" She lowered her voice, "A hookup with some tall, dark, and handsome stranger?"

Grace snorted and leaned toward Jill to whisper, "No, thanks. I think I'll stay away from men for the foreseeable future."

"Ooh, look. There's a card."

Grace looked at where Jill was pointing. A printed card with an image of Zamira the Gypsy on the back slipped out of a dispenser. Expecting the same generic enjoy-yourself-today fortune that the puppet had handed out, Grace picked up the card and read it.

Although you may not look for it, love will soon arrive, changing the course of your life. It might not look like a blessing at first, but remember that the greatest pleasures in life often come from unexpected sources.

She stared at the card for a moment.

"What is it?" Jill asked and tried to peer at the card.

"Nothing." Grace shook her head. It was just a generic fortune, not intended for her specifically. Everybody probably got the same card. She pocketed it and let herself be dragged away from the fortune-telling machine.

It was close to eleven already, but the party still showed no signs of winding down. Everywhere Lauren looked, celebrities, entertainment professionals, and reporters were still playing with abandon.

Jill sidled up next to her and bumped Lauren with her hip. "Looks like Operation Fun Birthday is a success. And Katherine hasn't killed you either."

"She's just waiting until we're back outside, where the blood won't be so hard to remove from the floor," Lauren said.

Jill laughed. "It was worth it, though, wasn't it?"

"Yeah. It definitely was." The joy on Grace's face as she played had made it all worthwhile.

As if conjured up by Lauren's thoughts, Grace appeared behind Jill and pressed a bottle of water into her hands. "Here. Drink this."

"Yes, Mom." Jill emptied half of the bottle in several big gulps.

Lauren studied her and lifted a brow at Grace, silently asking whether everything was okay with Jill.

Grace subtly shook her head. "How about we wrap up this party?"

"Now?" Jill asked. "But everybody's still having so much fun!"

"Yeah, but now that I'm thirty, I tire more easily," Grace said without missing a beat.

Lauren hid a grin. She liked the unobtrusive way Grace took care of her friend without making her feel as if she were being treated like a child.

"Spoilsport," Jill grumbled. "All right. But first, I want to play one last game with you two. Your pick, Lauren."

146

After letting her gaze roam over the nearby games, Lauren pointed decisively. "How about pinball?"

"Do you know how to play?" Grace asked, eyeing the vintage pinball machine.

"Please. I'm a lesbian. We're contractually required to be good at pinball, or we lose our lesbian card."

"Is that so?"

Grace's drawl made goose bumps erupt all over Lauren's body.

"Yes," she croaked out and sent Jill an imploring gaze. "Right, Jill?"

Jill looked back and forth between them. "Right. Go ahead and start."

Lauren cracked her knuckles and stretched her fingers like a piano player preparing for the concert of a lifetime.

"Uh-oh," Grace said. "Why do I get the feeling we're about to be hustled?"

Lauren just grinned and popped two tokens into the machine, which lit up and started playing eighties music. She pulled the plunger and flung the silver ball into play.

Her first ball quickly escaped through the paddles. Christ, it had been some time since she'd last played pinball. She tried to remember how long it had been since she'd taken any time off to just enjoy herself, but other than a few hours of writing on Sundays, nothing came to mind. Maybe Grace was right. She was a workaholic.

She propelled her next ball upward, this time getting back into the rhythm of the game, pressing the buttons at exactly the right moment. The ball banged and bounced against the rubber bumpers, and then she flung it up into the megapoints zone.

Lights flashed, and bells rang.

Lauren lost herself in the game, no longer keeping track of time. When she finally straightened and stepped back, she felt gazes on her and turned.

"Not bad for an old woman," Jill said. She gestured at Grace to go before her. "Age before beauty."

Grace stepped forward and bent over the pinball machine, involuntarily drawing Lauren's gaze toward her firm backside.

She quickly looked away, just in time to see Jill winking at her. Scowling, she kept her gaze directed at the pinball machine.

Grace sent the ball flying the way she'd seen Lauren do it, but it quickly rolled down a gutter. The second ball fared no better. Grace's shoulders slumped. "Good thing I'm not a lesbian, or the committee would revoke my card," she mumbled.

"Let me show you." Lauren stepped behind her before she could stop herself.

"Hey, no helping allowed," Jill said.

"I'm her publicist. It's my job to make her look good with so many journalists around."

Grace turned her head and grinned over her shoulder. "Yeah. We wouldn't want Lauren to have to handle headlines about Grace Durand sucking at pinball, would we?"

Jill flung up her hands. "Whatever."

Grace slid her feet shoulder-width apart and braced herself for the next game. She felt Lauren step up behind her, so close that her front almost touched Grace's back. Then Lauren reached around her and her hands covered Grace's on the red buttons that moved the flippers.

Part of Grace wanted to protest this closeness. What if one of the reporters saw them and misunderstood? She told herself she was overreacting. It was just a game after all. Even the journalists would see that, and her mother was no longer here to watch her every move.

"Ready?" Lauren asked from just inches away, her breath hot on Grace's ear.

A shiver went through Grace. *Just the excitement of the game.* Focusing on the pinball machine in front of her, she nodded.

The silver ball streaked up the ramp and ricocheted its way down.

"Wait, wait," Lauren whispered. "Wait…now!" Her left hand pressed down on Grace's.

The flipper snapped up, hitting the ball at exactly the right moment and volleying it up. It careened through a ramp and hit a couple of targets, which lit up in red, white, and blue colors.

Sirens and bells went off.

The ball bounced back and forth between bumpers before dropping down.

With one quick squeeze of their hands, Lauren catapulted it back up.

It clanged through a series of bumpers and bells, quickly making the number on the scoreboard climb.

Her skin warming and all her senses involved now, Grace pressed the buttons along with Lauren. They managed to keep the ball in play for quite some time until it finally dropped straight down.

"Oh, shit." Helplessly, Grace watched as the ball came down right between the flippers, where she couldn't reach it.

Just when she thought it would be game over in a second, Lauren thrust her hips against her from behind, nudging Grace against the pinball machine.

The ball changed its trajectory, and Lauren shot it back up with one flick of the right flipper. "You have to play with your entire body, not just your hands," she said right into Grace's ear. "Try it."

148

Her body felt as if it was on fire. *Game fever.* Grace waited until the ball was on its way down again before she rocked her hips against the machine.

The scoring lights went out, and "tilt — game over" flashed on the scoreboard.

Lauren dropped her arms from around Grace and stepped back.

Dazed, Grace turned. Her cheeks were hot, and she felt flushed with the excitement of the game. "What happened?"

"You nudged it too hard and triggered the tilt mechanism, which shuts the game down," Lauren said and took another step back. Even in the bluish light of the arcade, her face looked flushed too.

No wonder. It was pretty warm in here. Grace turned toward Jill. "Not bad for an old woman, huh?"

"Not bad at all." Jill grinned broadly and shouldered past them. "My turn now."

It was after midnight when Grace finally stepped out of the arcade. The ocean breeze ruffled her hair and cooled her overheated body. She was exhausted, but at the same time, she was sad to see the evening end and the last of her guests leave.

Her mother had fled back home with the first person leaving the party, and Grace hadn't seen Lauren since she'd walked Jill to her car. Just when she started to wonder how she'd get home, a quiet voice reached her.

"Grace, over here."

She peered into the almost darkness at the edge of the pier.

Lauren stood at the railing, leaning against it with one hip.

Smiling, Grace walked over.

"Who's your cute friend?" Lauren asked.

For a moment, Grace had no idea what she meant, but then Lauren gestured at the stuffed animal that Grace had just traded for her stack of tickets at the prize counter. She held it out for Lauren to see. "I think she's a lynx."

"She?"

Grace shrugged and stroked one of the soft, bushy ears. "I don't know. She just looks like a female to me." She leaned against the railing next to Lauren. "Didn't you get yourself anything for the tickets you won?"

"I gave them to one of the journalists I know. He has three kids at home," Lauren said.

Grace smiled. For someone who showed the world just her tough publicist persona most of the time, Lauren sure had a soft heart.

They both listened to the sound of the waves rolling in and the bustling of the people in the amusement park still open somewhere behind them. After a while, Grace spontaneously turned and pressed the lynx into Lauren's hands. "Here."

"For me?" In the dim light, Lauren's eyes looked just as big and round as those of the stuffed animal. "But it's your birthday, not mine."

Grace glanced at her wristwatch. "Not anymore. It's five minutes past midnight."

"Still. You won it fair and square." Lauren tried to give back the lynx, but Grace refused to take it.

"Please. Keep it. At least until I can come up with a better idea to say thank you."

"You don't need to—"

"Yes, I do. I want to. This was by far the best birthday I ever had, and I know you risked my mother's wrath by making it possible."

Lauren's brow furrowed. Did she find it pathetic that a day at the arcade was Grace's best birthday of all time? Finally, she nodded, accepting the stuffed lynx and cuddling it to her chest. "Thank you."

"No, thank *you*."

They looked at each other, then Lauren pushed away from the railing. "Come on. The limo is waiting to drive you and Betty home."

Grace frowned at the mention of her birth name. "Betty?"

Grinning, Lauren lifted the little lynx.

"Oh, no. You did not name her Betty!"

"Oh, yes, I did."

They playfully argued about it all the way to the limousine.

CHAPTER 15

LAUREN HAD WORKED ON THE electronic press kits for *Ava's Heart* all morning, putting together a series of sixty-second clips of the movie and behind-the-scenes footage the studio had sent. She laughed at a blooper in which a hen kept pecking at Grace's leg. It clucked and thrashed its wings when a production assistant tried to grab it and drag it away from Grace.

"Grace Durand, chick magnet." Lauren laughed and shook her head. The memory of the magnetic effect Grace had exerted on her in the arcade last week resurfaced. Showing her how to play pinball hadn't been one of her better ideas. As soon as she felt Grace's heat against her body, she'd wanted to wrap her arms around her and press even closer.

Thank God the remainder of her professionalism had kicked in before she could make a fool of herself or draw the attention of a journalist. How would Grace react if she ever found out how much Lauren had enjoyed their semi-embrace? *You'd better make sure she never finds out, or her mother won't have to bother trying to get you fired.*

Not wanting to linger on those thoughts for too long, she double-clicked on the next video. It was a day-in-the-life segment that followed the actors of *Ava's Heart* through an ordinary day on the set. The footage started at five o'clock in the morning, with Grace entering the makeup trailer, carrying two paper cups of coffee.

Two? Even a known coffee addict like Lauren usually contented herself with one cup on the way to work.

When Grace placed the second paper cup next to the makeup case, Lauren understood. She'd brought in coffee for the makeup artist. The logo on the cup indicated that it wasn't the free swill from the studio's catering area but a rather expensive designer coffee. With every other actress, Lauren would have snorted and assumed that she'd done it just this once to make herself look good on camera, but Grace seemed like the kind of woman who'd do that every day.

In the video, Grace settled in the makeup chair.

The makeup lady spun her into position in front of a backlit mirror and started applying concealer and foundation. Then a close-up of Grace's full lips followed as a medium pink lipstick glided over them, following their gentle curves. Grace's mouth opened slightly.

Blindly, Lauren grabbed for the nearest piece of paper on her desk and used it to fan herself. Maybe this would be a good clip to include in the press kit. If it had this effect on her, it might work for Grace's male fans too.

Her phone rang, interrupting her in-depth study of Grace's lips. She reached for it without looking away from the screen. "Chandler & Troy Publicity, Lauren Pearce speaking."

"Hello, Ms. Pearce. This is Katherine Duvenbeck."

The cool voice made Lauren sit up straight and close the video that was playing on her computer screen. She felt like a teenager who'd been caught watching porn. "Uh, hello, Mrs. Duvenbeck. What can I do for you?"

She waited, almost afraid of the answer. Since Grace's mother had stomped out of the arcade, Lauren hadn't heard from her, but she hadn't forgotten Mrs. Duvenbeck's promise that she'd talk to her later.

"I want you to call my son-in-law and set up a date for him and Grace in a place where they will be photographed together," Mrs. Duvenbeck said.

Lauren took a pen from her desk and started fiddling with its clip. "Is that really necessary?"

"I thought you agreed on that strategy?"

"Well, I didn't outright object to it. But the fundraiser at the arcade gave Grace a lot of positive press, making the public forget about the mud the media was slinging before. A fake date won't be necessary." After seeing Grace and Nick together at the birthday party, Lauren wasn't eager to look at photos of them playing the happy couple.

"Leave that for me to decide," Mrs. Duvenbeck said.

The clip broke off the pen and ricocheted across the room. "I'm just saying. If the media finds out that they're going through a divorce, this date will make them look like they've been pretending all along."

Mrs. Duvenbeck seemed to think about it for a few seconds. "No, we're going through with this. Who knows, maybe when they start spending some time together, they'll reconcile and forget about this stupid divorce."

Oh, come on. She couldn't really believe that, could she? Grace had appeared quite certain that her marriage was over for good.

"So go ahead and call him," Mrs. Duvenbeck said, making it sound like an order—which it was. "You have his number, don't you?"

"I do." Lauren gritted her teeth. *Who does she think I am—a pimp?* Why didn't Mrs. Duvenbeck call her beloved son-in-law herself if she was so eager for them to go out? Then she understood. This was Mrs. Duvenbeck's revenge—her way of showing Lauren that she wouldn't allow her to ignore her orders.

"Good. Talk to you soon."

Not if I can help it. Lauren hung up after a stiff good-bye. Her jaw muscles bunched as she held the phone in her hand for a few moments. *Come on. Get it over with.* She scrolled through her contact list and called Nick to set up a date for Grace.

Nick instantly agreed. "I need to talk to her anyway," he said.

Lauren furrowed her brow, wondering what a couple about to divorce could possibly have to talk about. Was he indeed aiming to reconcile, as Mrs. Duvenbeck hoped? She rolled her eyes at herself. Christ, when had she become so curious? Grace would tell her whatever she needed to know as her publicist. The rest was none of her business.

She kept repeating that to herself as she called Grace to let her know about her date.

"Hi, Lauren." Grace sounded happy to hear from her. "How are you?"

"Uh, I'm fine."

"Good. And how's Betty doing?"

When Lauren realized Grace was talking about the stuffed animal, she had to laugh. "She's doing fine too. Reigning over my couch and demanding lots of adoration and many hot dogs."

"What? The couch? She's not allowed in your bed?"

Lauren bit back a comment about reserving her bed for women. *She's a client, remember?* "Um, listen, I'm calling about a date...uh...about your date with Nick." God, what was it about this woman that made her stammer like a starstruck girl?

"Do you really think that's still necessary after *Entertainment Weekly* published the photo of Nick teaching me how to shoot in the arcade?" Grace asked.

"I personally don't think it is, but your mother insisted."

"Gosh, this feels like being sixteen again and having Mom pick my dates," Grace mumbled.

Lauren felt her eyebrows creep up her forehead. *Her mother picked her dates for her?*

"She wanted me to be seen with all the right people," Grace explained as if sensing the unasked question. She was silent for a few moments before saying, "Okay. If she thinks it's for the best, then let's do it. When and where?"

"Saturday at eight in The Aerie," Lauren said.

"That posh rooftop sushi bar in Venice Beach?" Grace sounded less than enthusiastic.

"Well, if it's any consolation, the sushi is supposed to be good, and you can watch the sunset from the top of the building."

Grace sighed and mumbled, "I'd rather join you and Betty for hot dogs on the couch."

Lauren was stunned into silence. Did Grace really mean that? Of course, she couldn't ask.

"Okay," Grace said. "I wrote it down. Tell Nick he's got a date."

Okay, that's it. If she drags out one more thing, I'll just go naked. Grace stared at the stack of clothes piled on her bed. Her mother had regarded each item for a second before declaring it not good enough. "Mom," Grace said before her mother could pull out the other half of her closet too. "It's just Nick." If left to her own devices, she would have grabbed the article of clothing on top of the pile and put it on. Case closed.

But with her mother, things were never that easy. "Just Nick?" She shook her head. "That's the kind of attitude that made your marriage fail."

Maybe she was right. While Nick had always been important to her, he'd never played first fiddle in her life. She itched to remind her mother that she'd encouraged Grace to put her career first but knew it wouldn't do any good. Trying to be patient, she watched her mother rummage through her walk-in closet.

Finally, she handed Grace a fiery-red dress with a plunging neckline.

Grace held it to her chest and peeked down at herself. "Isn't that a little over the top for a sushi bar?"

Her mother sent her a gaze that made Grace duck her head.

"Okay, I'll wear it."

At least she would make some paparazzi happy.

Grace knew something weird was going on with Nick even before their date started. He called her the day before, asking if she would mind driving and picking him up so he could have some sake with his dinner.

Normally, he didn't drink around her. But apparently, he thought he needed alcohol to make it through dinner with her. Grace frowned. Were things really that bad between them? They were still friends, weren't they?

They found a parking spot not too far from The Aerie.

A horde of fans and paparazzi surrounded them as soon as they got out of Grace's SUV. Someone—probably her mother—must have tipped them off. Camera shutters clicked, and strobe flashes went off as Nick gallantly wrapped one arm around her.

Grace slung one arm around Nick's athletic middle and put on her infatuated-wife smile. *There, Mom. Happy now?*

Young women, barely out of their teens, screamed and waved pen and paper at Nick, wanting his autograph. A few of them seemed to want more than just autographs, as a red lace bra arched through the air.

Nick caught it, grinning, and blew a kiss at the overeager fan.

Grace just shook her head and signed some autographs of her own. She realized that she wasn't jealous anymore. After considering it for a moment, she discovered that she'd never been jealous of young women throwing their underwear at her husband. Maybe that should have been a clue.

Finally leaving their fans behind, they veered around a couple of skateboarders and strolled toward the sushi bar. Perched atop a hotel, it offered a great view of the palm tree-lined beach and the Pacific.

A cool breeze from the ocean made Grace wish she hadn't listened to her mother and had worn something other than the revealing dress. Nick seemed too distracted by whatever was on his mind to appreciate it anyway. But then again, she was wearing the dress for the media, not for Nick, and the paparazzi who'd followed them up to the rooftop certainly seemed to like it. They snapped picture after picture. When two waiters descended on them, they finally left.

Grace allowed herself to relax and tipped the waiter generously as he brought her a blanket. While she looked over the menu, her mind went to the hot dogs Lauren had served her last month.

They nibbled on shitake tofu, spicy tuna rolls, and yellowtail carpaccio and talked about the party at the arcade, Nick's new movie, and Grace's upcoming trip to Las Vegas. Nick downed his sake in one shot and poured himself another from a small ceramic bottle.

The sun sank lower and dipped below the horizon, coloring the ocean and the clouds in shades of orange, gold, and crimson. Grace leaned her chin on her hand and gazed toward the horizon, but Nick didn't seem to even notice the beautiful view.

Finally, Grace leaned back and regarded him across the table. "What's wrong?"

His head jerked up. "Excuse me?"

"I asked you what's wrong."

"Nothing. Not really."

Grace shook her head at him. "You might be an actor, but you can't fool me. Something's going on."

He glanced left and right. "Not here. I'll tell you in the car."

The tension at the table rose. Grace's mind churned, coming up with all kinds of things he might have to say. Was he sick? Giving up on acting? Or maybe he wanted to have the cottage instead of the house once the divorce was final?

Whatever it was, it was probably bad if he didn't want to tell her in public, afraid she'd make a scene.

She quickly finished her water so they could pay and leave.

"Would you like to get the rest of that to go?" the waiter asked as he brought them the bill.

"No, thanks," Grace said while Nick answered, "Yes."

The waiter looked back and forth between them.

"Yes, please," Nick repeated.

Grace gritted her teeth. Now they'd have to wait for the waiter to wrap the tuna rolls. Was Nick trying to delay the inevitable?

Ten minutes later, they finally left the sushi bar. Neither of them said anything until they got into the SUV and pulled out onto the street. Now no one could overhear what Nick was about to tell her.

Grace glanced into the rearview mirror but couldn't make out any cars following them as they drove toward Silver City. She gripped the steering wheel with both hands. "Tell me."

He rubbed his mouth as if trying to hold back the words. "I don't know how to say it."

"Just say it. Whatever it is, I won't bite your head off."

Nick glanced at the dashboard, the rearview mirror, the back of Grace's seat… everywhere but at her. "Shailene is pregnant."

Grace nearly hit a telephone pole before she got control of herself and the SUV again. The words echoed through her head on auto repeat, so she shook her head to stop the audio loop. "How the hell did that happen?"

"Uh, the usual way," he said, one corner of his mouth quirking up into a small smile.

Grace braked at a red light and turned her head to glare at him, making the smile drop off his face. "You think this is funny? Let's see if you'll keep your sense of humor once the media starts writing crap about you. Now we'll never be able to sell them that neither of us was having an affair."

His jaw muscles clenched. "I know. But don't worry. This won't fall back on you. I'll be the cheating husband, and you'll be off the hook with the media and the public."

It wasn't that easy. At least some of the gossip rags would try for a different angle. "That's what you think. I can already see the headlines: Poor Nick. Grace was so focused on her career that she refused to give him kids. He couldn't help going elsewhere to start a family."

The light turned green. Grace stomped her foot down on the accelerator.

"What would you have me do?" A little anger crept into his tone. "Pressure Shailene into getting an abortion?"

156

"Jesus, no. I never said that."

"I'm sorry, but it happened and I can't undo it," Nick said stiffly. "I'm not even sure if I'd want to. You know I always wanted kids."

That had been the only bone of contention in their marriage. Nick wanted children—the more, the better—but Grace was ambivalent. If she ever had kids, she didn't want them to grow up the way she had, on movie sets. That meant giving up her career. Grace hadn't been ready for that.

Her mother had advised her to wait and said that she could always start a family later, but if she hadn't made it in Hollywood by the time she was thirty, she'd never make it.

Now she was thirty, and her soon-to-be ex-husband was having a baby with another woman.

She shook her head at the irony of it all.

"I want to marry her as soon as the divorce is final," Nick continued.

Grace clutched the steering wheel more tightly. "Of course," she answered stiffly. She tried to be happy for Nick, even though this was going to be a public-relations nightmare for her. This was what he'd always wanted. He'd been the one who had wanted to get married while Grace had been content to just live together. Finally, she'd given in at her mother's encouragement, even though part of her had always known she'd never be happy having 2.5 kids and a house with a white picket fence with Nick.

She pulled onto I-405 and headed north, keeping an eye on the rearview mirror. The same car had been behind them since they'd left the sushi bar. "Great," Grace mumbled. "There's a paparazzo glued to my rear bumper."

When they reached Nick's apartment, Grace stopped the SUV.

The paparazzo was still right behind them, probably snapping pictures.

Nick craned his neck. "Shit. He's watching us. I can't just say bye and get out."

No, he couldn't. If they wanted the media to buy that Nick was staying at the Silver City apartment only because it was closer to the studio, just a quick wave wouldn't do; they needed a more heartfelt good-bye.

"Well, we're actors, so..." Grace breathed in deeply and glanced at his lips. There had been a time when she'd liked kissing him, but she could barely remember. As much as she wanted to feel even one little spark of the old passion, it wasn't happening. *Method acting 101. Think of someone else.* But she wasn't interested in anyone else either. Sighing, she wrapped one arm around Nick and leaned across the middle console.

The familiar scent of his cologne brushed her nostrils. He slid one arm around her, so close now that she could feel his body heat.

An image flashed through Grace's mind—or more of a sensory memory, really—of Lauren's warm body pressing against her from behind while they played pinball. The mental picture surprised her, almost making her pull back, but then she calmed herself. No big deal. She had thought of the strangest things during her film kisses—fantasizing about how much she craved a chocolate bar, calculating camera angles, and brainstorming ideas for her mother's birthday present.

Nick pressed his mouth against hers and kissed her.

Jesus, this is awkward.

At least he was smart enough to know he'd lose his tongue if he tried to slip it into her mouth.

Flashes went off outside of the SUV.

Grace waited another second, until she could be sure the paparazzo had gotten a couple of good shots, and then pulled back, lightly grazing his cheek with her fingertips for effect as she did.

Nick cleared his throat. "Good night. And thanks for dropping me off." He reached for the door lever and climbed out of the SUV.

Just as he was about to close the door, Grace called, "Nick?"

"Yes?" He stuck his head back in.

Grace forced a smile. "Congratulations. I'm happy for you, even if your timing really sucks."

"Thank you. I really... That means a lot." He gave her a grateful nod and then closed the door between them.

For once, Lauren didn't have a red-carpet event or a promo op she had to attend on Saturday night. Finally a chance to get caught up on her e-mail! She rolled her eyes at herself. *That's your idea of a fun weekend? Wow, you really are a party animal, aren't you?*

Shaking her head, she settled down on the couch with her laptop and a glass of red wine. Once she was done with her e-mail, she opened her screenwriting program, rubbed her fingers together to warm them, and then touched them to the keyboard.

But again, the words wouldn't come. Writer's block still had her tightly in its clutches. No matter how hard she tried, she couldn't come up with a satisfying ending for this damn script.

Instead of seeing her main characters in the burned-down San Francisco, the only image that formed in her mind's eye was of Grace out on a date with her husband. Lauren wondered how that was going. Were they having a good time, or could Grace barely wait to get back home? Had they taken separate cars, or would Nick drive her home, maybe come in for a cup of coffee...or more?

Growling, she refilled her glass and took a big sip of wine, then a second and a third.

She rarely drank, so just a glass and a half of wine made her a bit tipsy. Since she was at home, she didn't mind but resolved to nurse the remainder. The wine didn't help with her writer's block anyway.

Just when she contemplated giving up for today and heading to bed to catch up on some much-needed sleep, the doorbell rang, making her jump.

Jesus. Who could that be at this hour? It was close to eleven already. Barefoot, she marched to the door and peeked through the peephole.

Even though her famous face was distorted by the fish-eye glass, it was unmistakably Grace standing in front of her door.

Lauren looked down at the pair of pajamas she was wearing. Not exactly the kind of clothing she wanted to wear while talking to a client. But then again, Grace wasn't visiting her at the office. After a second's hesitation, she slid back the deadbolt and pulled the door open.

Grace stood in front of her in a crimson dress that ended mid-thigh. Its plunging neckline gave a stunning view of her ample cleavage. A pair of blood-red stilettos made her legs look even longer.

Her mouth suddenly dry, Lauren had to swallow and look away before she could say, "Isn't it a little late to come over for hot dogs?"

Grace didn't smile.

"What's wrong?" Lauren asked, alarmed.

"I'm sorry. I know it's late, but... Can I come in?"

"Of course." Belatedly, Lauren stepped back and closed the door behind Grace before leading her to the living room. "Make yourself at home."

Grace plopped down onto the couch and eyed Lauren's half-full glass of red wine.

"Uh, let me get rid of that." For a moment, Lauren contemplated just gulping down the rest of the wine. Somehow, she had a feeling she would need it in a minute. But she didn't want to drink in front of Grace, so she carried it to the kitchen and poured it down the drain.

When she returned, Grace had picked up Betty from the corner of the couch and cuddled the little plush lynx against her chest.

Lucky cat. Lauren gave herself a mental slap. *Stop it, idiot. Mind on the job!* She sat across from Grace in the armchair. It was better to keep her distance while she felt a bit intoxicated by the red wine and the sight of Grace in the stunning dress.

"I'm really sorry to just drop by on a Saturday night, but this is something that I didn't want to discuss on the phone," Grace said. "I also didn't want you to be blindsided by it, so..."

After all the things Grace had kept from her in the beginning, Lauren appreciated being kept in the loop. But what was it that Grace had come here to say? What could be so urgent? "Did something happen while you were out with Nick?"

Grace stalled by putting the lynx down and smoothing its tufted ears.

Lauren slid onto the edge of the armchair. "Did he…try to get back together?"

"Oh, no. That ship has sailed—for both of us," Grace said. "It seems Shailene isn't just his rebound girlfriend after all."

"Shailene?" Who the heck was that?

"His new girlfriend. She's pregnant."

For a second or two, Lauren was relieved. Nick and Grace wouldn't get back together. Then her slightly buzzed brain grasped the meaning of what Grace had just said. She jumped up. "Jesus! We get one nightmare with the press cleaned up and now this. It's starting to feel like being stuck in a soap opera."

"Tell me about it," Grace muttered.

"How are we supposed to sell it to the media that it's an amicable divorce?"

"Why are you asking me?" Grace grumbled. "You're the public-relations expert, not me."

Lauren sank back into the armchair. "I'll think of something. Don't worry." Her mind was spinning, already putting together a media strategy and brainstorming the best news outlets for an exclusive interview. After a minute or two, she remembered that she wasn't alone and glanced over at Grace.

Her skin looked a little pale against the deep red of her dress, and her full lips were compressed into a thin line, but otherwise she appeared perfectly composed.

"Do you think this could end up hurting my career?" Grace asked, a tiny wrinkle between her brows.

"Ultimately, I don't think so. Nick is the one who got involved with someone else while you're still married, not you."

"Yeah, but he's an action star," Grace said. "People expect him to be a virile macho who has women throwing themselves at him wherever he goes. Fathering a baby with another woman won't ruin his image. But if people start thinking I'm a cold-hearted career woman who denied him the chance to have a family…"

"That won't happen. When the time comes, we'll go public with some interviews that will have even his fans wanting to castrate him with a blunt, rusty instrument."

Grace cracked a smile but then shook her head. "No mudslinging, remember? I want this to be a clean divorce, despite everything."

She sounded so reasonable, so levelheaded. What was really going on inside of her? "How are you doing with this?" Lauren asked quietly.

"Like I just said, I'm worried about how this will affect my career."

Lauren shook her head. "I'm not talking about your career. I'm talking about how it affects you as a person. As a woman. I mean, your husband just told you he's going to have a baby with another woman…"

Grace shrugged, her expression calm. "Nothing I can do about it."

"You know, there are no cameras in my apartment," Lauren said.

"Excuse me? I don't understand what you mean."

"I mean that you can stop acting," Lauren said. "You don't need to put on a show for me. You have a right to be hurt and angry."

For a moment, Grace looked as if she would rebuke her for her open words. "You want anger?" Her cheeks flushed, and her eyes hurled daggers at Lauren. "All right. I wanted to ram the goddamn chopsticks the waiter put into the doggie bag down Nick's throat and kick him where it really, really hurts." She kicked out as if demonstrating. Her bare shin hit the coffee table. Moaning, she bent over and clutched her leg. "Ouch. Dammit. See? That's why I try not to get angry. The only person who ends up getting hurt is me."

Lauren hurried over, pushed the coffee table out of the way, and knelt. "Let me see."

"I'm fine."

"Let me see," Lauren repeated and gently pushed her hands away.

Grace let go of her leg and leaned forward to inspect the damage too.

Their heads hovered inches from each other, so close as if they were about to kiss. Now it was Lauren's turn to flush. She quickly inspected Grace's shin, trying to ignore the smooth skin under her fingers. "It's perfect. Uh, I mean, it doesn't look as if you hurt yourself."

Grace leaned back. "Thank you."

Was she thanking Lauren for checking her leg for injuries or for the involuntary compliment? Lauren couldn't figure her out.

"You're right," Grace said, her voice so low that Lauren had to strain to hear. "I am angry and hurt. I mean, I knew he had a new girlfriend, but I thought it wasn't very serious between them, just a rebound fling or something. But, no, he wants to marry her and have the 2.5 kids, the dog, and the white picket fence." She shook her head. "Maybe it's just my Hollywood ego, but it's really a slap in the face that he'd get over me so fast."

Marry her? Wow. Lauren didn't know what to say to that. She certainly didn't understand it either. If she were involved with a woman like Grace and their relationship ended, she wouldn't get over it anytime soon. Belatedly letting go of Grace's leg, she got up and settled on the other edge of the couch. She picked up Betty the lynx and put her on the cushion between them. *Need a chaperone, Lauren Pearce?*

"But then again," Grace continued, "I'm the one who filed for divorce, so I can't blame him for finding someone else. I just wish he'd have waited a little longer. It makes me wonder if what we had was ever real or just one of these Hollywood illusions."

"Was it real for you?"

Grace opened her mouth, and Lauren knew her well enough by now to see that she was about to give her a stock answer.

"Not the *Entertainment Tonight* answer, please." She wasn't asking because she needed to know as Grace's publicist; she was genuinely interested in the answer.

"I'm not sure, to be honest. There was a time in my life when I thought I was really in love with him, but..." Grace picked a piece of lint off Betty's fluffy tail. "Despite everything that's going on now, Nick is a decent guy. I loved his sense of humor from the start. But looking back, I'm not sure I was ever head over heels for him. Maybe I just confused caring for him with being in love with him."

Huh. Lauren wondered how that could happen. She had never fooled herself into thinking she was in love when she wasn't.

"He just seemed to fit into my life so well," Grace said as if guessing Lauren's thoughts and trying to explain. "He understood my career; he was busy with his own, and my mother loved me being with him. She still hopes that we'll reconcile."

Oh, yeah. Trust me, I noticed.

"Don't get me wrong," Grace said quickly, "that's not why I was with Nick, but when you're in the limelight all the time, your public and your private persona can get kind of mixed up."

Lauren had seen that more than once with her celebrity clients. That was one of the reasons why she avoided dating within the entertainment industry. It was too hard to tell what was real and what wasn't. "Maybe you should do what I'm doing."

"Which is?" Grace quirked a smile. "Dating women?"

Laughter burst from Lauren's throat. She tried to imagine Grace with another woman. To her surprise, the image came without effort. She tried not to dwell on the fact that Grace's imaginary lover had the same shortish, brown hair that she had. "No. Although I can personally recommend it, I wouldn't like it as your publicist. What I meant is staying away from Hollywood types romantically."

"Is that what you're doing? Not dating anyone in show business?" Grace tilted her head and regarded her with a curious gaze. "Did you get burned?"

"Oh, yeah. One of your colleagues left some third-degree burns. I dated an actress once, when I was just starting out as a publicist. Not one of my clients, mind you."

"What did she do?" Grace asked.

The memory still left a bitter taste in her mouth. "It turned out she was more interested in being introduced to my parents than in me."

"Ouch." Grace looked as if she wanted to pat Lauren's knee but then seemed to change her mind. "You can't judge all actresses by this one flake. We're not all like that, you know? There are some nice ones too."

"Yeah. I'm beginning to realize that." The more time she spent with Grace, the more she became aware of how different she was from other actresses and from her tabloid persona.

They smiled at each other.

"Still, I think I'll stick to my rules," Lauren said, partly so Grace wouldn't think she was interested in her. *Which you, of course, aren't.* She suppressed a snort. *Yeah, right.*

They sat in companionable silence until Grace sighed. "I'd better go. I see you're still working." She gestured at the laptop that sat open on the coffee table but made no move to get up. Slumped against the back of the couch, she looked as if she was running out of steam, emotionally exhausted from the events of the day.

"Oh, no, I wasn't working. I was…"

"Yes?"

Lauren wanted to slap herself for almost telling Grace that she'd been trying to write. "Uh, just looking at some stuff."

A teasing smile darted across Grace's face. "Stuff. I see."

Great. Now she probably thinks I was looking at porn or something. Her cheeks warming, she idly trailed her fingertips across the trackpad.

The screen came to life.

Lauren quickly closed the laptop before Grace could see what she'd really been doing.

But Grace had already seen. "Oh, you're reading a script for a client? Excuse me, but that counts as work in my book." She regarded Lauren with a shake of her head. "You really shouldn't work so much, you know? After all, where would it leave me if my publicist had to quit because of burnout?"

"I wasn't working, really," Lauren blurted out defensively. "That's just my script."

"Your script? You mean…you're writing one?"

Lauren didn't need a mirror to know that her face had taken on the color of Grace's dress. Where was the confident senior account executive, the seasoned PR veteran? She tried to shrug it off. "Yeah, but—"

"Wow." Grace's ocean-blue eyes gleamed with interest. "What's it about?"

Lauren looked away, pulled the laptop off the coffee table, and held it against her chest, needing the protective shield. She wanted to slap herself silly for telling

Grace about the script. "Nothing interesting. It's probably not very good. Just some way to while away the time on weekends."

"Why don't I believe that? You don't seem like a person who'd do anything halfway."

She wasn't, but it startled her that Grace apparently knew her that well already. "I think I have the dialogue down pat, but the plot sucks, so this," she gestured at the laptop, "will never see the light of day."

Instead of letting the subject drop, as Lauren had hoped, Grace asked, "What's wrong with the plot?"

"I have no idea, but I can't get the third act to work."

"Do you want me to read it?" Grace asked. "Maybe I can help. I mean, I must have read thousands of scripts in my life, trying to find the best roles for me."

God, no, Lauren almost blurted out. Just the thought of letting someone, anyone, read her script made her break out in cold sweat. It was too personal, as if she were revealing her inner self. Plus Grace was a client. Granted, she was starting to feel more like a friend. Still, Lauren hesitated.

"You don't have to. It was just an offer," Grace said, lightly touching Lauren's knee. "I understand if you'd rather not. It's pretty personal, right?"

It was. But then again, Grace had revealed things about herself that were about as personal as one could get. Was it fair to hold back? She struggled with the decision.

"It's okay. Really," Grace said. She glanced at her delicate golden wristwatch. "It's getting late. I should go." She patted Betty's head and then got up.

Lauren hesitated for another moment. Then, before she could chicken out, she logged into her e-mail program, typed in an address, and attached the document to a new message. Inflating her lungs, she clicked the send button and then blew out a breath. *Done. No way back now.* Acid burned in her stomach, and something heavy lodged in her chest, making it hard to breathe. "Grace?" she called.

Already at the door, Grace turned and smoothed her hands over her hips and down her half-bare legs in a gesture that looked entirely unconscious.

The sight of her made Lauren breathless for a different reason. "I just sent you the script."

"You...you did? Wow. I hope you didn't feel pressured to do that."

Lauren shrugged and wanted to shove her hands into her pockets before realizing that she was wearing pajamas, which had no pockets. Maybe a little pressure was just what she'd needed to get over her writer's block. "It's okay."

"Thank you," Grace said quietly, as if sensing what this meant for Lauren.

"It's not a romantic comedy, though."

A mild smile crossed Grace's face. "I do read other stuff, you know?"

"Sorry, I didn't want to imply..."

"It's okay. People know me for my rom coms. I'm fine with that."

Was she really? Or was she secretly wishing she could shoot a movie that would challenge her acting skills but afraid to lose her audience? Lauren bit her tongue before she could ask. Now was not the time to get into that topic. For tonight, they'd had enough discussions that crossed into personal areas.

She walked over and joined Grace by the door. "Drive carefully."

"I will. Getting home safely shouldn't be a problem. Even the paparazzo went home after he got the shot he wanted." Grace gave her a nod, said good night, and slipped out the door, leaving Lauren to wonder what shot that was.

Well, she'd find out tomorrow morning when she'd routinely check the gossip blogs and celebrity sites. Somehow, she had a feeling she wouldn't like it much.

CHAPTER 16

LAUREN FELT A MIGRAINE COMING on when she saw the name on her caller ID, even though she normally didn't get migraines. Pinching the bridge of her nose, she lifted the phone to her ear with the other hand. "What can I do for you, Mrs. Duvenbeck?"

"I want you to stop Grace from appearing on that lesbian show!"

The pressure behind Lauren's forehead spread to her temples. She bit back an aggrieved sigh. "What lesbian show?" She had all of Grace's appearances in her calendar, and there was no lesbian show among them.

"That *Central Station* thing, of course! As her publicist, you should really be more aware of her schedule, Ms. Pearce."

Lauren gritted her teeth. "It's *Central Precinct*, Mrs. Duvenbeck, not *Central Station*," she said as calmly as she could. "And it's not a lesbian show. It's a critically acclaimed crime show about a homicide detective who—"

"Who goes on a honeymoon with another woman! Didn't you read the episode's script?"

Lauren hadn't. It wasn't part of her duties as a publicist. Besides, she was working almost fourteen hours a day to coordinate campaigns for the worldwide premieres of *Ava's Heart*. "I assume Grace did, and she was in the third-season episode that started the same-sex romance between the detective and the medical examiner, so she's probably fine with it. Didn't you watch that episode?" Lauren asked, smirking at being able to give back the question.

"Of course I did. Well, I saw the scenes Grace was in. But if I had seen those other scenes, I would have never allowed her to guest-star again, especially now!"

Allow her? When would Mrs. Duvenbeck finally understand that her daughter wasn't eight years old anymore and could make her own decisions? "It's a little late to pull out now. She already signed the contract, and the cast is flying to Vegas tomorrow."

"There must be something you can do. After all, we're paying you a lot of money!"

We? Lauren suppressed a snort. "Grace is paying me to protect her public image—and I'm doing exactly that by not telling her to break the contract."

"Please." Her tone of voice made it clear that she was rolling her eyes. "How is that protecting her public image?"

"Grace has a stellar reputation in this town. Every director and producer in Hollywood knows that she always fulfills her contracts without any diva drama. They know they can rely on her to show up on set on time. If she backs out now—for no good reason, I might add—she loses that reputation. Is that really what you want?"

Mrs. Duvenbeck was uncharacteristically silent for several moments.

Lauren's throbbing head rejoiced.

"No, of course not," Mrs. Duvenbeck said gruffly. "But if being on that lesbian show starts that whole media circus again, I'll blame you."

Of course you will. Grace's mother always found someone else to blame. "Understood." As Lauren hung up, she made a mental note to buy season three of *Central Precinct* on her way home. She had a lesbian storyline to catch up on.

Dawn was just breaking as Grace's driver pulled the town car to a stop in front of the terminal at LAX. Knowing the paparazzi would descend on her as soon as she got out, she suppressed a yawn.

The passenger side door of the SUV in front of them opened, and a blonde woman climbed out.

Hey, that's Amanda! Most of the crew and cast of *Central Precinct* would probably be on the same plane.

A tall man climbed out from behind the SUV's wheel, walked around to Amanda, and pulled her into his arms for a tender kiss.

Grace grinned. Good to know at least one of them had some romance in her life.

They let go of each other with obvious reluctance, and he lifted Amanda's luggage out of the SUV's back for her. The movement stretched the fabric of his shirt across his chest—and Grace realized with a start that Amanda's boyfriend wasn't a boyfriend. A jolt went through her. Her co-star had been kissing another woman!

Someone cleared his throat next to her, making Grace jump. She realized that the driver was holding the door open for her—and probably had been doing so for quite some time. "Thank you," she mumbled and climbed out.

As expected, she was immediately bathed in a meteor shower of camera flashes.

The driver lifted her carry-on and the bigger suitcase out of the trunk.

"Thanks," she said and tipped him. "I can handle it from here."

"Hey, Grace!" Amanda waved and squeezed past the paparazzi to join her. The SUV with her girlfriend was gone.

More flashes went off as they greeted each other with a short hug.

"Grace, look up!" one of the paparazzi called. "Over here!"

"How are you, Grace?"

"Where are you two going?"

"Looking good, ladies."

She just kept smiling, gave them a quick wave, and tried to make it past the automatic doors into the building, but with the ring of paparazzi, fans, and curious onlookers surrounding them, it was almost impossible.

At times like this, Grace wished she had a team of bodyguards or at least an intimidating-looking personal assistant. But she didn't want to be one of the celebrities who had a gaggle of staff around all the time.

Almost inch by inch, they made their way inside. Once they entered the terminal, more of the paparazzi practically living in the airport joined them, surrounding them from all sides. Some of them walked backward so they could keep snapping pictures as they followed them through the airport.

Security and airport employees hurried over. "Move back, guys," one of them shouted. "Let them through."

Reluctantly, the paparazzi stepped back but kept following them for as long as they could. Grace was grateful for the help of the airport employees, who herded them through check-in and security in record time.

With twin sighs of relief, Grace and Amanda finally dropped into plush chairs in the VIP lounge.

"Jesus." Amanda wiped her brow. "Is it always like that?"

Grace gave her a tired smile. "Sometimes, it's worse. Just wait a year or two. I have a feeling you'll get there too." Even though Amanda was beginning to be quite well-known among crime show fans, it hadn't been that long since she'd starred only in commercials. But before too long, she probably wouldn't be able to kiss her girlfriend good-bye in front of the terminal anymore. If the tall woman actually was her girlfriend. Dozens of questions spun through Grace's mind, but she thought it impolite to ask about a colleague's sexual orientation. Still, she couldn't get over the fact that suddenly everyone she worked with seemed to turn out to be gay. *Must be something in the Hollywood air.*

"What's that grin for?" Amanda asked.

Grace put on her most innocent face. "Grin? What grin?"

Amanda gave her a look and got up. "I'm going to check out the buffet. Do you want anything?"

"A banana or an apple would be great. Thanks."

Minutes later, Amanda returned and handed Grace an apple before setting her plate down on the small table between their chairs.

Grace eyed the plate, piled up high with a Danish pastry, two muffins, some fruit, and a bit of cheese. "Are you sure you're an actress?"

Amanda chuckled. "Pretty sure. I just missed dinner last night and didn't have time for breakfast either."

Was that a blush dusting her cheeks? Grace bit her tongue and abstained from asking what had made Amanda miss two meals in a row.

As soon as the fasten-seatbelt sign turned off, Amanda started rummaging through her backpack and pulled out a slightly tattered script. The title on the cover page said "Lucky in Love," which was the name of the episode they'd start shooting tomorrow. "Do you mind?"

"Of course not. Go ahead." Grace had already studied her lines at home. She had fewer scenes than Amanda, so it wouldn't take long to go over them again tonight. When Amanda started studying her lines, she pulled out her laptop and opened the document Lauren had sent her. She'd been itching to read Lauren's script for days, but this was the first time she had to herself all week.

As they flew toward Vegas, she quickly became involved in the script, following along the adventures of the two heroines in 1906. Her finger clicked the button to turn the pages faster and faster as the earthquake struck.

"Hey, that's good."

Amanda's voice brought her back to the here and now. She turned her head and realized Amanda had put her script away and was reading over her shoulder. "Yes, it is. Very captivating."

"What is it?" Amanda asked. "Your next project?"

"I wish." As she said it, she realized it was true. The women she played never got to save themselves the way the two female main characters of Lauren's script did; they always had to wait around for their knights in shining armor to charge in and save the day.

Amanda peered at her with a curious expression. "Why are you reading it, then? Don't tell me you read scripts just for the fun of it."

Grace hesitated, knowing Lauren was quite shy when it came to telling others about her writing. Although after reading the first act of the script, she really didn't know why. The story was well written and engaging. It didn't read like the work of someone who was just dabbling in screenwriting to while away the time on weekends.

When Amanda kept looking at her, she finally said, "A friend gave it to me. She wants a second opinion because she thinks the third act isn't working."

"And? Is it?"

"I don't know. I haven't read that far yet." Grace pressed two keys and skipped ahead to the end of the document. After a moment's hesitation, she turned the laptop a little so that Amanda could read the last page too. The ending was, admittedly, a little dark. The two heroines had survived, but they were standing on a hill, looking down at the smoldering ruins of their once-proud city.

"Hmm. Pretty dreary ending," Amanda said.

"I wouldn't call it dreary. It's historically accurate." The need to defend Lauren's script surprised her.

"While I'm sure that would satisfy history aficionados, most people go to the movies to be entertained and forget their own troubles for a while, not to be educated about history."

Grace had to agree. That was the reason why her mother and George advised her not to stray from her romantic comedies. Escapist entertainment was always in high demand. "The script is entertaining. It just needs a more hopeful ending. Maybe L…the writer could show the cable cars start running again or something, just as a symbol that the city will survive."

"Ooh, that's good. But I think you'd need something else to balance all the destruction and the chaos in the rest of the script. How about adding a love story?"

"A love story?" Grace scratched her head. "Between who? There are no men in this script who'd make believable love interests." In fact, the story focused mostly on the two young women's struggle to survive, learning to overcome their class differences and their fears as they saved each other time and again.

Amanda gave her a pointed look. "I wasn't talking about one of the men."

"Oh." Grace stared down at the screen. "Oooh. You mean…?"

"Why not? I read only a little bit, but the chemistry between those two just jumps off the page. Didn't you think so?"

Grace clicked through a few pages and read bits and pieces here and there. Maybe Amanda was right. Very little was missing to make the audience believe that the two women were falling in love with each other while trying to survive the inferno. She rubbed her chin. "But wouldn't that narrow the commercial appeal of the script?"

"Maybe," Amanda said. "But I think it might be worth the risk. It still wouldn't be a lesbian movie, just a movie about two women who happen to be lesbians. I'd like to think that audiences could deal with that nowadays. I mean, just look at the episode we're about to shoot."

"Right. I almost forgot that you and Lorena are supposed to be honeymooning in Vegas before you get involved in that case."

"Well, Detective Halliday and Dr. Castellano, not really Lorena and I, but a lesbian storyline on a prime-time TV show is a good indication that including a little same-sex romance in a script like this," Amanda pointed at the screen, "is a viable option. Or do you think the writer would be adamantly against having a lesbian relationship in one of her scripts?"

Grace tried to hide her grin. "No, she definitely doesn't have anything against lesbian relationships."

"Good." Amanda reached for her own script again and started mouthing the words, making little gestures, as if she were already getting into character.

Grace watched her for a while. When Amanda paused at the end of a scene, she gathered her courage. "Can I ask you something?" She pitched her voice low so that the people surrounding them wouldn't hear.

With one finger between the pages, Amanda lowered the script. Her eyes twinkled. "No, I didn't get a boob job; yes, the scar on my shoulder really is from a camel that was co-starring with me in a commercial, and no, I didn't sleep with any of the producers to get the lead role in *Central Precinct*."

"Uh, thanks for that enlightening background information, but that's not what I wanted to ask."

"So what did you want to know?" Amanda asked, now with a more serious expression.

Grace nibbled her lip. "The woman who dropped you off at the airport earlier…"

"Her name is Michelle."

Amanda's tone was so soft that Grace didn't need to ask the other questions running through her mind. Clearly, the tall woman wasn't just a fling or a nice distraction between shoots for Amanda.

"You didn't know I'm a lesbian, did you?" Amanda asked.

Grace shook her head. "Why do people always think it's somehow tattooed on their foreheads and I should be able to tell?"

"People?"

"Jill."

"Aha. Well, Jill was deeply in the closet up until a very short while ago, but I never was. Every tabloid from here to New York City wrote about it when we first introduced the romantic storyline on *Central Precinct*."

"That may be, but I never read those gossip rags unless my mother brings them to my attention," Grace said.

Amanda shrugged. "Guess she missed those headlines."

Thank God. If her mother knew that she would be working with an actress who didn't just portray a lesbian on TV but was gay in real life too, she would have been even more insistent about Grace pulling out of *that lesbian show.*

They were silent for several moments, the muted conversations of other passengers and the hum of the engines filling the space between them.

"Doesn't it affect your career?" Grace asked after a while.

"Me being gay?" Amanda leaned her head against the backrest and seemed to think about it. "Hard to say. I've never been in the closet, so I don't know if it made any difference. Maybe it did. It took me forever to break out of commercials and tiny little walk-on roles. But in the end, it might have even helped me. When the powers that be were looking for an actress to play a lesbian detective, someone thought of me."

Grace considered it for a moment. "I doubt it would be like that for an actress in my genre. Tough, crime-fighting heroines can be gay, but the cute girl-next-door the hero is supposed to fall for? I think some people would have a problem with her being a lesbian."

"Well," Amanda flashed a grin, "good thing you're straight, then."

"Yes. Good thing I'm straight," Grace repeated and went back to reading the script.

God, what a day. Lauren felt as if she hadn't slept in days as she pulled into the parking garage of her apartment building. One of her clients had been caught buying cocaine, so Lauren and her team had worked their asses off trying to control the damage to the singer's career. When her cell phone started to ring, she jumped. "Jesus Christ!" She parked the car, turned off the engine, and then reached for the phone. If that was Marlene or a client, she might go ballistic.

A glance at the display made her frown. It was an out-of-town number that she didn't recognize. "Lauren Pearce."

"Hi, Lauren. This is Grace."

So it really was a client. Lauren smiled and released the seat belt. Well, she didn't mind hearing from this particular client. "Hi. How are things going in Sin City?"

"So far, so good."

"No ugly headlines for me to handle?" Lauren asked and grinned. "Drunken brawls in the hotel? Skinny-dipping in the Fountains of Bellagio? Losing millions in the casinos?"

"We don't have time for any of that. Oh my God, your father is a slave driver! He had us shoot eight pages of script today! Eight pages! If we have to do the same tomorrow, there will be a real murder to solve for Detective Halliday—even though she might be involved in the crime."

Chuckling, Lauren got out of the car. "Tell me about it. I grew up with that man." More or less. Her father hadn't been around much while she was growing up, always on location or traveling to promote a new movie. She closed the car door with more force than necessary.

"Where are you?" Grace asked.

Lauren started to wonder why Grace had called her. She didn't mind at all, but Grace had never called her just to chat. Did she feel lonely in her hotel room in Vegas? "Just getting out of my car and heading to my apartment." Lauren covered the phone with her other hand when she had to cough.

"You're just now getting home? You're really working too much."

The concern in Grace's voice warmed her, but she didn't want her to worry. "It's not that bad."

"Oh, no? Then why are you coughing?"

Damn. That weird little trait was a dead giveaway. "Maybe I'm getting a cold." She tried to sound innocent.

"Nice try, but you should leave the acting to me," Grace said.

Her other clients would have let her get away with her evasion, but Grace seemed to really care about her well-being. Usually, Lauren carefully avoided mixing her private and her professional lives and smothered any attempt by a client to become friends. With Grace, she didn't have the heart—or the will—to push her away.

Lauren unlocked the door to her apartment. She kicked off her shoes as she entered and padded to the fridge. After a day like this, she didn't have the energy to cook, so she began to slap a sandwich together, the phone tucked between her ear and shoulder. "Other than having to shoot eight pages a day, how do you like shooting a TV show?"

"It's definitely a change of pace," Grace said. "Very different from shooting a movie."

"How so?" The sandwich and a beer in hand and the phone still tucked against her shoulder, Lauren opened the balcony door and stepped outside.

"It's more intense. There's not much time to rehearse, and you can't do as many takes to get a scene just right."

Lauren took a big bite out of her sandwich and then set the plate onto the small table on one side of the balcony. She leaned against the railing and enjoyed the cool night air. "Sounds stressful," she said and sipped her beer.

"It is. But it's also fun. There's a great sense of camaraderie on set, and the script is good." Grace paused. "Speaking of scripts...I read yours."

Beer dribbled down Lauren's chin as she nearly choked on a mouthful. Her hands started sweating, even though she was clutching the cold bottle. The bite of sandwich sat like lead in her stomach. "Oh." So that was why Grace had called her. Maybe she was just as nervous as Lauren about it, so she'd struck up a friendly conversation first to soften the blow. "So what did you think?" She tried to sound confident, as if she let people read her scripts every day.

"It's wonderful."

"Really?"

Grace chuckled. "Don't sound so skeptical. It's great."

Lauren's tension receded. She wiped one palm on her slacks and took a swig of beer. So the friendly conversation wasn't just to soften the blow. Grace liked talking to her—and she liked the script. "I'm glad you think so."

"I do. Is this the first one you have written?"

"No. Not by a long shot." Over the years, she'd written dozens.

"Have you ever shown one of them to a producer or a director?" Grace asked.

"No."

"Not even to your parents?"

"Especially not to my parents," Lauren said, surprising herself with how openly she talked to Grace. While Grace was still a client, she was beginning to feel like a friend too. With her workload, Lauren didn't have many of those. "If one of my scripts is ever turned into a movie, I want it to be because of its quality, not because of who my parents are."

Grace made a sound of approval. "I respect that. And if I'm not mistaken, you don't need your parents' influence to sell this script."

"You really think so? But what about the ending?"

Something rustled on the other end of the line.

Bedsheets? Was Grace already in bed? Lauren tried not to dwell on that thought; she focused on the conversation instead.

"Yes, I think you were right about that. The ending needs to be revised. Maybe you could tweak it a bit, have it end on a high note, not with a shot of San Francisco lying in ruins. People need to see that the city will survive."

"So I end with a shot of the stores opening again or city hall being rebuilt?" Lauren's mind was already busy coming up with new scenes.

"Or maybe the cable cars start running again," Grace suggested.

Lauren abandoned the half-eaten sandwich and went back inside to get a sheet of paper and write it all down. "Ooh, I like that idea. They could catch the first cable car and..." She plopped down on the couch and started scribbling down ideas. Finally, she paused. "Do you really think that's all the script needs?"

"Well, it could do with a love story too."

Lauren laughed. "A love story? Are you a closet romantic, Ms. Durand?"

"As my publicist, you should know that I'm not in the closet about anything," Grace said with a faux haughty tone.

"Whatever you say. You're not romantic at all. Got it."

For a moment, only the sound of Grace's breathing filtered through the line. "Actually, I wasn't the one who came up with the suggestion to introduce a little romance into the script."

Lauren clamped her hand around the pencil so tightly that the writing utensil nearly snapped. "You showed it to someone else?"

"Yes. No. Well, not on purpose. I read it on the plane, so Amanda saw it."

Amanda. Okay, that wasn't too bad. She owed the actress one for saving her from Mrs. Duvenbeck.

"I'm sorry," Grace said quietly. "I know you didn't want anyone else to read it. I didn't tell her who the author was."

What was done was done. Lauren dropped the pencil and shook her stiff fingers. "It's okay. So, what did she think?"

"She just read a couple of scenes, but she loved it too."

A warm feeling spread through Lauren. Two experienced actresses couldn't both be wrong about the quality of a script, could they? Maybe her script wasn't that bad after all. She stretched out on the couch, folding her free arm behind her head. "So Amanda wanted me to write a romance into the script? Since the men in the script are mostly minor characters, are we talking about a lesbian romance?"

"Yes. She thought it was a really good idea."

"Of course Amanda would think that," Lauren said before she could stop herself. She hadn't meant to out Amanda, since she wasn't sure Grace knew her colleague was gay. "I mean…"

"I think it might be a good idea too," Grace said.

Lauren blinked. "You do?"

"Yes. Well, I'm not sure if it would make the script harder to sell, but it would fit the story and the characters."

Huh. What do you know? Grace Durand suggests a lesbian romance subplot for my script. Lauren still wasn't sure about it, though.

"You don't like the idea?" Grace asked.

"I'm not sure it's the kind of story I want to write."

"What kind of story do you want to write?"

Swirling her fingertips over the laptop on the coffee table, Lauren said, "Thrillers. Historical dramas. Stories about ordinary people going through extraordinary circumstances."

"Well, falling in love during a major earthquake could be seen as an extraordinary circumstance, couldn't it?"

"Depends on who you fall in love with," Lauren mumbled.

"Sounds like your relationships weren't all that extraordinary. Not that I'm one to talk, since I'm going through a divorce." Grace was quiet for a moment and then started to chuckle. "Maybe I should risk some of my millions in the casino. Unlucky in love, lucky at cards, right?"

If that was the case, maybe she should take up gambling too. "I'll think about rewriting the script, weaving in a love story."

"Let me know if you want me to reread anything," Grace said.

"Thank you." Lauren coughed and emptied her beer bottle to get rid of that dry feeling in her throat.

"I'd better let you get some sleep," Grace said. "I wouldn't want your boss to have to deal with headlines like 'Grace Durand's publicist collapses after working too hard.'"

She was right, of course. It had been a long, busy day, but Lauren still found herself reluctant to end the call. "When will you be back?"

"The day after tomorrow. We're shooting the big finale with a lot of stunt scenes tomorrow."

Last night, Lauren had watched the first *Central Precinct* episode in which Grace had starred, so she knew the kind of fast-paced action scenes the show was known for. "You're not going to do your own stunts, are you?"

"Just some of them," Grace said. "Nothing too dangerous."

Somehow, that didn't appease Lauren's worries. "Please be careful."

"Are you worried about me?" Grace sounded as if she was smiling.

Lauren tried to shrug it off. "Ah, you know. Just trying to spare myself the work of having to deal with—"

"The headlines about my unfortunate accident on set, I know."

Grace's laughter, warm and soft, trickled through Lauren, soothing her stressed nerves. She grinned into the empty living room. "Yeah, exactly."

They were both quiet for several moments, then Grace said, "Well, then... Good night, Lauren."

"Good night." Once the call ended, Lauren lay there and stared up at the ceiling, watching the fan move around in circles. She liked talking to Grace. *You like it a little too much.* Sighing, she squeezed her eyes shut. Just one more minute, then she'd drag herself into the bathroom for a shower and then to bed.

That was her last thought before she fell asleep.

The next morning, she woke up on the couch with a crick in her neck, still clutching the phone to her chest.

CHAPTER 17

At first, it had been a little weird to see her colleagues kiss, but after the first two takes, Grace realized it wasn't any different than watching a film kiss between a man and a woman. *Of course not. What did you expect, idiot?*

"Can you turn a little to the left, Lorena?" Leonard Pearce called from his director's chair while the prop people prepared the third take. "Slide your hand into her hair but don't hide her face."

Lorena followed directions, looking as if she didn't mind kissing another woman.

And why would she? Grace thought as she watched them do another take of the kiss scene. *This is probably more pleasant than having to kiss Russ.* With all his stubble, kissing her co-star in *Ava's Heart* had at times felt like kissing a hedgehog.

Amanda lay stretched out on a hotel bed, watching Lorena dress. "I don't like this. Why can't I be the decoy?"

Lorena slipped into her high heels and walked over to her. "Because you, my darling," she bent and pressed a kiss to Amanda's nose, "have a gambling problem that is pretty much common knowledge. He'd get suspicious if he saw you at a poker table."

"Don't think I'll let you out of my sight for even a second," Amanda said with a fiercely protective expression.

"I'm counting on it." Lorena looked down at her. "But don't worry so much. I can do this."

"Is the wire in place?" Amanda asked, still not looking happy.

Lorena nodded. "Yeah. But there's one more thing I need..." She bent and kissed Amanda, who immediately kissed her back. "For luck," Lorena breathed. She kissed her again and then turned and strode away.

"Cut!" Leonard called. "That's it! Great work, you two. Let's take a short break and then shoot the last scene."

Activity broke out all over the set as lights were adjusted and cameras rolled into new positions.

Amanda and Lorena walked over to Grace. "Nervous?" Amanda asked.

"No. It's not a dangerous stunt. I think I'd be more nervous about having to do a kiss scene."

"Oh, yeah." Amanda nodded vigorously. "I hate those too."

Lorena elbowed her. "Are you implying I'm a bad kisser?"

"I guess you do all right," Amanda said, trying for a bored expression.

Another elbow hit her in the ribs. "You didn't look like you were suffering much a minute ago."

Grace watched them banter back and forth, wondering if she would be as relaxed if she had to kiss a female colleague. She tried to imagine soft lips against her own, a hint of perfume teasing her nose, silky hair against her skin as she ran her fingers through the short, brunette strands. *Uh, short?* Lorena's hair was really long this season, brushing her shoulder blades. Maybe she'd thought of short hair because that was what she was used to—kissing men.

"Ms. Durand?" the stunt coordinator called. "We're ready for you."

Grace shook herself out of her daze and hurried over for some last-minute instructions.

Lauren had dredged up her admittedly rusty Spanish vocabulary to get one of her clients onto the cover of a Spanish-language lifestyle magazine. The call seemed to last forever. When she finally got an agreement and put the phone down, it immediately started to ring again.

Frowning, she looked at the caller ID. It was her father. He was probably calling because he needed a ride home from the airport tomorrow morning. She opened her leather-bound day planner with one hand to look at tomorrow's appointments while she answered the phone. "Hi, Dad. What time do you need me to be at the airport?"

"Uh… You heard already?"

"Heard what? That you'll be back from Vegas tomorrow?"

"No," her father said. "I'm not calling because of that."

Lauren closed her day planner. "No? So you don't need a ride home from the airport?"

"Not this time. Your mother is picking me up."

So this was an *on* phase in their on/off relationship. Lauren had long ago stopped trying to keep track of the status of their marriage. "Okay," she said and waited to hear what he might want. He'd never called her from a set just to say hello.

"Someone else could use a ride, though," her father said.

What the heck? Now he thought she was a shuttle service? He should know better than to add more items to her already long to-do list.

Before she could voice her complaints, her father asked, "Grace Durand is still one of yours, right?"

"She's my client. Why are you asking?" Lauren's hands went cold. Dread skittered down her spine. "What happened?"

"She got hurt during a stunt."

Lauren jumped up, hitting her knee on an open drawer. "What...? How...?" She hobbled around her desk without knowing where she wanted to go. To the airport maybe, to catch the next flight to Vegas. Images of broken bones and stab wounds flashed through her mind. What did her father have Grace do? Jump from a moving car? Hang from a burning building? Dammit, she should have read the script. She should have—

"Calm down." Her father's voice rumbled through the phone. "It's not that bad. She's got a black eye; that's all."

With legs that felt weak, Lauren sank onto the edge of her desk. "How could you let that happen?"

"Let that happen?" he echoed. "You know as well as I do that accidents happen on set."

"Yeah. To stuntmen and stuntwomen," Lauren grumbled. "She's an actress doing rom coms, for Christ's sake, not Tom fucking Cruise! Why did you let her do her own stunts?"

"Because she wanted to. She did just fine."

Anger throbbed in her temples. "A black eye isn't 'just fine' in my book!"

"Jesus, Lauren. I thought I could avoid some drama by calling you, but it seems—"

"Okay, okay." Clutching the edge of the desk, Lauren took several deep breaths. So Grace had some bumps and bruises. Not a big deal, right? She was hardly the first actress who'd wrapped up shooting with a few minor injuries. "What do you need me to do?"

"I thought maybe you would want to pick her up from the airport," her father said. "She handled it like a trooper and didn't want anyone to make a fuss about her, but I thought she might appreciate seeing the friendly face of someone she knows at the airport instead of a limo driver or—God forbid—her mother."

So he'd met Grace's mother. "I can definitely do that," she said without even consulting her day planner. "When does your plane land?"

"I'll be home the day after because we need to reshoot the opening scene, but Ms. Durand's plane touches down at LAX at eight forty tomorrow morning."

Lauren wrote it down next to the flight number he gave her. "I'll be there."

Lauren paced at baggage claim and checked the arrivals monitor for the tenth time. It showed the American Airlines flight from Las Vegas as having landed at eight forty-five. She checked her wristwatch. It was after nine.

The plane's other passengers had picked up their baggage already. Now the bustle and noise around her had stopped. Just one lone, silver suitcase made turn after turn around the conveyor belt. Was it Grace's? Had she been on the plane, or had she for some reason missed her flight?

Lauren pulled out her cell phone to call Grace or her father, but it had no reception. *Great.*

A commotion behind her made her whirl around.

Grace was coming down the escalator. Paparazzi seemed to appear out of nowhere, snapping away. Some of them pressed much too close, nearly unbalancing Grace as she stepped off the escalator.

Her hands curled into fists at her sides, Lauren rushed over. "Step back," she shouted. "Give her some space!"

At the sound of her voice, Grace's head jerked up. A large pair of sunglasses covered half of her face, but it couldn't hide the expression of relief.

None too gently, Lauren made her way through the crowd of paparazzi, lightly gripped Grace's elbow, and took the carry-on from her with the other hand. She wanted to wrap her arm around Grace and block her from the flashes going off around them, but she didn't know if Grace's jeans and long-sleeved blouse covered any other injuries and didn't want to hurt her.

Airport security hurried over, forcing the paparazzi back a few steps.

"Not that I'm not glad to see you, but what are you doing here?" Grace asked, her voice low.

"Picking you up."

"Don't tell me your father called you just because—"

"Not here," Lauren said with a glance at the paparazzi and airport security, who followed them at a slight distance as they headed over to the rotating carousel.

Lauren handed back the carry-on, lifted the silver suitcase off the conveyor belt, and led Grace to the parking garage.

"Where to?" Lauren asked as she pulled onto Airport Boulevard. "Do you need to see a doctor?"

So her father had told Lauren what had happened, and that was why she'd come to pick her up. "No. I'm fine. The set medic checked it out, and I put some ice on it last night."

"Are you sure?" Lauren asked, glancing away from traffic for a moment to search her face.

"I'm sure. It's just a black eye."

"So home, then?"

Grace nodded and turned to see if they were being followed. Thankfully, the airport paparazzi had stayed behind to photograph other celebrities arriving at LAX.

"That means the cottage, right?"

How well Lauren knew her already. Not many other people had guessed that the cottage was her true home, not the mansion in the Hollywood Hills. "Normally, yes. But I'm meeting with George tomorrow, so I think staying in the villa makes more sense."

Lauren stopped at a red light and looked over. "Can I see?"

Sighing, Grace pulled her sunglasses down just enough so Lauren could see the swollen, discolored skin under her left eye.

"Ouch." Lauren winced. "Someone nailed you good. What happened?"

Grace pushed the sunglasses back up her nose as Lauren navigated across the intersection. "We were shooting a scene in which the bad guy draws a gun in the casino and takes me hostage. Dumb little rich girl that I am, I try to wrestle the gun from him. Amanda was supposed to dive in and knock him out, but Cody— the actor who played the gunman—moved in the wrong direction, so she hit me instead."

"Christ. You really need to be more careful." Lines of worry crinkled Lauren's forehead. "If the press gets wind of it, can you imagine the headlines? They'll think Nick beat you up or something."

Yeah, sure. Grace hid a smile. *Keep pretending that you're only worried for professional reasons.* She had already seen the genuine concern in Lauren's hazel eyes.

"Does it hurt?" Lauren asked.

"It's a little tender." She didn't feel the need to pretend in front of Lauren.

"Want me to stop at a pharmacy to get something for the pain?"

Grace shook her head. "It's not that bad."

"Are you sure?"

"Yes. Stop being such a mother hen." Despite her complaints, Grace had to admit that Lauren's concern felt good.

Twenty minutes later, Lauren turned right instead of continuing straight ahead toward Grace's home. She circled the block in search of a parking spot.

"Um, what are you doing? I told you I don't need painkillers."

"I'm not getting painkillers," Lauren said. "Trust me. You need what I'm getting you." She gave a triumphant cry as another car pulled out of a parking spot on her third trip around the block. After competently maneuvering her Honda Civic into the small spot, she turned to Grace. "I'll be right back."

Then she was gone.

Grace craned her neck to see where she was going, but Lauren quickly disappeared around the corner. Grinning despite herself, she shook her head. Lauren Pearce was a force to be reckoned with when she was trying to take care of someone. She let her head sink against the backrest and closed her eyes.

She jumped as, seemingly only seconds later, the driver's side door was pulled open and Lauren dropped onto the seat next to her. "Here." With a proud grin, she held out a large chocolate waffle cone with two scoops of ice cream.

Her mouth watering, Grace stared at the decadent offering. "Oh my God, you're so bad for my diet. You bought me ice cream?"

Lauren grinned. "It's just what the doctor ordered."

"The set medic didn't say anything about ice cream."

"What an oversight." Lauren tsked. "Everyone knows that you need to cool a shiner like that." She pointed at Grace's eye with her own ice cream cone.

"With ice cream?"

Lauren lifted one shoulder into a half-shrug. "Whatever works, right?"

"And what excuse do you have for getting yourself some too?"

"None." Lauren happily swirled her tongue over her frozen treat. "I don't need an excuse for ice cream. But if you don't want yours…"

Grace snatched the second cone out of her hand before Lauren could pull it back. "I didn't say that. Do you know how long it's been since I last had ice cream?"

"About as long as your last hot dog, I'd guess."

There was no answer from Grace as she was busy sampling her ice cream.

Grace eating ice cream was quite possibly the most erotic thing Lauren had seen in her entire life. She almost groaned as she watched Grace's tongue swirl over her cone. The pink tip of her tongue darted out to lick a drop of cream from the corner of her mouth. Then she tilted her head back and moaned.

The sound went through Lauren, making heat pool low in her belly. *Oh, God.* Maybe getting Grace ice cream hadn't been such a good idea after all. Something cold dripped onto her fingers. When she wrenched her gaze away from Grace and directed it downward, she realized that her own ice cream was melting while she'd been busy watching Grace devour hers. She licked a bit of her peanut butter cup off her hands.

"God, this is so good." Grace moaned again. "What flavor is this? I don't think I've had it before."

Lauren shifted in the driver's seat. "One is pineapple coconut and the other white chocolate raspberry truffle."

"Yum. Pretty exotic choice, isn't it?"

"Would you have preferred something simple, like vanilla?"

Grace gave her a teasing smile. "You think I'm vanilla?"

Lauren nearly choked on a piece of almond. Was Grace flirting? "Uh, no, I just thought maybe you wanted to try something new, since there are so many different ice cream flavors just waiting to be explored."

"Good guess. When it comes to ice cream, I'm definitely open for experimenting."

Ice cream. She's just talking about ice cream. Lauren took a long lick of her cone. It tasted great but did little to cool her down. Not when her mind was busy imagining how sweet and cold Grace's lips would feel against her own.

"What did you get?"

"Excuse me?" Lauren's brain had trouble keeping up with anything but the erotic movements of Grace's tongue.

"Your ice cream. What flavors did you get?"

"Oh. Peanut butter cup and coffee with roasted almonds."

Grace laughed. "Coffee. I should have known." She didn't speak again until she had finished the last bite of her cone, lightly swaying back and forth and sometimes moaning, definitely in ice cream nirvana.

Lauren was still holding her melting ice cream, which was dripping all over her hands. "There are some napkins in my pocket." She'd stuffed a handful into the front pocket of her jeans before leaving the ice cream store. Studying her hands, she tried to decide which one was less sticky and wouldn't leave stains on her pants.

"Thanks. I got it." Grace reached over and pulled one of the napkins from Lauren's pocket.

Lauren's breath caught when Grace's fingers brushed her hip. She nearly dropped her soggy cone.

"Your ice cream is melting," Grace said while she wiped her fingers on the napkin. "Don't you like it?"

Drops ran down the outside of the cone, and Lauren quickly licked them off. "I do. It's delicious." She peered over at Grace. "Do you want to taste?" The moment she'd said it, she wanted to slap herself. *God, you really are a glutton for punishment, aren't you?* After suffering through watching Grace eat her ice cream, she'd have to watch her lick her cone.

With a smile that looked a little shy, Grace nodded.

Charmed, Lauren held out her ice cream cone. She was sure that not many people got to see this side of the famous actress.

Grace bent her head and swiped her tongue across the peanut butter ice cream. A moan escaped her. "Oh, wow. That's really good too."

"What can I say?" Lauren's voice sounded a little hoarse. She hoped Grace wouldn't notice or would think it an effect of eating something cold. "I'm a woman of taste."

When Grace straightened, she had a little bit of ice cream on her nose.

Lauren's overactive imagination showed her pictures of her leaning forward to lick it off. *Are you out of your mind?* "Uh, you have some..." She pointed.

Grace wiped at her nose with the napkin. "Guess I'm a messy eater."

No, you're a sexy eater. Lauren held out her cone. "Would you like to eat the rest?" On the one hand, she knew it would only prolong her torture, but on the other hand, she enjoyed the way Grace enjoyed her ice cream way too much to want it to end.

"Don't you want to finish it?" Grace asked.

"The coffee one is all gone, so if you like peanut butter, be my guest."

Grace looked back and forth between her and the ice cream. "I really shouldn't."

That was what she'd said before taking the second hot dog. Lauren grinned and pressed the cone into her hand. "Enjoy."

Within minutes, the remainder of her ice cream was gone.

Happily crunching the last bite of cone, Grace wiped her fingers on the napkin again and then touched Lauren's forearm.

Tingles spread through the upper part of Lauren's body.

"Thank you," Grace said. "I haven't had anyone bring me ice cream when I came home with a boo-boo since my father died."

Sticky fingers and tingles be damned, Lauren covered Grace's hand with her own and squeezed. "You're welcome."

CHAPTER 18

"I'M SO, SO, SO SORRY," was the first thing Amanda said when she called Grace later that day.

"Stop apologizing already." Grace tried to fluff the sofa pillow beneath her head. "It's not your fault. If Cody hadn't pulled me to the side at the wrong moment..."

Amanda sighed. "Still. I feel bad for giving you that black eye."

"Nothing a bit of concealer won't cure. Besides, it wasn't all bad."

"How's that?"

Grace closed her eyes and could almost taste the delicious ice cream melting on her tongue. "I got a double scoop of ice cream out of the deal."

"You? Getting ice cream?" Amanda let out a disbelieving snort.

"No, really," Grace said. "I did. Lauren bought it for me when she drove me home."

Only silence filtered through the line.

"Amanda?" Grace looked at the display to make sure they hadn't been disconnected. "You still there?"

"Um, yes. I'm just a little surprised she'd do that. Maybe I need to switch publicists, because mine sure never did something like that for me."

"Not even when that meanie of a camel bit you?"

"Nope," Amanda said. "Not even then."

Grace didn't know how to explain why her publicist would buy her ice cream and miss a few hours of work just to pick her up from the airport. These were just two of the many things that Lauren had done for her even though they weren't in her contract. They were becoming friends, but she felt as if she needed to protect that growing friendship from being trampled on by everyone else. "Maybe your publicist would if you paid her better," she finally quipped.

"Are you sure that's all it is? Lauren appreciating the paycheck she gets from you?"

"Yeah, okay, I think we're becoming friends too."

"That too, but I think it might be more than that."

At Amanda's suspicious tone, Grace's hackles rose. "What are you hinting at?"

"Well, if my gaydar isn't totally off, she's a lesbian, so…"

Grace sat up on the couch. "Oh, come on! Just because she's a lesbian doesn't mean she'd be interested in me. You of all people should know that."

"Yeah, why would she be interested in you, just because you're drop-dead gorgeous, rich, and one of the nicest people in Hollywood."

"That's nonsense," she said more loudly than intended. She normally didn't shout at people, but now it was hard to keep her voice down. "You're really selling Lauren short. She's more professional than most other people in Hollywood."

"I saw the two of you playing pinball at your birthday party, and excuse me for saying so, but that didn't look very professional to me. She seemed to have forgotten that you're not just her client but also a married woman."

The memory of Lauren's arms around her, their bodies pressing together as Lauren bumped the pinball machine made Grace flush. She told herself it was just anger heating her cheeks. The sofa pillow sailed across the room, nearly shattering the Chinese vase. "Bullshit! You don't know what the hell you're talking about."

"I'm sorry," Amanda said. "I didn't mean to upset you. It's not my place to say things like that to you. I know we haven't been friends for very long and haven't gotten to know each other that well. I should have kept my mouth shut. I just feel like you're one of the few fellow actresses I can really talk to."

Grace rubbed her face with her free hand and winced when she accidentally touched the tender, still-swollen area beneath her left eye. While it was true they hadn't been friends for that long, spending up to sixteen hours a day together for a week last year and then doing the same this year had brought them closer. They both shared the same work ethic and a similar sense of humor. She did consider Amanda a friend, even though they saw each other mostly at red-carpet events and on set. "I'm sorry too. I didn't mean to make you feel as if you couldn't be honest with me. It's just… Do you know how many people swarmed around me like bees to honey, pretending to care for me, just because I'm nice, rich, and…"

"Drop-dead gorgeous," Amanda said for her.

"But that's all just skin-deep. Everyone before Nick wanted just my money or my body or both, and I don't want to think that Lauren might be one of those people."

"That's not what I'm—"

The sudden bang of the front door made Grace jump.

Seconds later, her mother strode into the living room and dropped a stack of paper onto the coffee table.

Not again. "Amanda? I'm sorry, but I have to go."

"Are we okay? I really didn't mean to—"

"We're fine," Grace said. "It's just that my mother dropped by. There seems to be something important going on."

They said good-bye and ended the call.

"Mom, you'll give me a heart attack if you keep coming in like that."

"Do you see that?" Her mother waved her finger at the stack of printouts on the table, ignoring what Grace had said. "That's why I didn't want you to—" Her eyes widened and her mouth snapped shut as she caught sight of Grace's shiner. She rushed toward her. "Oh my God! What happened to your eye?"

Grace tried to fend off her mother's hands that were fluttering all over her face. "Nothing. Just—ouch, Mom, that hurts. It was just bad timing while we were shooting one of the action scenes."

"How often have I told you not to do your own stunts? They have stuntwomen for that."

"I know. But it looks more authentic if I do it myself, and it wasn't dangerous."

"Dangerous enough to give you a black eye," her mother muttered. "I told you that nothing good would come of you doing that lesbian show, and now look... you got hurt."

Grace shrugged. "It could have happened on any other set too. At least it wasn't my nose like that one time when I got hit by a champagne cork during the wedding reception scene and the director insisted on icing my nose with the entire cooler of ice."

They both laughed at the memory, and her mother finally let go of her face and sank onto the couch next to her.

"So what's this?" Grace pointed at the papers on her coffee table. They looked like printouts from websites. "Don't tell me the gossip sites are writing nonsense about me again."

"No. Not the gossip sites. Some other people."

Grace frowned. "What other people?"

"I don't know. Writers, I guess. They're writing stories about you...*homosexual* stories." Her mother nearly seemed to choke on the words.

Grace reached for the stack of paper and skimmed the first page. It was a short story written by someone using the pseudonym CPFan. The story was littered with typos and grammar mistakes but otherwise entertaining. The character Grace had portrayed in two episodes—the daughter of a casino owner—was a suspect in a murder case, and Detective Halliday was back in Vegas to investigate the case.

In an interview room in a police station, Detective Halliday towered over the suspect, who was sitting behind a metal table. Almost nose to nose, they were shouting at each other.

Grace turned the page.

And then they were kissing. The chair toppled over as Grace's character pressed the detective against the table and slid her hands under the other woman's shirt.

Heat crept up Grace's chest and into her cheeks. She stopped reading and fanned herself once with the stack of papers.

"See what I mean? That's porn! Lesbian porn!" Her mother paced the length of the living room. "We need to contact your lawyer right away. We'll sue. We'll…"

Grace pinched the bridge of her nose, wincing when pain flared through the area around her left eye. How she wished she were back in Lauren's car, eating ice cream, instead of dealing with this. "It's not porn, Mom. I think it's called fan fiction. These stories aren't written by professional writers. They're just fans."

Her mother snorted. "What fan would write something like that about you?"

"They're not writing about me. This is about Alexandra—my character."

"We need to tell the network, then. They can sue them for copyright infringement."

"I'm pretty sure they already know," Grace said.

Her mother stopped pacing and stared at her wide-eyed. "And they're just letting them write this…this…?" She gestured as if unable to find a strong enough word.

"I don't think anyone officially allowed it," Grace said. "It's more of a don't-ask-don't-tell policy. But if you think about it, isn't it a great compliment that the show and its characters inspired people to write stories about them?"

"Maybe. But did it have to be that kind of story?" Her mother resumed her pacing.

Grace shrugged. "I'm sure there are others too." She stood, walked over to her mother, and gently gripped her shoulders to make her stop pacing. "These stories have nothing to do with me. They are just fiction."

"Just fiction," her mother repeated as if trying to get it into her head. She inhaled and exhaled audibly. "Okay. So you don't think we should call your lawyer?"

Sometimes, Grace felt as if she were the mother and Katherine the child. "No," she repeated as patiently as she could, "we definitely shouldn't."

"All right. But you need to keep an eye on these crazy fans. I don't want anyone to take them seriously."

"Yes, Mom. Do you want a smoothie?"

Her mother looked at her dainty gold watch. "No, thanks. If I don't hurry, I'll be late for my mani-pedi." After two air kisses and a wave, she picked up the stack of printouts, holding them between two fingers, and swept out of the house as quickly as she'd come.

Blowing out a breath, Grace flopped onto the couch.

Grace saved the attachment with her travel itinerary the studio had sent. Seven premieres in as many days, waking up in a different city every morning... The weeklong tour to promote *Ava's Heart* would be exhausting. She took a sip of her green smoothie, for a moment wishing it were something stronger—or at least something more tasty. That made her think of the ice cream Lauren had bought her that morning, which in turn made her think of the fan fiction.

Thinking of Lauren makes you think of fan fiction? She raised an eyebrow at herself. Well, Lauren was a lesbian, so it was only natural to jump from thoughts about her to thoughts about lesbian fiction, right?

She opened a new tab in her browser and typed in a search for *Central Precinct* fan fiction. A number appeared above a list of links. "Two hundred forty-seven thousand hits? Wow."

A random click on one link revealed an entire archive of fan fiction. There had to be hundreds or maybe even thousands of stories. Grace's astonishment grew as she clicked on several and read a few of the descriptions.

Some stories took place in alternative universes in which Alexandra, her character, was a detective too. Others were crossovers that had the *Central Precinct* characters meet the heroes and heroines of other popular prime-time shows. Most were short; others had to be longer than some of the novels on her bookshelf.

Several of the stories paired Alexandra with Detective Halliday's male partner, but the majority were lesbian in nature, some about her character with one of the female leads, but most about the detective and the medical examiner.

This apparently was a world of its own. A world she'd had no idea existed, at least not to this extent.

She clicked on one of the Alexandra Eadington/Linda Halliday stories and started to read. Her mother had told her to keep an eye on the crazy fans and their stories, after all.

During the first chapter or so, it felt strange to read a story about the character she portrayed on TV, but then the fast-paced plot and the three-dimensional characterization quickly drew her in. Faintly, she worried that reading this author's interpretation of Alexandra Eadington would influence her portrayal should she be asked to guest-star in another episode, but then she pushed the thought aside and continued to read.

Some time later, she realized the sun had set outside and she was reading just by the glare of the laptop balancing on her belly. Not setting the laptop down, she stretched out one arm as far as it would go, turned on the light, and continued to read.

Unlike some of the stories she'd skimmed, this one was good. Really good. Better than some of the books she'd read in the past.

She grinned as for once, it was her character who was allowed to save the day. Much better than ending up with a black eye. She followed a link to the story's next chapter.

Detective Linda Halliday had invited Alexandra over for dinner as a thank-you for saving her life—and now she was watching her guest devour the chocolate mousse she'd made for dessert.

"You've got a little..." Linda pointed to the corner of her mouth.

Instead of using her napkin, Alexandra flicked her tongue along her bottom lip. "Gone?"

Linda had to clear her throat before she could answer. "Uh, no."

Again, Grace had to think of the ice cream they'd eaten that morning and of Lauren directing her to wipe some of it off her nose. She rolled her eyes at herself. *You're really obsessed with ice cream. Get it out of your head. It's salad and fruit for you for the foreseeable future.* She directed her attention back to the story on her laptop.

Alexandra licked her upper lip, her tongue dancing along the curved contours. "Now?"

Was Alexandra teasing her? Was she...flirting? Linda took a big gulp of her Coke, then another one, wishing she could fish the ice cubes out of her soda and slip them down her shirt to cool off. This had to end, or she'd do something stupid. Like walk around the table and wipe that bit of chocolate mousse off with her thumb—which she promptly did. Slowly, she put her finger into her mouth and then withdrew it.

Now just inches apart, they stared at each other, both flushed. Heat flickered between them, like the shimmering waves above a road leading through the desert.

Linda's breathing quickened. "Are you teasing me?"

"Don't you like teasing?" Alexandra's voice was as husky as her own.

"I like kissing better."

Alexandra's incredibly blue eyes glittered with desire. "Then what are you waiting—?"

Before she could finish the sentence, Linda pulled her up from the chair and surged forward. At the last possible moment, she tamed her passion and gentled her touch, brushing her lips over Alex's in a tender caress.

When Alexandra wound her fingers through Linda's hair, she came back for a second kiss. This time, the pressure of her lips was firmer. She nipped Alex's full bottom lip with her teeth and slid her tongue over the wet silk of her mouth, teasing it open.

Moaning, Alexandra parted her lips. One hand slid down Linda's neck and dug into her back, pulling her closer, while the other came up, cradling Linda's jaw, tilting her head so that their mouths fit together even more perfectly.

Their hips pressed against each other; their breasts melded together.

Linda's entire body came alive as she let her tongue entwine with Alex's. She kissed her slowly, unhurriedly, despite the urgent need pulsing through her body.

Grace paused and emptied her smoothie in one big gulp. She was as breathless as the characters. *Wow.* When had been the last time she'd been kissed like that? Her gaze already back at the screen, she slid her empty glass onto the table without looking.

Linda caught Alex's tongue between her lips and sucked. Then she circled that hot tongue with her own before pulling back to teasingly lick her bottom lip.

Alexandra's hands burned a path from Linda's shoulders down to her hips and then slid lower. She tore her mouth away, kissed and nibbled a path along Linda's neck, and nuzzled her ear.

Shivers of delight rushed through Linda. Her eyes drifted shut and then popped open when Alexandra grabbed her ass and squeezed with both hands, pulling their hips even closer together. Her clothes felt unbearably heavy against her hot, oversensitized skin. "God, Alex. I want to see you. Feel you. All of you. Now."

Looking as if she was beyond speaking, Alex answered nonverbally. With hands that were trembling with desire, she started unbuttoning her blouse.

"Let me." Lauren brushed her hands aside and took over.

Grace frowned. Not Lauren. Linda. It was Linda who was making quick work of Alexandra's buttons, ripping off the last one when it refused to cooperate fast enough. The names were just too similar; that was all. With a shake of her head, she dove back into the story, not stopping to examine why she kept reading this lesbian romance. A well-written story was a well-written story, no matter if the main characters were gay or straight, right?

Alexandra shrugged impatiently, letting the silk blouse slide off her shoulders. She reached out and pulled Linda's sweatshirt off over her head. Both articles of clothing landed next to each other on the floor.

"God." Linda groaned. "You're beautiful."

"So are you."

They came together in another heated kiss. Linda let her hands roam over the soft curves and dips of Alex's body. She pressed kisses to her ample cleavage and let her tongue flicker over the edges of the lacy bra. After sliding her hands up Alex's quivering belly, she teased her nipples through the material of the bra. They hardened immediately under her touch.

Alex threw her head back, baring her throat to Linda's kisses.

When she couldn't stand to have any kind of barrier between them anymore, Linda reached around her and expertly unhooked the bra with one hand while the other slid down Alex's belly and unbuttoned her jeans. With two of her fingers, she reached into Alex's open pants and dipped beneath a sexy pair of panties. A groan wrenched from her lips. "God. You're so wet."

Christ, so am I. Startled by the realization, Grace closed the laptop and put it aside. Her whole body felt as if she were running a fever, burning up, but it wasn't a fever making her sweat. *It's totally normal. Just a physical reaction to a well-written love scene.* Anyone—gay or straight—would react like that, right? After all, not all of the people who read and wrote these stories could be lesbians. So if the love scene between women affected her, it just proved that she still had a healthy sex drive, even if she hadn't seen much proof of it for the last year or two.

Deep in thought, she slid one hand under the waistband of her sweatpants. Her eyes fluttered shut at the wetness she found—and then popped open when the phone started to ring.

She jerked her hand out of her pants and pressed it against her thumping heart. With the trembling fingers of her other hand, she reached for the phone and groaned when she saw the name on the display. Why did Lauren of all people have to call now? "Hi, Lauren," she said into the phone, trying to sound normal.

"Hi," Lauren said. "Is everything all right? You sound a little…strange."

A flush swept up Grace's neck, adding to the heat coursing through her body. She slid one foot onto the floor to ease the pressure between her legs. "I'm fine." *You just caught me with my hand down my pants; that's all.*

"Are you sure? The set medic checked for a concussion, didn't he?"

"I'm one hundred percent positive," Grace said. "I don't have a concussion." She did feel a little dizzy, though, her mind still spinning with the powerful effect the love scene had had on her.

"Good."

"So, what can I do for you?"

"I'm just calling to see how your eye is doing," Lauren said.

Amanda's words reverberated through Grace's mind. Clearly, Lauren wasn't just concerned for professional reasons. *Oh, come on.* Why did suddenly everything Lauren did and said have to be suspicious, just because Amanda thought she might be attracted to Grace? She was a friend, period. Belatedly, she cleared her throat. "The eye is just fine."

"Glad to hear that. Uh, listen, there's something else…"

Grace held her breath. "Yes?"

"I don't want to risk another confrontation with your mother, but…could you please tell her to stop clogging my in-box?"

"My mother is sending you e-mail? Why? She didn't mention it when she was here earlier."

Lauren sighed. "She keeps sending me these links to *Central Precinct* fan fiction sites, telling me that they're harming your reputation and demanding that I do something about them."

Grace groaned and covered her face with her free hand, then quickly pulled her hand away when she caught a whiff of her own musky scent. "I'm sorry. I thought I'd convinced her they're harmless."

"Oh, so she brought them to your attention."

Oh, yes, the stories had caught her attention all right. "Yes. She came over with a couple of these *lesbian porn stories*."

Lauren laughed. "They're hardly porn stories."

"So you read them?" Grace asked before she could stop herself. Her cheeks flamed. She didn't want to think about her new friend reading these NC-17-rated stories.

"Well, I needed to take your mother's concerns seriously, didn't I? I read just enough to make sure the stories are not harming your reputation—quite the opposite," Lauren added with a laugh.

Grace didn't know what to say to that.

"These stories...do they bother you?" Lauren asked when Grace kept silent.

"Why would they? They're not stories about me."

"A few of them actually are," Lauren said.

Grace frowned. "Really? I didn't see any of those."

There was a short pause. "Oh, so you took a look at the stories too?"

"Well, I needed to take my mother's concerns seriously, didn't I?" Grace repeated Lauren's words.

"Right."

Did Lauren's voice sound a little husky?

It was probably just her imagination. Because of Amanda's implications that Lauren might be attracted to her and that damn fan fiction story, she was now overly aware of Lauren's sexual orientation. "So, there are actually stories about me? Not just about me as Alexandra Eadington?"

"Just a handful. They're called real-person fics."

"Wow. You certainly know a lot about these things." Grace immediately wondered why. Did Lauren read these lesbian stories in her spare time?

"I had to deal with a lot of upset Hollywood divas over the years, calling me to complain about all of these sex stories about them circulating the Internet."

Was that how Lauren saw her? As just one more Hollywood diva she had to deal with? The thought hurt. Grace shook her head. If Lauren did, she wouldn't talk so openly. "So what do you think we should do about these real-person stories?"

"Nothing," Lauren said. "As long as they're not becoming rampant, it's best to just ignore them."

"Because trying to get them pulled off the web would be like saying 'no comment'?" Grace asked.

"Something like that. It would just call attention to these stories. Plus lashing out at your fans is considered bad form."

Even fans who wrote dirty stories about her. It rankled Grace a little, but she knew Lauren was right. "Okay. I'll tell my mother to stop bothering you about it."

"Thanks. So, I'll see you next week, then."

"Uh, next week?" Had she forgotten an appointment?

Lauren chuckled. "Yeah. You, me, and about a dozen other people flying to the city of fish and chips?"

"So it's decided now? You'll accompany me and the rest of the cast on our promo tour through Europe?"

"Yes. The studio will send two people from their PR department too, but they didn't seem to mind letting me handle all of your publicity."

"Great." Grace much preferred working with Lauren to working with two PR consultants she didn't know. "No fish and chips for me, though. It's also considered bad form if my dress bursts while I'm walking down the red carpet."

Lauren snorted. "Like that would happen. Okay, I'd better get back to work now."

And this call wasn't work? Grace wondered.

When they'd said good-bye, she sat there for a moment and stared at the laptop, tempted to open it back up and continue reading. With a decisive shake of her head, she got up and marched over to the exercise room for a vigorous workout. She needed to burn off some calories—and some sexual frustration.

CHAPTER 19

"I hate this, I hate this, I hate this," Jill mumbled as she gripped the armrest of her seat with one hand and Grace's fingers with the other.

The plush leather beneath Grace vibrated as the eighteen-passenger corporate jet accelerated down the runway and then lifted off. The pressure on her hand increased. "Ouch, Jill. Ease up a little. I might need my hand again, you know?"

"You have two," Jill answered, unimpressed.

"Why are you so afraid of flying? You must have done it a thousand times."

Still keeping Grace's hand in a death-grip, Jill said, "I'm not afraid of flying. Just of crashing. Statistically, most airplane crashes occur during takeoffs and landings."

Grace peered at the two publicists who sat on the other side of the gleaming mahogany table. One seemed to be sleeping already while the other was engrossed in a file folder. Neither paid them any attention.

"Have you ever heard of fan fiction?" Grace asked, partly to distract her but mainly because she was curious. She hadn't visited that *Central Precinct* fan fiction archive again, but her mind was still processing the stories she'd found.

Her lips tightly pressed together, Jill nodded.

Finally, the small plane leveled off and Jill let go of Grace's hand.

Both of them heaved a sigh of relief as they settled in for the long flight to London.

"Of course I've heard of fan fics," Jill said, now her usual chipper self. "I used to read a lot of them when I first figured out my sexual orientation. I loved reading romances that I could enjoy without having to mentally replace the male part of the couple with a woman."

Hmm. Interesting. Grace didn't think she'd done that. She hadn't replaced one of the women with a man while reading the fan fiction. Well, she hadn't really pictured a woman looking like Amanda making love to her own lookalike either. In her imagination, the second woman had been taller, with darker hair—probably because she and Amanda looked too much alike. Having a bit of a contrast was more attractive.

"Why do you ask?" Jill regarded her with a curious expression.

"My mother somehow discovered a few stories about Alexandra, the character I play on *Central Precinct*, online."

Nodding, Jill stretched out in her upholstered seat.

"Lesbian stories," Grace added, pitching her voice low so the studio publicists across from them and their fellow cast members behind them wouldn't hear.

"Ooh." Jill laughed and slapped her thighs. She peered across the aisle to where Grace's mother sat on a comfortable couch, chatting off the ear of their poor director. "I bet she was not amused."

"That's the understatement of the year," Grace muttered.

"How about you?" Jill asked. "What did you think of the stories?"

To her annoyance, Grace felt her cheeks heat.

Jill nudged her and pulled up the armrest between them to lean closer. "Ooh! You read some of them!" She nudged her again. "Come on. Admit it."

"Stop poking me. I read one, okay? Just one of them."

"Aaaand?" Jill drawled.

"And it was a well-written story with a beginning, a middle, and an end. At least that's what I assume, since I didn't finish it."

"Not your cup of tea. I understand." Jill stopped poking her.

Grace considered leaving it at that. But after everything she and Jill had been through together, she didn't want to lie to her friend, not even by omission. "That's not it. I did enjoy the story." *Mom would have a heart attack if she knew how much.* Okay, maybe she would omit that bit of information after all. Jill would jump to all the wrong conclusions if she told her about the way her body had reacted. "I just had to stop reading because Lauren called."

"I packed my laptop." Jill pointed to the laptop case she'd stowed under her seat. "If you want, you can continue reading."

No way in hell would she read that story while Jill was looking over her shoulder. "Uh, no, thanks. I'll just try to sleep in a little while. We won't get much sleep for the next seven days."

Jill nodded and picked up a magazine from the table in front of her.

Grace rotated her neck, reached up to massage one stiff shoulder, and looked around the luxurious cabin. Her gaze found Lauren, who sat in a single seat toward the front of the plane. Her expression was tense, with a deep line forming between her brows. For a moment, Grace thought Lauren might be afraid of flying, but then she realized that her co-star, Russ, was sitting across from Lauren on the other side of a small table, chatting her up.

Now it was her turn to nudge Jill. "Do you see that?" She pointed. "Russ is trying to flirt with Lauren."

Jill glanced up from the magazine she was flipping through. "Can't blame him. She's an attractive woman. If I didn't have MS, I'd ask her out."

Something about that statement sparked Grace's ire. "Why do you keep saying that?"

"Saying what? You wouldn't want me to ask her out?"

"No, that's not it." Although, truth be told, thinking of Lauren and Jill dating was weird. "Why do you keep acting as if you don't have the right to date anyone, just because you have MS?"

Jill threw the magazine back onto the table. She regarded Grace with an uncharacteristically serious expression. "Because I don't. Not when my future is so insecure."

"No one knows what their future holds."

"That's not the same, and you know it. Who knows if I would be able to hold up my end of the relationship in a year or five or ten?" Jill shook her head, her eyes clouded over. "I refuse to be a burden to the person I love."

"So if you met a woman and fell in love, you'd just ignore your feelings?"

Jill lifted one shoulder into a half-shrug. "Probably."

"Even if you could have many happy years together? Even though you have so many other things to offer in a relationship? Any woman would be lucky to have you."

A slow smile spread over Jill's face. "Is that your way of saying you'd do me if you were gay?"

Grace poked her in the ribs. "It's my way of saying I don't want you to give up on love."

"Anything to drink?" A flight attendant stood in the aisle next to them.

They both ordered glasses of Diet Coke, which were promptly delivered.

When the flight attendant was gone, Jill leaned over and asked in a near whisper that only Grace could hear, "How about you? Have you given up on love after the Nick debacle?"

"I haven't even told you the newest development in that department," Grace answered, her voice pitched just as low. "Nick will be a father soon."

Jill nearly spat out a sip of Diet Coke. She pressed a napkin to her mouth and eyed Grace's belly.

"Don't look at me like that." Grace gave her a playful little shove. "I'm not the mother. Shailene, his girlfriend, is."

"Christ. What was he thinking? Once the media finds out…"

"Yeah, I wasn't exactly happy about it either. But it's the way it is, and now we'll have to deal with it."

Jill looked at her with a slight shake of her head. "Sometimes, I think you're way too Zen for your age."

"Thanks, I think."

Someone coughed softly next to them.

When Grace looked up, Lauren stood next to her seat, holding out a bag of chocolate-covered peanuts. "Nuts?"

"Is that an offer or a statement?" Grace asked.

Lauren laughed and glanced over her shoulder to where Russ was still sitting. "After having to sit next to your co-star, I'm actually not sure."

"Russ isn't that bad," Grace said.

"If he knows you're married or gay," Jill added. "If you're single and straight, all bets are off. Just tell him you're a lesbian and he'll stop chatting you up."

"I tried that." Lauren made a face. "He seems to think it's sexy."

"Hmm. He stopped flirting with me after I came out. Must be the MS, then. I bet he doesn't think that's sexy."

"What an asshole," Lauren said.

Jill reached out and patted her arm. "See?" she said to Grace. "She's not so Zen. Good for you, Lauren."

Lauren looked back and forth between them with a furrowed brow but didn't ask.

"Want to switch seats?" Jill asked.

Was she trying to avoid any further conversation about her reluctance to get romantically involved with anyone? Grace wasn't sure.

Lauren's eyes lit up, but she hesitated. "Are you sure?"

"Why not? He'll leave me alone, and I plan on sleeping all the way to London anyway."

"All right. Let me just get my laptop." Lauren darted down the aisle as if afraid that Jill would change her mind.

Chuckling, Grace watched her go.

"The two of you have gotten pretty friendly, haven't you?" Jill said.

Grace's head jerked around. "What do you mean?" She hoped this wasn't another attempt to warn her of Lauren's less-than-platonic intentions. One of her friends lecturing her about it had been more than enough.

"She offered you her snack. And I have rarely seen you so playful with anyone else."

"Can't I just be in a good mood?"

Jill lifted both hands. "Hey, no reason to get defensive. It's all good. I like knowing you have a friend beside me."

"Sorry. I didn't mean to take your head off. It's just…"

Lauren's return prevented her from having to explain.

Jill picked up her soda and the magazine.

With one hand, Lauren held on to Jill's elbow as she stood and accompanied her to her seat, carrying Jill's laptop case.

"I'm not a helpless old woman, you know?" Jill's complaint trailed back to Grace.

"I'm just carrying your laptop to make sure you stay in your new seat and don't want mine back," Lauren answered. A minute later, she returned and settled into the aisle seat next to Grace. She fished the bag of chocolate-covered nuts out of her pocket and slid them onto the table in front of Grace. "I come bearing gifts."

"Are you trying to fatten me up?"

"Just doing my duty, ma'am," Lauren said.

Grace gave her a skeptical look. "How is trying to fatten me up doing your duty?" Despite her protests, she opened the bag and began snacking on the nuts.

"I'm keeping you from fainting on the red carpet."

Gesturing at the aisle, Grace said, "There's no red carpet here. As a PR specialist, you should know that people stop desiring actresses when they're no longer perfectly thin."

"The only desire I have when I see one of those perfectly thin actresses is the desire to buy them a large pizza with double cheese," Lauren said.

Was she serious? Were lesbians so different from the men Grace knew? "Really?"

Lauren shrugged and stole a peanut for herself. "I like a woman who's comfortable in her own skin, even with a few extra pounds."

The simple declaration made Lauren even more likable to Grace. "I like that attitude, but I'm afraid the rest of the world doesn't share it, so you'd better take these." She pressed the rest of the candy into Lauren's hand.

"All right." Lauren poured a handful of the chocolate-covered nuts onto her palm and popped them into her mouth. Then she dusted off her hands, coughed once, and lifted her laptop onto the table in front of her. "Do you mind if I get some work done?"

"No, go ahead. I usually enjoy the time to myself on planes, since I get so little of it during promo tours."

"I'll work quietly, then."

Grace shook her head. "The typing won't bother me. In fact, if you want to write a little, that's okay too. I promise not to peek."

"Not here. I can't write while someone is watching." A hint of red dusted Lauren's cheeks at the admission. "Nothing personal," she added quickly. "It's just one of my little quirks."

"Like coughing when you're tired—which you're doing right now."

"I am? Sorry."

"You don't need to—"

The small plane abruptly lurched, dropping several feet. Glasses clanked. Books, glasses, and other items clattered to the floor.

The flight attendant rushed past them toward her own seat.

"Oh my God!" Grace's mother yelped from the couch in the middle of the cabin.

Startled, Grace gripped the armrest—or so she thought. After a second, she realized that it was Lauren's hand she was squeezing. She quickly let go. Before she could apologize, the plane plunged downward again.

A terrifying moment of weightlessness gripped Grace.

Their hands found each other on the armrest. Lauren's fingers were warm and soothing, so this time, Grace let go only when the plane steadied.

With a soft chime, the fasten-your-seatbelt sign came on. The captain's voice came over the loudspeakers, "Ladies and gentlemen, this is your captain speaking. As you probably noticed, we're experiencing some turbulence."

Grace snorted. "That's the understatement of the century."

"It's not that bad," Lauren said, her voice soothing. "It just feels that way because we're in a small plane."

"There's nothing to worry about, but please stay in your seats and fasten your seat belts," the captain said.

Retching sounds from the front of the plane made Grace turn her head.

Russ was heaving into a paper bag.

Across from him, Jill mouthed a "you so owe me" in Lauren's direction.

The corporate jet's second flight attendant, a young man, was really getting on Lauren's nerves. After serving their dinner and then collecting the empty trays, he had returned twice to ask if they—or rather Grace—needed anything else. Now he was heading in their direction a third time. Predictably, he stopped next to Lauren's aisle seat. "Is there anything else I can do for you?" He looked right past Lauren, talking only to Grace.

"Thanks, we're fine," Lauren answered for her.

"Don't hesitate to let me know if you need anything." After smiling at Grace again, he walked away.

"What was that?" Grace asked with an amused grin.

Lauren watched the flight attendant's retreating back. "Nothing. After I had to suffer through Russ's lines, his flirting was just getting on my nerves."

"Flirting? He wasn't flirting. He was just being friendly."

Was she serious? Judging from Grace's expression, she really meant what she said. Lauren started laughing. "Oh my God!"

"What?"

"You're not just missing a functioning gaydar; you also have no flirtdar whatsoever."

"You!" Grace reached across the armrest and pinched Lauren's leg.

Lauren rubbed the affected body part. The pinch had barely hurt, but now her leg tingled from Grace's casual touch. "Ouch. Hey, careful. You wouldn't want headlines about Grace Durand being kicked off the airplane for abusing her publicist, would you?"

An unladylike snort escaped Grace.

Her mother looked over from the couch and regarded them with a disapproving frown.

Like two kids being caught giggling at the back of the classroom, they stopped laughing and settled down.

"I think I'd better get some work done before you get me into trouble," Lauren whispered and took her laptop back out.

"Me? Getting you into trouble?" Grace whispered back. This time, she reached beneath the armrest, where her mother couldn't see it, and pinched Lauren's thigh again.

Lauren nearly dropped the laptop. "See?" She started to review the schedule of the upcoming days, and her smile slowly died away. It was grueling. Back-to-back interviews all day, then the premiere and the after-party, only to fly to the next city and do it all again the next morning. It was part of what actors did for a living, but she couldn't help worrying about Grace. *And about Jill, of course.*

She opened her e-mail and replied to the most urgent messages until the lights in the plane dimmed.

"Don't you want to sleep a little too?" Grace asked.

"In a moment," Lauren said and continued to work.

Grace lifted her head from the pillow the flirty flight attendant had brought her. "You know if you keep working, you'll keep me awake with your coughing."

Lauren knew when she was beat. Sighing, she stowed her laptop under the seat and obediently closed her eyes. She wouldn't be able to sleep, but she would rest her eyes for a moment or two. Once Grace had fallen asleep, she would get the laptop back out and continue to work. That was her last thought before the drone of the engines lulled her to sleep.

Grace couldn't sleep. The anticipation of what the next few days would bring was keeping her up. The premiere in London would be the first time *Ava's Heart*

would be shown in full length to journalists and film critics. The reviews and articles they wrote after attending the premiere would set the tone for how the movie would be received by the public. If they didn't like *Ava's Heart*...

She jumped, startled out of her thoughts when something softly hit her shoulder.

When she opened her eyes and carefully turned her head, she had to smile.

Lauren's head was resting against her shoulder. Even with the generous legroom in the luxurious jet, her tall body was crammed into a position that couldn't be comfortable. The armrest between them had to dig into her ribs.

Slowly, Grace moved back a little, creating some space between them so she could flip up the armrest.

Lauren mumbled a protest. As soon as the armrest between them was gone, she turned more toward Grace and cuddled closer. One of her hands came to rest on Grace's leg.

Grace tensed for a moment. Her gaze darted to the people around them. Had anyone seen? Then she relaxed. Everyone around them, including her mother, was either asleep or absorbed in their laptops or other digital devices. The two publicists across from them were snoring softly. With one hand, Grace reached for the blue blanket the flight attendant had given her and covered Lauren with it best as she could while serving as her pillow.

Lauren continued to sleep, which told Grace just how exhausted she had to be. During the past weeks, Lauren had worked almost nonstop to help organize the press junkets in Europe. Even in the dim light of the plane's cabin, Grace could see the dark smudges under her eyes.

A wave of protectiveness swept over her. She tugged the blanket more tightly around Lauren and nearly reached out to smooth back a strand of hair that had fallen onto Lauren's face but stopped herself at the last moment.

Someone passed them on the way to the lavatory, and Grace quickly pulled the blanket more toward herself, covering Lauren's hand, which still rested on her thigh. She didn't want to give anyone the wrong idea, but neither did she want to wake Lauren by removing her hand. Besides, she had to admit that the touch felt good, grounding her, letting her know that whatever came in the next few days, she wouldn't have to face it alone.

She sat watching Lauren sleep until she became almost cross-eyed. Finally, she let her tired eyes drift shut.

Lauren drifted in that pleasant state between sleep and wakefulness, content to just lie like this forever. She snuggled her cheek more deeply into the warm, soft material, breathing in the tantalizing mix of scents—perfume, lotion, and something that was just—

Grace! Her eyes popped open. From less than an inch away, she stared at Grace's light blue blouse…which was darker in one spot. *Oh, shit.* Not only had she fallen asleep on her—literally—she had also drooled on her. They were cuddled together under one blanket, their legs resting against each other along their lengths, the armrest between them gone. When she slowly lifted her head, she realized that this wasn't the worst of it. Her hand had settled into a comfy spot on Grace's thigh. *Christ. I practically groped her in my sleep.* She could only hope that Grace had slept through it.

Careful not to wake her, she pulled her hand away and retreated to her side with a vague feeling of loss.

And not a second too soon. As the flight attendant went down the aisle, asking for breakfast orders, people around them started to wake up and look around.

Lauren blew out a breath. If Grace's mother had caught them in this position, Lauren would have lost her job—or at least her hand.

The scent of coffee drifting through the cabin seemed to rouse Grace. Her nose twitched, and then she blinked her eyes open and sat up. With rumpled clothes, tangled hair, and her face lined from the small pillow, she was more beautiful than anyone who'd slept in her clothes could possibly be.

Mesmerized, Lauren stared at her.

Grace wiped her chin. "Did I drool in my sleep?"

Heat crept into Lauren's cheeks. "Uh, no." *But I did.* The spots on Grace's blouse hadn't yet dried.

"Did you sleep well?" Grace asked.

Which meant that she'd fallen asleep before Grace had. But if Grace had noticed her cuddling up, she didn't seem to mind. "Actually, yes." Amazing. Despite the awkward position she'd slept in, she felt refreshed.

"Could you let me through? I want to freshen up before breakfast." Grace tried to disentangle her hair with her fingers. "I must look horrible. Glad the paparazzi aren't here. A picture of this would go viral as the worst hair ever."

Lauren almost told her how beautiful she was but then bit her tongue and just said, "Sure." She stepped out into the aisle, and Grace squeezed past her, their bodies brushing in the tight space.

Once Grace was gone, Lauren dropped back into her seat. She felt like ordering an ice-cold drink for breakfast but knew it wouldn't help. She'd just have to be a professional and ignore this damn attraction.

CHAPTER 20

THEIR WING OF THE FIVE-STAR hotel in Mayfair, London, was bustling with journalists and entertainment reporters, who went from room to room, interviewing the stars and creators of the movie.

Lauren had been going back and forth between Grace's room and Jill's, making sure that the interviews didn't veer into areas she didn't want them to. When she quietly slipped back into Grace's room, the actress was in the middle of her tenth five-minute interview.

"What was it like to play a farmer from Texas?" the reporter asked.

"Actually," Grace said with a kind smile, "Ava—the farmer I played—is from Georgia. It was fun to slip into the skin of someone whose life is so different from mine. Getting her accent right wasn't easy, though. I went through weeks of dialogue training before we started shooting."

Lauren leaned against the back wall and watched her. Press junkets could be hell for actors. They were supposed to express their enthusiasm for the movie, even if the reporters asked idiotic questions or were horribly ill prepared, and to keep each interview fresh and fun, even though they were getting tired of answering the same old questions time and again.

"Your character finds love again after a personal tragedy, right?"

Grace nodded. "Yes. That's what I love most about the movie. It has such a positive message about not giving up on life and on love."

"What about your own life?" the reporter asked. "There were some rumors earlier this year that—"

Lauren pushed away from the wall. "Sorry," she said loudly. "It's time to wrap up the interview. We're running late for the next one."

The reporter grumbled but finally moved out.

"Here." Lauren handed Grace a fresh bottle of water.

"Thanks. And thanks for stepping in. Christ, did you hear that?" Grace groaned and rotated her shoulders to loosen them. "He thought the movie was about some woman from Texas. The questions are getting worse with each interviewer."

Lauren was tempted to reach over and massage Grace's shoulders for her but stayed where she was. Bad enough that she'd cuddled up to Grace on the plane.

Here, at the press junket, she had to be on her most professional behavior. "Just one more, then you're done for the day. At least with the interviews."

"Print or television?"

"A reporter from a national LGBT magazine. Her name is Chloe Davies," Lauren said.

Grace gave her a questioning look. "Why would an LGBT magazine be interested in a heterosexual love story?"

"I think they're less interested in the story than in Jill's recent coming out," Lauren said just as a knock on the door announced the journalist's arrival. "Ready?"

"Bring her on." Grace slid a little to the side so she wouldn't block the movie poster behind her.

Lauren greeted the reporter with a handshake, her gaydar pinging loudly. "Come on in. Ms. Durand is ready for you."

Chloe Davies introduced herself, shook Grace's hand, lingering a moment too long for Lauren's taste, and then settled onto a chair across from her. "Congratulations on the new movie."

"Thank you," Grace said.

"So, what was your favorite scene?"

"Oh, that's like asking a mother about her favorite child. I like them all."

"But if you had to choose, say because a reporter is asking you?" The journalist gave her a charming grin.

Grace returned the smile. "Then I'd probably say the scene toward the end, when Ava is standing in the middle of the field, with rain pouring down on her, and she finally decides to give this new love a chance."

Ms. Davies pointed to one of the movie posters behind Grace. "I saw that scene. It's a good one—and, if you allow me to say so, you look hot in that rain-drenched dress."

Grace threw her head back and laughed, taking the compliment in stride, as if she were complimented by lesbians every day. "Thanks. And please tell your editors they're not allowed to take this out."

They both laughed.

"Are you aware that you have a large lesbian following in the UK?"

"I do?"

The reporter nodded.

"I had no idea, but I'm happy to have anyone as a fan, gay or straight," Grace said. "It's good to know my movies appeal to a wide audience."

"Are you ever going to do a lesbian movie?"

If Lauren hadn't known Grace's body language so well by now, she would have missed the slight increase of tension in her shoulders.

"I don't yet know what movies I'll do next," she said. "But I actually just finished shooting an episode of *Central Precinct*, an American TV show with a fantastic lesbian storyline."

"Do you feel more pressure to pick only certain roles at this point in your career?" Chloe Davies asked.

Grace's shoulders stiffened a little more, but her smile never wavered.

Lauren kept an eye on her watch, preparing to step in the second the five minutes were up.

"Well," Grace said, "I want to do a good job in each of my movies, no matter what role I play. That hasn't changed. Luckily, *Ava's Heart* made it easy. The writing was stellar, and we had a very talented cast."

Well done. Lauren breathed a sigh of relief as Grace adroitly brought the topic back to her current movie, away from the more dangerous subjects. The time was up shortly after, and Lauren escorted the reporter out. "Well done," she said after she'd closed the door. "You're very good at this."

"I should be," Grace said with a tired smile. "I've been doing this for a quarter of a century."

"That makes you sound really old."

Groaning, Grace powered herself up from the chair. "Not as old as I feel."

Lauren lightly placed one hand on the small of Grace's back and guided her to the door. "Come on, old woman. Let's get changed for the premiere."

London didn't live up to its reputation as a rainy city at all. Sunshine filtered through the limo's windshield as the driver navigated the busy streets toward Leicester Square.

Despite the gorgeous weather outside, Lauren grew tenser with every second, not just because of the premiere but also because Mrs. Duvenbeck kept tugging on her daughter's dress and fussing over her hair and makeup. *If she starts licking a tissue, I'm out of here.*

It wasn't as if Grace needed any more help to make her look beautiful. In a backless burgundy dress, her golden-blonde hair falling in soft waves onto her shoulders, she took Lauren's breath away.

Grace didn't react to her mother's fussing. Either she had long ago gotten used to it, or she was too focused on her own thoughts to notice.

When the limo came to a stop, Lauren peered through the tinted window at the crowd outside. There had to be thousands of people lining the wide red carpet. Behind them, the Odeon cinema towered over the square, its neon-blue lights reflecting off the black, polished façade.

One of the security guards approached the limo.

"Ready, ladies?" Lauren looked from Jill to Grace. She caught Grace's eye and for a second saw a hint of the nervousness that Grace hid so well.

Grace gave her a nod and unbuckled her seat belt. "As ready as I'll ever be."

The security guard outside pulled the door open.

Pools of spotlights hit them as Grace climbed out, followed by her mother and Jill. Lauren got out after them.

"Smile," Mrs. Duvenbeck said every few steps, as if Grace needed the reminder. Lauren wanted to whack her over the head with the nearest object.

Camera flashes went off as Russ joined them, and the three Hollywood stars posed for the photographers. Fans screamed and waved, some of them holding up banners or movie posters. Once again, Lauren marveled at the craziness of the business they were in.

Grace and her colleagues approached the waist-high metal barriers that had been set up along the edge of the red carpet. Fans leaned across the barricades, holding out autograph books and cards. They signed autographs and posed with some of the fans so they could snap pictures, until one of the organizers—a woman with a clipboard—signaled them to move to the next section of the red-carpet course.

A girl of about twelve or thirteen sat in a wheelchair, which had been placed off to the side. She stared up at Grace with wide eyes. A man who was probably her father waited next to her.

"This is Emily," the woman with the clipboard said. "She's here through the Make-A-Wish Foundation because she wanted to meet you, Ms. Durand."

Grace waved at the TV crew following her around, asking them to stay back. She stepped up to the girl and pulled up her dress a little so she could go down on one knee to be at eye level with her, ignoring what it might do to her dress.

Lauren watched them with a big lump in her throat.

After a while, the woman with the clipboard tapped her wristwatch, signaling that it was time to move on. The entire red-carpet event was planned out down to the last second, with nothing left to chance.

"Give them a minute," Lauren said, knowing that every second with Grace would mean the world to Emily.

Grace hugged the girl and whispered something in her ear that made Emily beam. When she got back up, her eyes were damp.

Two men removed a section of the metal barriers.

After an encouraging nod from Grace, Emily maneuvered her motorized wheelchair onto the red carpet. Grace joined her, walking next to her and letting her experience how it felt to be treated like a Hollywood star, complete with having your picture taken and fans screaming.

When clipboard woman pointed over to the press area, indicating that they needed to go, Grace squeezed the girl's shoulder and smiled down at her. "I have to go, but I'll see you inside later."

Emily nodded eagerly.

Grace joined the rest of the group. She clutched Lauren's arm. "She's just twelve and in a wheelchair already," she whispered to Lauren. "Do you know how meaningless and stupid all of this," she indicated the red carpet and the paparazzi surrounding it, "feels compared to what that girl is going through?"

"I know," Lauren murmured. She wanted to pull Grace into her arms and hold her but knew she couldn't, especially with all the paparazzi around.

"Well, at least she's not giving up on her dream." Grace turned toward Jill and made eye contact with her. "She wants to be an actress one day."

The group was silent as clipboard woman ushered them over to the press area. Even Mrs. Duvenbeck stopped telling Grace to smile.

Jill and Grace posed for more pictures and were interviewed by a camera team. They answered all the usual questions about the movie and their choice of dresses with aplomb.

Just when Lauren was beginning to think they had made it through the press gauntlet, the reporter asked, "I notice you're here with your mother, Ms. Durand. Why isn't Nick escorting you today?"

Damn. Of course the media had noticed Grace's lack of male escort.

"He would have loved to be here, but he's busy crashing cars and blowing things up," Grace said, garnering a few laughs. "Seriously, he's in the middle of shooting his own movie, but he'll join us for the premiere in Los Angeles."

Then Russ moved up behind them and posed for more photographs with his co-stars before they finally made their way inside.

This was it—the moment of truth. In about one hundred and twenty minutes, she'd get her first real feedback about the movie that might make or break her career after her last one had tanked at the box office. Not that she'd get an honest opinion from most of the people crowding the theater's foyer. They would just put on their Hollywood smiles and tell her what they thought she wanted to hear, no matter whether they'd really liked the movie and her performance.

Not Lauren, though. She knew she could count on Lauren to give her honest feedback. In search of her publicist, she looked around the crowded lobby. It wasn't hard to find Lauren. In her black pantsuit, she stuck out of the mass of dress-wearing women and men in tuxedos. She stood holding a glass of champagne but didn't drink from it while she chatted with two British actresses.

The ushers started showing everyone to their seats, and Grace realized with disappointment that Lauren wouldn't sit anywhere near her. She would have liked to see her reaction while the movie played on the big screen.

Jill appeared at her elbow. "Are you okay? This is your big night, so why are you frowning?"

"It's nothing," Grace said, not sure how to explain what had been going through her mind. "I'm just beat."

"Oh, God, me too. Do you think anyone will notice if we sleep through the movie?"

Grace chuckled. "Probably. Come on. Let's take our seats. The ushers are getting antsy." With a quick glance back at Lauren, she led Jill toward the front and took her seat between her mother and Jill.

Minutes later, one of the producers took the stage and introduced the movie and then the actors and creators, calling them up to join him on stage one by one.

Stepping once more into the spotlight, Grace peered at the rows below and smiled at some familiar faces before saying a few words. She couldn't even remember what she'd said afterward. It took some effort not to fidget while she waited until they could finally take their seats again.

Her nervousness grew as the lights dimmed and the red curtain parted, revealing a huge screen.

When the opening credits rolled, Jill reached over and took her hand. It was a bit clammy, just like Grace's own. Good to know she wasn't the only one who was a little nervous, even after years in show business. Smiling, she squeezed her friend's fingers and focused on the movie. If she tried hard enough, she could almost forget that she was watching herself.

By the time they piled back into the limo, Jill looked exhausted.

Lauren and Grace exchanged worried glances. Just as Lauren was about to suggest that Jill should skip the after-party and head back to the hotel, Grace lowered the screen separating the back of the limousine from the front.

"Can we make a quick stop at the hotel?" Grace said to the driver.

"Of course, ma'am." The driver pulled out into traffic.

Grace's mother frowned. "Honey, we don't want to be the last ones showing up at the after-party."

"I'd really like to change before we head to the party," Grace said. "I wouldn't want to ruin this beautiful dress that you found for me."

Lauren bit back a grin and gave Grace a hidden little nod.

When the limo stopped in front of the hotel, Grace said, "Why don't you wait here? I'll make it quick. Jill, can you come and help me out of this dress?"

Her mother opened her mouth to protest, but Grace already climbed out of the limo, Jill in tow.

Ten minutes later, Grace returned in a silvery jumpsuit that clung to her curves—and without Jill.

"How did you manage to get her to stay behind?" Lauren asked as they headed toward the after-party, which was being held at another hotel.

"Oh, that was easy. I just had her lie down on my bed while I pretended to think about what to wear. By the time I had changed, she was fast asleep. I left her a note in case she wakes up, which I doubt."

Lauren knew Grace had to be just as exhausted and jet-lagged, even if she didn't show it. As the movie's lead actress, she had to make an appearance at the post-premiere party before she could get some rest, though.

The party was already in full flow when they arrived. The guest list looked like the who's who of British and international film stars, and Mrs. Duvenbeck instantly left them to mingle with the rich, famous, and beautiful. Buffet tables were set up around the edges of the room, featuring some of the Southern food that the characters had cooked in the movie—grits, cornbread, fried chicken, and peanut butter pie. Lauren grinned. At least she could make sure that Grace ate more hearty food than two leaves of salad.

"I know what you're thinking." Grace wagged her finger at her.

Lauren tried to look innocent. "Which is?"

"You want to get me a plate piled high with that admittedly delicious-smelling food. Don't even think about it, Lauren Pearce."

"Actually, I was just thinking about the movie." Well, the food in the movie, to be more precise.

"Oh." Grace seemed to instantly forget about the food. "What did you think?" She looked at Lauren as if world peace depended on her answer.

Lauren knew the feeling well. She'd felt the same while she'd waited to hear how Grace had liked her script. It amazed her that a seasoned actress like Grace still seemed to care so much about what others thought of her performance. "I liked it."

The tense set of Grace's shoulders didn't relax. "But?"

"Don't be silly," Mrs. Duvenbeck interrupted as she reappeared next to them. "There's no but. You were great, darling. Wasn't she?" She stared at Lauren, daring her to do anything but agree.

"You really were great," Lauren said.

"See?" Mrs. Duvenbeck patted her daughter's arm. "Even Ms. Pearce recognizes a talent of your magnitude when she sees it."

Even me? What's that supposed to mean? Lauren held back the reply at the tip of her tongue. She didn't want to spoil Grace's special night by getting into a fight with her mother.

"Oh, there's Lucius!" Mrs. Duvenbeck waved to someone across the room. "Come say hello to him, Grace."

"Go ahead. I will join you in a minute," Grace said. When her mother marched off, she turned to Lauren. "What did you really think?"

A passing-by waiter offered them glasses of champagne. Grace took a glass of orange juice instead, and Lauren followed suit.

"Well, you know that I'm not normally a fan of romantic movies, but I really liked this one. It was different from your other movies," Lauren said. The movie had its lighter moments, but as a whole, it had been more serious than Grace's usual romantic comedies—and more adult.

Images from the love scene still flashed through Lauren's mind. It had been tastefully done, more romantic than erotic, but the curve of a full breast and fake sweat glittering on creamy skin still made Lauren wonder whether that had been Grace in the love scene or whether she'd used a body double.

"Different as in worse?" Grace asked, a tiny wrinkle between her brows.

"No. Not at all. Quite the opposite. It's just my opinion, of course, but I liked this movie better than your others."

"My mother didn't think it was a good idea to take a chance on something different."

"Well, I do," Lauren said, not just so she wouldn't have to agree with Grace's mother. "No offense, but I think you're wasting your talent on the kind of movies you've been making so far. I know you've got a much broader range as an actress. Why don't you show it off more often?"

"Because…well, because it's a risk. People love me for my romantic comedies. There's no guarantee I'll do as well in dramas."

"True. But I think it's a risk worth taking. You were great in *Ava's Heart*."

Grace nodded slowly as if letting Lauren's words sink in. "Maybe we both need to learn to take more risks in our careers. I'll tell you what. If you sell that script of yours, I'll audition for the lead role."

Orange juice splashed over the rim of Lauren's glass. She gaped at Grace. "Are you serious?"

Before Grace could reply, her mother was back and dragged her across the room toward a silver-haired gentleman.

Stunned, Lauren stayed behind, staring after Grace.

By the time they made it home from the after-party, it was nearly one in the morning. Grace groaned when she remembered that they'd have to check out of the hotel to fly to Berlin at six.

Her mother staggered through their deluxe suite, mumbled "good night," and disappeared into her bedroom, where she started to snore so fast that Grace doubted that she'd even removed her makeup before dropping onto the bed.

Grace kicked off her high heels on her way to the bathroom. Once she'd removed the makeup, her face looked as tired as she felt. She headed toward her own bedroom. At the door, she remembered Jill was probably still sleeping in her bed. She opened the door an inch and peeked in.

When her eyes adjusted to the darkness, she could make out Jill's shape in the bed. She tiptoed in and retrieved her pajamas. For a moment, she considered rummaging through Jill's purse to see if she could find her key card, but she didn't want to invade her privacy or wake her. The promo tour was especially taxing on Jill, so she needed every little bit of sleep she could get.

Sighing, she turned back, changed into her pajamas, and made herself comfortable on the sofa in the living area.

Her mother's snoring drifted through the door.

Grace pressed a couch pillow over her face, hoping to drown out the noise, but it was no use. Her mother could outdo a lumberjack when it came to the volume of her snoring. Grace tossed and turned for a few minutes. She was exhausted and jet-lagged, but after the premiere and the party, adrenaline was still buzzing through her system. With her mother's snoring, she wouldn't be able to settle down and sleep.

She stared up at the dark ceiling. How the heck could Jill sleep through that racket? Either the second door drowned it out, or Jill was dead to the world. Grunting, Grace tossed off the afghan and put on the bathrobe the hotel provided. Maybe some nice, cold water would help. She slipped the key card into the bathrobe's pocket, took the ice bucket from the kitchenette, and softly closed the door behind her.

Someone else had apparently had the same idea. Lauren stood in front of the ice machine in sweatpants and a T-shirt. She coughed once, confirming that it was really her, even before she turned.

"What are you doing up?" Lauren asked. "Is Jill still in your bed?" She bit her lip as if only now realizing how that sounded. "I mean…"

"I know what you meant. Yes, she is, but that's not the problem. The sofa is pretty comfortable…if no one is snoring next door."

"Your mother?"

Grace nodded.

Lauren scratched her neck. She looked cute in a T-shirt that had an image of a yellow, downy chick and the words *PR chick* printed on the front. "Well, I would offer to let you bunk with me, but I don't have a suite and there's just one bed in my room, so…"

"It's okay." Grace didn't want to even imagine the drama if her mother found out that she'd spent the night with Lauren, no matter how innocently.

"Oh, but I packed some earplugs. Do you want them?"

It seemed Lauren had thought of everything. Grace wondered if she was always so well prepared. Probably. "Oh God, yes. I'd give my right arm for earplugs, maybe throw in the left one too for good measure."

"Nah. I think your fans like you better with all your body parts intact. Come on. Let's get you the earplugs so that you can get some sleep." Lauren led her to her room, which was just a few doors down from Grace's suite.

Her hand rested lightly on the small of Grace's back, warming her skin even through the thick terrycloth robe. Grace's fuzzy brain decided that it liked the feeling. She was almost disappointed when Lauren took her hand away to slide her key card through the lock. *Sleep. I definitely need sleep.*

They stepped into the room, which smelled faintly of Lauren's perfume.

Lauren bent and rummaged through her suitcase.

She had a nice ass, even in her baggy sweatpants. Grace roughly shook her head to get rid of the disjointed thoughts her overtired brain came up with.

"Here." Lauren turned and offered her the earplugs on her outstretched palm.

Grace walked over and took them, careful not to let her fingers linger. "Thank you. You're a lifesaver."

"All part of the service, ma'am," Lauren said with a tired grin. She accompanied Grace to the door and placed one shoulder against the wall as if she needed the support.

"You should try to get some sleep now too. Don't stay up working." Knowing Lauren, she'd start checking e-mail or something equally crazy the moment she left her.

"Okay, okay. I'm heading straight to bed, I swear."

Grace gave her a nod of approval. "Good night."

"Good night," Lauren said.

They looked at each other for a few moments longer; then Grace stepped past Lauren and opened the door.

"Grace?"

"Yes?" she answered, holding her breath for some reason she didn't fully understand.

"I really liked how you portrayed Ava."

A feeling of pleasure flowed through her, chasing away the exhaustion. "Thank you. That means a lot, coming from you, PR chick."

Peering down at her T-shirt, Lauren laughed.

With new energy in her step, Grace stepped into the corridor, softly pulling the door closed between them. After taking one deep breath, she turned—and nearly collided with someone.

"Jill!" At the last moment, she grabbed her friend's arms and held on before she could fall. "Jesus, what are you doing up?"

Still in her now-wrinkled dress from the premiere, Jill yawned and said, "Heading to my own bed. You tricked me, Betty Grace Duvenbeck!"

Grace winced at the name but then grinned unrepentantly. "You needed the sleep."

"Yes, I did. You look like you could use some too. Whose bed did you just get out of?" Jill asked in a teasing tone and pointed at the door behind Grace.

Heat flooded Grace's cheeks. She stammered out her answer before she could think about how it would sound. "Lauren's."

Jill's eyes widened.

"No, I mean her room. She was just giving me some earplugs because Mom is snoring like a bear in winter." Grace presented the earplugs like a piece of evidence, at the same time wondering why she felt the need to prove anything. She rubbed her overly warm cheeks. "I really need to get some sleep."

Jill gave her a quick hug and then a gentle push. "Go. We'll talk tomorrow."

Her fingers tightly gripping the earplugs, Grace trudged to her suite, where she fell asleep the moment her head touched the pillow.

CHAPTER 21

GRACE FELT AS IF SHE were moving in slow motion as she stuffed the rest of her belongings into her carry-on and tried to get the zipper to close.

A knock on the door interrupted before she could win the battle.

"Mom," she called on her way to the door. "I think it's time to leave for the airport."

When she opened the door, Lauren stood in front of her, wearing dark gray slacks and a white button-down. She balanced three paper cups of coffee in her hands while newspapers were tucked beneath one arm. "Good morning."

"Morning." Grace stepped aside to let her in and gratefully accepted the coffee Lauren handed her. "Oh, thanks. You're a lifesaver. We'll be ready in a second." She took a healthy sip of coffee before putting the paper cup down to fight with the carry-on.

Her mother bustled back and forth between the living area and her bedroom. "I hope you chose a better hotel in Berlin," she said to Lauren instead of a greeting or a thank-you for the coffee Lauren had brought her. "My mattress was too hard. I didn't sleep a wink."

Grace grinned. For a woman who hadn't slept a wink, her mother had snored pretty loudly. She turned away from the carry-on to search Lauren's gaze and share her mirth with her.

But Lauren wasn't looking at her face.

Did she just check out my ass?

"Um, let me try." Lauren set down her coffee and the newspapers and bent over the suitcase, forcing the zipper closed with brute strength. "There. Take a look at the newspapers before we head out."

Grace's hands went cold. She knew what the newspapers held—reviews of *Ava's Heart*. For a moment, she considered telling Lauren she didn't want to know, but then she'd only imagine all kinds of negative things. Besides, Lauren wouldn't bring over the newspapers first thing in the morning if the critics had torn the movie or her performance to pieces.

With slightly trembling fingers, she unfolded the first newspaper and skimmed the review, reading bits and pieces. *Given that I didn't care much for Ms.*

Durand's last movie, I attended the world premiere of Ava's Heart *with relatively low expectations.* She grimaced and read on. *Grace Durand and Russ Vinson star in an epic love story in which hope and grief collide... Bla, bla, bla...* She skipped ahead to where the critic talked about the performances of the actors. *The performances were a bit unbalanced. While Russ Vinson couldn't quite keep up with his co-stars, Jill Corrigan was a scene-stealer every time she appeared on screen. Grace Durand gave an outstanding performance as the movie's title character, displaying just the right mix of strength and vulnerability.*

Breathing more easily, she opened the next newspaper. *Grace Durand shines as Ava. This might very well be her breakthrough to a different kind of acting.*

When she dropped the newspapers back on the table, it was as if managing to throw off a big weight that had rested on her chest for the last few months. Laughter bubbled up from somewhere deep inside her. She spun around the room, spreading her arms wide.

"Careful." Lauren caught her before she could stumble over the suitcases and take a nosedive.

Grace gripped Lauren's upper arms. "They liked it! They liked me!"

Grinning, Lauren pulled her close in a jubilant embrace. "Of course they did."

Her voice rumbled through Grace, making her eyes flutter shut. Every last bit of stress and exhaustion left Grace's body as she rested against Lauren.

Loudly clearing her throat, Grace's mother brushed past them. "We need to get going. Ms. Pearce, could you take the dress bags?"

Grace felt as if she'd been immersed in the scene of a movie and now the director had called, "Cut!" A little disoriented, she let go of Lauren and went to get her suitcase.

Berlin, Rome, and Madrid passed by in a blur of PR activities for Lauren. In each city, they went through the same whirlwind of emotions—the stress of back-to-back interviews, nervousness right before the premiere, exhaustion during the after-party, and finally, joy and relief when the reviews came in the next morning. So far, the majority of the reactions from the press had been positive.

Lauren hadn't gotten another exuberant hug from Grace, but she'd dreamed about it. Twice. Of course, in her dreams, the hug hadn't ended with Grace's mother interrupting. Instead, Grace had kissed her and then dragged her to the bedroom and made love to her.

Maybe it was a good thing they'd fly back home tomorrow. Rooming door-to-door, spending every waking minute together had forged an unexpected closeness

216

that Lauren had never felt with any of her other clients. Just one more afternoon of interviews, one last premiere, one last after-party here in Paris and she could get some much-needed distance.

When the last journalist left, Grace sank against the back of her chair, arms dangling to both sides, her head tilted back in a way that exposed the length of her throat. Her very kissable throat.

Lauren quickly looked away.

"When he asked how I like the city, I really had to think about where I am for a second." Grace straightened and rubbed her eyes. "Can you believe I've been in Paris at least half a dozen times, yet all I've ever seen are the airport, a handful of hotels, and the theaters where the movies premiered? I spent some time in Spain and England, but except for work, I haven't been to France."

"Really? You haven't even seen the Eiffel Tower?"

"I've seen it—from the back of a limo. But even if I had the time, can you imagine what would happen if Grace Durand stood in line to get to the top of the tower like a mere mortal?" Resignation flickered in Grace's eyes. "Guess I'll have to shoot a movie on the tower, or I'll never get to see it up close."

Lauren frowned. When Grace left to get changed for the premiere, Lauren reached for her phone. "Sébastien? Hi, this is Lauren Pearce. Do you have a minute? I need a favor..."

Grace felt as if she would start to scream if she had to shake one more hand, kiss one more cheek, or make small talk with one more person. She had been circulating the banquet room where the after-party was held for what seemed like an eternity but was, in fact, only half an hour.

When someone called her name, she gritted her teeth, took a deep breath, and then turned with the friendliest smile she could muster. Relieved, she realized that it was just Lauren, who waved her over. Her familiar face was a welcome sight in this crazy circus of strangers.

"Ready to get out of here?" Lauren asked when Grace reached her.

Grace stared, for a moment not sure if she'd heard her correctly. "Please tell me you're not kidding."

"I'm not kidding," Lauren said with a grin.

"But I can't just leave this early...can I?"

"Sure you can. Who's gonna stop you?"

Grace grimaced and muttered, "My mother, for one thing."

"I don't think so. I told her I'm going to whisk you away for an interview with the French press. But don't worry; it's not true. We're going somewhere much more fun." Lauren guided her to the door, using the same excuse for anyone who wanted to stop them to chat with Grace.

Outside, a limousine with tinted windows idled at the curb. Lauren pulled open the rear door and ushered Grace onto the backseat before climbing in after her. The driver pulled away immediately, without having to be told where to go.

Grace squinted at Lauren. "This seems like a pretty well-organized kidnapping attempt. Where are you taking me?"

A hint of a smirk played around Lauren's lips. "What kind of kidnapper would I be if I told you?"

"A nice one." Grace batted her lashes at her. "Please?"

At first, Lauren shook her head, but then she melted under Grace's pleading gaze. "All right. But don't complain about me spoiling the surprise."

"I won't. So?"

"I thought you might like to go all the way to the top of the Eiffel Tower before we leave Paris."

Grace blinked. "You're taking me to the Eiffel Tower? Now?"

"It's open until midnight, so we should have enough time to make it to the top. Or would you rather go somewhere else?"

"I'm not exactly dressed to go up a one-thousand-foot tower, but what the heck..." She let out a giddy laugh. "Let's do this."

"Actually, I thought of that too." Lauren bent and pulled out a plastic bag from beneath the passenger seat. She raised the black privacy screen and emptied the contents of the bag onto the seat between them. A pair of jeans, a sweatshirt, a pair of sneakers, and a baseball cap slid out.

Grace groaned at the sight of the sneakers. Her feet had been killing her in her high heels for at least the last hour. "Oh my God. Just for this, you deserve a raise. A big one. How did you know what sizes to buy?"

"I googled it."

Grace thought she hadn't heard correctly. "Are you saying that information is on the Internet somewhere?"

Lauren nodded. "Right down to your shoe and bra size."

"Wow. That's amazing—and not in a good way." It probably didn't matter, but it still felt like an invasion of her privacy.

Lauren regarded her with a compassionate gaze. "It sucks; I know. But maybe you can console yourself with the fact that your measurements are a lot more flattering than those of most other people."

Grace tried to shake her feelings and focus on the moment. Eager to get out of the restricting clothes and into the more comfortable ones Lauren had provided, she peered around. She knew no one could see her through the tinted windows with the privacy screen up, but it still felt weird. "Should I just change here?"

"We don't have time to stop by the hotel. Sorry."

"It's okay." Grace kicked off her high heels. She'd shot love scenes in front of an entire camera team, for movies that were seen by millions of people, so getting changed in front of Lauren was no big deal, right? But for some reason, it was. *Oh, come on. She's seen a half-dressed woman before. Naked ones too.*

Then she realized that Lauren had turned away to give her some privacy. She had pulled a second plastic bag out from somewhere and was now struggling to get out of her pantsuit and into something more comfortable.

Quickly, Grace turned toward her own side of the limo. She twisted to open her dress but the zipper was somewhere between her shoulder blades, where she couldn't get to it. "Uh, Lauren? I can't reach the zipper. Would you mind?" She glanced over her shoulder.

Lauren had stripped off her blazer and blouse. Grace caught a glimpse of smooth-looking skin and firm breasts encased in a white bra before Lauren wrestled a sweatshirt over her head.

Cheeks flaming, Grace turned on the seat, presenting her back to Lauren.

"Oh, sure." Lauren moved Grace's hair out of the way, softly placing it over one shoulder. The fingers grazing the bare skin on Grace's back were warm and gentle.

Only when Grace had to suck in a lungful of air did she realize she'd held her breath. *It's just Lauren,* she told herself. *Why are you so nervous?*

Lauren took her hands away. "There."

A shiver went through Grace. She clutched the dress to her chest and cleared her throat. "Thank you." She dropped the dress and picked up the sweatshirt.

Quickly, Lauren turned back toward the window.

It took some maneuvering within the confines of the backseat, but finally, Grace had managed to shimmy into the jeans and the sweatshirt. "All done."

Lauren, now fully dressed too, turned to face forward. Were her cheeks flushed?

Before she could take a closer look, the limo stopped within direct view of the Eiffel Tower. Grace had never seen it so up close and personal. From the distance, it looked slender, almost delicate, but when they climbed out of the limousine, she stared at the tower's four massive legs.

"Wow."

Lauren laughed and led her across the street, toward the tower. "Wait until we're at the top to say that."

Even at this hour, there was a line in front of the ticket window, but Lauren held up two tickets and pulled her toward the elevator.

Grace kept her head down while they waited so that the bill of the baseball cap hid her features. No one seemed to pay her any attention. She marveled at the freedom of being just another tourist.

Finally, it was their turn to board the elevator. People crowded in after them, jostling Grace and pressing her against Lauren. The elevator climbed so fast that she was glad for Lauren's steadying support against her back. Excitement skittered up and down her spine as the elevator rose higher and gave her a glimpse of Paris from above. The illuminated steel beams they passed gleamed like gold against the backdrop of darkness.

At the second level, Lauren led them to another elevator, which carried them all the way to the top. A cool wind tugged on Grace's sweatshirt as soon as the elevator doors slid open. Ignoring it, she headed straight for the edge of the observation platform and looked through the wire cage.

From up here, she had a sweeping view of Paris. Glowing bands—the large boulevards of the city—stretched out below. Bridges spanned the Seine, their lights reflecting off the water.

Lauren stepped next to her, so close that their shoulders brushed, and pointed out some of the illuminated monuments to the north. "I guess that's why they call Paris the city of lights."

"I thought it's the city of love?"

Their gazes met; then Lauren directed her attention back to the city below. "That too."

After a while of silently enjoying the view, Lauren glanced at her wristwatch. "Ready to leave? We need to be down there before midnight."

"Why? Does the limousine turn into a pumpkin?" Grace asked.

"No. The driver will pick us back up whenever I call him."

"What happens at midnight, then?"

"You'll see," Lauren said, and this time, neither the eye-batting nor the pleading smile worked.

They made it back to ground level and strolled across a bridge leading over the Seine. Down here, the night was warm, and Grace was surprised to see how many people were still out and about, even though it was approaching midnight. Lauren seemed to know exactly where she was going. "Are you hungry?"

Grace's stomach rumbled as if on cue. "Well, you did kidnap me from the party before I could eat anything."

"Then come on." Lauren pointed to one of the cafés lining a square.

"Are you sure we can still get something to eat at this hour?"

"This is Paris. People eat pretty late here." Lauren asked the waiter for a table on the outside terrace.

Glad to sit, Grace stretched out her legs beneath the small table. She looked around, charmed by the atmosphere. On the square, crowds were gathering, and street performers were playing the pan flute and strumming a soft melody on a guitar.

Lauren looked over the menu, which at this hour was limited. "Oh, you should try the croque-madame. It's like a grilled cheese and ham sandwich, just better."

Grace's stomach growled its approval, but she shook her head and looked at their choices of salads. "I don't think so."

"Come on." Lauren gave her a gentle nudge. "We're in France. You need to try some of the local food and broaden your horizons."

"You mean broaden my waistline."

Before Grace could make a final choice, an ooh and aah went through the crowd on the square.

Grace looked up from the menu. Her breath caught. The Eiffel Tower was sparkling with thousands of lights that blinked on and off. A beacon on top of the tower sent out two light beams in opposite directions, sweeping the sky over Paris. The spectacle lasted for several minutes. When the glittering finally stopped, Grace turned toward Lauren. "You know, for a woman who refuses to write love stories, you're pretty romantic."

"No, I'm not. I just thought you might enjoy it. So, do you want to share the croque-madame?"

Grace sighed and gave in. Lauren wasn't just a romantic, she was also pretty hard to resist. If Grace were gay, she might really be in trouble.

They paused in front of the door to Grace's suite. Key card already in hand, Grace turned and looked at Lauren. "Thank you for kidnapping me. It was a wonderful evening." Her eyes shone.

Lauren could tell she wasn't acting now. She'd really enjoyed their adventure, and so had Lauren. She hadn't wanted the evening to end, and they had lingered over dessert—crème brûlée for her and fruit salad for Grace—until the café closed. "No need to thank me. I enjoyed it too."

They looked at each other.

This was starting to feel like a date, with neither of them knowing how to say good-bye. *It's not, so just say good night and leave, idiot.* Lauren shuffled her feet. "Well, then, good night."

"Good night. Sleep well." Grace hesitated, then leaned up and kissed Lauren's cheek before sliding the key card through the lock and disappearing into the dark suite.

Lauren stood staring at the closed door. Slowly, she lifted her hand and touched her overly warm cheek. *What the heck was that?* She shook herself out of her daze. *Just a simple kiss on the cheek, a gesture of gratitude, nothing more.* But as she walked toward her room, she trailed her fingertips over her cheek, where she could still feel Grace's lips.

Grace leaned with her back against the closed door and lifted her fingers to her tingling lips. She scolded herself for giving in to that spontaneous impulse. What if she was giving Lauren the wrong signals?

Calm down. She'd kissed Jill on the cheek many times, even after finding out that she was gay, and Jill had never mistaken it for anything more than what it was—a gesture between friends. But kissing Lauren had felt different from kissing Jill.

She pressed her hands against her temples as if that would stop the thoughts. Exhaustion swept over her, making her lean against the door more heavily. She couldn't deal with this now. It was probably just stress, lack of sleep, and all that talk about Lauren possibly being interested in her that made her so hyperaware of her interactions with Lauren. Reading that *Central Precinct* fan fiction hadn't helped either.

Without turning on the lights, she tiptoed across the living area so she wouldn't wake her mother.

The lights flared on before she could reach the safety of her room.

One hand pressed to her chest, Grace whirled around.

Her mother sat in the armchair, dressed in her nightgown and a bathrobe. Now she rose and walked toward Grace. All the Botox in the world couldn't hide the frown on her face.

Grace suddenly felt like a teenager who'd stayed out after curfew and had been caught sneaking back home. She tried to remind herself that she was an adult woman with the right to do whatever she wanted, but she couldn't help feeling guilty.

"What were you doing out at this hour? I was scared to death when you weren't back at midnight!"

"Mom, I'm sorry. I didn't think…"

"Obviously, you didn't, or you wouldn't go out alone in the middle of the night, in a city you don't know!" Her mother was shaking, but Grace wasn't sure if it was caused by rage or fear.

"Please calm down. I wasn't alone. Lauren was with me. We just went to see the Eiffel Tower. That's all."

If she'd thought that would soothe her mother's concerns, she couldn't have been more wrong. "So that was the 'interview' Ms. Pearce told me about."

Grace lowered her gaze to the carpet. She wasn't proud of lying to her mother. Well, strictly speaking, it had been Lauren doing the lying, but Grace knew she wouldn't have told her mother either, even if she'd known where Lauren intended to take her. "I'm sorry for not telling you, Mom."

"Then why didn't you?"

"Because I knew you wouldn't like it."

"Darn right. I don't like it one bit. You should be here in Paris, enjoying the city of love and the great reviews of your movie with your husband, not with... with that woman."

At her tone of voice when talking about Lauren, anger sparked inside of Grace. She struggled to keep her voice down. "Nick is shooting in LA, and he won't be my husband for much longer. You know that. And that woman is my publicist—and my friend."

"Well, if you enjoyed spending time with Nick as much as you apparently do spending time with that so-called friend, then maybe Nick wouldn't be your soon-to-be ex-husband," her mother said. "I always thought there was something strange about your marriage. You kept using your schedule and Nick's as a convenient excuse not to spend time together. I would give anything to be able to spend just one more minute with your father, but you..."

The rare reference to her father distracted Grace, so it took her several moments to realize what her mother had just said. "You knew I wasn't happy in my marriage? You knew and yet you never said one word, never asked me how I'm doing?"

Now it was her mother's turn to study the carpet. "I wasn't sure, and it's not my place to interfere with your marriage."

Since when? Grace almost asked. Such concerns had certainly never stopped her mother from interfering with her life before. She bit her lip, afraid what would happen if she started speaking openly. Something told her that it might start an avalanche that could ruin her relationship with her only remaining parent forever.

Her mother pulled her to the small sofa and sat next to her. "What's going on with you, darling?" She smoothed a strand of hair back from Grace's face.

Grace leaned into the motherly caress for a moment before pulling back. "What do you mean?"

"You lied to me. You left a party full of important people who could be essential to your career...just to do some sightseeing with...with Ms. Pearce. I don't understand."

If she tried to see it through her mother's eyes, Grace wasn't sure she understood it either. Her career had always been the most important thing in the world to her, more important even than her marriage. That was why she'd never seen the Eiffel Tower before. She'd been too busy working, attending red-carpet events, and schmoozing with the movers and shakers of the entertainment industry. Yet when Lauren had whisked her away from the after-party, she had followed her without much hesitation. "I don't know, Mom. Maybe...maybe my priorities are changing."

Her mother regarded her with an alarmed expression. "Changing? How? Why?"

"I don't know," Grace said again. "Maybe it's the upcoming divorce or Jill's diagnosis or turning thirty that made me think about my life for the first time." She gave a little laugh that sounded fake, even to herself. "Maybe I'm going through an early midlife crisis."

Instead of lecturing her about her priorities, as Grace had halfway expected, her mother surprised her by taking both of Grace's hands into hers. "Whatever it is, I'm here to help you deal with it, okay?"

Sudden tears burned in Grace's eyes. She didn't trust herself to speak, so she just nodded.

Her mother rubbed her hands and stood. "Now go to bed. We have a plane to catch early tomorrow morning."

When the bedroom door clicked shut behind her mother, Grace slumped against the back of the sofa, trying to keep up with all the emotions this evening had brought and failing miserably. Maybe she'd slipped in and out of too many roles over the years, and now she felt like a stranger in her own life.

She shook her head at herself. It was two o'clock in the morning, after a week of not enough sleep. Hardly the perfect time to reflect on her life. She forced her tired body up from the sofa. Her midlife crisis or whatever it was would have to wait until after *Ava's Heart* had been released.

CHAPTER 22

LAUREN PRETENDED TO PICK SOME morsels from the buffet table while she eavesdropped on a conversation between two film critics who'd just attended the premiere in Los Angeles.

"I wasn't sure I'd find her believable as a farmer," one of them said.

The other chuckled. "I know what you mean. With a body and a face like hers... That's just not how I imagine a farmer from Georgia."

Lauren gritted her teeth. People might think that Grace's looks had paved the way for her in Hollywood, but in truth, the way she looked made it difficult to be taken seriously—as more than just a pretty face and a hot body.

"But by the end, I really bought it," the film critic said.

Now more relaxed, Lauren filled her plate and looked around to find Grace and tell her the good news. Instead, she found Jill, who leaned against the other end of the buffet table, looking as if she were about to fall face-first into the shrimp cocktail.

Lauren put her plate down and hurried over. "Jill? Are you all right?"

Jill straightened and smiled. "I'm fine."

"Sure. And I'm a Catholic nun."

"I'm really all right, Sister Lauren."

"You don't look all right," Lauren said.

"You need to work on the way you're complimenting women."

Grace joined them as if sensing that something wasn't right with her friend. "Everything okay? You don't look so good, Jill."

A groan escaped Jill. "Not you too. I'm a little tired. That's all."

"Come on." Grace wrapped one arm around her and tried to lead her to the exit. "I'll take you home."

"Let me do it," Lauren said. "Your mother will have my head if I let you leave another after-party early."

"Don't I get a say?" Jill asked.

"No," Lauren and Grace said at the same time. They grinned at each other. Lauren added, "I need you bright-eyed and bushy-tailed for *Good Morning America* tomorrow."

Jill grumbled but finally gave in. "All right. I'll try to be bright-eyed, but I refuse to be bushy-tailed."

"We'll talk about it on the way to your house." Lauren turned toward Grace, trying to ignore the little jolt she felt every time she looked at her. Any lesbian would react to the sight of Grace in the emerald-green, strapless cocktail dress she'd chosen for the LA premiere. *Oh, yeah? Jill doesn't seem to have a problem keeping her eyes off Grace.* "Don't stay too late either."

"I won't. I'll try to make an escape in half an hour max."

Jill hugged her friend, and after a moment's hesitation, Lauren followed suit, managing to keep it short and not give in to the pull of gravity her body seemed to experience whenever Grace was near.

Even when they finally stepped outside, she could still smell Grace's perfume and feel her warmth imprinted on her body. *This is work. Focus.* As soon as they had settled on the backseat of a limousine and were on the way to Glendale, she pulled out her phone and reviewed the schedule for the next few days.

Good Morning America tomorrow. Then *The Today Show* and the premiere in New York City the day after. Once the movie was released to the general public this weekend, things would hopefully settle down a little.

"I bet that thing is very popular with your girlfriends," Jill said, breaking the silence in the back of the limousine.

Lauren looked up. "Excuse me?"

"That thing." Jill gestured at the cell phone in Lauren's hand. "I bet your girlfriends don't appreciate playing second fiddle to it."

For a moment, Lauren considered giving just a noncommittal shrug, but she knew such personal details about Jill's life that it didn't seem fair to just brush her off. "What can I say? I'm much better at building relationships with the press than with women."

"Have you ever tried to change that?"

Lauren dropped the phone to her lap. "Not really. I guess I just haven't—"

The phone started ringing.

"Um." Lauren itched to pick it up or at least check who was calling, but she didn't want to prove Jill's point, so she let it go to voice mail.

Seconds later, the phone rang again.

"I guess it's important," Lauren said.

Jill nodded at her to go ahead.

Half turning to face away from Jill, Lauren checked the caller ID and grimaced. Her boss calling her at this hour couldn't be good. She lifted the phone to her ear. "Hi, Marlene. What can I do for you?"

"Did you see the gossip blogs?" Marlene asked.

"No. I was at the premiere and then the after-party with Ms. Durand and Ms. Corrigan. Is something going on I should know about?"

"*Hollywood Affairs* just posted another article about Ms. Durand," Marlene said, ratcheting up Lauren's tension another notch. "Apparently, Mr. Sinclair's new girlfriend couldn't keep her mouth shut. One of her friends leaked the divorce to the press."

Shit, shit, shit. Lauren pummeled the leather seat with her free hand.

"What happened?" Jill mouthed.

Lauren held up one finger, signaling her to give her a minute. "What else does the press know?"

Marlene laughed without any humor. "What don't they know? They emphasize the being-left-for-a-younger-woman angle; they know that the girlfriend is a dancer...and that she's pregnant with his baby."

This time, Lauren cursed out loud. "I've got to call Grace right now and warn her before she leaves the party. Update you later." Not waiting for her boss's reply, she ended the call and lowered the privacy screen while dialing Grace's number with the other hand. "Turn around," she said to the driver.

He glanced over his shoulder. "You want me to—?"

"Turn around and drive us back to the party," Lauren shouted. "Now!"

Grace's relief at getting her mother to leave the party early lasted for exactly one minute. The moment she exited the expensive hotel, strobe flashes went off all around them, blinding her. She raised one hand to shield her eyes. "Come on, guys. Didn't you get enough photos of me earlier?"

The paparazzi continued snapping pictures. They pushed and shoved each other, trying to get the best vantage point. These weren't the well-dressed photographers who'd been at the premiere. This bunch wore jeans and looked hungry for pictures they could sell.

There was even a camera crew shoving a microphone into her face.

They were shouting questions, and it took Grace several moments to make any sense of the cacophony of voices and understand what they were asking.

"How do you feel about the baby?" the loudest reporter shouted.

"When will the divorce be final?"

"Is there something going on with Jill after all? Is that why he left you?"

"Is it true that she's expecting twins?"

Grace froze in her tracks. An icy hand closed around her heart and squeezed. *Oh God. They know. They know everything.*

Her mother grabbed her arm and tried to push and shove her way to the limousine waiting nearby.

The paparazzi didn't budge.

"Let us through, tabloid rabble!" Her mother swung her purse as if wanting to club them with it. "If you don't get out of our way, I'll make sure none of you take as much as a photo of a cockroach ever again!"

"Hey, Grace," one of the paparazzi shouted. "Is his bitchy mother-in-law the reason Nick wanted a divorce?"

The others laughed.

Grace pressed her teeth together so tightly she thought her molars would shatter. She wished Lauren were here to help her deal with this craziness.

The limousine driver must have realized what was happening. He backed up toward them, forcing the paparazzi to scatter.

Grace and her mother made a run for the limo. She shut the door as fast as she could. Her heart pounded so hard against her chest that it took her a moment to realize that it wasn't just her thrumming heartbeat—the photographers and reporters were slapping their hands against the glass, the force of their bodies making the limo wobble. With trembling hands, she reached for the seat belt and buckled up before gesturing at her mother to do the same.

The driver honked and finally managed to get them safely onto the street.

The paparazzi sprinted to their own cars to follow them.

Her mother waved two fifty-dollar bills over the half-raised privacy screen. "I'll give you a hundred-dollar tip if you can shake them."

Grace clung to the grab handle above the window as the driver stepped on the accelerator.

Her face ashen, Grace's mother turned toward her and gripped her arm with both hands. "What were they talking about? What baby?"

Grace's cell phone began to ring. Eager to escape her mother's question, she pulled it out of her clutch. *Lauren!* The relief at seeing Lauren's name on the display made her slump against the back of the seat. She slid her trembling finger across the display to accept the call and snatched the phone to her ear. "Lauren! They know! The paparazzi found out everything."

After a moment of silence, Lauren said, "I know. Where are you?" She sounded tense.

"We just left the party. They were waiting for us outside." The roaring of engines made Grace turn around.

The paparazzi must have called for backup. Other SUVs and cars had joined the pack tailing them.

"Great," Grace said into the phone. "Now there's a horde of them following us."

The limousine sped toward a traffic light, trying to escape. When it turned red, the car in front of them braked.

Their driver was going much too fast.

Oh God! Grace dropped the phone to hold on with both hands.

Her mother screamed.

The limo swerved to avoid the collision. They clipped the car of a paparazzo who was trying to overtake them.

They spun, rotating across the street like one of the silver balls in the pinball game she'd played with Lauren. Her heartbeat thundered in her ears. Strangely distanced, Grace wondered why her life wasn't flashing before her eyes. Was there nothing worth reliving?

The cars in the oncoming lane blared their horns. Brakes squealed and lights flashed as they spun. Then the limo crashed into something with a sickening crunch and came to a sudden stop.

Grace's head slammed against something hard. Pain seared through her temple, her arm, and her chest. Glass splintered, and broken shards rained down on her. Someone screamed. Then everything went black.

"Grace? Grace!" Lauren yelled into the phone.

There was no answer.

Her stomach twisted itself into knots. For a moment, she thought she might puke.

Jill pulled her back from her panicked haze by shaking Lauren's arm. "What happened?"

"I think they were in an accident," Lauren mumbled. "Grace said the paparazzi were chasing them. Then I just heard someone scream and a crash." She stared ahead through the windshield, willing their limo to move faster.

"I'm sure they'll be fine," Jill said, but her face had lost all color.

"Yeah." Lauren tried to tell herself that the last time Grace had been chased by paparazzi had turned out okay too.

But as they made their way back downtown, a fire truck and an ambulance passed them with wailing sirens.

Oh God, no. No. Not Grace. Lauren clutched the edge of the leather seat.

The sirens in front of them fell silent.

"There!"

The red-and-blue lights of police cruisers lit up the night. A battered-looking SUV blocked one lane. Then Lauren found the limousine. Smoke rose from its hood. It had slammed into a telephone pole, which had crushed one of the rear doors.

Where the passengers sit. A new wave of panic hit Lauren. "Stop!" she shouted at the driver. "Let us out here!"

"I can't stop here, ma'am," he yelled back. "Or I'll cause another accident."

As they passed slowly in the only open lane, Lauren watched helplessly as firemen surrounded Grace's limousine. Were they prying open the crushed door? Or getting people out on the other side? She craned her head but couldn't tell what was happening. It was driving her crazy.

"Turn!" she yelled at the driver.

"I can't. There's no place to turn here."

Lauren didn't want to hear a *no*. "Then find a place where you can."

Before the driver could follow instructions, an ambulance passed them with blaring sirens, heading away from the accident site. Several paparazzi chased after them in their cars.

"Follow them!" Lauren and Jill shouted in unison.

The driver mumbled something about not being James Bond, but he stepped onto the accelerator and followed the ambulance as fast as safety allowed—which wasn't anywhere near as fast as the ambulance went.

Lauren gritted her teeth as they lost sight of the ambulance, but by now, she could guess which hospital they were heading for. By the time the limousine pulled up to the hospital entrance, she was nearly jumping out of her skin with impatience and worry. She paid the driver, got out, and turned back to Jill. "He should drive you home."

"Oh, no. If you think I'll just go home, you need to think again." Jill climbed out after her. "I'm coming in with you."

"Okay. Then come on." They ran toward the sliding glass doors.

The ER waiting room was packed with people. The sharp sting of antiseptic and cleaning agents seemed to linger in the air, but maybe it was just Lauren's overactive imagination, which was busy showing her horrible images of Grace bleeding, screaming out in pain. She tried to shake these thoughts as they slid to a stop in front of the information desk.

A scrub-clad woman looked up from her computer screen. "Hi. What can I do for you?"

"We're here for..." Lauren leaned over the reception desk and lowered her voice so she wouldn't draw the attention of anyone around. "...Grace Durand."

The nurse eyed her sternly. "This is a hospital. Hardly the place for stupid pranks."

"What? No. This isn't a prank." Lauren pointed at her own grim face. "Do I look like I'm joking? She was just brought in by an ambulance."

Still not looking completely convinced, the woman typed something into her keyboard and shook her head.

"Try Betty Duvenbeck."

The woman hesitated for so long that Lauren wanted to jump the desk, push her aside, and take over the keyboard. Finally, the nurse typed again, read some information on her computer screen, and looked from Lauren to Jill and back. "Are you family?"

"Yes," Lauren said.

"No," Jill said at the same time.

Lauren groaned. "I'm her publicist, and she's her best friend."

"I'm sorry, but I can't give out information about a patient to anyone but an immediate member of her family."

Lauren put both hands on the reception desk. "Please. Just tell us if she's going to be okay."

"Sorry. I can't discuss a patient's condition with you. It's against hospital policy."

Lauren's hands on the reception desk curled into fists. "Listen," she said, barely keeping herself from shouting. "I was on the phone with her when the accident happened. I need to know if she's okay."

"Ma'am, I—" A commotion outside drew the nurse's attention.

Frowning, Lauren turned.

Nick rushed through the sliding doors while security guards pushed back a horde of paparazzi, stopping them from following him in.

Goddamn vultures. Lauren fought the impulse to storm out and knock some sense into them. They weren't important now. Her only concern was for Grace.

Nick headed straight for her. "Katherine called me just as I was leaving the party. I got here as fast as I could."

Katherine called him. So she was doing fine. But what about Grace?

"How is she?" Nick asked.

"I have no idea. They won't tell me anything because I'm not family."

"But I am." Nick turned toward the nurse behind the information desk. "I'm her husband."

Lauren had never been so glad that the divorce hadn't yet gone through.

The nurse gazed at him with starstruck adoration. "Hi, Mr. Sinclair."

"Can you tell me how my...how Grace is?" Nick asked.

"The doctors are still with her, so I can't give you any details. I'll show you to one of our conference rooms and let the doctors know you're there. Someone will be with you right away and give you an update on her condition." The nurse led them down the corridor and didn't say anything when Jill and Lauren followed Nick.

As soon as they reached the conference room and the nurse left them alone, Jill slumped into one of the chairs, but Lauren was too charged with adrenaline to sit.

Nick sank onto the chair next to Jill and ran both hands through his hair. "How the fuck did this happen?"

"Your girlfriend ran her big mouth to the press; that's what happened," Lauren ground out.

"Bullshit." Nick vehemently shook his head. "Shailene would never talk to the press."

"Yeah, but she bragged about her new family to a friend of hers."

Jill lifted her head from where she'd leaned it on her folded arms on the table. "Guys, please. Fighting each other won't help Grace."

She was right. Lauren snapped her mouth shut.

After what seemed like an eternity but was probably just half an hour, a doctor came in.

Lauren was next to him with two long steps. Jill and Nick jumped up.

"Mr. Sinclair? I'm Dr. Ramirez. I'm responsible for treating your wife."

Nick shook his hand. "How is she?"

"She's got a broken arm, which needs to be set, but we're sending her for a head CT first to make sure she only has a slight concussion. She's also got some bruises from the seat belt and a few very small cuts. It could have been a lot worse."

Lauren caught herself against the wall with one hand as relief weakened her knees.

"We'd like to keep her overnight for observation, just to make sure no complications develop," Dr. Ramirez said. "If you want to see your wife before she goes to CT, the nurse will take you to her."

Nick nodded and left with the doctor and a nurse.

Lauren stayed behind with Jill, wishing she could follow them to wherever Grace was and see for herself that she would be fine.

It seemed to take forever until a nurse finally came and said, "Ms. Durand is being moved to a private room, so if you'd like, you can see her now."

She led them to Grace's room.

Lauren's chest constricted as she entered and got a glimpse of the woman in the hospital bed.

Nick had taken up position at the foot end of the bed and Mrs. Duvenbeck sat in a chair next to the bed, looking none the worse for wear, but Lauren had eyes only for Grace.

Grace's face was as pale as the off-white walls of the hospital room. A couple of shallow cuts crossed her left temple. Her left arm, which rested on top of the covers, was encased in plaster. She smiled when she saw Lauren.

Jill rushed to her, interrupting the eye contact between her and Lauren. "Christ, Grace! You scared us. Are you in pain?"

"I'm fine." Grace returned her soft hug as best as she could with only one good arm. "They gave me some pretty potent stuff."

Hesitantly, Lauren stepped closer. "You'd do anything to get out of *Good Morning America*, wouldn't you?" she said around that giant lump in her throat.

Grace laughed and then winced. "Damn. You found me out."

"This is hardly the time or place for jokes," Katherine said sharply. "We could have died because you weren't there to do your job!"

"Mom, please. None of this was Lauren's fault." Grace raised her hand to her temple and nearly bashed herself in the head with her cast.

Her mother glared at Lauren but said nothing else.

"How's the driver?" Grace asked, looking from Nick to Lauren and Jill and then to her mother.

"He's fine," her mother said. "You were the only one who got hurt since we crashed into the telephone pole on your side."

"And the paparazzo whose car we hit? Is he fine too?"

Lauren stared at her. The paparazzi's chase had caused Grace's limo to crash, yet she was worried for their well-being? God, this woman was almost too good to be true.

"I have no idea," her mother said.

"I'll find out," Nick said and left, looking as if he was glad to have a good excuse not to stay, now that he'd seen that Grace was stable.

Lauren knew she should leave too, take Jill home, and then get started on all the things she had to do now—canceling Grace's interviews, taking a look at the social media sites and the gossip blogs to see how bad the damage to Grace's public image was—but she couldn't bring herself to move even one inch. She stood gripping the rail at the foot end of Grace's bed, drinking her in.

Finally, a nurse came and asked them to leave. "Ms. Durand needs her rest."

Jill bent and wrapped her arms around Grace in a gentle hug.

Then it was Lauren's turn to say good-bye. She stepped around the bed.

"I think we need to cancel *Good Morning America*," Grace said. "Probably *The Today Show* too."

"Don't worry. I'm on it. You just rest and get better, okay?" Lauren wanted to reach out and touch her so badly but was afraid of what she'd do once she felt Grace's warmth against her fingers.

Grace nodded and looked up at her, her gaze a bit hazy.

For a moment, Lauren thought she saw the same longing in Grace's eyes—the longing to be held and to forget the horror of the last few hours, but then she told herself that it was just wishful thinking. She lingered next to the bed, unable to tear herself away from their eye contact.

When Mrs. Duvenbeck loudly cleared her throat, Lauren turned away and followed Jill to the door, even though everything in her shouted at her to stay. *Get yourself together.* Now more than ever, Grace needed a professional, clear-thinking publicist, not an emotional wreck who'd gotten much too close to one of her clients. When she stepped out of the hospital, she squared her shoulders and put on her game face. It was time to worry about Grace's career, not just about Grace herself.

Smoke filtered through the broken window of the limousine's rear door, stinging Grace's nose. Panicked, she looked around. Flames were licking along the hood. She'd seen enough of Nick's action movies to know that the gas tank would explode within minutes. *Oh God, oh God!* She struggled to free herself of the seat belt, but the buckle wouldn't give. Pain shot through her arm as she pulled, throwing her full weight into an attempt to break free.

The buckle held. She was trapped in the burning car.

Someone pounded on the car door from the outside but couldn't get to her.

Grace screamed—and woke up. Her eyes popped open. It took her several seconds to realize that she wasn't in the limousine anymore. She was in the hospital—and in Lauren's arms.

For a moment, she thought she was still dreaming, but then the details filtered into her consciousness: the scent of Lauren's perfume and her leather blazer, her warmth against Grace's skin, separated just by a thin hospital gown, and the feel of the strong arms holding her.

"Are you okay?" Lauren whispered. Her warm breath washed over Grace's ear.

Grace burrowed deeper into the embrace, laying her face against Lauren's shoulder. "Oh God. I was trapped in the burning car."

"It wasn't real," Lauren said. "It was just a dream. You're safe. Nothing can hurt you here."

Grace allowed herself to remain in the comforting embrace for a little longer, until her racing heart slowed. Finally, she pulled back and peeked up at Lauren, hoping she hadn't embarrassed her with that moment of weakness.

All she could read in Lauren's hazel eyes was concern. There was no hint of judgment.

Her mouth dry, Grace looked around for some water.

"Here." As if guessing what Grace needed, Lauren poured her a glass of water from a pitcher on the bedside table and handed it to her.

Grace drank gratefully and glanced about the room.

Lauren's laptop lay abandoned on a chair next to the bed. She'd probably been here for a while, working and watching over her. Somehow, Grace wasn't surprised to find Lauren by her bedside, almost as if she'd sensed her presence in her sleep. The rapid-fire clickety-clack of Lauren's keyboard had even made it into her dream as someone pounding on the limousine door, trying to get in and help her.

"Where's my mother?" Grace asked.

Lauren moved back to the chair. "She left to get you some clothes to wear home, just in case they let you go later today."

Was it childish to instantly miss Lauren's warmth next to her? Wow, that must have been quite the hit on the head she'd taken. She'd never been this clingy in her life.

Lauren studied her. "How do you feel?"

Truth be told, Grace felt as if she'd had a close encounter with an entire football team tackling her, but she didn't want to worry Lauren unnecessarily, so she said, "Not too bad, considering how I probably look."

"You're beautiful." Lauren's cheeks colored as if she hadn't meant to say it. She rose and put the laptop away.

Grace suppressed a smile. For some reason, it pleased her immensely that Lauren still found her beautiful, despite the cast, the cuts, and the bruises.

Lauren returned and slid the chair closer to the bed. She looked at Grace with a serious expression. Shadows lurked beneath her eyes, indicating that she hadn't slept much.

"How bad is it?" Grace asked.

Lauren hesitated.

"The truth. Please, Lauren, tell me. I need to know."

"All right. As you can imagine, you're gracing the cover of every single gossip rag in Northern America."

"Probably in Europe too," Grace muttered.

"Probably. Most of them are on your side, though."

Grace shook her head. "I never wanted there to be sides."

"Hollywood's golden couple is going through a divorce, and there's a new girlfriend and a baby already on the way—of course the press will take sides and not report the boring 'amicable separation' angle."

A sigh escaped Grace. Maybe she'd been naive thinking she could get the press to not make a media spectacle of her divorce. "Sometimes, I think it wasn't one of my better ideas to file for divorce. At least not right now."

"Why did you?" Lauren asked. "I mean…you must have known that with the release of *Ava's Heart*, this would be the worst possible time to go through divorce proceedings. Why not wait?"

"I waited too long already," Grace said, surprising herself by answering honestly. "When Jill told me about her diagnosis earlier this year, it really got me thinking. What if I were in Jill's shoes? What if I were diagnosed with an incurable disease? It occurred to me that I wouldn't be able to look back at my life and say that I have no regrets. I feel like I've been sleepwalking through life the last few years, and Jill's diagnosis gave me the much-needed wake-up call."

"So you haven't been happy with Nick for quite some time?" Lauren said, making it sound like a question.

"I wasn't exactly unhappy. I made millions with my acting, lived in a house that most people could just dream of, had a handsome husband… I should have been ecstatically happy."

"But you weren't," Lauren said for her.

Grace shook her head. Her mother had asked her repeatedly why she wasn't happy with Nick and what they had, but she'd never been able to answer the question. Something had been missing. Sure, she loved Nick, but it had never been the all-consuming, head-over-heels, butterflies-in-the-stomach kind of love the characters in her movies got to experience. "Once I realized that, I told Nick that we needed to take a break."

Lauren leaned forward, her full attention on Grace. "How did he take that? Did he try to get you to change your mind?"

"No." Grace had expected a fight, but Nick had made it easy for her. "He was angry and confused, but I don't think I shattered his heart into a million little pieces. When I suggested some time apart to think, he looked at me and said, 'After three years together, what's there to think about? You either want to be married to me or you don't.' And I realized that I didn't. I just needed a little push to take that last step and file for divorce."

Grace leaned back in the hospital bed. *Wow.* She'd never talked so openly to anyone, not even her mother or Jill. She peered at Lauren, who looked back at her with an open, nonjudgmental expression.

"For what it's worth, I think you did the right thing, even if the timing wasn't ideal," Lauren said. "You deserve to be happy."

"Thank you," Grace murmured. "I haven't figured out yet what would truly make me happy."

"You will."

Grace trailed invisible patterns with her fingertips on top of the hospital covers. "What about you?"

"Me?"

"Yeah. Did you ever find that all-consuming, head-over-heels, butterflies-in-the-stomach kind of happiness in a relationship?"

Not looking at Grace, Lauren shook her head. "I can't seem to find a woman who's more important to me than my job."

Somehow that made Grace sad. She wanted Lauren to be happy in all aspects of her life, not just in her job. "Do you love your job that much?"

"Not everything about it, but yeah, I like it," Lauren said, now looking at her. "And it's what I'm good at. It's what I grew up doing."

Grace gave her a puzzled look. "How does anyone grow up in PR?"

"Easy. My parents always had a weird kind of on-again, off-again relationship. Both of them had numerous affairs over the years, not bothering to hide them, but unlike you, neither filed for divorce. To the public, they always presented the image of the happily married Hollywood power couple. I learned early on to play the game and cover their messes."

No wonder Lauren wanted to stay away from a relationship with anyone in show business. "I'm sorry you had to—"

A knock on the door intruded.

"Come in," Grace called, even though she didn't feel up to more visitors. She would have preferred to stay alone with Lauren and continue to talk.

Nick entered and closed the door behind him. He trudged over to the bed, looking worse than Grace felt. "How are you?" he asked.

"I'm okay, considering."

"That's good to hear." He smiled at her, but it seemed forced.

"How are you doing?" Grace asked.

Nick's face darkened. "How would you be doing if you were painted like a monster?" He looked from Grace to Lauren and then back. "This is hurting my career—and my relationship. Everyone thinks I've been cheating on you."

"Well, what else are they supposed to think?" Lauren said. "You're having a baby with your new girlfriend before the divorce has gone through."

Nick glared down at her. "Grace isn't paying you to judge me. She's paying you to—"

"Please, Nick." Grace pressed her good hand to her forehead. Her temples were pounding. "I can't take this right now. Let's talk calmly."

"Easy for you to say." Nick wrapped his hands around the bed railing as if he wanted to strangle it. "You can afford to stay calm. This isn't messing with your public image. People automatically assume that I'm the bad guy, especially now that you got hurt."

The pounding in Grace's head increased.

Lauren stood and leaned over Grace, her hazel eyes big and worried. "Are you okay? Do you want me to call a nurse?"

"No. I'm fine. Just incredibly tired."

"Close your eyes and go to sleep. We can talk about this later." Lauren's voice was soft, not like the voice of a tough PR specialist. She straightened and turned toward Nick. "I'll prepare a joint statement, but for now, Grace needs to rest."

Nick didn't look happy to be practically kicked out, but he walked around the bed and touched Grace's shoulder. "I'll be back tomorrow. Get some rest." He strode to the door without looking back.

"Maybe you should follow him and help him handle the paparazzi," Grace said halfheartedly. "I bet they're waiting outside."

"I'm your publicist, not his. Or do you want me to go?"

"No." That was the last thing Grace wanted. Drowsiness swept over her, but she fought against her exhaustion and tried to keep her eyes open, not wanting Lauren to leave. The painkillers they'd given her made any attempt to think feel like wading through molasses.

"Close your eyes," Lauren said. "You need to rest."

"Will you stay?" Grace hated sounding so needy, but she couldn't help it.

"Of course." Lauren perched on the edge of the bed. Hesitantly, she lifted her hand and smoothed back a strand of hair that had fallen onto Grace's face. Her fingers trailed over Grace's cheek on the unhurt side.

At the tender touch, Grace's eyes fluttered shut. "Don't stop," she mumbled. Seconds later, she drifted off to sleep.

Long after Grace's peaceful breathing indicated that she'd fallen asleep, Lauren sat on the edge of the bed and softly caressed Grace's golden-blonde hair. She took in every detail of Grace's face—the lashes resting against the soft cheeks, the sculpted cheekbones, the full lips, the downy hair near her temple, where tiny cuts marred her otherwise flawless skin.

Oh God. Lauren trembled at the thought of how close she'd come to losing Grace. *Losing her? Who do you think you are—her lover? You're friends at best.* But no amount of reason could change the way she felt, as crazy as it was.

The door opened, and Mrs. Duvenbeck swept into the room. "Thank God the paparazzi are—" She stopped in the middle of the room when she saw Lauren sitting next to her daughter.

Lauren suddenly became aware that her hand was still resting along the unhurt side of Grace's face, cradling it gently.

"What do you think you're doing?" Mrs. Duvenbeck glared at her like a chaperone intent on protecting her charge's virtue.

Careful not to wake Grace, Lauren took her hand away and got up from the bed. "I'm just providing some comfort, like any decent human being would."

"She's asleep. She doesn't even know you're here."

Grace moved restlessly in her sleep, her good hand trailing over the bed as if searching for something.

"She said she wanted me to stay."

Mrs. Duvenbeck took up position between Lauren and the bed. "I doubt she wanted you to touch her face while she sleeps."

Don't stop. Grace's whispered words echoed through Lauren's mind. Yes, Grace had wanted her touch. Was she just seeking some comfort from whatever source was available, or was there more to it? She shook her head at herself, knowing nothing good would come out of thinking like this. "What did you say about the paparazzi when you came in?"

"A few are still lurking in front of the hospital, but most retreated, and they didn't try to follow me in."

Lauren nodded grimly. "Good." So her none-too-subtle threats had worked. She'd been on the phone all morning, calling every magazine, blogger, reporter, and paparazzi she knew and telling them she'd make sure Grace would sue their sorry asses if they didn't back off after the accident they'd caused.

Under Mrs. Duvenbeck's watchful gaze, she packed up her laptop, walked to the door, and stopped to look back at Grace. She'd promised her to stay, but now she couldn't. Being close to Grace short-circuited every last bit of reason, especially now that her emotions ran so close to the surface. What she needed was more distance until she could be her professional self around Grace again. "Tell Grace I had to go."

After one last glance back, she fled.

CHAPTER 23

LAUREN HAD SPENT THE LAST two days at the office, only making it home to fall into bed and sleep for a few hours. She had e-mailed Grace and Nick the joint statement, assuring the press and the public that it had been an amicable separation long before Shailene had come into the picture and that they still had the deepest respect for each other and would remain friends.

Instead of Grace, her mother had responded to Lauren's e-mail, approving the press release. Even though Lauren missed Grace, she was secretly glad that she didn't yet have to deal with her. She hadn't seen her since Mrs. Duvenbeck had caught her caressing Grace's face, but Jill kept her up to date, so she knew Grace was home from the hospital and on the mend. Her heart ached with the longing to see for herself that Grace was fine, but she'd prescribed herself some distance. Maybe if she stayed away for a while, her attraction would die down.

The problem was just that getting away from Grace was impossible at the moment. She couldn't go anywhere without having Grace's face and those incredibly blue eyes staring back at her—and it wasn't just all in her imagination. Every time she opened Twitter, Facebook, or one of the celebrity blogs, Grace was there.

After work, she fled to the fitness center on the ground floor of the office building and pounded out her frustration on the treadmill. When she looked up, her gaze landed on a billboard across the street.

It was a giant movie poster of *Ava's Heart*, showing Grace on the veranda of the farmhouse, her face bathed in the orange glow of sunset.

Lauren's steps faltered. She almost fell off the treadmill, catching herself at the last moment. *Jesus!* For the rest of her workout, she forced herself to keep her head down and not look at the billboard again, as tempting as it was.

She ignored the movie poster too when she drove by it on the way home. Not that it did her any good. Grace's face seemed to be plastered on every damn billboard in the city.

Lauren stopped at a supermarket to get milk and some other essentials for her bare fridge. She would just hole up at home with a bottle of wine and her laptop, maybe get some writing done—anything but think of Grace and how she might be doing.

Determined, she steered toward the checkout line. Her gaze veered around while she waited and landed on the magazine display to her left. *Damn.* She clutched the cart with both hands. Several racks were filled with tabloids, all of the covers featuring Grace's picture. Lauren lifted one of the magazines from the rack and read the captions beneath Grace's photo. *Twins for Nick—heartbroken Grace is being treated for depression.* With a snort of disgust, she threw the tabloid back.

Her phone rang, and she pulled it out of her pocket. The name of the woman she'd been trying not to think of flashed across the display. Lauren knew she couldn't avoid Grace—or her growing feelings for her—forever. She was still her publicist, after all. "Hi, Grace," she said into the phone. "How are you doing?"

"I'm fine," Grace said.

It didn't sound like the warm-hearted woman Lauren had gotten to know during the past months. It sounded like the polite actress everyone else knew. Maybe Lauren should have been glad that Grace was putting some distance between them too, but all she felt was hurt.

"Can we talk?" Grace asked.

Fear clutched Lauren. Had Grace guessed her feelings and was now uncomfortable around her? Had Grace's mother told her about finding Lauren touching her face as a way to turn Grace against her? Was she about to fire her? She swallowed the lump in her throat. "Uh, sure. Now?"

"If that's a good time for you."

Lauren squared her shoulders. Better get it over with. "Now is fine. Do you want me to come over?"

"That would be nice," Grace said. "I've been cleared to drive, but to tell you the truth, I'm not too eager to get into a car again."

That sounded more like the Grace she knew—the one who trusted Lauren and talked openly to her. "I'll be there in twenty minutes." Leaving her cart behind, she squeezed past the people in the checkout line and headed to her car.

To Lauren's relief, only Grace's car was in the driveway when she arrived at the mansion. At least she didn't have to deal with Mrs. Duvenbeck on top of everything else. But then again, it meant she'd be alone with Grace. She climbed the stairs to the front door like a woman on her way to the gallows. *Ridiculous. Just act like a professional, and everything will be fine.*

But when Grace opened the door, every last professional thought disappeared from her mind in an instant. Grace was wearing Lauren's Boston University sweatshirt—the one she'd borrowed and never returned. Lauren had never considered that old thing sexy, but on Grace, it took her breath away. Somehow, having Grace wear her clothes was an unexpectedly strong aphrodisiac.

They stood rooted to the spot, regarding each other across the doorway.

Grace seemed to realize what had caught Lauren's attention. She tugged on the sweatshirt's sleeve with her good hand. "Sorry. I meant to give it back a long time ago, but I forgot. It's one of the few things I found that fits well over the cast."

Lauren finally managed to gather enough of her wits to say, "It's okay. I don't mind." That was the understatement of the century.

She followed Grace into the house. A couple of moving boxes stood in the corner of the living room, one of them still open. "You're moving out? Now?" Grace had been out of the hospital for barely two days.

Grace nodded. "I figured I might as well go ahead and do it now. At least then Nick and Shailene will have enough time to settle in and get the nursery done before the baby comes."

Wow. Lauren studied her closely. Was there really not the slightest bit of resentment or envy, now that Nick was having a baby and building a home with another woman?

"You can say it."

"Say what?"

"How stupid I am to just give him the multi-million-dollar mansion. My mother already told me so at least half a dozen times."

Lauren shook her head. "I don't think that. This"—she pointed at the modern furniture and the sterile living room—"just isn't you. I think you'll feel much more at home in the cottage."

Grace's eyes warmed. "Finally someone gets it."

Great. Another bonding moment. Instead of pulling back, Lauren felt herself drawn closer and closer. "Just be careful with your arm. Packing moving boxes can't be good for it."

"I'm not lugging around boxes, just putting some stuff in with my good hand. Jill will come over sometime this week to help me transport the boxes."

Lauren opened her mouth to offer her help but then snapped it shut. *Distance, remember?* "You wanted to talk to me?"

"Yeah, I..." Grace gestured at the couch. "Why don't we sit?"

Lauren settled on one end of the sofa, carefully leaving as much distance as possible between them.

"Do you want something to drink? I bought a great blend of coffee that should be right up your alley."

"No, thanks," Lauren said. She wanted to get this over and done with, but now Grace kept procrastinating.

With the fingers of her good hand, Grace tugged on her cast. A few strands of hair fell into her face, and she impatiently swiped them behind one ear. Finally, she glanced up. "I haven't seen you since I was in the hospital. Are you avoiding me?"

Heat rushed up Lauren's chest. "No, I was just busy with work. We're getting bombarded with media inquiries for interviews with you, and I'm trying to pick the best one for an exclusive." She forced a grin. "Being your publicist is a full-time job."

Grace's face fell. "I thought I was more than a job to you. I thought we were friends."

The hurt in Grace's voice clutched at Lauren's heart. God, how was she supposed to keep her distance if Grace looked at her like this? She wanted to slide across the couch and hold her. "Of course. I want that too, but..." She rubbed her face with both hands. "It's not that easy."

"Did I do something wrong?" Grace asked quietly. "Maybe I shouldn't have told you all the boring details of my marriage, but I just—"

"No. No, Grace, that's not it. I'm glad you felt you could talk to me openly. I want you to. It's just..."

"It's just what?"

"I'm not sure that you and I being friends is such a great idea." It pained her to say it. Everything in her rebelled against the words, but she forced them out.

Confusion and hurt flashed across Grace's usually controlled face. "Why not?"

"Our friendship could hurt both of our careers. It's hard to stay objective and professional if you're friends with a client."

"Who says I need you objective and professional?" Grace punched one of the sofa pillows with her unhurt hand. "What's wrong with having a publicist who's rooting for me for more than financial reasons?"

"Nothing. But now the media knows that Shailene wasn't the reason for the divorce. They'll keep digging, and they won't stop until they find something juicy."

"There's nothing to find," Grace said.

"Then they'll make something up. Remember what they wrote about you and Jill? They'll start those rumors all over again."

Grace had already opened her mouth for a reply. Now she snapped it shut and gave Lauren a disbelieving look. "That's what this is all about? You're afraid they'll photograph us getting ice cream together? That they'll say there's something going on between us just because we don't hate each other's guts?"

"Aren't you afraid of that happening?" Lauren asked quietly.

Eyes squeezed shut, Grace nodded. "Yes. I'm afraid of stupid headlines like that every time my mother marches in with a stack of gossip rags." She jumped up and started pacing in front of the couch. "But you know what? I'm sick of it. I'm sick of being just as trapped in that celluloid cage as I was in my marriage. At some point, any halfway intelligent person has to realize how stupid this is. Just because you're a lesbian doesn't mean you have feelings for me."

Silence descended on the living room.

Grace stopped pacing.

Lauren felt her gaze on her but didn't look up. "No," she said, trying to keep her face expressionless, "of course it doesn't mean that." It didn't sound convincing, even to herself.

When Grace didn't say anything, Lauren peeked up at her. Grace's forehead crinkled; then Lauren watched as realization dawned.

"Oh," Grace said and collapsed into the armchair.

A muscle jumped in Lauren's jaw. She instantly regretted leading the conversation down this road. If she'd just kept her mouth shut, Grace would have never found out. But there was no way to take it back. "I'd better go. I'll send you the best options for interviews." She stood and made a beeline for the door.

"Wait!"

Grace's shaky voice stopped her after just a few steps. Lauren hesitated, took a steadying breath, and slowly turned.

"I...I don't know what to say." Grace got up from the armchair and took a couple of steps toward Lauren but stopped before she reached her. "I just know that I don't want to lose you as a friend."

A groan was wrenched from Lauren's lips. "I don't want that either, but—"

"Don't you think two people can be friends despite having feelings for each other?"

Lauren stared at her. Surely Grace didn't mean it the way that had sounded, right?

Grace lifted her hands to scrub her face with both palms, nearly giving herself a black eye with the cast. "That's not... I... What I meant was, don't you think we can still be friends, even though you're attracted to me?"

It shouldn't be a problem. Lauren had been friends with women she was attracted to before and had always managed without much heartbreak. But this wasn't just about Grace being so damn attractive. Lauren was around good-looking women all the time. She was no stranger to desire, yet these feelings were new. This had disaster written all over it if she didn't distance herself now. She opened her mouth to tell Grace that it wasn't a good idea, but with one glance into Grace's pleading eyes, she found herself saying, "It's worth a try."

Grace rushed forward and right into Lauren's arms.

Lauren's arms came up. She cradled Grace carefully, mindful of her broken arm and the bruises the seat belt had left on her chest.

"Friends?" Grace asked close to her ear.

"Friends." Her eyes fluttered shut. *God, what are you doing?* She had a feeling she'd end up regretting this, but for now, with Grace in her arms, she didn't care.

CHAPTER 24

"Stop looking at the clock and start unpacking," Jill said for the third time. "If you're not done by the time your mother is back from the spa, she'll want to help and end up driving us crazy."

"There's not that much to unpack," Grace said. She had left everything but her books, clothes, and a few other personal items behind, preferring a fresh start.

"Still. There's no sense in watching the clock all the time."

"I'm not keeping an eye on the clock because of my mother," Grace said.

"I know, but it's still useless. The numbers will come in when they come in."

"Easy for you to say," Grace mumbled. "I've got a lot riding on that movie."

Jill stacked the books onto the cottage's floor-to-ceiling bookcase. "And I don't? People will keep an extra close eye on me in every scene I'm in, trying to find any sign of my MS or proof that I'm not fit to play the very cute, very straight best friend."

Grace wanted to club herself over the head with her cast. *God, how insensitive can you possibly be?* She put her good hand onto Jill's shoulder. "I'm sorry, Jill. That was stupid of me."

"No. I understand why you're worried. But look at it this way. What do you have to lose? You've got a few million stashed away. If push comes to shove, you can just retire."

"At thirty?" Grace gave her a skeptical glance.

Jill shrugged. "Why not? Just get yourself a hot lover to help keep you busy."

Laughter bubbled up from Grace's chest. "I'll take it into consideration." An image of Lauren formed in front of her mind's eye. She chased it away with a shake of her head. It was completely normal for Lauren to pop into her head a lot, right? After all, she was still stunned by that revelation two days ago. It didn't mean that she saw her as anything but a friend. A friend who had the hots for her. She still couldn't quite grasp that thought, and that baffled her even more. What was so extraordinary about it? She'd had acquaintances before who'd revealed a romantic interest in her. After telling them she thought of them just as friends, she hadn't wasted much thought on it anymore, so why couldn't she stop thinking about

Lauren's confession? Was it just because Lauren was a woman and all the others had been men?

"Where dos this box go?" Jill's question interrupted her thoughts.

Grace checked the label. "Up in the bedroom. But I'll unpack that one myself, if you don't mind."

"Ooh!" Grinning, Jill nudged her. "That's why you're not interested in finding a new lover! You've got an entire collection of sex toys!"

Grace's cheeks warmed. "It's hardly an entire collection."

"Hey, there's nothing to be embarrassed about. Toys are fun." Jill set the box aside and peeked into the other one. With childlike enthusiasm, she dug into the moving box and triumphantly lifted something in the air. "You've got Scrabble? Let's play!"

"Now?"

"Why not? You're practically unpacked, and it's going to be hours until we hear anything from the studio, if they even call today." Jill dragged her to the couch and set up the Scrabble board. "Come on. I'll even let you go first."

They each took seven tiles from the letter bag and arranged them on their trays.

Grace stared at her tiles, but they just wouldn't form any words. Not finding the right words seemed to be a common occurrence lately. She hadn't known what to say to Lauren's revelation either. *Stop thinking about it.* She arranged her letters this way and that and realized she could form a word after all. *Figures.* Making a face, she laid out three of her tiles on the star square at the center of the board. "S-E-X. On a double-word score, which gives me twenty points."

Grinning, Jill used the x to form out the word *boxers*. "I think that's fifteen points."

Grace looked down at the seven letters on her rack. Most of them were useless vowels. Just when she was considering trading most of her tiles for new ones, she discovered one option that might work. She picked up three of her wooden letters and placed them to the right of Jill's b.

"First *sex* and now *boob*?" Jill laughed. "Are you trying to tell me something?"

Blood rushed to Grace's cheeks. "It's just a stupid game, Jill," she said, a little more defensively than she'd wanted.

Jill held up both hands. "Hey, I'm just teasing. Jesus, you seem really tense today. I hope the studio doesn't make us wait too long to find out the numbers, or you'll be a nervous wreck."

Admittedly, it wasn't only waiting to find out the numbers of the opening weekend that made Grace so tense. She hadn't slept much the last two nights. "Sorry," she mumbled and busied herself reaching into the bag and drawing out three new tiles. She hoped none of them would form any more sex-related words.

After scribbling down the score, Jill studied her own tiles and then added an *ies* to Grace's *boob*.

When it was her turn again, Grace added a y to *sex*, which Jill then used to spell *naughty*. What a strange game this was turning out to be. Grace gave up on trying to find a word in the mess of letters on her rack and exchanged the tiles for new ones.

"Other than being worried about the opening-weekend gross, are you okay?" Jill asked.

Grace clutched the tiles in her hand so hard that the edges dug into her skin. She wanted—no, needed—to talk to someone, but how could she tell Jill what was going on with her without betraying Lauren's trust? "I'm fine," she finally said. "There's just a lot going on with the release of *Ava's Heart*, the divorce, the media nightmare, and all."

"Anything I can do to help?"

Sometimes, Grace didn't know what she'd done to deserve a friend like this. "You're already doing it, keeping me company and helping me move."

Jill nodded and laid out her next word, *aorta*.

Finally a perfectly innocent one. Grace took it as a good sign. "Did you ever have feelings—romantic feelings—for a friend?" she asked while Jill was distracted drawing new tiles.

"Besides you, you mean?" Jill said with a grin.

Grace threw a tile in her direction.

Jill was too slow to catch it, so it bounced off her chest and tumbled beneath the coffee table. She bent to retrieve it and handed it back to Grace. Now with a more serious expression, she nodded. "Once or twice. Falling in love with a friend is practically a lesbian rite of passage."

See? It's perfectly normal. Jill got over whoever she had feelings for. Lauren will too. Somehow, the thought did nothing to help improve her mood.

"Amanda and I were friends long before we became lovers too," Jill added.

The tiles she'd just picked up dropped from Grace's limp hand. "What? You and Amanda...you were lovers? Are we talking about the same Amanda? Amanda Clark?"

"The one and only."

Grace sank back against the couch. "I had no idea. When was that?"

"Hmm. About four years ago, back when no one had ever heard of Amanda... or me."

"What happened?"

Jill shrugged. "The usual."

"Which is?"

"We were both busy building our careers and didn't have much time for each other. Plus I was so far into the closet, I practically lived in Narnia. That can be really tough on a relationship. But at least we managed to stay friends after we broke up."

"Wow." Grace could only shake her head. "I had no idea."

"Why would you?"

Yeah. I'm not exactly the best at figuring out what my lesbian friends are feeling. This was the second confession this week that had blindsided her.

Jill studied her across the Scrabble board. "So, why the sudden interest in my romantic past?"

"Can't I just be curious?" Not looking at her, Grace trailed her fingers over the tiles on her rack.

"The reason for your curiosity wouldn't, by any chance, have anything to do with Lauren, would it?"

Grace's wooden rack toppled over, spilling tiles all over the table. "Why would you say that?"

"You should have seen her when you had the accident. I mean, I was pretty worried too, but Lauren… She was frantic. She would have mowed down every paparazzo in LA to get to you. I know you think I'm imagining things, but I really believe our favorite publicist has a pretty big crush on you."

Instead of answering, Grace started picking up her tiles.

"She told you?" Jill said, her voice reflecting her surprise.

"I didn't say that."

"No, but you also didn't deny it, which speaks volumes." Jill slid a little closer on the couch and covered Grace's hand with hers, stilling it. "How do you feel about it?"

Grace let go of her letters and clutched Jill's hand instead. "I have no idea. I'm trying not to think about it too much."

"Why not?"

That was the million-dollar question. Why had she so far avoided looking at her own feelings too closely?

The doorbell interrupted before Grace could answer.

"Damn. Saved by the proverbial bell." Jill pointed a finger at her. "But don't think for a minute I'll just let this go. I want to know every last detail."

"There's nothing to know," Grace grumbled and got up to open the door.

A quick glance through the peephole showed her that Lauren had braved the drive up to the cottage.

Grace's heartbeat accelerated. It was just because she knew Jill would tease her mercilessly, she told herself. She slowly pulled the door open.

"Hi," Lauren said. She shifted her weight from one leg to the other.

"Hi." Grace stood rooted to the doorstep, taking her in.

Lauren's hair was windblown as if she'd had the window open on her drive up, and the sleeves of her blouse were wrinkled from being pushed up her forearms earlier. Her hazel eyes behind the horn-rimmed glasses were red and surrounded by dark shadows. Had she lain awake the last two nights too? And if yes, was it because she worried about having ruined their friendship or was she just working too much, as usual?

"Can I come in?" Lauren asked.

"Oh, yes, of course. Sorry." Grace quickly stepped back and let her in.

"Hi, Jill," Lauren said as she walked into the living room. "I thought that might be your car in the driveway."

Jill got up and greeted her with a quick hug.

Sudden envy gripped Grace. She wanted to hug Lauren too, but with this new awkwardness between them, she wasn't sure it was a good idea.

Lauren looked around the cottage, taking in the two remaining moving boxes and the Scrabble board on the table. "I hope I'm not interrupting."

Oh, please, please, Jill, don't say anything. Grace sent a panicked look toward her friend.

"No," Jill said. "We finished unpacking most of Grace's stuff. Now we're just killing some time while we wait for the studio to call with the opening-weekend numbers."

"That's why I'm here." Lauren pulled a piece of paper from her back pocket and unfolded it. "I've got the numbers and thought you might want to know."

Grace hurried toward her. "The studio called you?"

"No. I called in a few favors because I knew you'd be biting your nails until you found out how *Ava's Heart* has done. These aren't the official numbers, just an early estimate, but they should be pretty accurate."

They both jumped around Lauren like boisterous puppies, making her laugh. "All right, you two. Sit down before you pass out."

People usually told others to sit down when they had bad news, didn't they? Grace collapsed onto the couch and gripped it with her good hand.

Lauren looked at the piece of paper. "According to the CinemaScore polls, the people who saw the movie gave it an average grade of A minus."

Jill pumped her fist. "That's fantastic!"

Yes, it was. But Grace couldn't relax yet. Audience ratings weren't what really counted in Hollywood. For producers and studio executives, a movie's success was measured only in dollars. "And how much did it gross at the box office?"

"It's hard to tell if all the media circus harmed the movie or not. If it did, the numbers would have been spectacular otherwise." A big grin spread over Lauren's face. "The three-day opening gross will be about twenty-five million dollars."

It wasn't Grace's most successful movie of all time, but it was more than respectable. The film had even almost earned back its production budget already. No tabloid would be able to write that Grace's career was going down the toilet, just like her marriage. Relief weakened Grace's muscles, but she jumped up nonetheless and stumbled through the living room toward Lauren.

Lauren caught her and whirled her around, both of them laughing like maniacs.

When they stopped in the middle of the living room, Grace felt so dizzy she had to clutch Lauren's shoulders to stay upright. Lauren gripped her hips. The warmth of her hands filtered through Grace's jeans. Grace stared into Lauren's eyes, fascinated when she discovered that tiny green flecks sparkled in the hazel irises.

Jill squeezed past them. "I think I'll head back to the city now. Call me when you get the official numbers from the studio, okay?"

Lauren and Grace looked at each other, then at Jill's retreating back. They let go and stepped back at the same time.

"What the...?" They were still in the middle of a Scrabble game, and she hadn't even given Jill a congratulatory hug yet. Why the sudden hurry to leave? Was Jill hurt that she'd hugged Lauren and not her? She hurried after her and caught up with her at the door. "What's going on? You didn't feel left out, did you?"

"No, that's not it. I promise." Jill glanced over to Lauren, who'd stayed behind in the living area of the cottage. She lowered her voice and added, "I just think that the two of you could use a moment alone."

"What? We don't need... It's not like that, really."

"Who are you trying to convince—me or yourself?" Jill asked.

Before Grace could think of an answer, Jill squeezed her shoulder and was gone.

Her head buzzing with thoughts, Grace trudged back to the living room. "Um, can I offer you something to drink? Coffee?"

"No, thanks. I drank too much of it already, even by my standards." Lauren glanced in the direction of the door. "Is everything okay with Jill?"

"Yes. She's just... She's fine."

Silence spread through the cottage like a physical entity. It was so unlike the effortless conversation and the teasing banter they'd exchanged in the past. Grace hated this sudden awkwardness between them, but she had no idea how to change it.

"So," Lauren said and massaged the back of her neck with one hand, "you're all moved in already?"

"Yeah. I just had a few moving boxes."

"Need any help with these?" Lauren pointed at the last two boxes.

"No. This one is just some board games that will go into the closet down here, and the other one goes up in the bedroom."

"And how are you supposed to navigate the ladder with the moving box and just one good arm?"

Grace hadn't thought of that. "Uh…"

Lauren grabbed the moving box labeled *bedroom* and swung it up onto one shoulder, leaving one hand free to navigate the ladder.

"Please be careful." Grace clutched the ladder with her good hand while she watched Lauren climb rung after rung.

"Yeah, I know," Lauren called down. "Headlines about your lesbian publicist falling to her death from your loft bedroom wouldn't look good."

"Uh, yeah. Exactly." Grace realized that her position at the bottom of the ladder made her stare directly at Lauren's ass. She wrenched her gaze away.

"Do you want me to unpack the box and bring it back down?" Lauren called from the loft.

Heat shot through Grace's body. "No! I mean…no, thanks. That's not necessary. Just put it down somewhere."

Lauren climbed back down.

Since Grace was still holding on to the ladder, even though it was firmly attached to the loft and didn't need to be held, their bodies came within inches of each other.

Grace hastily let go of the ladder and stepped back. God, why was she so jumpy and overly aware of Lauren's physical presence all of a sudden? Why couldn't she just relax around her, as she had in the past?

"Are you sure you want to stay here tonight?" Lauren's brow wrinkled. "It's not safe to climb the ladder with your cast."

Lauren's concern warmed her. She wanted to reach out and touch Lauren's arm but held back. "I'll sleep on the couch."

"Good." A cough shook Lauren's body. She pressed her hand to her mouth.

Grace watched her with a frown. "You're working too much. Now that the marketing campaign contributed to the movie's success, you should really cut down on your hours. Maybe you could even take a vacation."

"Are you trying to get rid of me?" One corner of Lauren's mouth curled into a half-smile, but the expression in her eyes showed that she wasn't just teasing.

"No! I just…" She lowered her gaze to the cottage's hardwood floor. "I worry about you."

"No need. I'll take a few days off, but not right now. At the moment, we need to keep you in the press for things other than your divorce."

In the past, Grace would have been happy to have a publicist who focused on her career above everything else, but now she couldn't help worrying about Lauren. "Just don't overdo it, okay?"

"I won't."

Another moment of silence between them seemed to last forever.

"I'd better head back. I don't want to navigate the dirt road in the darkness."

Grace followed her to the door.

Lauren opened it and then turned back around but didn't say anything.

"Uh, drive safely," Grace said because it was the only thing coming to mind.

"Will do. And I'll call you about rescheduling *Good Morning America*." Then the door closed behind Lauren.

Grace went to the window and watched the Honda Civic slowly make its way down the dirt road. She stood there, clutching the windowsill, until long after the car was gone and the clouds of dust had settled back down.

Finally, she turned and restlessly roamed the living room. The piece of paper Lauren had brought over still lay on the coffee table. Grace picked it up and stared at the numbers, written in Lauren's bold handwriting. The opening-weekend gross was great. She'd made the goal she'd worked on for so long. That would put her in the running for even larger, better roles. She should be happy, ecstatic even.

Then why on earth did she feel so unsettled?

CHAPTER 25

ONE GOOD THING ABOUT LIVING up in Topanga Canyon was that her mother didn't drop by quite as often. At least that was what Grace thought—until her mother came by unannounced a week after *Ava's Heart* had been released. Once she stopped complaining about the "homicidal excuse for a road" leading up to Grace's property, she perched on the couch and handed her a business card. "Here," she said with obvious pride. "Look what I found for you."

Grace glanced at the card. Richard Lomas, PR consultant and manager, it read. Her fingers tightened around the card, and she barely resisted the urge to crumple it up and throw it into the nearest garbage can. "I don't need a new publicist. I already have one that I'm very happy with."

"But I—"

"No, Mom. This isn't up for debate. Lauren really did a great job with the marketing campaign, and she went above and beyond the call of duty to make sure I got positive press after the tabloids found out about the divorce. I'm not going to fire her, no matter what you say."

Her mother clutched her chest as if Grace had driven a dagger into it. "I said nothing of the kind. Why are you getting so defensive?"

Grace slumped against the armrest. "I'm sorry. I thought you wanted…"

"Well, I still think Ms. Pearce isn't the best choice of publicists for you, but I guess for the time being, she'll have to do," her mother said.

Biting her lip to keep from defending Lauren again, Grace held up the card. "What's this, then?"

"He's Todd Walbert's manager." At Grace's blank stare, she added, "The soccer player."

"I know who he is, but why do I need the contact data for his manager?"

"Well, as you would know if you followed the celebrity news, Todd recently had some PR problems too…"

Grace nearly snorted. Hitting a paparazzo could be called a PR problem all right. Not that she couldn't understand the impulse at times.

"Richard and I got to talking, and we thought that Todd and you could help each other out."

"Help each other out," Grace repeated. "How?"

"What better way to show the media and the public that you're not depressed about the divorce than going out with a handsome young man like Todd?"

Grace groaned. She should have realized where this was going. "I know you mean well, but I don't want to go out with Todd or any other handsome young man."

Her mother regarded her with a sorrowful expression. "And that's exactly the problem. What's the media supposed to think if you become a recluse, living hidden away in the wilderness—"

"Mom, we're just forty minutes from LA. This is hardly the wilderness."

Waving her objection away, her mother continued, "Spending most of your time with your lesbian friends?"

"They're my friends, Mom. Yes, they happen to be lesbians, but that's not why I'm friends with them, and I'm not spending that much time with them lately." It had been five days since she'd last seen Lauren and three days since she'd last heard from her. Not that she was keeping track or anything. She hadn't seen much of Jill either. Truth be told, she'd avoided Jill, knowing she'd insist on talking about Lauren.

"But you're not spending much—or any—time with anyone else either. You don't go out."

"I just haven't felt like it with the cast and everything." Grace rubbed her fingers over the cast she'd been wearing for nearly two weeks now.

Her mother continued as if she hadn't spoken. "You show up at red-carpet events without a male companion. You don't have the slightest interest in any man. How long do you think it will be until the rumors about you being gay start again?"

Damn. As much as she hated to admit it, her mother was right. "So you and your new best friend, Richard, want me to do...what exactly?"

"Go have dinner with Todd. I hear he's nice. Maybe you'll like him. And if not..." Her mother shrugged. "Well, you're an actress. Act. You'll still get some gorgeous photos of the two of you in the press."

For a moment, Grace considered suggesting they call Lauren and ask her opinion about this publicity stunt, but she could vividly imagine what her mother would say to that idea, so she just nodded. "All right. I'll do it."

Her mother delivered a smacking kiss to her cheek. "Wonderful. I knew you'd be reasonable."

Reasonable, yeah. Grace watched as her mother pulled out her phone and went outside to the patio, the only place up here where the cell phone reception wasn't so spotty. She'd always been reasonable when it came to relationships—she'd gone out with Nick when a studio executive introduced them and she'd married him because it seemed like the right thing to do and because her mother had started to get worried about her squeaky-clean girl-next-door image after two years of living together. Reasonable Grace Durand would never do something stupid, would never act on impulse. What the heck did Lauren even see in her?

She shook her head at herself. Why was she thinking about Lauren again?

Her mother returned to the living room. "You've got a date. Saturday, at seven."

Grace inwardly groaned.

When Lauren passed Tina's desk on the way to get herself another cup of coffee, her colleague was clicking through celebrity gossip websites as part of her morning work routine.

Lauren's step faltered when one of the pictures on the gossip blog caught her attention. She would know those incredibly blue eyes smiling into the camera anywhere.

Tina turned. "Good job," she said, pointing at the blog. "Making her go out with the hottest hunk in soccer was a genius idea. The media is eating it up."

Lauren narrowed her eyes at the picture of Grace with that soccer Adonis. "I sure as hell didn't come up with this harebrained scheme. You should know me better than that. No publicist worth her money would suggest a stunt like that."

"Maybe it's not a PR stunt," Tina said. "They look pretty...friendly together."

Yeah, they did. Lauren took in the way Todd Walbert had his muscular arm wrapped around Grace's waist and the way she smiled up at him. It made her want to barf, even if a voice deep down whispered that this was how Grace smiled at the leading men in her movies too. It wasn't the kind of smile Grace had given Lauren when she'd kidnapped her to see the Eiffel Tower.

"Excuse me. I need more coffee." She walked past Tina without another glance at the picture on the computer screen.

By the third date, Grace had to admit that her stereotypical notions of what a sports star might be like had been completely wrong. To her surprise, Todd wasn't a chauvinist who talked about soccer all the time. He was funny, a great conversationalist, and as handsome and nice as her mother had said.

But there was no spark, no butterflies when he called to set up another date, no damp hands and weak knees when he said good-bye with a brief kiss on the lips, and definitely no desire to ask him in for anything more.

Todd nudged the dessert menu in her direction. "Come on. I need to keep my weight in check too, but making an exception every now and then can't hurt."

Grace regarded him with her arms crossed over her chest. "What is it with people always trying to get me to eat things that are bad for me?"

He shrugged and gave her a boyish grin. "Maybe we just don't want you to miss out on the little pleasures of life."

That sounded like something Lauren might have said. Sighing, Grace opened the dessert menu. Taking a look couldn't hurt. *Oh, they have coffee crème brûlée. Lauren would love that.*

"I'm having the banana custard pie," Todd announced. "How about you?"

"I'm not sure I should—"

The ringing of her cell phone interrupted. She pulled it out of her purse with an apologetic look. "Sorry. I forgot to turn it off." When she flipped the cover open to reject the call and turn the phone off, she saw the name on the display. *Lauren.* Her breath hitched. "Uh, it's my publicist. I have to take this."

Todd leaned back. "Go ahead."

Turning a little to the side for privacy, Grace accepted the call. "Hi, Lauren."

"Sorry to interrupt your evening," Lauren said. Her voice sounded a little husky, sending a shiver through Grace.

Oh, come on. She had worked with some of the most beautiful actresses in Hollywood. There had never been the slightest bit of attraction to any of them. Surely her weird reaction to Lauren, who by Hollywood standards was merely average-looking, was just a fluke. *You're imagining things. You're attracted to men. Just not Todd.*

"Grace?" Lauren's voice came through the phone.

"Uh, sorry. It's okay," she said, sounding a little raspy herself. "What can I do for you?"

Lauren coughed.

Had she been working late again? Grace frowned.

"You know how I've been trying to get you a new spot on *Good Morning America*?" Lauren said.

"Yes."

"Well, one of their guests canceled, so they have an opening, but it's the day after tomorrow."

"Are they pretaping it?"

"No. I want you to do it live," Lauren said. "That way, they can't edit anything out or present things out of context."

"Good thinking."

"Yeah, but it means you'll have to fly to New York tomorrow." Lauren coughed again. "Can you meet Tina at the airport tomorrow at ten? She'll have the interview questions and go over them with you. They're all pre-approved, so there won't be any surprises."

"Tina?"

"She's one of our account executives. Very competent."

Grace didn't care how competent Tina was. Why was Lauren suddenly trying to push her interviews off on a colleague instead of handling them herself? Was this how it would be between them from now on? Anger gripped her. "You know what? Maybe we should just forget about it."

"What? Why? Grace, *Good Morning America* is important. It could give the movie a new push."

"Well, it can't be that important if you're not even handling it yourself."

Static filtered through the line; then Lauren's husky voice was back. "Oh. You thought... Haven't you read my e-mail?"

"What e-mail? I went to one of Todd's games and now I'm at a restaurant, so I haven't checked my e-mail all day."

Another pause from Lauren. "I see. I sent you an e-mail this morning, telling you that I'm out sick for the rest of the week."

Grace's anger evaporated in an instant and was replaced by worry. "I didn't know. I thought you're coughing because you're tired."

"Not this time."

"Is it bad?" Grace asked.

More coughing rang through the phone. "I'll survive."

What was that supposed to mean? And why the hell was Lauren still arranging interviews for her when she was sick? "Have you seen a doctor?"

"Grace, I'm fine. You just worry about the interview, okay?"

"Yeah. You're completely fine. That's why you're out sick."

"It's just a stupid throat infection. No need to worry, really," Lauren said.

"Of course I worry," Grace said with more heat than intended. More calmly, she added, "I can't afford headlines about Grace Durand working her publicist to death."

Lauren's chuckle turned into a cough. "Right." She paused. "Good luck for the interview. Although you won't need it. You'll do just fine, even without me."

"I'm not worried." At least not about the appearance on *Good Morning America*. "You take good care of yourself, okay? No working."

"Yes, ma'am. I mean, no, ma'am."

"Why do I get the feeling that I'd have to court-martial you for disobeying orders if you were a soldier?"

Lauren laughed. "I have no idea."

For a moment, things were as they used to be between them, and Grace realized how much she'd missed their easy interaction. She didn't share that kind of friendship with anyone else. *Not even Jill?* a voice in her head asked. She thought about it for a moment. No, her friendship with Jill was different somehow.

They said good-bye and ended the call.

Grace put away the phone and faced Todd at the table. She'd almost forgotten that she was in a restaurant with him. "Sorry."

"Is everything okay?" he asked. "I didn't want to listen in, but you sounded pretty alarmed."

"I just found out that I have to fly to New York tomorrow for an appearance on *Good Morning America* and my publicist is sick."

Todd reached across the table and squeezed her hand. The touch didn't set off any sparks. "And now you're worried about being unprepared for the interview?"

"No. All of the questions are pre-approved, so it should be fine." Grace glanced at her watch. "Listen, could we cut this short and get the desserts to go? I'll have to get an early start tomorrow."

"Sure." He immediately signaled their waiter. "Would it be possible to order our desserts to go?"

"Of course," the waiter replied. "What would you like?"

"A piece of the banana custard pie for me, please, and..." Todd gestured at Grace.

She hesitated. *You're crazy. Just go home and get some sleep.* But for once, she didn't listen to reason. Instead, she heard herself say, "I'd like to have the coffee crème brûlée, please."

Paparazzi swarmed around them as soon as they left the restaurant.

"Is Todd the new man in your life, Grace?" one of them shouted while snapping away.

"Does Nick know?" another asked.

Grace ignored them and walked toward the town car the service had sent.

"I could have driven you home, you know?" Todd said.

"If you'd done that, the paparazzi would have kept following us, hoping to get a picture of a juicy good-night kiss."

Grinning, he wrapped one arm around her and pulled her against his side. "Well, then maybe we should give them what they want so they'll stop following us around."

Flashes went off all around them.

Grace turned toward him. When he leaned forward, she put one hand on his chest, stopping him while trying to make it look like a caress to the paparazzi. "Todd," she murmured. "You know this isn't real, right?"

"It could be," he whispered back.

She shook her head. "You're a nice guy, but…"

He groaned. "Don't give me the I-just-think-of-you-as-a-friend speech."

Grace poked him in the ribs in a buddy-like way. "Oh, come on. I don't imagine you hear that speech too often. I bet women are crazy for you."

"Just not you."

"Not me." Grace tried not to think about why that might be.

When Todd left, some of the paparazzi followed him. A few trailed the town car, but none braved the drive up to the cottage in the dark. Grace wanted to believe that they'd learned their lesson after her accident and would now stop hunting her no matter what, but the truth was that they were probably just worried for their cars.

She waited until she was fairly sure no paparazzi were hanging around on the main street, then got into her SUV. *This is crazy. Driving all the way back to LA for a dessert… Completely nuts.* On her way to Brentwood, she almost turned back around twice. But every time, an image of Lauren, suffering alone at home, urged her to continue. She found a parking spot a block away from Lauren's apartment building and kept her head down, hoping no one would recognize her as she carried the wrapped crème brûlée through Lauren's neighborhood. Even when she stood in front of the door, she wasn't sure she'd ring the doorbell or turn back around.

No big deal, she tried to tell herself. It was just dessert. Lauren had bought her ice cream when she'd been injured on location, and now she was returning the favor. Nothing more to it.

She pressed the buzzer before she could change her mind.

It seemed to take forever until Lauren's voice came through the intercom, sounding even hoarser than before. "Yes?"

Had she been sleeping? *God, this was a bad idea.*

"Who's there?" Lauren asked.

"Um, Lauren, it's me. Grace."

After an audible intake of breath, the buzzer sounded.

When Grace reached the apartment on the first floor, Lauren was waiting in the doorway, holding on to the door. Her short hair was tousled. She was wearing shorts and a T-shirt but no socks.

Grace immediately wanted to lecture her and then send her back to bed, but she bit her tongue. She wasn't Lauren's mother or her girlfriend.

"What are you doing here?" Lauren asked with her raspy voice. "I thought you were out with what's-his-name?"

As her publicist, Lauren had to know Todd's name, so Grace didn't supply it. She lifted the container with the crème brûlée. "Bringing you dessert."

A slow smile spread over Lauren's flushed features. "Ice cream?"

"No. Damn. I should have gotten that. It would have been better for your throat, right?"

Lauren pulled her into the apartment. "I'll take whatever I can get. I didn't feel up to grocery shopping today, and my fridge wasn't that well-stocked to start with."

Grace shook her head at her. "God, you really need a girlfriend to take care of you."

Lauren didn't answer, reminding Grace of where her romantic interests lay at the moment.

Great. Now things were awkward again. Grace looked around the apartment, anywhere but at Lauren.

The laptop stood open on the coffee table. Lauren had dragged the bed covers into the living room and had created herself a little nest on the couch. Grace gently pushed her toward it, guiding her with one hand against her back.

Lauren's body felt overly warm where she touched it. When Lauren sank onto the couch, she peered down into her flushed face and frowned. "Are you running a fever?"

"I don't think so."

"Let me see." She put the container down on the coffee table and bent over her. Lauren pulled back. "You don't need to…"

"Come on. Trust me. I once played a doctor on TV, you know?"

The husky sound of Lauren's laughter created goose bumps all over Grace's arms.

"Well," Lauren said, "since you're so highly qualified, go ahead." She held still as Grace softly touched her forehead. Her flush deepened and then slowly lessened when Grace took her hand away and stepped back.

It took a few seconds for Grace to understand. *Oh.* Lauren wasn't running a fever. Her body was just reacting to Grace's closeness.

"What's the diagnosis, Doc? Will I live?"

"I'm pretty sure you'll survive." Grace turned away and searched the small kitchen for a spoon. She took her time, using the minute alone, where Lauren couldn't see her, to get herself back together. *We're adults. We can deal with this.* Spoon in hand, she marched back to the couch. "Here."

Eagerly, Lauren removed the aluminum foil from the container and peeked in. "What is it? Crème brûlée?"

"Not just any crème brûlée. It's coffee crème brûlée."

"Ooh!" Lauren dug in, breaking the crust, and lifted a spoonful of the dessert to her mouth. Her eyes fluttered shut, and a moan escaped her lips. "Oh my God," she mumbled around the spoon and then slowly withdrew it. "That's so good."

Her throat suddenly dry, Grace swallowed. "I'm glad you like it."

"Like it?" Lauren shook her head and took another spoonful. "I love it. This is exactly what the doctor ordered." She lowered the container for a moment and looked into Grace's eyes. "Thank you."

"You're welcome," Grace said. She watched Lauren enjoy her treat for a few moments longer and then tore herself away. "I should go. If I don't get enough sleep, the makeup artist at the interview won't be very happy with me."

Lauren put the container down. "Are you sure it's safe to drive up to the cottage in the darkness?"

"It's no problem at all. I've done it a thousand times."

The worried frown didn't disappear from Lauren's face. "Not with just one arm."

"The SUV has power steering," Grace said.

"Still. A while ago, you didn't even want to get in a car."

Grace didn't like the reminder, but she appreciated Lauren's concern. "That was four weeks ago, right after the accident. I'm over it now."

"Just be careful, okay?"

"I promise to be careful if you promise to stop working and go to bed." Grace pointed at the laptop. "Deal?"

Lauren hesitated. "I need to finish—"

"Please. For me."

"You're fighting dirty," Lauren grumbled but obediently reached out and closed the laptop. "There. Happy now?"

"Yes. Thanks." Grace slowly made her way to the door. When Lauren moved to follow her, she waved her back, not wanting her to step onto the cold tiles by the entrance with her bare feet. At the door, she turned.

Their gazes met across the room.

A thousand thoughts rushed through Grace's mind. She latched on to a straightforward, uncomplicated one and said, "Get better soon."

"I'll do my best. Have a safe flight."

After one last glance, Grace stepped outside and closed the door. She stood in the corridor, staring off into space for God knew how long.

One of Lauren's neighbors went by with a garbage bag and did a double take when he saw Grace.

She kicked herself into motion and hurried back to her car.

CHAPTER 26

THIS ATTRACTION WAS REACHING A ridiculous level. Lauren shook her head at herself. Grace had been back from New York for a couple of days already, but Lauren still hadn't talked over the fall schedule with her. She had even contemplated having Tina take over as Grace's publicist for good, but how could she justify it to her boss?

Sorry, Marlene, but I have trouble thinking straight—pun intended—whenever she's around? Lauren made a face. No, she couldn't do that, especially not now that Marlene had started talking about promoting her as a reward for how well she'd handled Grace's marketing campaign. She'd just have to grin and bear it. At some point, this damn attraction had to fade away if she just gave it time, right?

But the more time went by, the more Lauren began to doubt whether it was really just physical attraction. This wasn't some starstruck infatuation with a gorgeous celebrity. When she thought of Grace—which was more often than she liked to admit—she didn't think of her all made up in a cocktail dress and stilettos, showing off her curves and her famous smile on the red carpet. She thought of the travel-weary woman with the black eye who had enjoyed her ice cream with childlike glee. She thought of Grace hanging on to the ivy-covered wall for dear life, peering down at the lights of Paris from the Eiffel Tower, watching the sun set over Topanga Canyon, and doing the dishes after having hot dogs with Lauren.

She longed for one more of those moments with Grace, but since she'd blabbed her less-than-professional feelings, they both didn't know how to act around each other anymore.

With a frustrated growl, she grabbed her keys and the thick, red folder on her desk and headed out.

"Hi." Lauren stood on the cottage's doorstep, holding a red file folder with both hands.

The flush was gone from her features, and the dark circles under her eyes had faded. Relief trickled through Grace at seeing her look so healthy. "Hi. Come on in. You look good... I mean, healthy." She mentally rolled her eyes and told herself to relax. It was perfectly okay for a straight woman to tell a friend she looked good, wasn't it?

"Yeah. Thanks. I feel much better," Lauren said as she followed her to the stone patio.

A small lizard fled as they stepped outside and settled at the table.

"How's the arm?" Lauren asked.

"Itching like crazy." Grace trailed her fingernails over the cast as if that would help. "I can't wait to get this thing off."

A wrinkle formed between Lauren's brows as she stared at the cast.

Grace followed her gaze and realized Lauren was looking at the autograph Todd had insisted on placing on the cast. She covered it with her hand and barely resisted the urge to explain. Lauren wasn't her girlfriend or anything; Grace didn't owe her an explanation.

Lauren tore her gaze away from the cast and placed the red file folder on the table. "Shall we get started?"

Her businesslike tone was unexpectedly hurtful. Grace bit her lip and nodded. She opened her day planner so they could go over her appointments and promo opportunities for the next three months.

Lauren leafed through calendar pages. "The awards season starts in November, so we should have you sit down for interviews with *Entertainment Tonight* and all the other big outlets next month."

"All right." Grace didn't look forward to more interviews, but they were part of her job.

Clicking her pen on and off a few times, Lauren said, "There's one thing we should talk about before that." More clicking. "Now that the media knows about your impending divorce, they'll pepper you with questions about your private life. What are you going to tell them about Todd Walbert?"

Grace sighed. "What do you think I should tell them?"

Lauren dropped the pen on the open file. "Depends on what's going on between the two of you."

"Nothing. I mean, we went out three times, but I don't see it going anywhere."

"So you'll stop seeing him?"

If only she could do that. "My mother thinks I should keep going out with him."

"That's what your mother thinks, but what do you think?" Lauren asked.

"I don't know." Grace put her elbow on the table and rubbed her forehead with the base of her thumb. "I don't want to go out with him, but—"

"Then don't do it."

"It's not that easy."

"Yes, it is." Lauren snapped the folder closed. "You're an adult and don't have to do what your mother tells you."

"You don't understand."

"Damn right." Lauren's voice became louder. Her eyes sparked. "I don't understand why you keep letting your mother run your life and pretending to be fine with whatever she wants."

What the hell was going on with Lauren? Where was all that anger coming from? Grace had done nothing to deserve that kind of treatment. She felt her own temper rise too. "I'm not letting her run my life; she just guides my career."

"Yeah, and what exactly qualifies her to do that?" Sarcasm dripped off Lauren's words. "The fact that she's a former actress that never amounted to anything? Can't you see that not all of her advice is based on what's best for your career? She just wants you to date that soccer player because—"

"Oh, so that's what this is really about. This isn't about me or my mother. You're just jealous of Todd!"

"Bullshit!" Lauren smashed the folder onto the table, making it rattle. "I'm trying to do my job as a publicist."

Grace snorted. "Oh yeah. That's why you're shouting at me. Very professional."

"I wouldn't need to shout if you'd listen to me. Your mother's advice is bringing you right back to the tabloids' attention, and I know that's not what you want. But your mother doesn't give a damn about what—"

"Don't talk about my mother like that! She gave up everything for me—her own career, her friends, and her home back in Illinois—to focus on my career."

"You never asked her to do that."

"No," Grace said, struggling not to shout, "but she did."

"And now you have to give up your own life in return?"

"Who says that's what I'm doing?"

Lauren raised her chin and looked into her eyes, challenging her. "When was the last time you ordered dessert without earning a dirty look from your mother or feeling guilty?"

Grace opened her mouth to say something, but Lauren just kept talking.

"When was the last time you did something, anything, just because you felt like it, without wondering what your mother or anyone else would think?"

"I do that all the time," Grace said. Goddammit, Lauren was making her sound like a child who couldn't even decide what clothes to put on in the morning without her mother's approval! She shoved her chair back from the table and marched to the edge of the patio, staring down at Topanga Canyon without really seeing it.

Lauren's chair scraped over the stone floor as she got up and stormed after her. "No, you don't. Even now when you're spitting mad at me, you walk away and avoid any conflict instead of saying what you're really thinking."

Hands clenched into fists, Grace whirled around and found herself almost nose to nose with Lauren. Her perfume mingled with the canyon's sage scent and teased Grace's flared nostrils. The fine hairs on her arms prickled with the tension between them.

"You're acting and pretending all the time. Why don't you turn off the stage instructions in your head for once and show some real emotion?"

Blood roared through Grace's ears. The urge to slap Lauren or do something, anything, to make her stop talking gripped her. "You want emotion?" she ground out through gritted teeth. "How about this?" She grabbed Lauren by the lapels of her leather blazer and roughly pulled her forward.

Their bodies collided; then Grace's lips were on Lauren's.

She'd meant for it to be hard, punishing, but at the touch of soft lips against hers, something ignited inside her. The kiss gentled. It lasted for only a couple of thudding heartbeats, not long enough for Lauren to push her away—or kiss her back.

Heat zinged through Grace. She pulled back with a gasp.

In the sudden silence between them, Lauren's sharp intake of breath sounded overly loud. She reached up and touched her lips. Her fingers trembled. She stared at Grace with wide eyes, her pupils so large that only hazel rings remained of her irises.

Grace pressed her hand to her own mouth, where the kiss still seemed to sear through her. "Oh God. I'm so sorry. I didn't…"

Lauren reached for her, but Grace quickly stumbled back, almost afraid of what would happen if she let Lauren touch her now.

"Grace, please. Talk to me."

She roughly shook her head. "I can't. Not now." Her brain was on overload, and she struggled to form even one halfway clear thought. "Please. Can you…? I need some time alone."

Still breathing heavily, Lauren searched her face or maybe searched for something to say. Finally, she just nodded. "Once you can talk about it, please call me."

Her lips pressed together, Grace made a vague sound of agreement.

Lauren lifted one hand as if to touch Grace's arm before seeming to change her mind and making it a short wave. Then she was gone. The sliding door clicked shut behind her.

Grace collapsed onto one of the patio chairs and let her head drop onto the red file folder Lauren had left behind.

CHAPTER 27

LAUREN HID IN THE SMALL kitchen, preparing the dressing for the salad and trying to ignore her parents' arguing in the living area. For once, it was easy to do since her mind wasn't on what was going on in her apartment anyway.

In between adding vinegar, olive oil, and salt, her hand kept returning to her lips. She could still feel Grace's mouth on hers, even after two days, seven hours, and about twenty minutes. To say that the kiss had thrown her for a loop was an understatement. It hadn't been just the kiss itself, that all-too-short contact of their lips, but the fact that Grace had chosen that way to end their argument.

What did it mean? If the kiss was supposed to prove that Grace wasn't always acting, did it indicate that Grace felt something for her too? Or had it just been Hollywood's age-old method of manipulation, an attempt to win the discussion by whatever means available?

Lauren shook her head. She couldn't make herself believe that Grace would manipulate her like that and use Lauren's feelings against her. Besides, Grace had appeared just as shaken by her actions as Lauren. Confusion and panic had been obvious in her widened eyes, forcing Lauren to back off and leave.

Even if Grace felt something more than friendship for her, the chances that she would ever act on her feelings again were slim to none. Doing so would seriously affect her career. *And yours too. Getting involved with a client—and not just any client...* Marlene wouldn't tolerate it. No matter how she looked at it, there just wasn't any future for her and Grace. Lauren slumped against the kitchen counter.

"Can the salad go on the table?" her mother asked right next to her.

Lauren jumped and dropped the spoon she'd been holding. She quickly poured the dressing over the salad and tossed it. "All ready."

They settled at the dining table and started to eat. Her parents discussed upcoming red-carpet events they would attend together, as usual giving the impression of a happily married couple. Lauren knew that they'd fight in the limo, up until the moment they stepped into the spotlight. It was a reminder not to get involved with an actress. Nothing was real in Hollywood.

That brief kiss, the heat of Grace's body against hers, and then the confusion in Grace's eyes had felt real, though.

Lauren pushed her food from one side of the plate to the other, making herself crazy with what-ifs. She listened to their conversation with one ear while half her attention remained on her cell phone, in case Grace called.

Her father let out a gasp, reached for his glass, and gulped down the wine. When they stared at him, he waved at his plate with flushed cheeks. "What the hell did you put in that salad?"

"The usual." Lauren carefully tried a bit of the salad—and nearly spat it back out. The dressing tasted as if she'd used an entire bottle of vinegar. "I'm sorry. I must have lost track of how much vinegar I put in." *More like you've lost your mind.*

The ringing of her cell phone made her jump. Her knee hit the table, making the plates rattle. *Grace!* With trembling fingers, she pulled out her phone. When she saw that it was Jill, relief and disappointment warred within her.

Her parents had always found it perfectly normal to answer business calls during dinner, so she lifted the phone to her ear. "Hi, Jill," she said, trying to sound cheerful, as if she hadn't been moping around for the last two days. "What can I do for my favorite client?"

Jill let out an unladylike snort. "Don't bother. I know who your favorite client is, and it's not me."

Was she that obvious? *Shit.* None of her clients had ever been privy to her personal feelings, and now not one but two clients had breached that barrier. The thing that had always been most important to Lauren—absolute professionalism— had gone out the window the moment she'd met Grace.

"Lauren? Is everything all right?" Jill asked when Lauren remained silent.

"Yeah. Everything's fine. It's just... I have guests over for dinner."

"Oh. Sorry. I didn't mean to interrupt," Jill said quickly. "I just wanted to talk to you about a fundraiser I thought Grace and I could do. I'll run it by Grace first and then get back to you."

It was crazy, but just the mention of Grace's name made Lauren's heart beat faster. She even found herself a little jealous. Jill could call Grace while she had to wait for Grace to contact her. She suppressed a sigh. "Sounds good."

When they ended the call, she considered turning off the phone before returning to her dinner. Her finger hovered over the power button. No. She couldn't do it. Reason might tell her to stay away from Grace, but her heart said something else. Besides, one of her other clients—or even Grace, if she had a media emergency— might try to reach her, so she couldn't just turn off the phone. Whatever happened, she had to be as professional as possible. She put the phone on the table, where she could see it while she continued to poke at her now nearly cold food.

Grace had probably lost a few pounds pacing the cottage in the last three days. She couldn't sleep. She couldn't eat. All she could do was replay that moment out on the patio over and over again. Sometimes, her tired mind showed her alternative endings to the encounter—once or twice, imaginary Lauren pushed her away, but most often, she wrapped her arms around Grace and kissed her back with a passion that made Grace's head spin.

At night, when she lay on the sleeper sofa and stared at the dark ceiling, her amazingly clear memory of the softness of Lauren's lips, the smoothness of her skin, the heat of her body mingled with scenes from that damn fan fiction story she'd read.

Had that been why she'd reacted so strongly to the lesbian love scene in that story? Was she attracted to women—to Lauren?

Impossible. She had spent her life around beautiful women. If she were gay or bisexual, she would have noticed by now. There'd been nothing more than fleeting glances and professional admiration for other actresses who knew how to make the most out of what they had. That was perfectly normal, even for straight women, right?

But that kiss... Straight women didn't do that. They didn't feel what she'd felt when they touched the lips of another woman with her own—if they'd ever do such a thing.

Grace groaned. Maybe a soak in the hot tub, with her cast carefully wrapped in a plastic bag, would help her clear her head. But when she pushed open the sliding doors and stepped onto the patio, her gaze landed on the spot where she'd kissed Lauren.

The ringing of her phone interrupted another replay.

Her heartbeat sped up at the thought that it might be Lauren. *God, I'm not ready for that conversation.* She pulled the phone out of her pocket and walked to the corner of the patio with the best reception before answering the phone.

"Hi, stranger," Jill's voice came from the other end of the line. "I haven't heard from you in a while. How are you doing?"

"I'm fine," Grace said before she could even think about her answer. God, Lauren was right. She was acting a lot, even when she talked to her best friend.

"So, what's new with you?" Jill asked.

Everything. Nothing seemed to be the same anymore. Even things she'd always taken for granted were now called into question. "Not much," she answered and wondered whether that sounded as lame to Jill as it did to her. "I decided not to go out with Todd anymore."

"Good," Jill said. "I never understood why you thought going out with him just for appearance's sake was a good PR strategy. I bet Lauren didn't like it either."

"No, she didn't." Before Jill could delve into the reason Lauren didn't like her dating Todd, Grace said, "Enough about me. What have you been up to?"

Jill blew out a noisy breath. "Not much. My career seems to be in a lull at the moment."

A bitter taste flooded Grace's mouth. "Do you think that's because you came out?" One more reason why she had to get these crazy thoughts about Lauren and their kiss out of her mind. Her career had been the focus of her life for thirty years. She couldn't risk that now.

"Hard to tell. Whatever it is, I'm not going to sit around and feel sorry for myself while I wait for the rest of Hollywood to get their heads out of their asses."

The way I do. Despite the MS that sometimes weakened her body, Jill was so much stronger than she was. "Have I ever told you how much I admire you?"

"Enough to wait tables with me?" Jill asked.

Grace frowned. "Uh, things aren't that bad financially, are they? Because you know I could always lend you—"

Jill's laughter interrupted her. "No. That's not what I meant. There'll be a benefit dinner in two weeks where celebrities will wait tables. The money raised goes to unemployed actors and their families."

Grace had been lucky. Unlike many of her colleagues, she'd never had to work in a restaurant or at any job other than acting. "That sounds like a good thing. Count me in. Maybe we can even get Amanda to join us."

"I already asked her, but with her shooting schedule, she can't make it. But we should get Lauren to beat the big advertisement drum so we'll get some big tippers at the tables."

Just when Grace had stopped thinking about her for a second, Jill had to mention her name again.

"Knowing you, you'll talk to Lauren before I do," Jill said. "Can you let her know? I tried to call her yesterday, but she had someone over for dinner and couldn't talk."

Lauren had had dinner with someone? Grace immediately started wondering whether it had been a woman. *Oh, come on. You're not jealous, are you?*

"Earth to Grace? You'll ask her, won't you?"

"Um, can't you do it?"

Jill was silent for a moment. "Did you and Lauren have a fight or something?"

"Or something," Grace muttered.

"What happened?"

Grace couldn't talk about it yet, not even to her best friend. Not when she barely understood it herself. "Nothing."

"You don't expect me to believe that, do you? I know you better than that. You usually go out of your way to avoid conflicts, so if you and Lauren got into a fight, something must have happened."

Her friend wouldn't let it go. Grace knew that. "Lauren said something she probably shouldn't have said. And then I did something I *definitely* shouldn't have done."

"Did you slap her?" Jill asked.

"What? No!"

"Then it couldn't have been that bad."

Grace sighed. "You have no idea."

"I don't. Because you won't tell me anything." A bit of hurt vibrated in Jill's tone.

"It's not that I don't want to. I just… I can't."

"Then at least go and talk to Lauren. She sounded a little off when I talked to her. Whatever happened affected her too. You need to clear the air."

Jill was right; Grace knew that. She had kissed Lauren out of the blue, in the middle of an argument, and then sent her away. Poor Lauren was probably just as confused as Grace was. She had to face her sooner or later. Her stomach tightened at the mere thought. "I will."

"Good. And if you need someone to talk to—someone other than Lauren, I mean—let me know."

"Thank you," Grace said around the big lump in her throat.

When they ended the call, she stood on the patio and stared at the phone in her hand. Should she call Lauren? But what would she say?

Finally, after ten minutes of internal debate, she decided to drive to Brentwood and see if Lauren was home. *What if she doesn't want to see me?* She hesitated, then decided to try anyway. Anything was better than sitting around in the cottage, driving herself crazy for three more days. At least the drive to Brentwood would give her forty more minutes to think about what to say—or to change her mind and turn back around.

For the first time in her life, Lauren couldn't focus on work, so she left the office on time for a change. At home, she tried to write a little and revise her script, but all it did was remind her of Grace, who'd been the one to suggest the rewrite.

Groaning, she pushed the laptop away and ran both hands through her hair. It seemed Grace had finally succeeded in stopping her from being such a workaholic—just by kissing her. That single touch of Grace's lips had turned her life upside down in a way nothing else ever had.

The doorbell rang.

Her heart beat a rapid staccato against her ribcage as she walked to the intercom. *Calm down. That's probably just Mrs. Tuckerman needing to borrow a cup of sugar or something.* But that internal reprimand didn't stop her from half-hoping, half-fearing that it might be Grace. Every phone call or new e-mail she had received during the last three days had started that wild rush of emotions. Each time, it had been someone else, though.

"Yes?"

Only silence answered.

She peered through the peephole. The corridor in front of the apartment was empty, so it couldn't be her neighbor.

Just when she was about to put it off as some prank from the neighborhood kids and return to the couch, the intercom crackled to life.

"It's me. Grace."

Lauren stood at the door, frozen. Now that Grace had finally contacted her, she didn't know what to say, afraid to scare her away.

"Lauren?"

"Uh, yeah," Lauren said into the speaker. "Sorry. Come on up." She pressed the buzzer to let her in. Her gaze darted from the dishes in the drain board to the papers strewn across the coffee table. Too late to clean it all up. Grace would be here in a minute. She glanced down at her T-shirt and shorts, making sure there were no stains. *Christ, calm down. I doubt Grace cares about what you're wearing or what the apartment looks like.*

A light rap sounded on the door.

Lauren wiped her damp palms on her shorts and opened it.

After not seeing her or speaking to her for three days, being in Grace's presence again was electrifying. Lauren drank her in—the tousled hair, the makeup-free face, the dark circles around her eyes. She was beautiful, but it was easy to see that Grace hadn't been sleeping either. What did it mean?

"Um, hi," Grace said.

"Hi."

When Grace shifted her weight, Lauren realized they were still facing each other across the doorway. "Oh. Please, come on in."

Grace entered and looked around as if she'd never seen Lauren's apartment before. Or maybe she was just trying to avoid looking at Lauren.

"Why don't we...?" Lauren pointed at the couch.

They sat at opposite ends of the sofa, the still-open laptop between them.

Lauren peered over at her, wishing Grace would say something, but at the same time afraid of what it would be. "Do you...do you want something to drink? Coffee or water or...I'm not sure what else I have, but I can take a look." She leaned forward to get up.

Grace reached over and clasped her sleeve, holding her in place, and then quickly pulled her hand back. "No. I...I just want to get this over with."

Lauren's entire body went cold. That didn't sound promising. "O-okay." She sank back against the couch cushions. Half turning, she stared at Grace and waited for what she would say. *Breathe, you idiot, or the only thing she'll say is that your lips are turning blue.*

After endless seconds of just staring straight ahead, tugging at the frayed gauze on the edge of her cast, Grace finally looked at her. Her blue eyes had darkened to the color of the ocean during a storm. "Maybe I shouldn't have come. I don't know if I can talk about this. Not in a way that makes sense."

Lauren gripped the armrest. She didn't want Grace to leave, damning her to stay in that perpetual loop of hope and fear. "Please. Try."

Grace nodded. She pulled Betty from the back of the couch and buried her face against the lynx's soft fur.

It hurt to see her struggle like this. Lauren nudged the laptop toward Grace. "Do you think this would help?"

Grace lifted her head and glanced at the screen, where Lauren's script was still open. Her brow furrowed, and she sent Lauren a questioning gaze. "Your script? How's that supposed to help?"

"Not the script. Writing. If you can't talk about it, maybe writing will be easier. It always helps me think more clearly." Lauren took the laptop, opened a new document, and typed a couple of lines before handing it back.

> LAUREN
> See? This is what I mean.
> Talk to me. Please.

A slow smile chased away some of the tension on Grace's face. "You're such a geek."

The warm affection in her voice gave Lauren hope. "Is that a good thing?"

"I think so." Grace pulled the laptop closer and let her fingers hover over the keyboard. They were trembling.

Lauren wanted to place her hand over Grace's fingers and give them an encouraging squeeze, but she forced herself to sit still and wait.

Slowly, using only her good hand, Grace started typing. She hesitated often as if fighting with every word. Finally, she paused and turned the laptop a little.

Lauren slid closer so she could read what Grace had written. Since she was wearing shorts, she could feel the warmth of Grace's leg against hers. *Focus.* She drew a deep breath and then looked at the screen.

> GRACE
> I really need to apologize for
> ambushing you like that. I didn't…

> I don't know what I was thinking. I
> just wanted you to stop talking.

Lauren pulled the laptop over so she could type her reply.

> LAUREN
> Yeah, that certainly shut me up. But
> was that really all there was to it?

She handed the laptop back to Grace, who sat staring at the screen and gnawing on her lip for several seconds before slowly starting to type.

Lauren waited with bated breath until she could finally read Grace's answer.

> GRACE
> At that moment, I didn't think so.
> But now…I just don't know. God, I
> can't believe I just kissed you.

Too impatient to keep passing the laptop back and forth, Lauren cleared her throat and asked, "Do you regret it?"

> GRACE
> Yes. No. I don't know up from down
> right now, Lauren. I've never been
> attracted to another woman before.

Never before… Lauren latched on to those words with the desperate hope of a drowning woman grasping a lifeline. "And now?" she asked. "Are you…do you think you could be attracted to me?"

With fingers that were visibly trembling, Grace typed three words.

> GRACE
> (whispering)
> Yes.

She closed the laptop with a soft click and looked up at Lauren. "I don't know what this is or where it'll go. I don't know if it can go anywhere. I mean, the two of us just spent the last three months denying to the press and the world that I'm gay, and now…"

Lauren reached out and gently laid one finger against Grace's mouth, interrupting her. As her fingertip touched the soft lips, she had to stop herself from stroking them. "Let's not think that far ahead. For now, this is between you and me. No press. No world. Can you do that?"

Grace's shuddery exhale brushed her finger, and she pulled it back so Grace could answer. "I think so." She closed her eyes for a moment as if letting what she'd just said sink in. When she opened them again, her expression was so vulnerable that Lauren wanted to hug her close. "Right now, I'm not sure of much, not even of my own feelings. But I know one thing for sure: I don't want to end up hurting you or our friendship."

"Me neither."

Their hands found each other, and both squeezed softly.

If Lauren forced herself to be realistic for a second, she knew the chances that they would ever be more than friends were slim. Even if Grace was attracted to her, she might run, scared of her own feelings and their consequences; her boss might fire her; Grace's career might suffer. There were a thousand reasons why she shouldn't even think about pursuing anything more than friendship with Grace. It was crazy, really, but for now, she didn't want to think about any of that. All she wanted was to focus on the way it felt to hold Grace's hand and let herself imagine that this little bit of intimacy was just the beginning. "I don't want to pressure you into anything you don't want. If this," she pointed back and forth between them with her free hand, "isn't right for you, then I'll deal with it and be your friend. But I'd really like to see where things are going, if you're willing to do that."

Grace looked at her for a while. Lauren had no idea what answers she was seeking and if she found them. Eventually, Grace whispered, "Okay."

Joy flowed through Lauren. She felt like jumping up and doing a jig through her apartment, but she knew it was much too soon for any sort of celebration. Grace still looked tense. Time to lighten the mood. "Good. Now that we've got that settled..." Lauren gave her an exaggerated leer and a wink. "Want to make out?"

The tension in the room broke when Grace burst out laughing. She let go of Lauren's hand, grabbed Betty the lynx, and hit Lauren with the stuffed animal. "You!"

"What!" Lauren warded off the playful attack with both hands. "It's what the characters in love stories always do after heartfelt discussions like the one we just had, isn't it?"

"I thought you don't write love stories?"

Lauren's lips curved up into a soft smile. "I'm thinking about changing that."

"Yeah?"

Lauren nodded. Inadvertently, her gaze was drawn down, to Grace's mouth. God, she wanted so much to lean over and kiss her, but she knew she had to let Grace take that step. She forced her gaze away from those tempting lips.

Grace placed the laptop on the coffee table and got up. "I think I should go. It's getting dark and I'm pretty tired. You look like you could use some sleep too."

Truth be told, Lauren was exhausted, but she still didn't want Grace to go. She also didn't like the thought of her making the drive up the canyon alone. "I know you love staying at the cottage, but I really don't like the thought of you driving up the dirt road at night."

"I told you I've done it a thousand times before."

"Yeah, but you look like you haven't slept in days." Images of Grace falling asleep at the wheel and crashing darted through her mind.

Grace rubbed her eyes. "I haven't."

"Me neither."

With a wry grin, Grace shook her head. "We're quite the pair, aren't we?"

"I think we could be," Lauren said quietly.

Their gazes met. Something sparked between them; then Grace looked away. "I could stay with Jill tonight, if that would make you feel better."

"Or you could sleep here, with me," Lauren said.

"Uh…" Grace stared at her.

Lauren laughed. "Get your mind out of the gutter, superstar. I'm talking about a perfectly innocent sleepover, nothing else. We wouldn't even sleep in the same room."

Grace blushed a lovely shade of fuchsia, making Lauren smile.

"So," Lauren said, deciding to go easy on Grace and not tease her any further, "what do you think? Would you like to stay?"

Wordlessly, Grace nodded.

"Come on, then. Let's get you settled in the bedroom. I'm sleeping on the couch."

Grace stared into the darkness. The bedroom surrounding her was as unfamiliar as the feelings coursing through her. *God, what am I doing?* A part of her wanted to rush out into the living room, shake Lauren awake, and tell her that this was crazy and they could never be anything but friends.

But was that really what she wanted—or was that just her fear talking? If there were no cameras, no pressure from her fans, the media, and the studio, no mother with high expectations of her only offspring, what would she, Grace, want for herself?

She realized that she had never before allowed herself to think about it. When she'd found out about Jill's diagnosis, she had thought about her regrets and the things she *didn't* want in her life—being married to a man she was fond of but didn't love with all her heart—but she had never wondered what it was she wanted instead.

For close to thirty years, a successful career as an actress had been all she'd wanted. At least she had thought so. *Okay, so maybe you want more from life, but...a woman? Really?*

She buried her face in the pillow, as if that would help drown out her racing thoughts. All it did was make her inhale a whiff of Lauren's scent, which clung to the pillowcase. It was soothing and exciting at the same time.

Grunting, she turned onto her back. She was exhausted but still couldn't sleep. Her brain bombarded her with all kinds of thoughts and questions. What would her mother say when she found out where she'd spent the night? What would happen to her career if she did get involved with Lauren? What would it feel like to kiss her again?

Whoa. Sleep. You need sleep.

The bedroom door creaked open, and Lauren tiptoed inside.

Grace sat up in bed. "Lauren? What are you doing up?"

"Oh. Sorry. I didn't want to wake you. I just need the bathroom." Her bare feet padded closer. The light on the bedside table flared on, and they both blinked into the sudden brightness. "Are you okay?"

"Yeah. I just couldn't sleep."

"Me neither." Lauren shuffled her feet and coughed once. Without her glasses, in just a T-shirt and a pair of boxer shorts, she looked young and vulnerable.

Adorable. Grace couldn't help smiling.

"Well, it's still pretty early." Lauren pointed toward the living room. "Want to watch a movie with me?"

Grace nodded.

"Great." Lauren smiled like a little girl who'd been promised a visit to the fair. "Why don't you look through my DVDs to see if there's anything you'd like to watch while I use the bathroom?"

Grace climbed out of bed and tugged on the T-shirt Lauren had given her, very aware of the fact that it ended mid-thigh. When Lauren entered the bathroom, she went outside to the living area and looked through her DVD collection.

Most of the DVDs Lauren owned were thrillers, mysteries, and science fiction movies. She didn't even seem to have any lesbian romance flicks. Grace shook her head at herself. It was probably better that way. She didn't need any more images in her head, or she'd never go to sleep tonight.

"Found anything interesting?" Lauren asked behind her.

Grace jumped. *Relax. It's just Lauren.* But she knew she was lying to herself. It being Lauren was what made her so nervous. "Uh, not yet." She pulled out a familiar-looking DVD, then another and stared down at her own face. "I thought you're not that fond of romances?"

"I'm not." Lauren flushed as she added, "I'm just fond of the lead actress."

"Oh."

Before the silence between them could go on for too long, Lauren said, "Although your hair in that one movie nearly turned it into a horror film." She tapped one of the DVD boxes.

Grace groaned. "Oh God, yes. I kept wondering what drugs the hair stylist was taking, but whatever it was, everyone else on set seemed to be on the same stuff, because they kept telling me how great I looked."

"Want to watch that one?" Lauren asked.

"No, thanks. I can't relax when I watch my own movies. I keep critiquing myself, finding ways I could have made the scene better."

Lauren nodded. "I know what you mean. I can't read one of my own scripts without doing that either."

See? This isn't so bad. Despite the turbulent emotions coursing through her, they were still friends who could relate to each other in ways that Grace had rarely experienced before. "Why don't you pick the movie? I haven't seen most of these, so I'd be fine with whatever you want."

Lauren stepped next to her to look at the shelf. Their shoulders brushed, making Grace's breath catch. "How about *Gravity*?"

Grace raised one brow. "Sandra Bullock as an astronaut?"

"She was really good in that role. I'd love to see you doing what she did some day."

"Fight for my life in outer space?"

"Go from starring mostly in romantic movies and comedies to taking on more challenging roles."

"You want me to stop playing it safe," Grace said.

Lauren gently pulled her around to face her. "If you're happy with the kind of movies you've been making, then you should stick with them and I'll fully support you. But I think you have a lot more in you. You shouldn't be so afraid to try something new."

Were they still just talking about her career?

Lauren plucked the DVD from the shelf and held it up for Grace to see. "So?"

"*Gravity* it is."

They settled on the couch, their feet up on the coffee table and Lauren's blanket covering both of their laps. After a while, Grace's feet got cold, so she curled them under her.

Lauren did the same.

Their bare knees brushed. If Lauren noticed, she didn't seem to mind. Grace found that she didn't mind either. Quite the opposite. She enjoyed the touch, innocent and strangely intimate at the same time. Neither of them moved her leg away.

Lauren seemed to fully immerse herself in the movie despite her occasional coughing. She flinched when space debris almost hit the astronauts and raised her hands as if to protect her own face from the impact.

Grace watched her as much as she watched the movie, smiling at how involved she got. Lauren had been right, though. Sandra Bullock was good in this movie. And she looked fantastic for a woman approaching fifty. Grace tested herself by studying her fellow actress when she was stripping off her spacesuit a little later in the movie, wearing just a tight tank top and boy-cut panties.

Nothing. The sight left her as unaffected as George Clooney, who played the commander of the space mission.

The warmth of Lauren's knee against her own, however, made her heart beat a little faster.

An hour into the movie, she realized that Lauren had gone quiet, no longer commenting on the scenes or rooting for the characters. She had even stopped coughing.

Grace turned her head to look at her.

Lauren's head had fallen back against the couch. Her eyes were closed and her mouth slightly open. Her chest rose and fell in the peaceful rhythm of sleep.

The movie forgotten, Grace sat watching her sleep. She took in her features—the strong jaw, the stubborn chin, the thick lashes that fluttered behind the glasses Lauren had put on to watch the movie. Grace's fingers itched to trace the curve of Lauren's cheekbones.

Lauren murmured something and smacked her lips in her sleep.

A smile tugged on the corners of Grace's mouth. *Too cute.*

Lauren's head slid lower, resting in an uncomfortable angle against the back of the couch.

Grace reached for the remote control and turned off the movie and the TV. The room went dark, the only light now coming from a streetlamp somewhere outside. She slid from the couch and bent over Lauren, gently trying to pull her around and down into a lying position. But Lauren was unexpectedly heavy. "Come on, Lauren. You can't sleep this way. You need to lie down."

"Hmm?"

"Lie down," Grace repeated.

Lauren peered up at her through barely open eyes and mumbled something that sounded like, "You too."

"Um, the couch is too small for the two of us."

Lauren blinked up at her, clearly not understanding a word Grace said. A smooth seductress Lauren was not.

Grace grinned and finally got Lauren to stretch out on the couch. Gently, she removed Lauren's glasses, folded them, and placed them within easy reach on the coffee table.

When she turned back around, Lauren's eyes were now fully closed. Grace hesitated, but with Lauren sleeping she had the courage to give in to the impulse to bend down and kiss her forehead, lingering against the warm, smooth skin for a moment before straightening.

"Good night," she whispered, even though she knew Lauren couldn't hear her. She stood in the near darkness for several more moments, looking down at her, before she finally made her way back to the bedroom and slipped into Lauren's bed. This time, she fell asleep within seconds.

CHAPTER 28

An incessant ringing woke Grace from a dream in which she was snuggling with Lauren in a space capsule, both of them wearing only tank tops and boy-cut panties. At first, she thought it was an alarm warning them of space debris, but then the haze of sleep retreated and she realized that it was her cell phone.

Groaning, she reached out a hand from under the covers and placed the phone against her ear. "Yes?" she croaked, her voice rough from sleep.

"Uh, this is Jill. Sorry to call you so early on a Saturday. Did I wake you?"

"Yeah. But it's okay." Yawning, Grace sat up against the headboard and pulled the covers up over one shoulder. "Is there a special reason why you're calling me"—she glanced at Lauren's alarm clock—"at eight thirty on the weekend?"

"The people who're putting together the celebrity waiter dinner would like to get some input from Lauren. Did you talk to her yesterday?"

"I did, but I forgot to ask her about the dinner." As soon as she'd entered Lauren's apartment, the benefit dinner had been the last thing on her mind.

"Did the two of you at least kiss and make up?"

"Uh... No. I mean, yes. I mean...yes, we made up, but we didn't..." Grace snapped her mouth shut.

A soft knock sounded at the door to the living area before it was opened. Lauren padded in, still not looking fully awake. "Good morning. Are you talking to me?"

Grace pressed her palm over the phone's speaker. She shook her head and whispered, "I'm on the phone with Jill."

Lauren's eyes widened. She mouthed, "Sorry," tiptoed back out, and softly closed the door between them.

When Grace returned her attention to the phone, Jill was eerily quiet on the other end of the line. Then a salvo of questions was fired through the phone. "What the hell is going on? Was that Lauren? What is she doing at the cottage this early on a Saturday? Did she...stay over?"

"No."

"Come on, Grace. I'm not stupid. If you're not ready to talk about it, just say so, but don't lie to me, okay? I'm supposed to be your best friend. I deserve better than that."

Grace squeezed her eyes shut. "You're right. You do. But I didn't lie to you. Lauren didn't stay over. I'm not at the cottage. I slept with her last night. I mean... stayed with her. Jesus." She sounded like a stuttering teenager.

"You...?"

"She slept on the couch," Grace quickly added. "She didn't want me to drive up to the cottage in the dark."

"Ah. So there's nothing going on?"

It was tempting to just agree and avoid this conversation for a little longer. But it wasn't fair—not to Jill and not to Lauren either. She pulled the covers more tightly around herself and whispered, "I kissed her."

For several seconds, silence was her only answer; then Jill let out a piercing wolf whistle. "Woohoo! You go, girl!" Finally, she sobered and asked quietly, "Does that mean you want something more than friendship with her?"

Grace grabbed two handfuls of her hair and moaned helplessly. "I don't know. I'm trying not to think about it. I'm trying not to think, period. This is scary as hell. I mean, I'm not gay. At least I never thought I was. And now..."

"Now?" Jill prompted.

"Now I met this person who makes me laugh, who gets me, who supports and encourages me, who sees me—the real me, not just the Hollywood persona...and it's a woman."

"Does that really matter so much?" Jill asked.

Did it? "Maybe it wouldn't if it were just her and me, but... God, can you imagine what my mother would say? Or Nick? And I don't even want to think about what the media would write..."

"You know, if having MS taught me one thing, it's living my life to the fullest, not caring too much about what other people might think."

Grace knew Jill was right; she knew it, but she couldn't help how she felt. "But I care, Jill. I can't help it."

"What about Lauren?" Jill asked. "I take it I was right and she really thinks you're hotter than a walk through the Sahara in a turtleneck?"

Her friend's colorful choice of words made Grace smile despite her tension. "I wouldn't put it like that, but...yeah. She wants to see where this is going."

"And you?"

"I'm scared," Grace whispered. "But I think I'd end up regretting it more if I let this slip through my fingers without even trying. She's...special."

"I'm there for you, okay? If you need a hug, a kick in the butt, or lesbian sex tips, let me know."

Heat flared through Grace. "Jill!"

"Just saying," Jill said, the grin obvious in her voice. "I might be celibate right now, but I'm still highly qualified to give the talk about the bees and the bees...or would that be the birds and the birds?"

Grace had to laugh. Talking to Jill, with her fun, no-nonsense approach to life, always made her feel better. "Thank you."

"You're welcome. Now let me talk to your girlfriend."

"She's not my—" Grace bit her lip. *Is she?* The thought made her head spin. Without another word, she padded out into the living room.

Lauren sat on the couch, looking as if she'd been waiting for Grace's phone call to end.

Grace held out the phone. "Jill wants to talk to you." The alarmed expression on Lauren's face made her laugh. She patted Lauren's bare arm and retreated into the bathroom to take a shower and get dressed.

Lauren gripped the phone with clammy fingers. She tried to tell herself she had nothing to be afraid of. Grace probably wasn't ready to tell anyone about them, not even Jill. Not that there was much to tell. *Oh, yeah? You're about to risk your career and everything you've worked for—for a woman who might or might not be straight.* Even though they hadn't slept together or even really kissed, if Lauren was honest with herself, she knew that she was already in, heart, body, and soul.

"Hi, Jill," she said, trying to sound casual.

"Morning, Lauren. So, you and Grace, huh?"

If Lauren were a cartoon character, her eyes would have popped out of her head. "Uh…she told you?"

"More or less. It wasn't hard to guess with the way the two of you have been interacting lately. When you fell asleep on the plane and used her as a pillow, she looked at you with a tenderness I've never seen when she looked at Nick or anyone else."

Warmth spread through Lauren's chest. She loved knowing that she was special to Grace, but at the same time, it made her worry. "Do you think others noticed it too?"

"Amanda, maybe. And it won't be long before Katherine figures it out."

"Do you really think so?" So far, Lauren had thought that Mrs. Duvenbeck was so homophobic that she would deny and ignore any hints that her daughter might not be totally straight.

"Oh, yeah. Don't underestimate her," Jill said. "Part of her probably already suspects that Grace isn't so defensive of you just because you're the world's best publicist. Why do you think she keeps pushing Grace to date men? It's not just about the media."

Oh, shit. If her mother forced Grace to make a choice, Lauren wasn't sure Grace would choose her over the approval of her mother. She sighed. "Is this the part where you tell me you'll kick my ass if I hurt her?"

"No," Jill said. "This is the part where I tell you to make her happy."

How ironic. All her life, Lauren had tried to stay away from actresses because she thought they were shallow, incapable of selfless love and loyal friendship—and now it turned out that she'd been the one harboring shallow prejudices. "I'll try my best."

When she didn't hear Lauren talking anymore, Grace peeked into the living room.

Lauren sat on the couch, the phone hanging limply from her hand.

Grace walked over and sat next to her. "Sorry if I ambushed you with that phone call."

"I admit I liked your first ambush better, but it's okay," Lauren said with a small grin.

"I hope Jill didn't say anything to scare you off."

Lauren shook her head. "I don't scare easily."

"Good." It had occurred to Grace that Lauren had just as much at risk as she did. Her reputation and her career were on the line too. For the first time, she realized that it could be Lauren, not she, who would want to back out and go back to being friends. The thought made her insides clench. *Give her some credit. Lauren isn't the type to give up on something just because things are getting tough. For now, you're just friends anyway. Don't make yourself crazy over things that didn't happen yet.*

The loud growling of her stomach interrupted her brooding.

Lauren laughed. "I was just about to ask if you're hungry. It seems safe to assume that you are."

Grace rubbed her belly. She hadn't eaten much the last few days.

"How about I make you breakfast? It's the least I can do after I fell asleep on you last night."

"Are you going to corrupt me again with some of your unhealthy food?" Grace asked.

"If I'm going to corrupt you, it won't be with food."

Lauren's husky drawl made goose bumps erupt all over Grace's skin. She shivered in the most pleasant of ways.

"Come on. You can help me in the kitchen and make sure I don't go overboard." Lauren got up and held out her hand.

Grace took it, enjoying the way Lauren's long fingers felt wrapped around her own. Even Grace's goose bumps now had goose bumps. Okay, that answered that question. She had wondered how it would feel to have Lauren touch her, even in such a small way, now that she'd admitted her attraction.

Neither of them let go as they walked over to the kitchen.

Lauren opened the fridge, and they both peered in.

"I have eggs," Lauren said. "How about French toast?"

"I won't even dignify that with an answer." Grace pointed at a bowl of strawberries and two bananas. "How about a fruit salad with some yogurt?"

Lauren let out a suffering sigh. "Oh, the sacrifices we make for love."

Grace froze, but Lauren didn't seem to realize what she'd just said. *Oh, for Christ's sake. It's just an expression. She didn't mean it like that.*

While Lauren washed the fruit, she said over her shoulder, "Jill told me about the benefit dinner."

At least she hadn't offered to have the birds-and-the-birds talk with her too. "What do you think?"

"It sounds like a good idea. I'll put together a promotion package later."

"Today?" Grace wagged her finger at her. "It's the weekend."

Lauren turned and leaned against the kitchen counter. A smile played around her lips. "Well, I might be convinced not to work today...if you can provide a better way to keep me busy."

Suddenly, every word seemed to be full of innuendo and hidden meanings to Grace's overactive brain. "I'm sure I'll think of something." She turned away and searched Lauren's kitchen drawers for a cutting board.

"Want me to cut the fruit?" Lauren asked.

"No, thanks. I think I can manage." Admittedly, it was a bit awkward since she tried not to use the fingers of her broken arm too much.

"How about I at least lend you a hand?" Lauren said. "I mean, since you only have one good one..."

"Uh, yeah, why not."

Lauren stepped closer and reached around her. One of her arms brushed Grace's.

Heat suffused Grace. She flashed back to her birthday party, when Lauren had pressed close to show her how to play pinball. She remembered feeling overly hot then too. Had this...this pull between them existed even back then? Had her body known long before her head had gotten the message?

"Uh, Grace?"

Lauren's breath moved the hairs on the back of her head, making her body temperature rise even more.

"Yeah?"

"Slicing the fruit only works if you actually use the knife."

Grace bumped her with her behind, shoving her back a little. "Smart-ass."

Chuckling, Lauren moved closer again and held one end of the strawberry so Grace could chop it.

Preparing breakfast this way wasn't the most effective. With Lauren this close, Grace's hands weren't exactly steady, and Lauren kept reaching around her to steal a piece of fruit.

But finally, they had a pile of cut fruit and retreated to the table to eat.

When the last piece of fruit was gone, they worked together to do the dishes and clean the kitchen.

Finally, Lauren dried her hands on a dishtowel and leaned against the kitchen counter, regarding Grace. "I know you probably have things to do, people to see, mothers to appease, but...do you think you can stay a little longer?"

Grace wasn't yet ready to give up her company either, so she nodded. "George sent me two new scripts he wants me to read. If you could print them out for me, I could do that here. Or..." She hesitated. "I'd love to see the revisions you made to your script."

"I haven't made that many changes yet. I kind of had other things on my mind." A tinge of red colored her cheeks, and she turned away to wipe down the kitchen counter. "But if you want to see what I have so far..."

"I would love to." Grace could tell how much trust it took for Lauren to let her see her work, and she valued it.

"Okay. Just don't expect too much." Lauren printed out the pages for Grace, and they settled on the couch, with Lauren checking her e-mail and Grace reading.

Every now and then, their feet, which lay on the coffee table, brushed. Whenever Grace looked up, she found Lauren's gaze on her. Finally, Grace finished the last page of the revisions.

"And? What do you think?" Lauren looked like a puppy that didn't know if its owner was about to hand out praise or punishment.

"I have just one question for you."

Lauren licked her lips and nodded, signaling for Grace to go ahead and ask.

"Why the heck aren't you doing this for a living? It's great!"

"Yeah? Really? You think it works better now?"

Grace nodded. "It works like a charm. The emotions between them are so... real." It made her wonder if Lauren had based that part of the script on her own feelings for her.

Lauren beamed. "Thanks. It's great to hear that. It was all there in my head, but I wasn't sure if I managed to put it on the page."

"You did. Now you just need a title."

"I was thinking of *Shaken to the Core*," Lauren said. "Is that too corny?"

"No. It fits." Not just the script. It fit how Grace felt too.

With a happy grin, Lauren returned to her e-mail and Grace started reading one of the scripts that George had sent her. Every now and then, she paused and looked at Lauren, watching her long fingers fly over the keyboard.

Lauren seemed to sense her gaze. She lifted her head and smiled. "What?"

"Nothing."

"This isn't exactly an exciting Saturday, is it? Watching me answer e-mails..."

"No, that's not it." God, this was embarrassing. "It's just... This feels so... normal."

"You didn't expect it to be? Grace, just because I'm a woman...we're both women doesn't mean that this"—Lauren pointed back and forth between them—"is abnormal in any way."

"Oh, no, that's not what I meant. Sitting here with you, spending some quiet time together... I never had this with Nick or anyone else. One of us was always running out for a location shoot, a lunch meeting, or some promo event."

Lauren closed the laptop to give Grace her full attention. "I'm not going to lie to you. It'll probably be like that a lot of the time with me too...when...I mean, if..."

Grace wanted to reassure her but knew she couldn't. Not yet. For now, she would just try to focus on enjoying Lauren's company.

They spent the day in Lauren's apartment, not venturing outside. In here, just with Lauren, she could relax and be herself, while outside, the media and the expectations of the world were waiting. Grace wasn't eager to face them, but as the afternoon progressed, she knew she had to go. By now, her mother was probably wondering where she'd been all day. "I should go," she said and got up from the couch. "Otherwise, it'll get dark and I'd have to stay here for another night."

Lauren looked over with an almost shy smile. It was endearing to see the usually confident publicist so timid. "Well, I wouldn't mind. You're welcome here any time."

"To be honest, I wouldn't mind either. But I'm going to have to face the rest of the world sometime."

Lauren searched her face as if trying to decide whether she should attempt to change Grace's mind, but then she said nothing and just walked her to the door.

"So..." Grace jingled her car keys in her hand, unsure how to say good-bye. A hug? A kiss on the cheek? Or...? She glanced at Lauren's mouth.

"So..." Lauren shuffled closer, peering at Grace from under a stray lock that had fallen onto her forehead.

"Don't work too much, okay?"

"I won't," Lauren said.

"Liar."

Lauren chuckled. It sounded nervous. "Drive safely, okay? And call me once you make it home."

"Okay." Now there was nothing more to say. Grace slid her good arm around Lauren's shoulder so she could keep her balance as she was about to lean up and kiss her cheek.

But Lauren, probably thinking she was aiming for a hug, reacted instantly and pulled her close.

With a mental shrug, Grace sank into the embrace. God, this felt good. Safe, comfortable, and exciting, all at the same time. She burrowed her face against Lauren's worn T-shirt, washed to a velvet softness, and inhaled deeply. The urge to kiss the smooth skin of Lauren's neck overcame her, but that was way out of her comfort zone. She pulled back a little and instead aimed for bussing Lauren's cheek.

Lauren turned her head in exactly that moment, nearly making their mouths collide.

They both pulled back before it could happen.

"Sorry," Lauren mumbled. "I wasn't trying to—"

Grace leaned up a second time to kiss her cheek. *Oh, to hell with it.* At the last moment, she changed course, brushed her lips against Lauren's in a fleeting touch, and then moved back, just enough to look into Lauren's radiant eyes.

Faces just inches apart, lips parted, they looked at each other.

Then, as if pulled in by a common center of gravity, they both leaned forward at the same time and their mouths met in a longer kiss.

Lauren wrapped her arms more firmly around her and pulled her closer.

A wave of heat rolled through Grace. Her eyes drifted shut. She melted against Lauren, pressing closer as if trying to imprint the feel of Lauren's body against her own.

Lauren's lips were warm and soft and tender. She kissed her slowly, almost shyly.

With her cast resting along Lauren's back, Grace's good hand came up, and she wove her fingers through Lauren's silky hair.

A moan from Lauren vibrated against Grace's lips, sending a quiver through her. She let go of Lauren's hair and clutched her shoulder to keep herself upright while she deepened the kiss.

Lauren's tongue brushed against hers, caressing with gentle strokes.

Grace's body felt as if it would spontaneously combust in about three seconds. She pulled back with a gasp and tried to slow her breathing. Despite the growing attraction she felt, she hadn't expected Lauren to have such a powerful effect on her. Her head might be slow to adapt to the thought of being with a woman, but her body was willing to jump in with both feet. *Oh, yeah. Willing. Definitely willing.*

She leaned against the doorjamb and needed a few seconds until she could form a halfway intelligent thought.

Lauren touched Grace's cheek with her fingertips. "Are you okay?"

"Yeah. Okay. You...this...just...wow."

A broad smile chased away the insecure expression on Lauren's face. "Ditto."

Grace's gaze darted down to Lauren's lips. It was almost scary how much she wanted to kiss her again.

Lauren groaned. "Don't look at me like that, or you won't be going anywhere anytime soon."

And that would be a bad thing...why? Grace shook herself out of her kiss-induced haze. As much as she wanted to, she knew she couldn't hole up with Lauren forever. Reality was waiting for her on the other side of this door. She had to figure out a way to deal with it. "I'll call you later." Before she could change her mind, she pulled the door open and stumbled into the corridor on legs that felt weak. Outside, at a safe distance, she turned.

Lauren stood in the doorway as if it were an invisible barrier she couldn't cross. Her gaze was like a caress. She lifted her hand for a silent wave.

Grace waved back.

They stood like that for several seconds before Grace finally kicked herself into motion, turned, and walked down the corridor without looking back.

CHAPTER 29

ON THE WAY TO THE restaurant where the benefit dinner would be held, Jill bounced in the passenger seat. "Do you think they'll give us one of those sexy little aprons?"

Grace gave her a quick glance. "You think they're sexy?"

"If the right woman wears them, sure. I bet Lauren would think so too."

Grace didn't comment, not yet sure what Lauren would or wouldn't consider sexy. She could feel Jill's gaze on her.

"How are things going between the two of you?" Jill asked.

A blush rose up Grace's neck.

Jill laughed. "That well, hmm?"

"We're taking it slow," Grace said, hoping Jill would leave it at that. Normally, while she was private, she wouldn't mind discussing her love life with her best friend, but what she had with Lauren felt like something special and vulnerable that needed to be protected.

Jill reached over and put her hand on Grace's cast for a moment, now no longer teasing. "That's good. Are you okay with it all?"

"It feels so...different," Grace said in a near whisper.

"I'll have to take your word for it. I never really dated a man, so I wouldn't know."

"I'm not sure that's what makes it so different. I mean, it's probably a part of it, but... Most of the men I dated treated me like a goddess. It's flattering, really, but it's not... It never felt real. Lauren isn't intrigued by my Hollywood persona. She wants to be with the real Grace."

"Why does that make you frown? I'd think that's a good thing."

"It is." Grace nibbled her bottom lip. "It's just that sometimes, I feel like I've forgotten who that really is."

Jill shrugged. "So you'll get to rediscover it with Lauren."

Another blush warmed Grace's cheeks at the thought of all the other things she wanted to discover with Lauren. If things continued like this, her blush would soon become permanent. "Yeah. But it makes everything we do or say feel so important, larger than life. There's no acting or hiding behind my movie star persona with her. It makes me wonder how much longer I can hide this from the public."

"Is that what you want to do?" Jill asked. "Hide it?"

"A part of me does. I'm not sure I'm ready to risk everything—my career, my fans, my relationship with my mother."

They reached the restaurant before Jill could ask another question.

Grace handed her car keys to the valet and turned toward Jill. "Ready?"

"Yeah. But you aren't." Jill reached out and opened one more button on Grace's blouse. "Now you're good to go."

"Isn't that a little too much?" Grace lifted her good hand and tried to redo the button.

Jill slapped her hand away. "It's perfect. Remember, we're doing this for a good cause, so you want to earn lots of tips."

"Why do you get to keep your button closed, then?"

"I don't have that much to flaunt."

"Oh, come on. You certainly can't complain in that department."

Jill grinned. "Well, thank you, ma'am. I didn't think you noticed."

"I didn't... I mean, I did, but not—"

"Relax." Now serious, Jill looked into her eyes and lowered her voice. "Just because you're attracted to a woman doesn't mean you're attracted to every other female too. Although I am pretty irresistible."

"You're nuts; that's what you are." Laughing, Grace followed her into the restaurant.

The regular restaurant staff had already set up the tables. Everything was ready for the guests who'd start to arrive soon.

The restaurant owner greeted them with so much enthusiasm that Grace thought he was about to fall to his knees and kiss her feet. He handed them each a white waitress apron.

When Grace struggled to tie it with one arm still in the cast, Jill took over and did it for her.

The owner of the restaurant presented Grace with an order pad and a pencil.

"What about me?" Jill asked.

"Uh..." The man visibly squirmed. He turned and pointed behind the bar, where the cash register sat. "We thought it might be better if you would mind the cash register. To avoid accidents with the china, you understand?"

The muscles in Jill's jaw bunched. "I understand," she said stiffly.

Grace stared at him. He wanted her, who had one arm out of commission, to wait tables but not Jill, just because she had MS? "I think Jill would do just fine. Better than me with my arm in a cast."

The restaurant owner avoided her gaze. "I don't mean to offend anyone, but I'm a little concerned about liability if Ms. Corrigan got hurt carrying plates."

Jill put a hand on Grace's shoulder. "It's okay. I don't mind manning the register. That way, I can at least keep an eye on you and make sure no one is grabbing your ass."

"I think that's a very good idea," someone said behind them.

The restaurant owner used that opportunity to escape to the kitchen.

Grace whirled around.

Lauren stood in front of her, wearing dove gray slacks and a baby blue blouse with short sleeves that showed off her athletic arms.

"Lauren? What are you doing here?" Despite her surprise, Grace couldn't help beaming at the sight of her.

A soft smile curved Lauren's lips upward. "Well, after beating the advertisement drum for this event, I thought I might as well put all the money I make as your publicist to good use and buy myself a ticket too."

Grace wanted to hug her, but with so many people bustling around, she didn't dare.

"Well, if you tip well enough, I might make an exception for you and let you grab her ass," Jill said, her voice pitched low so that only they could hear.

"Jill!" Grace slapped her with the order pad.

"Don't worry," Lauren said. "I'll be on my best behavior. I hear your mother bought a ticket too."

As if on cue, Katherine entered the restaurant, and Grace went to greet her, but not before sneaking another look at Lauren.

By the time dessert was served, Lauren wasn't only pleasantly full, she was also exhausted. Keeping her eyes off Grace was a Herculean feat. It seemed everyone else in the room was watching her. The conversation at the table, which Lauren shared with a writer, a physician, and a member of the city council, rushed by her without her contributing more than a few sentences. She was much too busy trying not to watch Grace—and failing miserably.

With her arm in a cast, Grace couldn't carry as much as the other celebrity waitresses and waiters, so she was constantly bustling back and forth, serving meals, clearing plates, bringing new beverages. Her cheeks were flushed, and a few damp curls had escaped her ponytail. Somehow, it only added to her attractiveness. She looked so damn sexy in the crisp white apron wrapped around her waist that no one in the room seemed to be able to look away.

Even some of the other celebrities waiting tables—a local news anchor, a basketball player, two singers, a couple of actors, and several models—were watching Grace work.

You'd better get used to half the civilized world wanting her.

As if conjured up by Lauren's thoughts, Grace stepped up to the table. "Can I get you anything else?" Her question was directed at the entire table, but she looked directly at Lauren.

How about a kiss? Lauren wanted to say. But, of course, she kept her mouth shut, very aware that they weren't alone. Grace's mother was sitting just one table over. Jill's warning about Mrs. Duvenbeck figuring it out soon still rang in her ears. It was incentive enough to keep her eyes on her grilled snapper fillet and not on that open button on Grace's blouse that revealed just a hint of her cleavage.

The other people at the table declined.

"A cappuccino for me, please," Lauren finally managed to say. Did her voice sound as hoarse to everyone else as it did to her?

"Caffeine in the evening?" Grace paused with the order pad resting against her cast.

"Don't worry. It won't keep me up." Her fantasies about Grace in the white apron maybe, but not the caffeine.

"All right. One cappuccino, coming right up." Grace gave her a smile, not the Hollywood one, but a smile that was a little different, without Lauren being able to say what exactly it was that made it so.

Minutes later, Grace returned, carefully balancing the cup on a saucer.

Not wanting Grace to hurt herself, Lauren reached out and took the cup from her.

Their fingers touched.

It took a few seconds for Lauren to realize that the hot milk froth had spilled over and was now burning her fingers. "Ouch." She quickly put the cup down on the table.

"Careful," Grace murmured.

Yeah. Careful or I'll get burned by more than coffee. She wiped her fingers on her napkin. "Thank you."

Grace nodded and walked back to the kitchen.

Lauren managed to keep her gaze on the cappuccino.

"What the hell was that?" Jill whispered as Grace passed the bar with the empty tray.

"Cappuccino," Grace said.

Jill shook her head. "Something hot was going on at that table, but I'm not talking about the beverages. Lauren tried to hide it, but she looked at you like you're dessert." When Grace opened her mouth to protest, she waved her away. "Don't bother. I'm happy for you. Which is more than can be said for your mother."

Oh, shit. Under the pretense of putting the tips she had gotten this far into the register, Grace moved behind the bar and peered over to her mother's table.

A lemon sorbet was melting in the glass bowl in front of her mother while she was busy glaring at the unsuspecting Lauren, looking as if she wanted to march over and plunge the fish knife that Grace had forgotten to clear from the table into Lauren's chest.

The blood drained from her head, leaving Grace light-headed. "Oh God. Do you think she saw?"

"Your back was to her, so Katherine didn't see you make googly eyes at Lauren, but I'm sure she saw Lauren look at you—and let's just say it wasn't a gaze I've ever gotten from my publicist."

"I'd hope not," Grace muttered.

Jill looked at her blankly, as if she needed a moment to remember that Lauren was her publicist too; then she laughed. "Jealous?"

"No, I... Dammit." Grace ducked behind the cash register to hide her blush from her mother and the rest of the room.

Jill covered the fingers of Grace's good hand with both of her hands. "It's wonderful to see you like this. Don't let your mother or anyone else spoil this for you."

Grace sighed. "I'll try not to, but—"

They were interrupted as several guests, including her mother, signaled for their checks.

"Time to see if your show-some-cleavage strategy worked," Grace said. She took care of her other table first, ignoring her mother's and Lauren's tables for now. Finally, most other guests had left and she couldn't avoid her mother any longer.

"What is that woman doing here?" her mother asked, her voice lowered to a quiet hiss.

Grace didn't need to turn to see where she was pointing. "She's my publicist, Mom."

"Well, there's no need for publicity in here, is there?"

"She's my friend too, and she wanted to support a good cause, just like you did."

The disapproving expression on her mother's face remained. "You're too naive, just like your father." She looked around, making sure no one was listening in on their whispered conversation. "Don't you understand? She's one of those women.

293

The way she was looking at you earlier... That's not how one friend looks at another. I'm pretty sure her intentions toward you are less than honorable. She only wants one thing from you."

Grace's spine stiffened. She started shaking but wasn't sure if it was anger or fear or a mix of both. "That's not true, Mom. Lauren is the most honorable person I know. She—"

"Why don't I take over here?" Jill said as she showed up next to Grace. "The people at table three are in a hurry to leave. Could you collect their tips?"

Not managing more than a nod, Grace hurried away.

Lauren nursed her cappuccino, taking only tiny sips of the by-now cold beverage while she waited for the other guests to leave. She wanted to give Grace her tip without witnesses around.

Mrs. Duvenbeck was the last one to get up from her table. When she passed Lauren on the way out, she gave her a look that nearly had Lauren ducking for cover beneath the table.

What crawled up her ass now? She couldn't possibly know, could she? Their fingers had brushed once, but otherwise, Lauren had been careful not to touch Grace in any way or look at her for too long—at least in comparison to how long she wanted to look at her.

When she was the last guest in the room, Lauren signaled for the check.

Instead of Grace, Jill appeared at her table.

"Where's Grace?" Lauren asked.

"Back there." Jill pointed at the kitchen. "Hiding from her mother."

Lauren slapped a bundle of fifty-dollar bills into Jill's hands and hurried toward the kitchen. A member of the regular restaurant staff tried to stop her. "I'm Ms. Durand's publicist," she said and pushed past him through the swing door.

Grace sat on a stool in one corner of the kitchen, looking as if she was trying to make herself invisible. Not that it would ever work for a beautiful celebrity like her.

Wordlessly, Lauren took her hand and, after a quick glance around to make sure no one was watching, pulled her around the corner and through a door labeled *storage*. "What's wrong?" she whispered as soon as the door closed behind them. She turned on the light in the small room so she could see Grace's face.

Her lips compressed into a line, Grace shook her head. "Nothing."

"No acting, remember? Please, tell me. Did your mother do something?"

Grace sighed. "She saw the way you looked at me. Let's just say she wasn't amused."

"I'm sorry. I tried to be inconspicuous, but I guess my acting skills suck." Head down, she regarded the gray-tiled floor.

A soft touch to her hand made her look back up. "Don't apologize," Grace said. "I...I like the way you look at me."

Warmth flowed through Lauren. "You do?" She knew she was fishing for reassurance, but she couldn't help it.

Grace nodded. "I wish the same could be said for my mother. She's very suspicious of your intentions toward me. God, Lauren, she will never accept this... us." Her shoulders slumped.

"Come here." Lauren pulled her close and immediately felt Grace bury her head against her shoulder. Her heart was beating fast against Lauren's chest, and so was Lauren's—not just because of having Grace's body pressed against hers, but also because she was afraid. It would be so much easier for Grace to just ignore whatever feelings she might have for her and continue to let others perceive her as the perfectly straight star of romantic comedies.

Lauren wanted to beg her not to do that, to give them a chance, but what right did she have to ask Grace to risk her career and her relationship with her mother for her? She bit her lip and continued to hold Grace, who clutched her in a grip that felt almost desperate.

After a while of just standing there, between large plastic containers, cases of olive oil, and a shelf full of paper towels, Grace's grip on her finally eased. "Thanks," she whispered, but instead of letting go and moving back, she continued to hold Lauren close.

Lauren certainly wasn't about to object.

Tentatively, Grace ran her hands along Lauren's back, making shivers rush through her body. "I couldn't tell you earlier, but you look nice."

"Me? I could barely keep my eyes off you the whole evening. You look so damn sexy in this apron."

Grace grinned. "Jill thought you'd think so. Is this a lesbian fetish I'm not aware of?"

"I don't think so, but I just added it to my list of personal fantasies."

Instead of an answer, Grace leaned up and kissed her, first almost shyly, then more deeply.

Lauren struggled to hold back a moan and returned the kiss. God, she could kiss Grace forever.

But all too soon, Grace pulled back. Her chest heaved as if she'd just run a marathon. "This is crazy," she whispered.

"Kissing me?" Lauren asked, still not sure what Grace was feeling.

Grace shook her head. "Kissing you in a storage room, with people right outside." She touched Lauren's cheek and looked into her eyes. "But I just couldn't resist."

A groan wrenched from Lauren's lips. She was a writer and a publicist, a woman who made her living with words, but for once, she was speechless.

"Come on. Time for us to"—Grace chuckled—"come out of the storage closet. Figuratively speaking, of course."

Lauren grinned and then sobered. "You're a wonderful woman. Don't let your mother tell you otherwise, no matter what happens, okay?"

Every hint of her smile faded from Grace's face. She nodded. "I'll try."

After one last squeeze of Grace's apron-covered hip, Lauren moved past her. "Give me a two-minute head start, then come out."

"Okay."

If only she were as willing to come out of the proverbial closet too. Lauren rolled her eyes at herself. She knew she was putting the cart before the horse. Years ago, she hadn't been ready to come out within just a few weeks of finding herself attracted to a girl for the first time either. Vowing to be patient, even if it killed her, she pushed the door open and stepped back into the kitchen.

CHAPTER 30

GRACE SAT WITH HER MOTHER, enjoying low-carb cheesecake and tea at Katherine's home in Beverly Hills, when her cell phone rang. Okay, maybe she wasn't enjoying the cake so much, but now that she had Lauren in her life, she needed to provide some balance to the ice cream and hot dogs that Lauren kept feeding her.

With an apologetic glance at her mother, she pulled the phone from her back pocket. It was Lauren. Just the name on her phone display made Grace's heart beat faster.

"Hi," Lauren said when Grace answered the phone. "I'm back safe and sound."

God, it was good to hear her voice. Since Lauren had been out of town at a seminar, they hadn't seen each other or spoken much this week. "Give me a second." She couldn't talk to Lauren while her mother listened to every word. After the celebrity waiter dinner last week, her mother was already suspicious of Lauren. With another apologetic glance, she got up from the couch and went to the patio, where her mother couldn't hear her. "Sorry I couldn't pick you up from the airport."

Lauren chuckled. "It was for my own good. Can you imagine the headlines if the airport paparazzi caught us kissing each other hello?"

Grace's stomach first got butterflies at the thought of kissing Lauren and then churned when she thought about the headlines it would cause. She quickly changed the topic. "So, how was the seminar?"

A long groan reverberated through the phone. "You could fit everything I learned in the past five days into one e-mail—and not a very long one either. But I didn't call to talk about work." Her voice lowered to a more intimate purr that made a shiver run through Grace.

She sat at the edge of her mother's pool and dangled her bare legs in the water. "So there's a special reason for the call?"

"Yeah." Lauren sucked in an audible breath. "Well, I was wondering...if you don't have anything else planned this weekend, would you maybe want to go on a date with me?"

Grace's mouth went dry. She stopped moving her legs in the pool. "A date?"

"Yeah. You know, that thing where two people who like each other go to a restaurant to eat." Lauren's obvious nervousness was replaced with gentle teasing.

"No," Grace said. "That's called grabbing a bite to eat with a friend. A date is a little different, isn't it?"

"You're the queen of romantic movies, so I'll bow to your superior knowledge. I'd very much like to take you out on a date, not just a bite to eat with a friend. So, what do you think?"

All sound ceased at the other end of the line, as if Lauren was holding her breath.

"I'd love to go out with you, really, but do you think that's a good idea? I mean, out in public, we couldn't do any of the things all the other couples do. No holding hands, no loving gazes, no kiss good night." She felt bad for having to point it out but knew it was a reality they had to face.

Lauren sighed. "I guess it was a pretty dumb idea."

"No," Grace said quickly. The disappointment and dejection in Lauren's voice hurt. "No. It wasn't. How about we have our date up at the cottage? Just you and me. I'll even cook."

"Real food?" Lauren sounded suspicious. "Not that low-carb, low-taste, low-everything stuff you Hollywood stars call food?"

Grace laughed. "Real food. I might even go all out and make a dessert."

"Ooh. Well, in that case, I wouldn't miss it for the world. Not just because of the dessert."

Giddiness, mixed with just a bit of nerves, rushed through Grace at the thought of having an intimate dinner with Lauren.

After a moment of silence, Lauren cleared her throat. "Don't take this the wrong way, but should I bring my pajamas?"

Grace's breath caught as she thought of Lauren in her pajamas—and out of them. "Uh…"

"I'm just asking because I'd rather not navigate the dirt road in the dark. I'll sleep on the couch, of course."

"Um, that's where I'm sleeping while I still can't climb up to the loft because of the cast. But you can have the bed." Somehow, offering Lauren her bed felt intimate.

"Okay," Lauren said, her voice a bit husky. "If you're comfortable with that."

"I am." To her surprise, Grace found it was the truth.

"Thanks. So, how does tomorrow at seven sound?"

Grace didn't have to think twice. "Sounds good. Do you want wine with dinner?"

"No," Lauren said firmly. "I'll have what you're having."

Her consideration warmed Grace's heart. She smiled. "Sounds like that famous line from *When Harry Met Sally*."

They both laughed.

"God, I'm dating someone who's in showbiz," Lauren said. "I never thought that would happen again, but I'm really glad it is."

"Me too," Grace said. They were both quiet for several moments, just enjoying their connection and listening to each other breathe. "Sorry, I need to get back inside. I'm at my mother's. By now, she's probably wondering if I fell in the pool and drowned."

They said good-bye, and Grace padded back inside with her feet wet. If she was lucky, her mother would focus on the mess she made on the tiles in the living room instead of her phone call.

"Who was that?" her mother asked immediately, pointing at the phone that Grace was pocketing.

No such luck. Grace resisted the urge to grimace. "Uh, just Lauren."

Her mother's forehead crinkled as much as it could. "What did she want?"

"Oh, just to set up an appointment. We'll meet this weekend to go over promo events for the awards season." They'd already done that, although her mother didn't know. She felt bad about lying, but what choice did she have?

Her mother let out a long-suffering sigh. "I really wish you wouldn't spend so much time with that woman. I have a bad feeling about it."

"Mom..."

"All right, all right." Her mother held up both hands, palms out. "You're an adult. I trust you to take care of yourself should she..."

Grace's hackles rose. "Should she...what?"

"Should she try anything."

Her cheeks burning with the heat of anger, Grace put her hands on her hips and faced her mother fully. "What has Lauren ever done to make you think such a thing about her? She would never..." So far, Grace had been the one to initiate all of their kisses. Lauren had always let her take the first step, making sure it was really what Grace wanted.

"I get a strange vibe every time I see her looking at you," her mother said. "I don't like it."

For one terrifying moment, Grace wanted to stop her mother's accusations against Lauren by confessing her feelings, but her fear of the consequences was too strong. Her mother would have a nervous breakdown if she confessed to even the slightest attraction to another woman, much less that she had kissed her several times—and fantasized about doing a whole lot more.

"Mom, listen to me." She took her mother's hand. "Lauren is my friend. She's also one of the most honorable, decent people I know. She would never touch me in any way without my consent."

Her mother didn't seem particularly reassured. Did she already suspect Grace might give her consent? "Let's not talk about it anymore," her mother finally said. "So, will you take care of the house while I'm in the Caymans? You know I don't trust hired people with the house for that long."

Every year in October, her mother spent two weeks at a luxury resort in the Cayman Islands.

"I will. But now I have to go." She had a date to plan, after all.

Lauren couldn't remember when she'd last taken so much time to dress for a date. Normally, she just picked something from her closet that seemed to fit well together and was ready to go within ten minutes.

Now, she agonized over what blouse would bring out the golden sparks in her eyes, what pair of slacks would make her thighs look most slender, and how many buttons on her blouse would be appropriate to leave open. She tried to tell herself it didn't matter. After all, Grace would look beautiful to her even if she wore a burlap dress made of a potato sack, so she hoped Grace would find her attractive, no matter what she wore, too.

But her attempts to reassure herself did nothing to settle her nerves. She felt as if all the other dates in her life had merely been playacting. This one really counted.

Finally, with the clock urging her on, she decided on a pair of tailored slacks and a blouse that was a bit sexier than anything she wore at work. It had the exact color of Grace's favorite shade of lipstick. She grabbed the bottle of nonalcoholic wine she'd bought and sprinted to her car. Just as she got behind the wheel, she realized she'd forgotten to bring her sleepwear.

God, you're really losing it! She hurried back inside, needed another two minutes to decide between pajamas versus boxer shorts and a T-shirt, and finally sprinted back to the car with the pair of pajamas.

Traffic was bad until she got closer to Topanga. As she crawled up the dirt road toward the cottage, she realized she was still on time. *Phew!* She'd been late on so many dates because she'd gotten held up at work, but she didn't want to be late for this one.

When she reached the cottage's front door, she took a moment to smooth any wrinkles out of her slacks and make sure her blouse was properly buttoned.

The door opened before she could ring the doorbell. Had Grace already been waiting, maybe because she was just as nervous?

Then she caught sight of Grace, and any halfway intelligent thought died away. Her mouth went dry as her gaze traveled up a pair of formfitting jeans and a crimson halter top that showed off Grace's sculpted shoulders and arms. Grace wasn't wearing any makeup as far as she could see. Lauren preferred it that way. She wanted to spend the evening with Grace, the woman she was starting to fall in love with, not the movie star.

"I...uh...hi." Helplessly, Lauren held out the bottle of nonalcoholic wine.

Grace took it, cradling it to her chest. "Thank you." Her gaze lingered on Lauren's blouse before she blinked and tore her gaze away. She was wearing flat sandals, so she had to lift up a little to greet Lauren with a quick kiss on the mouth.

It was over much too fast but still left Lauren's head spinning.

"Um, come on in." Grace stepped back. "I'm running a little late, but dinner should be ready in about ten minutes."

Had she taken forever to get dressed too? Well, in Lauren's opinion, it had been worth every minute—especially when Grace turned around to lead her into the cottage. Her top was held up by just a neck strap, leaving her upper back bare. Was she even wearing a bra? If she was, it had to be a strapless one.

Stop thinking about her bra...or lack thereof! Lauren tried to keep her gaze in a more respectable area as she followed Grace inside. "Oh, wow, something smells heavenly. Don't tell me you can cook!"

Grace reached back and lightly pinched Lauren's upper arm. "Don't sound so surprised."

"Hey, stop manhandling the hired help!" Lauren rubbed her arm but was secretly glad that Grace seemed to feel more relaxed around her, resuming the kind of playful interaction they had shared when they'd been just friends.

Grace turned. Instead of the teasing answer Lauren had expected, she regarded her with a serious expression. "You're not here as my publicist."

"No. I'm not."

"For tonight, let's just be Grace and Lauren, not an actress and her publicist. Can we do that?"

Her throat went tight, so Lauren just nodded. Finally, she managed to say, "I'd love that." She followed Grace to the small kitchenette. Sauce simmered on the stove, but there were no dirty pots stacked in the sink, so Grace had apparently cleaned up the kitchen before Lauren arrived.

Grace moved back to the stove to stir the sauce.

Lauren stepped up behind her, peered over her shoulder, and deeply inhaled. She wasn't sure what smelled better—the sauce or Grace. "Anything I can help with?"

A visible shiver went through Grace. She turned slowly. Her eyes glittered like the surface of the ocean on a gorgeous day. "You could go out to the patio and make yourself comfortable. You're much too distracting to stay in the kitchen."

"Am I?" Lauren murmured. She couldn't look away from Grace's eyes.

Grace nodded. Her tongue darted out, wetting her full bottom lip.

The air between them was charged with a heat that had nothing to do with the nearby stove.

"Okay. I'll go," Lauren said. "But how about a kiss to tide me over until din—"

Grace's lips were on hers before she could even finish the sentence.

Something clattered to the floor. It might have been the wooden spoon Grace had been holding. Lauren didn't care. She wrapped both arms around Grace and pulled her closer as the kiss deepened. The fingers of her one hand came to rest against Grace's bare upper back, and she allowed them to wander just a bit, tracing the soft skin with her fingertips.

Grace gripped Lauren's hips with both hands, even the one in the cast, as if she needed to hold on so she wouldn't fall. Her lips and tongue moved against Lauren's in a slow, erotic dance. Finally, she pulled back, her hands still clutching Lauren's blouse. "There," she said.

Lauren had never heard her voice so husky and breathless, not even in one of her more passionate movie scenes.

"Now outside with you before I burn dinner." Grace gave her a gentle push in the direction of the sliding glass doors.

On legs that felt slightly unsteady, Lauren stumbled out of the kitchenette and toward the stone patio. She sank onto one of the chairs and looked back through the glass doors.

Grace still stood where she'd left her, staring back and meeting Lauren's heated gaze for a second before she turned toward the stove.

"Oh, wow." With the strong pull between them, she wondered how she'd ever make it through dinner. *Take it slow. This is your first date, remember? If it's meant to be, you'll have all the time in the world.* She tried to make herself believe it, even though she knew how fleeting things were in Hollywood. She clung to the belief that Grace was different and wouldn't change her mind about them.

The light breeze on the patio finally helped clear her head, and she looked around for the first time.

Grace had set the small table with a white linen tablecloth and laid out elegant glasses, starched napkins, and nice cutlery. She'd even put candles on the table; they were as red as her lips.

First her bra, now her lips. Stop thinking about anything to do with her body! She shook her head at herself.

The glass doors slid open, interrupting her thoughts. Grace carried a steaming plate to the table and set it down in front of Lauren, then went back inside to get her own.

Lauren jumped up. "Want me to get the wine? It's nonalcoholic."

"Sure." Grace squeezed past her with her plate, nearly making Lauren swoon with that moment of closeness.

She marched to the fridge and took out the wine she'd brought, using the time it took to open the bottle to clear her head.

When she returned, Grace had lit the candles. Crickets chirped, providing them with nice background vocals.

Lauren poured them both a bit of wine and then lifted her glass. "Let's drink to this evening and to my lovely hostess. Everything looks great."

Grace grinned. "You haven't even looked at the food yet."

Heat crawled up Lauren's neck. "I wasn't talking about the food." She glanced at her plate. Grace had arranged roasted potatoes, stuffed chicken in a sauce, and glazed carrots on each plate in an appetizing way. "But it looks wonderful too."

"Charmer," Grace said.

Lauren shook her head. "I know you get thousands of compliments about the way you look every day. But I really mean it. You're beautiful, inside and out."

For a moment, Grace looked as if she might be about to cry, then she smiled. "Thank you. It's the first time in a decade that I believe those words. With anyone else, there's usually a hidden agenda, but with you..."

"No hidden agendas. Not all publicists are spin doctors, you know?"

"I thought we wanted to try to be just Lauren and Grace tonight, not a publicist and an actress?"

"Right." Lauren clinked her glass to Grace's. "I'll drink to that too."

Their gazes met over the rims of their glasses.

Lauren tried not to notice a drop of wine wetting Grace's lips and chose to focus on her food instead. "Wow, this is delicious," she said after the first bite. "Who taught you to cook? Don't tell me it was your mother?"

"No. My mother can pick a five-star restaurant with the best of them, but I can't remember her cooking anything, even when my father was still alive. I learned bits and pieces from our housekeepers and, would you believe it, from cooking shows."

Lauren laughed. "Well, never let it be said that television isn't good for your education." She realized they were coming too close to professional territory, so she steered the topic in another direction.

They talked about favorite foods, cities they'd visited, and even touched on past relationships. By the time they had finished dinner and settled back with a glass of wine, the sun was setting over the canyon.

"Remember how we watched the sunset together the first time I brought you up here?" Grace asked.

Lauren nodded. She remembered every moment, every word they'd spoken, the way an actress would remember the lines in a script.

"I was amazed that having you here, in my refuge, didn't seem like an intrusion." Grace looked down and trailed one fingertip along the rim of her wineglass. "I normally don't like having people in my home, but with you, it felt... It just felt right."

"And now?" Lauren asked quietly.

"It still feels right. I like having you here, but I admit now that we're...dating, it also makes me a little nervous." Grace looked past Lauren, down into the canyon.

Lauren put her glass down and reached for Grace's hand. She squeezed softly until Grace looked at her. "There's no reason to be nervous. Nothing will happen that you don't want."

"That's not what's making me nervous. Well, not *just* that," Grace added with a wry smile.

"What is it, then?"

Grace hesitated. The breeze blew a few strands of golden hair onto her forehead, covering her magnetic eyes for a moment.

Lauren wanted to reach out and smooth back the errant locks, but she resisted the urge, sensing that she shouldn't interrupt Grace now.

"I've been a public figure pretty much since I was a baby. After a while in the business, you learn to recognize what people want and present that side of your personality. Don't get me wrong," Grace said with a slight shake of her head. "I'm not saying that I'm lying or acting all the time. I just never showed my real self—all of it, with nothing held back—to anyone. But I want to do it with you. And it's scary as hell."

Lauren's breath caught in her chest. "Yes, it is." She entwined their fingers until, in the fading light, she could no longer tell which were hers and which were Grace's. "But you're not the only one who's scared, and I promise not to violate your trust. I want to see you. All of you." She cracked a smile, trying to break the tension. "And that's not an attempt to get you out of that sexy top."

Grace smiled, a bit of her normal confidence shining through. She trailed her thumb along Lauren's index finger, sending a tingle down the rest of her body. "Dessert?"

Lauren understood. Grace needed a moment to get herself back together after revealing so much of herself. "As long as it's not some size-zero-approved watery sorbet."

"Guess you'll just have to wait and see."

Lauren's gaze followed her as Grace got up and went inside. The glass doors had barely closed between them when Lauren's cell phone began to ring. Suppressing a curse, she fumbled it out of her pocket. She hadn't even realized she'd left it on. Apparently, old habits really did die hard.

She stared at the display. It was one of her top clients.

Her gaze went toward the cottage. Grace was still busy in the kitchen, getting something out of the fridge. If she was quick, Grace would never even need to know she had taken a work-related call.

Her finger hovered over the green button that would accept the call. *No. This is Grace. New leaf for her. New leaf for you.* She stabbed the reject button with more force than strictly necessary, then turned the phone off before putting it away. For one moment, she felt strangely naked with all her connections to the outside world and her clients cut, but then she straightened and grinned. To hell with the outside world. Everything that counted was here, in this small cottage.

She jumped up to open the glass door for Grace, who stepped through carrying two bowls of white chocolate mousse with a strawberry sauce. "Everything okay? I thought I heard your phone ring."

"Not important," Lauren said.

In a reversal of her first stay at the cottage, this time Lauren slept up in the loft while Grace bedded down on the couch.

"Come on," Lauren said when Grace stepped out of the bathroom. "I'll tuck you in."

Chuckling, Grace slipped beneath the blanket.

Lauren perched on the edge of the couch and studied her. With her cheeks flushed either from Lauren's closeness or from washing her face, Grace looked as attractive as she'd ever seen her. There were so many things Lauren wanted to tell her—her fears and hopes for the future, but finally she just said, "Good night."

"Good night," Grace whispered back.

They kept staring at each other.

Slowly, Lauren leaned down, tucked one strand of hair behind Grace's ear, and then kissed her. She'd meant to make it a sweet, tender kiss good night, but when Grace returned the kiss, it quickly became more passionate.

Grace moaned beneath her and threaded her fingers through Lauren's hair, holding her against her.

Lauren wanted to press closer and stretch out on top of her but held herself back. *Slow. Don't spoil this.* Gasping, she pulled back.

Grace slumped back against the couch and blinked up at her. She looked dazed, as if part of her hadn't yet processed what was happening—and that was why Lauren needed to rein herself in. Grace needed time.

"Good night," Lauren said again. On legs that felt like a wobbly mass of Jell-O, she climbed the ladder to the loft and crawled into Grace's bed.

She chuckled to herself. *I'm in Grace's bed.* It wasn't quite what she had imagined, but it was nice nonetheless. Even though Grace hadn't slept up here in several weeks, her scent still seemed to cling to the pillowcase. Maybe it was just Lauren's imagination. She snuggled against the pillow while she listened to the soft sounds Grace made downstairs as she tried to find a comfortable position.

The lights went out in the living room.

"Good night, Lauren," Grace's voice trailed up to the loft.

"Sweet dreams."

Sheets rustled downstairs; then everything went quiet.

Lauren lay with her eyes open, still too charged up after her evening with Grace—and from that last kiss—to just go to sleep. She peeked up at the window and counted the stars shining down on her. After a while, her eyes finally closed.

Just when that heavy, peaceful feeling of falling asleep settled over her, Grace's soft voice came from downstairs. "Lauren?"

"Yes?"

They were both whispering.

"Do you remember what you said when I told you that Nick and I are getting a divorce?"

Lauren shook off the traces of sleep and searched her memory. "I said a lot of things during that meeting. That you can't be caught lying to the press?"

"No. You told me that if there was ever someone new in my life, you needed to know before I even told my mother or my best friend." Grace paused. "I think you should consider yourself notified."

The meaning of Grace's whispered words hit Lauren, leaving her staring up at the stars with her mouth open for several moments. Then she scrambled out of bed and to the edge of the loft, where she peered down into the nearly dark living room.

The only light in the cottage came from a night-light next to the bathroom, but Lauren could still make out Grace's form on the couch. She thought Grace might be smiling up at her, so she smiled back.

"Careful up there," Grace said. "I don't want you to fall."

Too late. She'd already fallen—hard. Shaken by that realization, Lauren crawled back into bed.

When Grace woke, the sun had already risen. Light was streaming into the cottage through the glass doors. She lay still, snuggling more deeply under the blanket, and listened.

Everything was quiet up in the loft. Even though Lauren was still asleep, the cottage felt different with her here. Or maybe Grace was the one who felt different.

A very short time ago, Lauren had been nothing more than her publicist and friend, and the rumors about Grace's being gay had been just that—rumors. Now everything had changed. Grace got up, tiptoed into the bathroom, and stared at the mirror above the sink while she brushed her teeth, almost amazed when her reflection looked the same as it always did.

Was this who she had been all along—the woman who had eaten white chocolate mousse without wasting even one thought on how many calories it had and who had passionately kissed Lauren last night—and she just hadn't known?

Realizing the mirror wasn't likely to answer her question, she put her toothbrush back into its cup and went to the kitchen to make breakfast.

She felt more than heard Lauren climb down from the loft, make a quick trip to the bathroom, and then step up behind her. Every cell in her body was aware of Lauren's proximity.

"Good morning," Lauren said.

Grace turned down the heat and leaned against the counter, smiling at the sight of Lauren, who stood in front of her, still in her pajamas, rubbing her eyes like a sleepy child. "Morning. I hope I didn't wake you?"

Lauren shook her head. "The scent of grilling bacon woke me. Sleep well?"

"Yes. How about you?"

Shuffling her feet, Lauren nodded. "Like a baby."

"Do you have time to stay for breakfast?" Grace asked, knowing Lauren usually reserved weekends for writing and catching up on e-mail. "I'm making bacon and pancakes."

"I'll make time. I can't stay too long, though. One of my top clients called last night, and I ignored him, so now I have to deal with it."

Lauren had ignored a call from a client? *Wow.*

They chatted about the weather up in the canyon while Grace poured pancake batter into the pan.

Why are we making small talk? Grace wondered. What she really wanted wasn't polite conversation. She wanted Lauren to take her into her arms and kiss her again.

But when Lauren finally bent to kiss her, it was just an almost shy brush of her lips, as if she didn't know if Grace would be comfortable with anything more.

Hell! If growing up in Hollywood had taught Grace one thing, it was that life didn't hand you anything; you had to reach for what you wanted. So she did.

Ignoring her cast, she grabbed two handfuls of Lauren's pajama top and pulled her down. For a moment, she caught a glimpse of Lauren's widened pupils, then both of their eyes fluttered shut as their mouths met.

Grace's body molded into Lauren's. She explored softly, nibbling on Lauren's bottom lip, kissing her upper lip, stroking Lauren's tongue with her own. Her hands lost their grip on the pajama top and instead slid around to flutter over Lauren's back and down. God, she loved how the curve of Lauren's hips felt beneath her hands.

A part of her—the part that could still think—was surprised at the intensity of her own reaction, but for once, she shut down that analytical part and allowed herself to just feel.

Lauren's warmth, the touch, the taste, and the scent of her filled her senses.

Then something else intruded. Dimly, she became aware of a much less pleasant smell.

Damn, the pancakes! She whirled around and pulled the pan from the stove.

Too late. When she flipped the pancake, its bottom was coal-black. "Sorry." She sent Lauren a sheepish glance. "Looks like I ruined breakfast or at least part of it."

Lauren shook her head and caressed Grace's cheek with the back of her hand. "No," she said, sounding a bit hoarse. "Trust me. You didn't ruin anything. Quite the opposite. From now on, this is my favorite kind of breakfast and these," she gestured at their sleepwear, "are my favorite date outfits."

They grinned at each other.

Grace marveled at how easy it felt to be with Lauren—at least as long as they were alone. As soon as they headed out into the real world, things would be different, though. She pushed the thought away. For now, all she wanted was to enjoy the time she had with Lauren. She'd deal with everything else later.

CHAPTER 31

"How does it feel?" Lauren asked.

A long moan escaped Grace. "Heavenly."

Only silence answered on the other end of the line.

Grace tapped her phone that was connected to the SUV's speakers. "Lauren? Are you still there?"

"Um, still here. You were saying…?"

"How wonderful it feels to finally get rid of the cast. You wouldn't believe how weak my arm is, though. I'll start physical therapy next week, and now I'm on my way to my mother's to take advantage of her pool while she's gone. The doctor said swimming would be good to strengthen the muscles."

More silence from Lauren.

Is she imagining me lounging by the pool in my swimsuit? Grace grinned. Most of the time, she preferred to pretend that no one ever fantasized about her, but the thought of Lauren thinking about her… She fanned herself with her still-weak left hand.

"If your arm is still not back to normal, isn't it dangerous to get into a pool alone?" Lauren finally asked.

"No," Grace said before her brain caught up with her mouth. "Oh. Yeah, now that you mention it, a closely supervised first swim might be better."

"Exactly my thought."

"You wouldn't happen to know anyone willing to supervise, would you?"

"Well, as your publicist, it's my duty to avoid any headlines about Grace Durand drowning in her mother's pool, so…"

Grace laughed at their old joke. "So you'll sacrifice yourself."

"I wouldn't call it that, but yes, I'll be over as soon as I wrap up work."

Which, as Grace knew, could be any time between now and midnight, even though it was Friday. Lauren's workaholic tendencies made her worry, but with her own work schedule when she was on location, she had no right to make Lauren feel guilty. "When you come over, don't forget to stop at your apartment first to get your swimsuit."

"Oh?" Lauren sounded a little breathless. "You want me to join you and not just supervise?"

"Well, we wouldn't want any headlines about Grace Durand's publicist having to dive into the pool fully clothed to rescue her client, would we?"

Lauren laughed. "No, we certainly don't want that. See you later, then."

"See you later." Grace ended the call and wondered how much of Lauren she'd be seeing. An image of water droplets running down Lauren's smooth shoulders, trickling down her cleavage, formed in her mind.

How weird. Fantasizing about a woman—about Lauren—felt a little strange and entirely natural at the same time.

A car honked behind her, making her realize that the light in front of her had turned green.

Rolling her eyes at herself, she cleared the intersection.

Briefcase in hand, Lauren walked past Tina's desk. "I'm leaving for the day."

Tina looked up from her computer screen. "Are you okay?"

"Sure. Why wouldn't I be?"

"Well, this is the second time this week that you left work on time," Tina said, looking a little embarrassed. "I thought maybe you aren't feeling well."

Lauren couldn't help staring. Her colleagues thought there was something wrong with her because she left work on time. Had her workaholic tendencies really gotten so bad? "Never been better. I just have an appointment." *With a swimming pool and a beautiful woman.*

"Okay. Just making sure."

"Thanks. I appreciate it."

Tina went back to the press release on her screen, and Lauren took the elevator down to the parking garage. On her way home, she found herself singing along with a love song on the radio.

Without stopping to eat or read her mail, she took a quick shower and went in search of her swimsuit. Where was that damn thing? Admittedly, it had been some time since she'd last needed it. *If push comes to shove, you could always wear your birthday suit.*

The thought of being naked in the pool with an equally naked Grace made her need another shower—a cold one.

"Aha!" She finally found her swimsuit underneath a pile of socks. Triumphantly, she pulled it free and put it on. That way, she didn't need to change when she got to Mrs. Duvenbeck's home. She stood in front of her mirrored closet and eyed her reflection. Her breasts were downright modest by Hollywood standards and her hips a little too full. She wondered what Grace would think of her body, compared to those of her fellow actresses.

Just as she ran her hands down her thighs, testing their firmness, her cell phone rang.

Not now! The thought that it might be Grace made her go in search of her phone anyway. On the last ring before voice mail picked up, she dove onto the bed, where she'd left her pants, and pulled the phone from her pocket.

She realized too late that her boss's name was displayed on the small screen; she'd already accepted the call. "Hi, Marlene," she said, hoping she wasn't needed back at the office.

"I wanted to check in with you, but Tina said you'd already left."

For the first time, Lauren realized what a strange profession she was in—she almost felt guilty for having a life. "I have an important appointment, so I left on time."

"I won't keep you. I just wanted to know how things are going with the Durand account."

"Oh, I think Grace is pretty happy with me." Lauren suppressed a grin at her choice of words. "Things have calmed down a little after her appearance on *Good Morning America* and the exclusive with *ET.*"

"Good," Marlene said. "I don't need to tell you how important it is having Ms. Durand as a client. Not just because of her generous retainer. Ten new A-listers have signed with us since we're representing her."

Lauren swallowed. If things between her and Grace didn't work out, she had much more to lose than just her heart. "I know," she said quietly. "I'm giving it my best."

"I didn't expect anything else from you. Come see me in my office on Monday morning. We should finally talk about that promotion."

A few months ago, that word would have made Lauren do a victory dance around the apartment, but now she just said, "Will do" and ended the call as quickly as possible.

Damn. She really deserved that promotion. It wasn't as if she had gotten it by becoming involved with a client. But if her boss knew about her relationship, she would view things in a different light.

Sighing, she put on her clothes over her swimsuit and headed out.

Grace had just finished watering her mother's plants when the doorbell rang. That couldn't be Lauren already, could it? A glance through the peephole made her heart beat faster. She quickly pulled the door open.

Lauren stood on the doorstep, the buttons of her polo shirt casually open and her sunglasses shoved up on top of her head, keeping her tousled hair out of her eyes.

Excitement hummed through Grace. Instantly, she wanted to pull Lauren into the house and into her arms. Her immediate, almost visceral reaction to Lauren surprised her. "That was fast," she said when she finally got her dry mouth to work.

Lauren gave her a slow grin. "I had the right motivation."

After grasping Lauren's arm, Grace pulled her into the house and closed the door behind her. "Hi."

"Hi." Lauren stepped closer. Now that Grace wasn't wearing high heels, Lauren was several inches taller than her.

Somehow, there was a physicality about her that robbed Grace of breath. The warmth that seemed to radiate from her ratcheted up Grace's body heat.

Lauren wrapped her arms around Grace, making her sigh. After looking into her eyes for several seconds, Lauren bent her head and kissed her. Her lips moved over Grace's in a tender caress.

Groaning, Grace wound her fingers through Lauren's hair. The sunglasses clattered to the floor, but neither of them broke the kiss.

This was it, Grace realized—the kind of kiss the characters in that fan fiction story had shared: slow and with a passion that made her head spin and her body pound.

Finally, they pulled back but didn't let go of each other.

It took Grace a while to realize that Lauren wasn't carrying a bag. "No swimsuit?"

Grinning, Lauren tugged on her polo shirt. "I'm already wearing it."

"I still need to change into mine."

"Want me to give you a hand?" Lauren's hazel eyes twinkled. "After all, I don't want to risk headlines about Grace Durand re-injuring her arm trying to get into her bikini."

"Who says I'll wear a bikini?"

"A woman can hope, can't she?" Lauren murmured.

The heat in her gaze made Grace's pulse speed up. She directed Lauren toward the pool and went to get changed. By the time she stepped outside, Lauren was waiting by the pool, looking a little uncomfortable, as if she expected Grace's mother to return any moment.

When the glass doors clicked shut, she turned and stared.

Grace gestured at her one-piece swimsuit. "No bikini. Disappointed?"

"Never," Lauren said. Her expression didn't leave any doubt about her sincerity. She unbuttoned her jeans and pulled her polo shirt up over her head.

Grace had never understood what men found so sexy about women undressing for them. Now she did. She held her breath as Lauren's efficient strip revealed a dark blue swimsuit. Her gaze took in the flare of Lauren's hips and the toned muscles in her arms and legs.

"Sunscreen," Lauren said and pointed at the bottle of sun lotion as if she weren't capable of more than one-word sentences while she stared at Grace.

Knowing she was having the same effect on Lauren that Lauren had on her soothed the butterflies in Grace's belly. She watched as Lauren spread suntan lotion over her arms and legs and finally her chest.

"You should have some," Lauren said.

Grace wrenched her gaze away from the hypnotizing circles Lauren's hands made over her skin. "Excuse me?"

"You should put on some sunscreen too." Instead of handing over the bottle, Lauren approached her. She squirted a bit of lotion into her palm, warming it, and then softly rubbed it into the dry skin of Grace's newly healed arm.

Grace's arm started to tingle, along with the rest of her body. She stared down, watching Lauren's fingertips glide over her skin. A shiver raced through her.

Lauren paused. A bead of perspiration trickled down the side of her face, indicating that she was feeling the growing heat between them too. "Does that hurt?"

"No." Quite the opposite. She took the bottle from Lauren. "I think I'd better do the rest myself, or my poor arm will get much more of a workout than the doctor recommended for the first day out of the cast."

Lauren's eyes widened. "I can't believe you just said that."

Grace couldn't believe it either. She finished putting on lotion and then dove into the pool, letting the water cool her heated cheeks.

Kicking the bottle aside, Lauren followed her in.

They playfully splashed each other, but Grace could tell that Lauren was gentle with her and held back, mindful of her mending arm. Grace swam a few laps while Lauren drifted on her back next to her. Every time her head came up to draw breath, Grace glanced over at her, peeking at the curve of Lauren's breasts just above the water line. God. She felt like a teenager again. *Not that I ever ogled women as a teenager...*

Finally, as if by silent agreement, they stopped their laps at the deep end of the pool and treaded water next to each other.

"We should probably get out and not overtax your arm," Lauren said. Droplets of water clung to her dark lashes.

Grace wanted to kiss them away. They were so close that she felt the currents created by Lauren's hands and feet moving underwater. The water around them seemed to heat up. Lauren's calf brushed hers. Grace wasn't sure who moved first, but their mouths found each other in a passionate kiss.

Moaning, Lauren parted her lips and slid one arm around her to pull her closer.

Their breasts pressed against each other, separated by just the thin fabric of their wet swimsuits.

Grace's nipples hardened. Need pulsed through her body. She pressed even closer.

Water surged around them.

Their legs entwined underwater, Lauren's thigh slipping beneath hers.

Oh, God. For a moment, Grace forgot where she was, forgot to tread water, forgot everything but the feel of Lauren.

She started to go under, but Lauren grasped the edge of the pool with one hand and pulled her even closer with the other.

Heat coiled in Grace's belly. Not breaking the kiss, she trailed her fingertips over each inch of bare skin she could find. One of her hands brushed the side of Lauren's breast.

Lauren gasped and lost her grip on the edge of the pool for a moment before clutching it again. "God, Grace. We need to stop."

Grace blinked water out of her eyes and stared at her. Her dazed brain couldn't do much more than repeat Lauren's last word. "Stop?"

"I want you, but I don't want our first time together to be a quickie in your mother's pool."

Grace let go of Lauren and held on to the edge of the pool instead. With that little bit of distance between them, her body started to cool down and her brain began to work again. "You're right." Of course she was. Still, Grace couldn't help feeling rejected. Maybe it was just her Hollywood ego, but it stung.

"Hey." Lauren moved closer until their legs brushed, starting the pounding in Grace's body again. "Don't think I'm not tempted. God, you're temptation personified, and knowing that you want me too is the most powerful aphrodisiac you can imagine. But I want this to be right for both of us."

A smile tugged on Grace's lips. "And you say you're not a romantic."

"I'm getting there." She placed a whisper of a kiss on Grace's mouth and then heaved herself out of the pool. Water sluiced down her body, and Grace's gaze followed the path of each droplet down.

Lauren walked around the pool toward the shallow end, where the stairs were. She held out a towel for Grace. "Come on, mermaid. Time to get out."

Grace swam over, climbed out while holding on to the handrail with her right hand, and let herself be enveloped by the towel and Lauren's arms. She closed her eyes. This felt right. It *was* right. But she wanted much more than a quickie in her mother's pool too. She wanted to wake up in Lauren's arms without fearing that her mother would drop by for an early-morning visit. She wanted to kiss Lauren hello at the airport without being scared that paparazzi would spot them. She wanted to thank Lauren in the acceptance speech for any future award she might get without risking another media feeding frenzy.

But maybe such happy endings didn't exist outside of her movies.

Sighing, she took the towel from Lauren and wrapped it around herself. "Come on. Let's see if my mother left any food in her fridge."

Lauren gave her an alarmed look. "You want me to try the food in your mother's fridge? Now I'm scared. I bet all she has are diet products."

"She's not that bad."

"Oh, really?"

"Yeah, really." Grace pulled the damp towel free, snapped it at her, and chased her into the house, leaving behind her morose thoughts.

The next day, Grace was lounging by her mother's pool again, enjoying the sun. Hard to believe that it was October already. This time, Jill was keeping her company. Grace's gaze kept veering toward the deep end of the pool. Scenes of her and Lauren kissing flashed through her mind on auto repeat.

"You should get out of the sun," Jill called from beneath the sun umbrella. "Your face is turning beet-red."

Grace bit back a grin and abstained from telling her that her flushed features had nothing to do with the sun. She closed the script she'd been reading, got up from the lounge chair, and joined Jill at the table in the shade. "How are you doing?"

"The ice helps." Jill nodded at the ice chips that she kept running over her pulse points. "But I should head inside in a little while. I don't want the heat to trigger a flare-up."

"I'd invite you inside for dinner, but Lauren and I pretty much emptied my mom's fridge yesterday."

Jill wriggled her eyebrows. "Ooh. So the two of you worked up an appetite?"

"I wish." The words were out before Grace could hold them back.

Jill's grin turned into a frown. "I take it things between the two of you aren't going so well?"

"No. Yes. Things between us are wonderful, but… Let's just say if they were handing out Oscars for restraint, Lauren would definitely deserve one." She couldn't hold back a frustrated sigh.

A chuckle escaped Jill. "Not used to someone telling you no, are you?"

Grace grimaced. "Thanks for making me sound like a spoiled Hollywood diva."

"So, why do you think she's holding back? I don't think this is about her not wanting you. I've seen the way she looks at you." Jill fished more ice chips out of the bowl and ran them over her arms and neck as if the mere thought made her need to cool down. "Do you think I need to have the birds-and-the-birds talk with her?"

"No. She doesn't need that talk, believe me. She knows exactly what to do." Her mind again shifted into an auto repeat of their hot kisses in the pool. *Oh yeah. She so knows.* Grace reached over and took a handful of ice for herself.

Jill grinned. "Glad to hear it. So, what's the problem, then?"

"I think she's afraid I'll regret it in the morning."

"Do you think you would?"

"I'm sure physically I would have no regrets at all." Grace shivered at the thought of how her body had reacted to Lauren. *Oh yeah. None at all.*

"But?" Jill prompted.

Grace crunched one of the ice cubes, taking out her frustration on it. "I'm just wondering what would happen afterward."

"More of the same, of course," Jill said with a broad grin and a wink. "You're two women, after all. You're not limited to one orgasm."

Grace threw an ice cube at her. It slipped down the V-neck of Jill's shirt, making her screech. "You know that's not what I meant."

After shaking the ice out of her shirt, Jill regarded her with an uncharacteristically serious expression. "Let me ask you one question."

Her heart beating rapidly, Grace nodded at her to go ahead and ask.

"What is she to you? I mean, is it a rebound thing? A little bit of excitement? The thrill of dating someone you really shouldn't be dating? A ride on the wild side for the nice celebrity with the boring girl-next-door reputation…?"

The mere suggestion of Lauren being just a diversion made Grace hurl an angry glance her way. "No! God, no, Lauren is… She's much more to me." She stared at the bowl of ice cubes in the middle of the table, watching them melt.

Jill waited, not saying anything.

Grace peeked up. "I think I'm in love with her."

"I knew it!" Jill hurried around the table, nearly stumbling over her own feet in the process, and threw her arms around Grace. "I'm so happy for you."

Grace returned the embrace for a moment before pulling back. "What am I going to do?"

Jill shrugged. "Love her. Be happy."

"It's not that easy. I'm not as strong as you are."

"Strong?" Jill snorted and gestured at her body. "If I stay out here much longer, you'll have to carry me in."

Gripping the bowl of ice with one hand, Grace pulled her inside with the other, into her mother's air-conditioned living room. "You're strong where it counts. You don't care what the media writes about you or what anyone else thinks."

"I care. I put up a good front, but believe me, deep down, I care. Every time I see or hear one of the reporters referring to me as 'the actress with MS,' I wince." Shadows of hurt darted across Jill's face, darkening her eyes.

Grace put the bowl down and gripped Jill's hand with both of hers, wanting so much to take away her pain. "Do you regret telling the press?" she whispered, knowing Jill had only told the media to protect her.

"No," Jill said without hesitation. "It's not always easy, but I realized that having to look over my shoulder all the time, being afraid that someone might find out, was much worse."

Was that true just for Jill's MS or also for Grace's relationship with Lauren? If she told the media, her mother, the whole world, would she be able to look back, the way Jill did, and say that she didn't regret it? If she didn't tell anyone, how would she be able to have a meaningful relationship with Lauren? She remembered what Jill had told her about her relationship with Amanda—that they had broken up because Jill had been deeply closeted. Grace didn't want that to happen to her and Lauren.

"If you keep frowning like that, you'll end up with a permanent wrinkle." Jill pointed at Grace's forehead. "Your mother won't like it."

"She doesn't like most of what I'm doing nowadays," Grace muttered and went to get them something to drink.

CHAPTER 32

THE NEXT DAY, SUNDAY, GRACE sat on her couch and reshuffled the stacks of scripts on the cottage's coffee table. "Okay. I narrowed it down to three."

Lauren put her laptop away to give Grace her full attention. "Which ones?"

"This one," Grace tapped one script, "is a romantic comedy about a thirty-something who starts speed dating."

"Hmm." Lauren picked up the script and flicked through it, reading bits and pieces. "I don't want to influence you, but…"

Grace took the script from her, threw it on the floor, and slid closer on the couch. Their bare knees touched, warming Lauren's entire body. "I want you to influence me. Your opinion is important to me."

"Thank you," Lauren said quietly. "That means a lot. I just don't want to be like your mother, getting you to do whatever I think is best, regardless of what you want."

A slow smile spread over Grace's face. "You're not like my mother at all. Trust me. So, that one is out, right?"

Lauren nodded. "You've been in movies like this one before. Don't get me wrong, you were good, but I think it's time for something different."

"How about this one?" Grace handed her another script. "It's about a lady thief in nineteenth-century England."

. *Ooh. Grace with a British accent…* Lauren fanned herself with the script. "Is there any romance in there?"

"I thought you don't like romances?"

Lauren grinned. "I'm rethinking that attitude."

"Oh, really?" Grace drawled.

"Yeah, really."

The script forgotten, they looked into each other's eyes and then leaned toward each other at the same time. Their kiss started slowly but quickly escalated.

This time, instead of keeping her hands on Lauren's back or weaving her fingers through her hair, Grace slipped one hand beneath Lauren's T-shirt.

Heat spread through Lauren's body as Grace ran her fingertips up and down her side, veering close to her breast but never quite fully touching it. She groaned.

"God." She knew Grace was exploring, working up the courage to touch her more intimately, not teasing her on purpose, but still... "If you keep doing that, I'm not going to be held responsible for what I'll do."

Grace paused with one hand under Lauren's T-shirt. Her eyes were smoldering and her cheeks flushed. "What if I don't stop? What would you do?"

"I'd get up, push you down on the couch," Lauren said and did it, "and cover your body with mine." She sank onto Grace, holding herself up with one arm so she wouldn't put her full weight on her.

Grace parted her legs, setting one foot on the floor, to make room for Lauren between her thighs. "And then?" she whispered, sounding breathless.

"Then I'd lean down and kiss your neck." She placed her lips against the warm skin of Grace's neck. A strong pulse thudded against her mouth. "And then lick it and nibble it." She flicked out her tongue and gave a deliberate lick before gently nipping.

A groan came from Grace. She clutched Lauren's shoulders with both hands and pulled her down more fully.

Lauren waited for the next question, but Grace seemed to have forgotten their little game. She grinned against Grace's skin, proud of herself for being able to make Grace lose her train of thought. It was wonderful to know that she could arouse Grace without any problems.

Deciding that there were better uses of her mouth than attempting to talk, Lauren leaned down and kissed her.

When their tongues touched, Grace groaned into Lauren's mouth.

God. She couldn't get enough. Being with Grace was addictive. *More.*

Grace's hands trailed down Lauren's back and then clutched her ass.

Not interrupting their kiss, Lauren arched against her. Her thigh pressed more firmly against Grace, making her gasp against Lauren's lips.

A shrill screech from the cottage's front door made them flinch apart. "Get off my daughter! Now!"

Her chest heaving, Lauren sat up and helped Grace do the same.

Mrs. Duvenbeck stood in the doorway, her face going from deathly pale to apoplexy red.

Shit, shit, shit! What the hell was she doing here? Wasn't she supposed to be in the Caymans or someplace else—any place but here?

"Betty Grace Duvenbeck! What in God's name are you doing? I get a call from Todd's manager, telling me that you're refusing to go out on another date with him, and now I find you with...with her, doing God knows what!"

"Mom, I...I... It's..." Grace tried to straighten her clothes with trembling fingers.

Mrs. Duvenbeck put her hands on her hips in a confrontational stance. "It's what? A sin? A result of a relapse with a bottle of champagne?"

Lauren got up and stepped between them, both hands raised in a placating gesture. "Why don't we all sit down and talk like adults?"

Looking as if she wanted to scratch Lauren's eyes out with her blood-red nails, Mrs. Duvenbeck glared at her. "Stay out of this, you...you corruptive bitch! I warned Grace from the start to stay away from you. I just knew you would manipulate her into—"

"Manipulate?" Lauren echoed. "I know that's what you want to believe, but I'm not the one trying to manipulate Grace all the time. Grace and I—"

Mrs. Duvenbeck slashed her hand through the air, cutting her off. "I don't want to hear one more word from you. This is between my daughter and me. I'm sure you can find the way out on your own."

If Mrs. Duvenbeck thought she'd leave her alone with Grace, she clearly didn't know Lauren at all. She opened her mouth to say just that.

"Lauren," Grace whispered behind her. "I think it's best if you leave us alone."

Lauren turned and stared at her.

For once, even Grace's acting skills weren't enough to conceal her panic. She looked as if she were about to face a firing squad.

"Are you sure?" Lauren asked.

Her lips compressed into a tight line, Grace nodded. She reached out to touch Lauren's arm reassuringly, but one searing glance from her mother made her stop before she could complete the movement.

"I don't like it," Lauren whispered. "Not one bit. But if that's what you want... Call me, okay?"

Grace nodded, her fearful gaze already on her mother.

On her way to the door, Lauren passed Mrs. Duvenbeck and sent her a warning glare. The next thing she knew, she was outside in her car, sitting in the middle of the dirt road. Being sent away hurt, but the fear was worse.

For thirty years, her mother had run every aspect of Grace's life. Would Grace be strong enough to pull free of that influence?

As the door closed behind Lauren, Grace tried to use her acting training to calm herself—or at least appear reasonable and collected—but it wasn't doing her any good. At least Lauren had respected her wishes and left. Grace didn't want her hurt by whatever her mother would say next. She gestured at the couch. "Why don't we sit and—"

"No. I can't sit there." Her mother stared at the sofa as if it would give her herpes. "I just can't." She broke down, crying.

Oh Christ. That familiar mix of compassion, guilt, and anger at being manipulated swept over Grace. Hesitantly, she went over to her mother and put one hand on her shoulder. "Mom, please. Don't cry. This isn't the end of the world."

Her mother looked up, her mascara running down her face. "Yes, it is! What do you think the media and your fans will say if they ever find out about your... indiscretion?"

Grace pulled her hand back from her mother's shoulder and curled it into a fist. "It's not an indiscretion. Lauren...she...we..." She closed her eyes for a moment, opened them again, and looked directly at her mother. Through the giant lump lodged in her throat, she said, "She means a lot to me." She drilled her fingernails into her palm. What she'd really wanted to say was, *I love her,* but she'd chickened out at the last second, trying to soften the blow for her mother.

"You don't mean that." Her mother stubbornly shook her head. "She just manipulated you into believing that."

Anger sparked inside her. She wouldn't let her mother think that about Lauren. "No, she didn't," she said with a firmness that made her mother's eyes widen. "I was the one who kissed her first."

A faint gasp came from her mother. She clutched her chest as if she were suffocating. "If you're doing this to spite me because I wanted you to go out with Todd..."

"No, Mom. This has nothing to do with spite or with Todd. Or with you. I..." *Love her.* God, why couldn't she just say it?

Her mother's mascara now dripped onto her blouse. "How can this be happening? You...you aren't"—she lowered her voice—"like that."

"I don't know. I never thought so, but—"

"You're just confused by everything that happened this year. The separation from Nick. The media nightmare. The accident. It was just too much for you, and that woman was all too willing to take advantage of it." Her mother stopped crying. A determined expression settled on her face. She patted Grace's arm. "Don't worry. We'll find you a therapist. There are therapists for that kind of thing, you know?" She pulled her planner out of her purse and started a frantic search through the contact information section, as if she had a gay deprogrammer ready in her contact list.

"Stop. Mom, please." Grace clung to her mother's hand. "I don't need a therapist." In fact, she'd never felt as normal and happy as when she was with Lauren.

"But...but we need to do something!"

Grace shook her head. "There's nothing to do." *Just let me live my life,* she wanted to say, but it would have felt like kicking a person who was already down.

Her mother gave her a fearful look. "You're not planning on telling anyone, are you?"

"For now, just Jill knows."

"You told her? And she didn't try to talk you out of this craziness? What kind of friend is she?" Before Grace could answer, she waved her away and said, "Oh, right. She's a lesbian too. Whatever you do, just don't tell anyone else."

"I'm not sure what I'll do. I've been thinking about it a lot, but... I just don't know."

Sobbing, her mother collapsed onto the couch and then cried even harder as if only then realizing where she was sitting.

Grace sank onto the sofa next to her and put one arm around her. It was going to be a long afternoon.

It was after ten when Grace finally called. Lauren answered on the first ring. "Hi," she said, making her tone as soothing as she could. "How are you?"

For a moment, only Grace's shuddery exhale echoed through the line. "I'm okay," she finally said.

"Hey, this is me you're talking to. No acting, please."

"Sorry. I... I'm emotionally exhausted. Seeing my mother crying her eyes out was hard to take. I went back and forth between wanting to hug her and wanting to slap her."

I vote for the latter. Lauren didn't say it, though. Grace needed her support now, not sarcastic comments. "God, I hate it that you had to go through that alone." She paced through her apartment, from the balcony to the kitchen and back. "Do you want me to come over?"

Grace sighed. "I wish you could, but my mother is sleeping over. I didn't want her to drive home in the state she's in. She cried herself to sleep on the couch, and I went to the patio to call you."

So her mother was still there. No doubt she'd again try to get Grace to break things off with Lauren the moment she woke up. "Grace? You're not...?" She bit her lip and trailed off. Grace didn't need to deal with her insecurities on top of everything else.

"What? I'm not...what?"

Lauren hesitated, but that worry gnawed at her belly, and she knew she wouldn't be able to sleep before getting an answer. "You won't let her convince you that you're just confused and need to stay away from me to save your career, will you?" She wanted to take it back the moment she'd asked. What chance did their relationship have if she doubted Grace like this? "Forget I asked that."

"No," Grace said. "I won't."

Which of her questions was she answering? "Leave me? Or forget I asked?"

"Both. It hurts that you even need to ask, but I understand. I haven't given you much indication that I want more than just a secret little tryst, have I?"

"That's not it. I know we have more than that, but when you're forced to make a choice between…us and your career and the relationship with your mother…"

"I still hope it won't come to that. My mother isn't totally unreasonable. Maybe she just needs time."

Lauren suppressed a snort. So far, she hadn't seen much indication of Mrs. Duvenbeck being reasonable. "I hope you're right."

They were both silent for a moment. Crickets chirped in the background.

"God, I wish so much I could be there with you right now and just hold you," Lauren said, cupping her palm around the phone as if she could cradle Grace closer.

Grace sighed. "I would love that. How about you sleep over tomorrow?"

Was Grace trying to reassure her? "You don't need to—"

"I want to. So?"

"Yes," Lauren said. Yes to anything Grace wanted or needed. Things wouldn't be easy for them in the future, but Lauren was determined to be there for her, no matter what.

CHAPTER 33

WHEN LAUREN STEPPED OUT OF the elevator and entered the CT Publicity offices on Monday morning, Carmen looked up from the reception desk. "Morning, Lauren. Marlene wants to see you in her office right away."

Marlene had already told her so on Friday, so Lauren just nodded. *God, Friday.* So much had happened since she had kissed Grace in the pool. Normally, she would have gone to see Marlene with more enthusiasm, knowing her boss wanted to talk about the promotion, but right now, all she could think of was Grace and how much she worried about her.

The door to Marlene's office stood open.

Lauren knocked on the doorframe and peeked in.

"Come on in and close the door behind you," Marlene called.

The male Siamese fighting fish flared his gills at Lauren as she passed the aquarium and settled in the chair in front of Marlene's desk. Tina and the rest of her colleagues kept saying that the fish could sense Marlene's mood and reacted with aggression whenever Marlene was about to reprimand an employee, but in this case, the fish's emotional radar had to be way off.

Marlene steepled her fingers on the desk and regarded her for several seconds. "You know how much I value you as one of our top publicists."

Lauren tensed. If this was supposed to be a conversation about her promotion, why did it feel as if there was a *but* coming?

"But," Marlene said, just as Lauren had feared, "no matter how much I appreciated your work over the years, I can't ignore this."

"Ignore what?"

"I got a call from Grace Durand's mother at six o'clock this morning," Marlene said. "She wants you removed as Ms. Durand's publicist immediately. She said she caught you kissing and pawing her daughter, pressuring her into having sex."

Goddammit. That bitch! Lauren's opinion of Grace's mother hadn't been very high to start with, but she hadn't thought Katherine would go that far. She gripped the edge of the chair with both hands, forcing herself to stay seated and not jump up and pace in outrage.

Marlene held up her hands. "I know she's prone to exaggerations and to taking action over her daughter's head, so I'm trying not to jump to conclusions, but this is an accusation I have to take seriously, especially after the Tabby Jones situation."

Lauren was sick of people bringing up that damn singer. So far, she had gritted her teeth and ignored it, but enough was enough. "Marlene, with all due respect, I don't know why we have to keep talking about Tabby Jones. I always conducted myself in a professional manner when I was on tour with her. She was the one who got drunk and made a pass at me, not the other way around. Ms. Durand is not like that at all."

Marlene relaxed against the back of her executive chair. "I didn't think she was. Listen, Lauren. It's not that I don't believe in your professionalism. But if a client's manager tells me she caught you taking advantage of her, I can't just let it go without asking some tough questions first. I tried to call Ms. Durand earlier to clear this up but couldn't reach her."

Lauren clenched her teeth so hard that her jaw started to hurt. "Taking advantage?" The words tasted bitter in her mouth. "That's not what happened. Once you reach Ms. Durand, she will confirm what I'm saying."

"Are you sure she'll side with you, not with her mother?" Marlene asked.

"I'm sure," Lauren said without even a hint of hesitation. Mrs. Duvenbeck had a lot of influence on her daughter, but Grace wouldn't betray her.

"So what really happened? Why is Mrs. Duvenbeck making these unfounded allegations against you?" Marlene asked. "What is it that she dislikes so much about you that she would try to ruin your reputation?"

A hundred thoughts tumbled through Lauren's mind. Her brain had trouble catching up with what was happening. She'd thought she would be getting a promotion, and now she was on the edge of being fired if she couldn't answer the question to Marlene's satisfaction. Only the truth could save her reputation, but it would mean outing Grace.

"Lauren?" Marlene prompted when Lauren kept hesitating. Her boss's gray eyes narrowed.

"There are many reasons why she doesn't like me," Lauren finally said. It sounded lame, even to her own ears.

"Such as?"

"My sexual orientation, for one thing," Lauren said, hoping her boss would leave it at that.

Marlene squinted over at her. "But there's more to it than that, isn't there? Why would Mrs. Duvenbeck feel so threatened by your sexual orientation?"

Damn. She should have known Marlene wouldn't buy it. "Mostly because she built her whole life on being the mother and manager of a beautiful, straight movie star and now she's deathly afraid that her daughter might be gay."

Marlene swished her leather chair a little to the side, tilted her head, and regarded Lauren with a frown. "Why is she still concerned about that? I thought we laid those rumors to rest once and for all?"

"We did, but…"

"But…what?" Marlene waved her fingers at her, her patience clearly wearing thin. "Come on. Out with it. What the hell is going on?"

Lauren tightened her grip on the chair until her fingers started to hurt. She wanted to scream at the unfairness of it all. If she refused to answer, Marlene would think there was at least some truth to Mrs. Duvenbeck's allegations. Her career and, what was more, her reputation would be ruined. Besides, how could she keep hoping that Grace might one day find the courage to publicly acknowledge their relationship when she herself was denying it, even in the face of such serious accusations? She leaned forward, a heavy weight on her shoulders, and regarded Marlene with an intent gaze. "This is totally off record, okay?"

Marlene nodded her assent.

She was one of few people in Hollywood Lauren trusted to keep a secret, especially since it was in Marlene's own best interest. She hesitated for a moment longer but knew the truth would come out once Marlene talked to Grace anyway. "I'm not sure Grace would put a label on herself, but…" Lauren squared her shoulders and willed her thudding heartbeat to slow. "She and I…we've recently gotten involved."

Sudden silence settled over the office. Only the soft whir of the aquarium filters drifted over.

"She's a client, Lauren," Marlene said, sounding as if she were laboring to keep her voice calm.

Lauren swallowed. "I know. Trust me, I didn't plan on falling in love with her. I tried to keep my distance, but…"

"Love?" Marlene repeated, her frown deepening. "So this isn't just a fleeting Hollywood thing or a bi-curious experiment?"

"No," Lauren said forcefully. Then, more softly, she added, "It's much more than that. Like I said, this isn't anything like the Tabby Jones situation."

"But Ms. Durand isn't thinking about making this public, is she?"

"We haven't talked about it yet." Truth be told, Lauren had been afraid to bring it up or make any demands, not wanting to put Grace in a position where she had to choose between their relationship and her career. "But I wouldn't rule it out at some point in the future."

"Christ." Marlene raked her hands through her graying hair, messing up her stylish hairdo. "You're putting me in an impossible situation, especially if you make your relationship public at some point. I don't want to lose you as an employee, but how can I keep telling our staff that getting involved with a client is a big no-no when I turn a blind eye to your involvement with a very prominent client?"

There was just one way out of this dilemma. Well, two, really, but if she had to make a choice between her career and Grace, her job would lose. For the first time in her life, her relationship was more important. Lauren knew that, but she still couldn't believe what she was about to say. "You'll have my resignation on your desk by the end of the day. I'll put notes in every client file before I go so Tina or someone else can take over."

Marlene stood and came around the desk. She looked down at Lauren with an incredulous shake of her head. "Are you sure that's what you want to do? I always saw a bright future for you at CTP, and now you want to give up your job...your career in PR...over a woman?"

"She's not just any woman," Lauren said quietly.

"No, she isn't."

They were probably talking about two different things, but Lauren didn't correct her. She stood and held out her hand. "Thanks for everything. I liked working here."

Marlene shook her hand. For the first time in the eight years that Lauren knew her, she looked as if she didn't know what to say.

With slow steps, Lauren walked past the Siamese fighting fish to the door. Her colleagues—well, former colleagues—were right. The flared gills weren't a good omen.

Grace and her mother had been a team her entire life. They had never lacked for things to talk about over breakfast. But now silence ruled on the patio as Grace poked around in her kiwi/blueberry yogurt and her mother sipped her smoothie.

When the phone rang, she got up, glad to leave the tense situation at the small patio table.

The number on the display looked familiar. *Oh, that's a CT Publicity number.* A warm feeling settled over her. Was Lauren calling her from work to see how she was doing? She slid her finger over the display to accept the call. "Hi."

"Good morning, Ms. Durand. This is Marlene Chandler from CT Publicity."

Grace's brows shot up. Why was Lauren's boss calling her? A cold shiver went down her spine. Had something happened to Lauren? *Nonsense.* Ms. Chandler wouldn't call her, then. She thought Lauren was nothing but her publicist to her. Grace drew a deep breath. "Good morning."

"I'm sorry to call you this early, but I was wondering if you have some time today to meet with me," Ms. Chandler said.

Grace frowned. If this was about a marketing campaign for her, why wasn't Lauren calling her? "What's this about?"

"Um, I'd rather not talk about it on the phone, if you don't mind."

That didn't sound good. Grace pinched the bridge of her nose. She so didn't need more problems in her life right now.

"I could meet you at your home at whatever time is convenient for you," Ms. Chandler said.

Grace didn't like strangers in the cottage. "Why don't I drop by your office? I could be there in about an hour."

"Sounds good. Thank you."

They ended the call.

"Who was that?" her mother asked.

"Ms. Chandler. She wants to meet with me."

Her mother emptied her smoothie and stood. "I'll come with you."

Grace didn't have the energy to protest. "Okay, then let's get going."

When the receptionist led them to Ms. Chandler's office, Grace kept an eye out for Lauren, hoping to catch a glimpse of her. But Lauren was nowhere to be seen, and her office door was closed.

With a longing glance, Grace walked past it.

Ms. Chandler greeted them with a friendly smile and offered them coffee, but Grace shook her head. She wanted to know what was going on—now. "What is this about?"

"Let me start by saying that we at CT Publicity are very proud to represent you and hope that you've been happy with our services so far." Ms. Chandler tugged on her silk scarf as if it were a noose around her neck.

"Ms. Pearce has done an excellent job with everything," Grace said.

"I'm sure she has. But given the nature of your relationship with her, I'm sure you'll agree that it would be for the best if someone else took over as your publicist."

Her words hit Grace like a punch to the stomach. Even nearly thirty years of experience as an actress didn't help to hide her shock. She stared at Ms. Chandler. "How...? Who told you that?"

Ms. Chandler didn't say anything, but her gaze went to the left.

Grace glanced in the same direction.

Her mother, who sat next to Grace, licked her lips and clutched her purse with both hands.

White-hot anger shot through Grace. For a moment, she felt as if she would black out. She swayed on her chair. "You...you told her about Lauren and me?"

Somehow, her mother must have called Ms. Chandler without her noticing, maybe when she'd been in the shower.

"I told her that Ms. Pearce has been taking advantage of your vulnerable emotional state," her mother said. "She's not the kind of person we want as your publicist."

"Taking advantage?" Grace repeated, her voice becoming louder. "That's not true! Lauren and I...we're in a relationship." She glared at her mother. "A consensual relationship."

"Lauren cleared that up already," Ms. Chandler said. "Listen, Ms. Durand, whatever is going on between the two of you is none of my business, but Lauren can't continue as your publicist. She knows that too. She quit her job this morning. But that doesn't mean we want to lose you as a client."

A roaring started in Grace's ears. Lauren loved her job. She'd worked hard for many years to be where she was today—and now she had lost everything because of her mother. *Because of me.*

Her mother reached over and patted Grace's arm. "I'm sure CTP can offer us the services of a publicist who's just as good if not better than Ms. Pearce."

Ms. Chandler nodded. "I could even take over your account myself."

The white-hot anger was replaced by cold determination. She had to pry apart her gritted teeth before she could speak. "With all due respect, Ms. Chandler. I'm sure you're really good at what you do, but I don't want you as my publicist. I already have one—Lauren Pearce. If CTP can't offer me her services, I'm done with your firm."

"My daughter doesn't mean that. She's just upset. Maybe you could—"

"I mean it more than I ever meant anything in my life." Grace whirled to face her mother and shoved her patting hand from her forearm.

"You're not thinking clearly, darling. As your manager, I advise you to—"

"You're no longer my manager. You're fired."

Silence descended on the room.

Even Grace was shocked by what she'd just said, but she refused to take it back.

Her mother's strangled gasp echoed through the office. "You can't do that! Just think about where you'd be without me—probably waiting tables, like so many other struggling actresses!"

"Maybe," Grace said. A strange calm settled over her, giving her the strength to face her mother and go on. "Maybe not. I'm grateful for all you've done for me over the years, Mom. But somewhere along the way, you being my manager stopped being good for me. You're my mother. You should be concerned with my happiness, not with my box office numbers or—"

"How can you say that I'm not concerned with your happiness?" Big, fat tears smudged her mother's mascara.

"Because Lauren is what makes me happy and you just got her fired."

"She resigned," Ms. Chandler said, as if that made any difference.

"Then hire her back." Grace stood. Her legs were shaking, and so was the rest of her, but she ignored it and tried to keep her voice steady as she said, "I'm leaving. Are you coming, or do you want Ms. Chandler to call you a cab?"

Her mother looked at her as if she were a total stranger.

Forcing herself not to look back to see if her mother would follow, Grace strode to the door.

For once, the Siamese fighting fish didn't flare his gills when Lauren walked past the aquarium a few hours later to hand over her resignation letter. Maybe he wasn't as good at predicting the atmosphere in Marlene's office as everyone thought.

Her heart tightened at the thought that this was the last time she would ever walk past the fish, would ever be in Marlene's office. Still, she wasn't as devastated as she had thought she would be. As long as she had Grace, she would be fine.

When she reached the desk, she held out the envelope. "My resignation letter. All of my files are in order, and I left detailed instructions for my replacement."

Marlene took the resignation letter and studied it for a moment before tearing it into little pieces. She swept them into her garbage can and looked up at Lauren with a grim expression. "There."

Lauren stared at her. "I thought you wanted me to resign?"

"You know what I always say: the customer is king. Ms. Durand insists on keeping you as her publicist."

Grace knew about all of this—and had put her foot down and stuck with Lauren, against her mother's wishes? Elation swept through Lauren.

"Make no mistake about it; I don't appreciate being blackmailed into making personnel decisions that go against company policy, but we can't afford to lose Ms. Durand as a client." The hard lines of Marlene's face softened a bit. "And, to tell you the truth, I wasn't happy to lose you as an employee anyway. But maybe you could talk to your...to Ms. Durand. I'd like to make Tina her official publicist while you supervise behind the scenes."

It sounded like an acceptable solution. Lauren hesitated. Did she really want her job back under these circumstances? She had worked hard to earn a reputation as a publicist who was not only competent but highly professional too. If she now got to keep her job just because the woman she was involved with had blackmailed her boss...

She slowly shook her head. "I'm not sure staying would be the right thing to do. I think I should take this as a chance to think about where I want to go with my life." She stood and clutched the back of the chair with both hands. "I'll go print out my resignation letter again."

"People will want to know why you're leaving CTP," Marlene said.

"I know. I'll think of something we can tell them. Something that won't harm your reputation—or my own—or make people suspect what's really going on." The first step toward the door felt shaky, but with every further step, she gained confidence in her decision.

"Lauren," Marlene called.

A little warily, Lauren turned.

Marlene regarded her across the room. "If you ever need a referral, let me know. I'll highly recommend you to anyone."

Lauren nodded and walked out. Before she closed the door behind her, she caught a glimpse of the Siamese fighting fish. The male and his harem floated peacefully, as if agreeing that it had been the right thing to do.

CHAPTER 34

FOR ONCE, LAUREN SPED UP the dirt road to the cottage, not caring about any damage it might do to her car. She couldn't wait to find out exactly what had happened and how Grace was doing. After parking next to Grace's SUV, she hurried to the front door and rang the doorbell in a rapid rhythm.

Grace opened the door, looking pale and beautiful. She was wearing Lauren's Boston University sweatshirt as if she'd needed the comfort.

Wordlessly, they came together in a tight embrace, clinging to each other. Lauren felt Grace tremble against her and held her tenderly. "What happened?" she whispered into Grace's hair.

"My mother called your boss and accused you of—"

"No reason to repeat it," Lauren said quickly. "I know what she said. My boss called me into her office and confronted me with her accusations. I'm so sorry, Grace. I tried to call you afterward to tell you...to warn you, but my calls kept going to voice mail."

"I turned my phone off after Ms. Chandler called. I could tell something serious was going on, and I didn't want to be interrupted."

"I'm sorry," Lauren said again. "I know it should have been your decision, but I had to tell Marlene about us or she would have thought—"

Grace squeezed her softly. "I know. It's okay. I'm so sorry for what my mother did. After I talked to your boss, she hired you back, right?"

"She wanted to, but I resigned anyway."

"You did...what?" Grace let go of her and took a step back to stare at her.

Lauren entered the cottage and closed the door behind them. "I don't want to keep my job because my girlfriend used her influence with my boss." She faltered when she realized what she'd just called Grace, but when Grace didn't object, she continued. "Can you understand that?"

"Yeah, but—"

"Besides," Lauren reached out and tucked an errant strand of hair behind Grace's ear, "it's almost never a good idea to mix business with pleasure. Just look at what having your mother as your manager did to your relationship. I'd rather be your partner than your publicist."

"But...but I need a publicist—and a new manager."

For a moment, Lauren thought she had misunderstood. "You fired your mother?"

Grace nodded. "I should have done it a long time ago. So you can see that I need a good publicist by my side—especially now that I'm thinking about coming out to the public."

Lauren felt her mouth move, but no words were coming out. She gaped at Grace for several moments. Her head was spinning. She stumbled over to the couch, pulling Grace with her, and plopped down on it. When she was safely sitting, she clutched Grace's hand with both of hers. "You're thinking about coming out?" Her voice squeaked like that of a teenager whose voice was breaking.

A faint smile ghosted over Grace's face. "Jill says if my fans and the studios don't like it, I could always retire and take a hot lover to keep myself busy."

"Grace, you and I...we're still pretty new. I don't expect you to make such a life-changing decision right now."

"I don't think I can avoid it for much longer," Grace said. She looked resigned but not upset.

Lauren's brow furrowed. "Why not?"

"Because I'm head over heels in love with you, and unless I want to do some serious acting in my spare time, anyone with eyes will soon figure it out." As soon as she'd said it, Grace sat stock-still, not even breathing while she waited for Lauren's response.

Any thought of their jobs withered away. A strangled sound of joy escaped Lauren. She felt as if her chest would burst with happiness. Her vocal cords refused to work, but her lips were still functioning, so she did the only rational thing—she pulled Grace close and kissed her.

Grace's hands came up, cradling Lauren's face as she opened her mouth and their tongues made contact.

Nothing had ever felt so good as kissing Grace, knowing she returned her feelings. Lauren shifted on the couch, never interrupting the kiss, to bring their bodies even closer. Her fingers slipped beneath the sweatshirt Grace wore, encountering warm skin.

Grace sighed into the kiss.

When the kiss finally ended, Lauren cradled Grace's face between her palms and looked deeply into her eyes. "Just in case my body language didn't make it one hundred percent clear—I love you too."

Grace's face shone with happiness. She ran her fingers up the back of Lauren's neck, threaded them through her hair, and pulled her down for another kiss.

This time, Lauren let her hands explore a little more, caressing the smooth skin of Grace's back and sides.

Grace moaned and then gasped when Lauren slid one hand up Grace's belly, brushing the underside of her breasts.

The erotic sounds made Lauren's head spin. She pulled away but kept one hand resting on the small of Grace's back. She searched Grace's face, trying to find out whether she was going too fast, but all she saw was the passion smoldering in her ocean-blue eyes. "God, Grace. I want to make love to you. But I know that after everything that happened today, you might not be ready or in the mood to—"

Grace shook her head. "If we wait any longer, I'm going to spontaneously combust."

A smile grew on Lauren's lips. "Well, in that case, what do you say we move this to the bedroom? I want to do this right, and I'm too old for the couch."

Instead of a verbal answer, Grace got up and pulled Lauren by the hand to the ladder leading up to the loft.

Lauren gripped her hips from behind, steadying her for as long as possible as Grace climbed up. She let her hands trail over Grace's shapely ass and then down her long legs until Grace disappeared over the edge of the loft. Quickly, she followed her up.

They stood in front of each other in the small space under the roof. It felt as if they had entered a world completely of their own, where nothing existed but the two of them and the love they shared.

Lauren trailed her fingertips down the side of Grace's face and then cradled her cheek in one palm. She took in every inch of Grace in breathless awe. "I had no idea I could love someone this much. Let me show you."

Looking into Lauren's eyes, Grace nodded.

Grace had heard words of love from Nick and from the few boyfriends before him, but this was different—not just because Lauren was a woman but because, for the first time in her life, her heart reflected what she saw in Lauren's eyes. It was wonderful and scary at the same time.

The confidence she usually felt when making love was gone. Every muscle in her body trembled.

Then Lauren slid her hands down, over Grace's shoulders and along her arms until she grasped her hands and tenderly pulled her closer. She rested her forehead against Grace's. "You're not scared, are you?" she whispered.

The warm breath bathing her face made Grace shiver. She started to shake her head but then stopped herself. No acting. Not with Lauren. "A little. This is so... overwhelming."

"Being with a woman for the first time?"

"No." Grace licked her lips. "Being with you for the first time."

Lauren tugged her even closer by their entwined hands and kissed her, just a short touch of her lips to Grace's. "This is new for me too. I've never been with someone I cared for so much."

This time, it was Grace who pulled her closer and kissed her.

The kiss started out slow and tender but quickly grew demanding as Lauren took charge.

Grace had appreciated Lauren always letting her make the first move and set the pace, but now she realized how hot it was to have Lauren take the lead. She groaned in protest when Lauren broke the kiss. It turned into a sound of pleasure as Lauren traced a line up the side of Grace's neck with her lips and then nipped at her earlobe.

"As much as I love seeing you in my sweatshirt, it has to go," Lauren whispered against her ear.

A shiver went through Grace's body. She reached down to grasp the edge of the sweatshirt and pull it over her head, but Lauren covered her hands with her own and stopped her.

"Let me." Lauren stripped off the sweatshirt and dropped it to the floor. She bent her head and again kissed Grace's neck while her fingertips slid over Grace's back, her arms, and then up her side, leaving goose bumps in their wake. With one hand, she cupped Grace's bra-encased breast and stroked the nipple through the lacy material.

It hardened instantly. Grace swayed and clutched Lauren's shoulders with both hands. Aching for more, she reached back to unhook her bra, but again, Lauren took over.

"Mine." She growled against Grace's neck. One flick of her fingers opened the clasp of the bra. It fell on top of the sweatshirt. Lauren's heated gaze swept over Grace's body.

The awe in her eyes made Grace's cheeks flush.

Lauren slowly lowered her head and kissed the slope of one breast. "Beautiful," she whispered.

"I want to see you too," Grace said.

Her air of confidence seemed to waver as Lauren paused and hesitated. Her fingers retreated from Grace's body and played with the collar of her blouse. "Just don't expect me to look like an actress, okay? I can't compete with—"

"Shut up," Grace said, her voice low and rough, but her hands gentle as she pulled Lauren close and kissed her. "I don't want an actress. I want you. You're perfect to me."

Lauren claimed her lips in a heated kiss. When the kiss tapered off, Lauren took a steadying breath and started to unbutton her blouse. One button refused to cooperate, so she pulled the blouse up over her head and tossed it on the growing heap on the floor.

Without thinking, Grace reached out and ran her fingertips along the edge of the plain, white bra, fascinated by the goose bumps that rose beneath her touch. She only realized that Lauren had opened her bra when it fell, baring small but perfectly shaped breasts to Grace's gaze. God, how could Lauren think she was anything but beautiful?

Gathering her courage, she touched one of Lauren's breasts. She slid her fingertips over its side, following the pleasing curve, then cupped it in her palm experimentally. "Oh. This is…"

"Weird?"

Grace shook her head. "Wonderful. I never got what's so special about breasts, but now…"

"Breasts are wonderful—especially yours." Lauren bent and nuzzled Grace's cleavage. She kissed a trail down Grace's breastbone and then, after a quick peek up at her face, flicked her tongue over one nipple.

A jolt of arousal hit Grace right between her legs. She arched closer and groaned.

"Is this okay?" Lauren whispered.

Her breath brushed over Grace's wet nipple, making her shudder. "God, do you really have to ask?"

"Guess not."

Grace felt her smile against her skin; then Lauren took her nipple between her lips and sucked gently. Grace's vision went out of focus. With a gasp, she raked her nails down Lauren's bare back.

A low, hungry sound escaped Lauren. She swiped her tongue over Grace's nipple again. With one hand, she held Grace against her, while the other hand slid down Grace's quivering belly and unbuttoned the fly of her jeans. Her fingertips grazed the upper edge of Grace's panties, dipped below, and then paused.

Grace reached down and grasped Lauren's wrist, not sure if she wanted to pull her away or push her hand down. She felt too close to losing all control already.

As if sensing her conflicting urges, Lauren slid her hand around to Grace's hip and let it rest there. "Are you okay?"

Grace nodded. "You just make me feel so much. I'm this close to losing control already."

"You don't need to control yourself. Not with me." Lauren caressed Grace's belly. "Just relax and enjoy. Why don't we move this to the bed?"

Grace's legs felt wobbly, so the bed was definitely a good idea. She nodded.

But instead of moving to the bed, Lauren first sank to her knees and eased down Grace's jeans, taking the panties with them and leaving them in a puddle at her feet. She leaned forward and kissed Grace's belly.

The hammering beat of Grace's heart thudded through her body. She wove her fingers through Lauren's hair and held her against her. The whispers of kisses against her overheated skin were driving her crazy.

Lauren's lips wandered lower, brushing the curly hair at the apex of Grace's thighs.

Heat shot through her.

Lauren pressed a kiss to Grace's lower abdomen and then stood, dragging her hardened nipples against Grace's front.

When their bare breasts touched, a low, guttural sound escaped Grace. She had dreamed about this the past few weeks but had never thought it would feel this good.

Their mouths found each other again, and their moans mingled.

"Bed," Lauren whispered urgently.

"Wait." Grace pointed at Lauren's slacks. "These need to come off first. I want to feel you. All of you."

Lauren's slacks hit the floor in less than two seconds. Her panties followed. Then Lauren reached for her.

The intimate contact of skin on skin made Grace suck in a breath. She strained against Lauren, feeling as if she couldn't get close enough.

Lauren walked her backward and eased her down onto the bed. For a moment, she knelt on the bed and looked down at her with an expression of wonder.

Grace reached up and drew her down.

Balancing on one arm, Lauren settled on top of her. One of her legs slipped between Grace's thighs.

Both of them moaned.

Grace pressed herself against her, aching for her touch.

Lauren leaned down and kissed the hollow of Grace's throat, then her neck, where her pulse thudded, and finally her lips.

Her fingers dug into Lauren's back. Grace lost herself in the kiss and restlessly moved against Lauren. A faint throbbing was already starting low in her belly.

Gasping, Lauren broke the kiss. "Tell me what you like," she said, her voice husky.

"Everything," Grace answered, a catch in her voice. "I like everything you're doing."

Lauren groaned. "I wanted to take my time and worship every part of you, but... God, you're driving me crazy."

"I don't need to be worshipped. I just want to be"—she gasped as Lauren cupped her breast with one hand, leaned down, and sucked part of it into her mouth—"Loved. Oh!"

"You are," Lauren whispered against her breast. She trailed her fingers down Grace's side, over her hip, and along the outer side of her thigh. Then, with a very light touch, she stroked up the inside of her thigh.

Grace stopped breathing in expectation of where that hand would end up. At the first touch of Lauren's finger against her, she sucked in a shuddery breath. Moaning, she opened her legs wider.

Lauren took the unspoken invitation. Her finger skimmed Grace's clit.

Grace moved against her. *More. Harder.* Her nails skated down and then dug into Lauren's back when that finger moved over her again.

"Like this?" Lauren asked.

Grace was beyond speech. She reached down and pressed Lauren's hand more firmly against herself.

A moan drifted through the loft. Had that been her or Lauren? Grace was no longer sure. She didn't care. All she cared about was Lauren—Lauren moving against her, then slipping into her with one finger, withdrawing, and finally coming back with two.

"Oh God. Yes." Grace rocked against her, meeting each of her thrusts. Her hands trailed up and down Lauren's sweat-dampened back.

Lauren curved her fingers and hit another area inside Grace.

A strangled shout escaped Grace's raw throat. Her hips jerked against Lauren as a throbbing started deep in her belly, quickly spreading outward.

"That's it," Lauren whispered against her lips. "Come for me."

And as she flicked her thumb over Grace's clit, Grace did. Her muscles contracted sharply around Lauren's fingers. She surged upward, clutching Lauren to her, and then fell back.

Before Grace had fully recovered, Lauren moved down and lifted one of Grace's legs over her shoulder. Her hot breath washed over Grace's swollen sex.

Through a fog of pleasure, Grace stared down at her. "What...?" It took her a moment to realize what was happening. She was about to pull Lauren back up and tell her she couldn't come twice in a row, but before her foggy brain could find the right words, Lauren lightly swept her tongue over her still-throbbing clit.

"Oh God!" Grace arched up as another wave of pleasure rushed through her.

"So good," Lauren murmured against her. "You taste so good."

Grace tangled her fingers in Lauren's hair and pulled her closer. Looking down at Lauren, she got out, "Don't...don't stop."

Lauren flattened her tongue, still keeping her touches light and then gradually making them firmer until Grace's entire body seemed to be throbbing. Gently, she nudged Grace's legs open wider.

Grace's breath came in ragged gasps. The muscles of her abdomen clenched. Her legs convulsed around Lauren, drawing her closer.

When Lauren closed her lips over Grace's clit and sucked gently, another orgasm hit her.

"Lauren!" She arched off the bed as shockwaves of pleasure swept through her.

Lauren crawled up Grace's body, trailing kisses over every inch of her skin.

Grace lay limply beneath her. Every muscle in her body had turned to mush. She blinked, trying to get her eyes to focus.

Lauren's flushed face appeared in her line of sight. "I hope that was okay. Maybe I should have asked first, but I just couldn't help myself."

Unable to form a coherent sentence, Grace merely nodded and drew her down for a kiss. She moaned when she tasted herself on Lauren's lips.

They lay in a sweaty tangle of arms and legs until Grace became aware of Lauren's wetness against her thigh. Her hands shook with a mix of desire and nervousness as she slid them down Lauren's body. She just hoped she'd be able to please Lauren at least half as much as Lauren had pleased her.

Lauren shivered as Grace slid her hand down her sweat-dampened side.

"Show me," Grace whispered against her neck and then gave it a little nip. "Show me how to please you."

"You do already." Making love to Grace had been a dream come true. God, the way Grace had responded to her touch... She had almost come with Grace the second time.

Grace pushed one leg between Lauren's to maneuver her around, onto her back.

Lauren groaned at the pressure and moved her hips against Grace's thigh. "Jesus, I'm so close already. It won't take much."

"Oh, no." Grace rolled off Lauren and lay next to her. "I don't want this to be over so fast. I want to touch every part of you."

Another groan escaped Lauren as Grace's words pushed her even closer to release.

Grace paused, leaning over her on one elbow, and swept her gaze down Lauren's body as if she couldn't decide where to touch her first. She softly caressed the shoulder closest to her, then leaned down and let her lips follow the path of her fingers.

Clutching the sheets with both hands, Lauren lay still and let Grace do whatever she wanted.

Grace stroked and kissed along Lauren's collarbone and then flicked out her tongue to taste a drop of sweat pooling at the hollow of Lauren's throat.

Strands of Grace's long, blonde hair tickled her overly sensitized skin as Grace covered every inch of her upper chest with kisses and careful little nibbles. Shivers ran through Lauren's body, and she was already breathing hard. She reached up with one hand and gently tried to guide Grace toward her breast, but Grace didn't seem to be in a hurry.

She explored leisurely, tracing the curve of Lauren's ribs with her fingertips and then circling one breast. Finally, she cupped it in one palm and looked up at Lauren, an expression of awe on her face. Then her hair fell like a curtain around her, hiding her features, as she bent and pressed a gentle kiss to Lauren's breast. She rubbed her cheek against it, first one side, then the other. "Oh. Your breasts are so soft."

The sight of Grace making love to her breasts was almost too much for Lauren. She felt as if she were melting from the inside out. "Not every part of them," she said, her voice raspy. Her nipples were rock-hard and ached for Grace's touch.

"Oh, you mean...this?" Grace took one nipple between thumb and index finger and rolled it gently as if trying to test its hardness.

Lauren flung her head back. "Yes! God."

Leaning down again, Grace took Lauren's nipple into her mouth and laved it with her tongue. She licked with the same hums of pleasure that had escaped her when Lauren had bought her ice cream. After a while, she tried to switch to the other breast but couldn't comfortably reach it, so she rolled on top of Lauren and nestled between her legs. Then the sweet torture continued.

Lauren writhed beneath her, holding Grace against her breast with both hands. Having Grace's curvy body on top of her felt heavenly, and what Grace did with her mouth... She took several shuddering breaths, fighting for some semblance of control. But it was a losing battle. Her control faded quickly under Grace's slow explorations.

When Grace gently raked her teeth over one nipple, Lauren's hips arched up. She hooked one leg around Grace and rocked against her abdomen, desperately seeking some pressure against her clit. "God, I need..."

Grace let go of her nipple and looked up. Her cheeks were flushed, and her eyes clouded with passion. "What? What do you need?"

"Touch me," Lauren said. She barely recognized her own voice.

Now looking a little apprehensive for the first time, Grace trailed her fingers down Lauren's stomach and, after looking back up into Lauren's eyes for reassurance, ran them through Lauren's curls.

Both drew in a sharp breath.

Lauren already felt herself hovering on the edge of climax.

"Oh, wow," Grace whispered as she started to stroke Lauren, her touch first tentative, then increasingly bolder.

Groaning, Lauren pulled her down and kissed her. Her hips rocked against Grace. Sensation built deep inside of her. She gripped Grace's hip with one hand, urging her on. *Oh God.* This was going to be fast. She broke the kiss to gasp for breath. Incoherent sounds tumbled from her lips.

Grace moved her fingers faster and then dragged them over the very tip of Lauren's clit with a little more pressure.

Lauren's stomach tightened. Orgasm hit without any further warning. "Grace!" She surged up against her. Her entire body shook and quivered as waves of pleasure rolled over her.

Then Grace was there, in her arms, holding her close. Her thigh pressed against Lauren, prolonging the pleasure.

When Lauren's muscles started working again, she weakly lifted her head and kissed Grace's lips, her cheek, her temple. Burrowing her face against Grace's damp neck, she mumbled breathlessly, "I'm not...usually...that...quick."

Grace guided Lauren's mouth to hers and kissed her. Her eyes shone with excitement, glowing against her flushed cheeks. "I take it I did okay?"

"Okay?" Lauren dazedly shook her head. "Let me put it in a way you'll understand best." She pretended to open an imaginary envelope and pull out a card. "And the Oscar for best performance goes to...Grace Durand."

"You!"

They wrestled playfully until the slide of skin against skin ignited their passion again.

Definitely Oscar-worthy, was Lauren's last coherent thought for quite some time.

Night had fallen while they'd made love, so now the cottage lay in darkness except for the soft glow coming from the loft. Lauren, who had gone to get them something to drink, climbed back up the ladder, two small bottles of water clutched in one hand. On the last rung, she paused to take in Grace.

She lay stretched out on her belly, the covers pooling at her waist. The smooth skin of her back called to Lauren, and she almost couldn't believe that she would get to crawl back into bed with this wonderful woman. A rush of love swept through her. Giddiness bubbled up, and she let out a laugh, amazed at her good fortune.

Grace turned onto her side and lifted up on her elbow. A slow smile spread over her face and lit up her eyes. "What are you doing down there? Come back to bed."

Lauren didn't have to be told twice. She climbed the last rung and slipped under the covers.

They sat side by side, leaning against the headboard, and emptied the bottles of water before sliding down in bed and cuddling close.

Grace settled half on top of Lauren, with her head on Lauren's upper chest and one leg across her thighs. Her eyes were closed, and she looked more relaxed and at peace than Lauren had ever seen her. "This is wonderful," Grace whispered. She opened her eyes and looked at Lauren. "I love you."

They had repeatedly whispered it to each other earlier, but Lauren's breath still caught. "I love you too." She smiled and let her fingers drift through Grace's soft hair. "What happens now?" she asked after a while of just enjoying the closeness.

"Well, as a very wise friend of mine once pointed out, we're women and can have multiple orgasms, so...more of the same." Grace grinned and trailed her hand down Lauren's belly.

"Oh God." Lauren trapped Grace's hand beneath hers, stopping it from sliding any lower. "I think I created a monster."

"Are you complaining?"

"Hell, no!" But for the moment, they were sated, so they just lay in each other's arms. Lauren craned her neck so she could place a kiss on Grace's head. "I meant, what happens in the future? Do you really think you're ready to make our relationship public?"

Grace lifted her head off Lauren's chest and looked into her eyes. "I don't know if I'm ready. But I want this. I want us. I want to go to sleep with you and wake up with you and spend as much time as I can in between with you. And that's not going to happen unless we make it official."

Lauren's heart ached with longing. She wanted the same things. It would have been so easy to be selfish and say yes to everything, but she wanted Grace's happiness even more than her own. "I'd love to do that, but is this really the best time for you...for your career?"

A sigh fluttered across Lauren's bare chest as Grace laid her head back down. "I don't know. I don't even know if there *is* a best time. So we might as well do it now."

"I'd need to media-train you first, teach you what to say and what not to say. Jill forced my hand, but with most of my LGBT clients, I prepare their coming out for months."

"I thought you resigned as my publicist?"

Lauren grinned ruefully. "Right. I did. But if you hire Marlene—and I would recommend it—she will tell you the same."

"Months," Grace murmured. She peeked up at Lauren. "Can you wait that long? I know you're out and proud. Stepping back into the closet with me would be awful for you."

Lauren linked her hands in the small of Grace's back and drew her even closer. "Don't worry, okay? You won't get rid of me just because I can't kiss you or even hold your hand in public right now. I know it won't be easy, but some things are worth waiting for."

A smile curled Grace's full lips. "There you go again, being romantic."

"I told you I was rethinking my attitude. It's difficult not to when you're in love with the most wonderful woman in the world."

Grace rolled her eyes but then grinned and kissed her. "Charmer. Speaking of rethinking... Now that you're rethinking your professional future, maybe you should think about sending your script to a couple of producers."

Lauren paused her gentle caresses to Grace's back. "I don't know."

"If you're worried about money... I have more than enough for the two of us."

"Thanks," Lauren said. "But that's not it. I have enough saved to live off of for a while."

"What is it, then?"

Lauren reached up and rubbed her nose, almost embarrassed to admit it. "I'm afraid of rejection. What if they don't like my script?"

"You'll never find out if you don't try. They'll love it; believe me." Grace's eyes glittered with conviction. "Besides, I promised to audition for the lead role if you ever made your script into a movie. I don't think you'll have any problems selling your script if you tell producers who comes attached with it. Well, that is, if coming out won't put me on the list of people not to cast."

"No," Lauren said firmly. "You're past the stage in your career where something like that would happen. You just have to pick your next two or three movies carefully, and you'll be fine. That means no lesbian movies, though, including mine."

"Oh." The happy glow on Grace's face dimmed. "But I promised you—"

Lauren kissed her tenderly. "I really appreciate your willingness to keep your promise. But if I do this, I need to do it on my own. I want producers to buy my script because it's good, not because of who my parents are or what actress supports it. Can you understand that?"

Still leaning over her, Grace caressed Lauren's face with a tenderness that made Lauren's breath catch. "Yes. But if there's ever anything I can do to support you, let me know, okay?"

Lauren cradled Grace's face in both of her palms and softly brought their lips together. "Thank you. You're wonderful. Your support means the world to me."

"So you'll do it?" Grace whispered against her lips. "Send your script out to producers?"

Lauren inhaled and exhaled deeply. With Grace by her side, it didn't seem so scary anymore. "I'll do it."

EPILOGUE

Three months later

GRACE STARED AT THE AUTOGRAPHED posters of former talk show guests covering the walls of the backstage greenroom, wondering if any of them had been as nervous as she was. She wished the greenroom had a window so she could watch the snow drift down on Rockefeller Plaza.

A large flat-screen TV was blaring behind her, and an intern chattered nonstop, trying to calm down one of the other guests.

"You should eat something, darling." Her mother stepped next to her and pointed at the snacks the studio provided.

"No, thanks. I'm too nervous to eat."

"Are you sure you want to go through with this?" her mother asked. "I really think you should—"

Grace turned her head and gave her a stern look. "Mom, we've talked about this. You're not my manager anymore."

"I'm still your mother. I worry about you."

"I understand that." Grace reached out and squeezed her mother's arm. "I wish this weren't necessary, but it's something I have to do."

Her mother bowed her head and fell silent.

Wow. That's a first. Sometimes, Grace couldn't believe how much her life had changed in the last few months—and it was about to change even more radically. Her stomach churned.

Marlene joined them. "Are you ready?"

She didn't feel ready at all, but her new publicist didn't want to hear that, so Grace nodded.

"Remember not to—"

"Use the word *admit*. It's a relationship, not a crime," Grace repeated what Marlene had told her during their media-training sessions.

"Good. I know you'll do just fine." Marlene patted her shoulder and left Grace to her appraisal of the autographed posters.

Someone else stepped up behind her, and Grace knew who it was even before two warm hands came to rest on her shoulders, massaging gently for a few moments.

With a soft groan, she leaned back into Lauren.

"It's getting close to airtime," Lauren said. "Marlene, your mother, and I have to take our places in the audience now."

Grace covered one of Lauren's hands with her own, not wanting to let her go.

"You can do this," Lauren whispered into her ear. "I'll be right there in the first row the entire time."

Grace gratefully squeezed her hand. The talk show would be just the beginning, though; a new media circus would follow. While she worried about what was coming, at least the hiding would be over. Sneaking around for the last three months had been hard on both of them, even though they'd known they were working toward this moment.

She nodded numbly.

Lauren pulled her around and looked into her eyes. "Do you want—?"

"No," Grace said, knowing what Lauren was about to say. "I want to do this." Not caring that the other guests were gaping at them or might even tweet about it, she wrapped her arms around Lauren, pulled her down a little, and kissed her. "For good luck," she whispered when the kiss ended.

Grace's mother watched them with the same expression she used to wear when she had watched Grace rehearse a scene and didn't approve of her performance, but once again, she said nothing.

Lauren caressed Grace's cheek and brushed her lips over Grace's again before stepping back, still holding her gaze.

Not saying another word, they nodded at each other.

Then Lauren turned and left, along with Grace's mother and Marlene.

Grace wrapped her arms around herself, instantly missing Lauren's comforting presence. She paced the room and finally forced herself to settle down on one of the red-and-black-checkered sofas and to chat with the other guests.

After about ten minutes, Steven Ryland, the host of the daytime talk show, appeared on the flat-screen TV and greeted the audience.

The other guests chuckled about something Steven said, but Grace was too tense to laugh.

A production assistant with a headset entered and gave Grace a nod. "You're up in five minutes." She escorted Grace to the stage curtain.

Grace rubbed her damp palms over the above-the-knee skirt that Marlene had chosen for her to wear. She peeked through a gap in the curtain, into the audience below.

The studio easily seated two hundred, but her gaze immediately zeroed in on Lauren, who was listening raptly when Steven started to introduce Grace as the first guest and talked about *Ava's Heart*. Next to her sat Jill; Marlene; Grace's mother; George, her agent; and Barbara, her new manager, all there to show their support.

Her nerves settled a little.

She returned her attention to the host just in time to hear him say, "Please welcome the lovely Grace Durand!"

With her heart beating overtime, she stepped out from behind the curtain and into the bright lights. She put on her most convincing Hollywood smile and waved at the audience as she stepped onto the set, which looked like a cozy living room with two slate-blue armchairs placed at an angle to each other.

People clapped, stomped, and whistled.

She greeted Steven with two air kisses before settling into one of the armchairs. When she crossed one leg over the other, her skirt slid up and revealed a bit of thigh. Each of her moves had been carefully planned by Marlene and the rest of the team—and their plan seemed to work so far.

The audience clapped even more loudly.

"They love you," Steven said with a grin as he sat in his own armchair.

Let's hope they still do once this is over. "Thank you," she said, again waving at the audience.

"You look incredible." Steven gestured at her. "Divorced life certainly seems to agree with you. I heard you recently joined the club of divorcees."

"I did, although I can't quite match your platinum membership," she said, earning her laughter and applause from the audience.

Steven clutched his chest. "Ouch. At least my exes still love me…and my alimony payments. So, what was your divorce like? *The War of the Roses?*"

"No, I'm happy to report there were no run-over sports cars or crashing chandeliers," Grace said. Well, for a moment, Nick had looked as if he wanted to drop a chandelier on her when she'd told him about her and Lauren, but in the end, he'd told her to do whatever made her happy.

"But I hear there'll be chandeliers in your next movie," Steven said. "Can you tell us a bit about it?"

"It's a historical adventure drama called *Like Diamonds*. Shooting will start next week, and I'm very excited about it. I'm playing Abigail, the daughter of a rich banker in nineteenth-century England. She's raised to be just a beautiful ornament in his house, but it turns out she's really good at stealing diamonds."

"So she's a kleptomaniac?" Steven asked.

"More like a female Robin Hood."

Steven nodded. "I see. So who's playing your Maid Marian…or should I say Mario?"

"No one. There's no love story in this one, just great action scenes, rich historical details, mixed with a bit of social criticism."

"No love story?" Steven widened his eyes comically.

Grace shrugged. "I'm ready to branch out a little. Don't get me wrong; I still love the romantic movies I'm known for, but I'd like to explore more diversity in my roles."

"So it's not that you're fed up with love stories, now that you're divorced?"

"Not at all. In fact…" She took a deep breath. "I'm living my own love story right now."

Steven leaned forward. "Ooh, do tell! Who's the lucky guy? A fellow actor?"

"Actually…" Grace clutched the armrests with both hands. Her heartbeat thrummed in her ears. She looked toward the audience, seeking Lauren. Their gazes locked. The connection centered her, reminding her what really counted in her life. She took a freeing breath, turned back to Steven, and said with a smile that wasn't the Hollywood kind, "She's a screenwriter."

For a moment, Steven's cheerful grin wavered. He blinked rapidly. "Did you just say…she?"

Grace swallowed. "Yes, I did."

The ensuing silence probably lasted for just a second, but to Grace, it seemed to go on forever.

Then all hell broke loose. The audience cheered and applauded. Someone was booing, though, and for some reason, that voice seemed so much louder than the others.

"This isn't a publicity stunt or a joke because the tabloids kept making up stories about you and Jill Corrigan, is it?" Steven asked.

Marlene had told her a question like that would be coming. "No," Grace said, more calm now. "Jill and I really are just friends. Best friends. This isn't a publicity stunt. It's the real thing."

"Wow." Now Steven's wide-eyed gaze was real. "I didn't see that coming."

"Neither did I, Steven," she said. "Neither did I." When she and Lauren had first met, she hadn't even been sure if she wanted to hire her as a publicist. Never in a million years had she thought she would fall in love with her. But now, just seven months later, she knew one thing with crystal clarity: nothing would ever be as important to her as Lauren, not even her career.

She looked toward the first row, where Lauren gave her a tremulous smile. Grace smiled back, and even though the cameras were rolling and probably millions of people were watching, she didn't have to act for once. No matter what the future would bring, she looked forward to spending it with Lauren.

If you liked reading about these characters, you might want to check out *Departure from the Script,* the first book in Jae's *Hollywood Series*, which tells the story of Grace's friend Amanda.

ABOUT JAE

Jae grew up amidst the vineyards of southern Germany. She spent her childhood with her nose buried in a book, earning her the nickname *professor*. The writing bug bit her at the age of eleven. For the last eight years, she has been writing mostly in English.

She used to work as a psychologist but gave up her day job in December 2013 to become a full-time writer and a part-time editor. As far as she's concerned, it's the best job in the world.

When she's not writing, she likes to spend her time reading, indulging her ice cream and office supply addictions, and watching way too many crime shows.

CONNECT WITH JAE ONLINE

Jae loves hearing from readers!

E-mail her at: jae@jae-fiction.com
Visit her website: jae-fiction.com
Visit her blog: jae-fiction.com/blog
Like her on Facebook: facebook.com/JaeAuthor
Follow her on Twitter: @jaefiction

OTHER BOOKS FROM YLVA PUBLISHING

http://www.ylva-publishing.com

DEPARTURE FROM THE SCRIPT

Jae

ISBN: 978-3-95533-195-5
Length: 240 pages (approx. 52,000 words)

Amanda isn't looking for a relationship—and certainly not with Michelle. She has never been attracted to a butch woman before, and Michelle personifies the term butch. Having just landed a role on a TV show, Amanda is determined to focus on her career.

But after a date that is not a date and some meddling from her grandmother, she wonders if it's not time for a departure from her dating script.

UNDER A FALLING STAR

Jae

ISBN: 978-3-95533-238-9
Length: 369 pages (approx. 91,000 words)

Falling stars are supposed to be a lucky sign, but not for Austen. The first assignment in her new job—decorating the Christmas tree in the lobby—results in a trip to the ER after Dee, the company's COO, gets hit by the star-shaped tree topper.

There's an instant attraction between them, but Dee is determined not to act on it, especially since Austen has no idea that Dee is her boss.

GOOD ENOUGH TO EAT

Jae & Alison Grey

ISBN: 978-3-95533-242-6
Length: 223 pages (approx. 64,000 words)

Robin is a vampire who wants to change her eating habits. To fight her cravings for O negative, she goes to an AA meeting, where she meets Alana, who battles her own demons.

Despite their determination not to get involved, the attraction is undeniable.

Is it love or just bloodlust that makes Robin think Alana looks good enough to eat? Will it even matter once Alana finds out who Robin really is?

BITTER FRUIT

Lois Cloarec Hart

ISBN: 978-3-95533-216-7
Length: 224 pages (approx. 50,000 words)

Jac accepts an unusual wager from her best friend. Jac has one month to seduce a young woman she's never met. Though Lauren is straight and engaged, Jac begins her campaign confident that she'll win the bet. But Jac's forgotten that if you sow an onion seed, you won't harvest a peach. When her plan goes awry, will she reap the bitter fruit of her deception? Or will Lauren turn the tables on her?

BARRING COMPLICATIONS

Blythe Rippon

ISBN: 978-3-95533-191-7
Length: 374 pages (approx. 77,000 words)

When a gay marriage case arrives at the US Supreme Court, two women find themselves at the center of the fight for marriage equality. Closeted Justice Victoria Willoughby must sway a conservative colleague and attorney Genevieve Fornier must craft compelling arguments to win five votes. Complicating matters, despite their shared history, the law forbids the two from talking to each other.

COMING FROM YLVA PUBLISHING IN SUMMER 2015

http://www.ylva-publishing.com

DON'T BE SHY
A Collection of Erotic Lesbian Stories
Volume I & II

Astrid Ohletz & Jae (editors)

A collection of short stories that focus on the sensual, red-hot delights of sex between women and the celebration of the female form in all its diverse hedonism.

You'll find intimate encounters between strangers, couples playing out their most titillating fantasies, one-night stands, and stories featuring slow, sultry weekends. Are you up for toys, hot sex, and fun?

Don't be shy.

ALL THE LITTLE MOMENTS

G Benson

Anna is focused on her career as an anaesthetist. When a tragic accident leaves her responsible for her young niece and nephew, her life changes abruptly. Completely overwhelmed, Anna barely has time to brush her teeth in the morning let alone date a woman. But then she collides with a long-legged stranger...

DELIBERATE HARM

J.R. Wolfe

US soldiers Portia Marks and Imma Thoms found love during the second Iraq War, after Imma, a combat surgeon, saved Portia's life from a roadside bomb. Immediately inseparable, the two of them returned to civilian life engaged and followed Portia's postwar dreams to Zimbabwe, where they brought humanitarian aid to the struggling nation. But when Imma is arrested on false charges and executed for trying to escape prison, Portia returns home to Chicago bereft, numbing her grief by day with work and by night with alcohol.

Until one night, Portia is stopped by a stranger in the street who tells her that Imma actually escaped death and has been on the run ever since. But before Portia can find out anything else, the man is killed before her eyes.

Unable to dismiss the chance that Imma may be alive, Portia turns to two old friends from her Army days, now in the CIA, to help her find out the truth. Her search leads her to Zimbabwe, then to South Africa, and finally to London. Along the way, she stumbles upon plots within plots involving not only the People's Revolution—a radical terrorist organization—but also the CIA and a mysterious Russian crime syndicate.

When Portia discovers that the People's Revolution has a dirty bomb that they plan to set off at a highly public event somewhere in London, her search for her fiancée becomes a race against time.

Damage Control
© by Jae

ISBN: 978-3-95533-372-0

Also available as e-book.

Published by Ylva Publishing, legal entity of Ylva Verlag, e.Kfr.

Ylva Verlag, e.Kfr.
Owner: Astrid Ohletz
Am Kirschgarten 2
65830 Kriftel
Germany

http://www.ylva-publishing.com

First edition: April 2015

Credits
Edited by Nikki Busch
Proofread by Gillian A. McKnight
Cover Design by Streetlight Graphics

CPSIA information can be obtained at www.ICGtesting.com
Printed in the USA
BVOW03s0622290715

410885BV00002B/270/P